A Debt to Pay

ALEXANDRA MILLER

Dove Christian
Publishers

Dove Christian Publishers

A Division of Kingdom Christian Enterprises
PO Box 611
Bladensburg, MD 20710-0611
Copyright 2024 by Alexandra Miller

All rights reserved.

This novel is a work of fiction. Names, characters, places, and incidents either are products of the author's imagination or are used fictitiously. Any resemblance to actual events or locales or persons, living or dead, is entirely coincidental.

The views, opinions, and actions expressed in this novel are those of the characters and do not necessarily reflect the official policy or position of any person or entity mentioned within. Any resemblance to real persons, living or dead, or actual events is purely coincidental.

No part of this work may be reproduced or transmitted in any form or by any means, electronic or mechanical, including photocopying and recording, or by any information storage or retrieval system, except as may be expressly permitted by the 1976 Copyright Act or in writing from the publisher. Requests for permission can be addressed to Dove Christian Publishers, P.O. Box 611, Bladensburg, MD 20710-0611, www.dovechristianpublishers.com.

Paperback ISBN 978-1-957497-31-0

Inscript and the portrayal of a pen with script are trademarks of Dove Christian Publishers.

Printed in the United States of America

A Debt to Pay

I want to give a loving thank you to my husband Tyler and my children Eden, Wesley, and Jade who very generously gave me the time I needed to write this novel! And a special thank you to Eden, whose interest in what would happen next kept me working toward the next chapter.

Chapter One

Chicago, Illinois
1875

With a weary sigh, Claire Wallace leaned against the bar counter and, for a moment, closed her eyes to the familiar scene of the overcrowded, noisy saloon. Her feet were throbbing, reminding her that she'd nearly worked another twelve-hour shift. Rubbing her temples, she opened her eyes and saw a man at a nearby table gesturing for her to come over.

"Another drink?" Claire asked once she stood beside him.

"If you'll share it with me."

Claire Wallace looked at the half-drunk regular and feigned a smile. "I've got work to do, Charlie, but I'll go and get it for you." She returned a moment later with a glass of whiskey before moving on to another man trying to get her attention.

"What do you need, Sam?" she asked, balancing the tray of drinks in her hand.

"Another one of these," he slurred as he lifted his glass toward her. Claire lifted a glass off her tray and set it in front of him, promptly taking the coin he had dropped onto the table.

A Debt to Pay

"Now, that oughta be your last one," she told him, although she knew it was her job to sell drinks for as long as the men were buying. She had worked at Rudy's Saloon for over a year, long enough to know the regulars and their limit. "You best get home before you can't find it," she advised him, but he only chuckled and lifted the glass to his lips.

Returning to the bar, Claire set her tray down and leaned on one of the stools. A yawn escaped, and she covered her mouth with her gloved hand.

"Ain't quitting time yet," Maggie Clemmins said as she came alongside Claire.

Claire smiled at her friend, who had been working at the saloon a few years before she got there. Claire glanced toward the clock on the wall behind the bar. It hung just above a mirror that reflected a hazy room full of men and commotion. The shouts and laughter were only matched in volume by the ragtime piano that accompanied the men as they drank, smoked, and gambled.

"Just a few more minutes," Claire said, looking toward the upstairs landing where she and Maggie rented a room. "I can't wait to get off my feet."

"Who's that fellow over there? The one that keeps staring at you."

Claire followed Maggie's gaze to where it rested on a nicely dressed man just a few tables away.

"He's a wealthy-lookin' gentleman," Maggie said, noticing his silk vest, three-piece suit, and top hat.

"From what I've seen, he's no gentleman," Claire replied. "His name is Frederick Harris, and he owns that big jewelry shop a few streets over."

"I think he's gesturing for you to come over," Maggie said.

Claire sighed with irritation, wanting to be done for the

night, but lifted her tray and headed toward the man anyway. "What can I get you?" she asked, trying to sound more cheerful than she felt.

He used his foot to slide the chair beside him from under the table. "Sit down, hunnie." Although obviously wealthy, he was not an attractive man; the wrinkles and bags under his eyes suggested he was somewhere in his early fifties.

"I'm just about done my shift," Claire told him, lifting a glass from her tray. "Do you want one of these?"

"I'll give you extra if you sit down and keep me company while I drink it."

Claire hesitated, not liking the sense the man was giving. She'd seen him there half a dozen times, and each time, it seemed he made an effort to talk to her. "I suppose I can sit for a few," she said, slipping into the chair and setting her tray on the table. She slid one of the glasses of whiskey toward him.

"Your name's Claire, isn't it?"

She nodded absently, picking at a broken fingernail.

"I haven't been in Chicago all that long, but so far, I like what I see." He winked at her, and Claire shifted, a bit uncomfortable under his wandering eyes.

"You own that jewelry shop, don't you?" she asked, trying to make conversation that would distract him from gawking at her.

"Yes, ma'am," he replied proudly. "Largest one this side of the city."

"You got any family?" she asked, although she couldn't have cared less. She had a few more minutes before she could go up to bed, and if this fellow was going to pay extra for conversation, she'd take it.

"Nope. Just me and my money." He lifted his glass, fin-

A Debt to Pay

ished the rest of his drink, and then gestured for the other one on her tray. She slid it toward him and watched as he dipped his finger into the alcohol and then circled it around the rim. Looking up at her with squinty eyes, he said, "Does this saloon sell anything besides drinks?"

On that note, Claire came to her feet. "No, it does not," she replied in a rigid tone. She extended her palm toward him. "I think that's long enough."

He grinned slightly as he dropped some coins into her hand.

Claire could feel his eyes follow her as she returned to the bar. She turned in the money from the night and was glad to finally escape to her room a few minutes later. Sitting on the edge of the bed, with her back to the door, she began to unlace her boots. She didn't look up when she heard the door open, assuming it was Maggie.

"I wasn't done with our conversation."

Claire gasped when she heard Frederick Harris' voice. "What are you doing in here? Get out!"

He closed the door behind him and walked toward her, a voracious look in his eyes. "I just want to pay for a few more minutes of your company."

Claire instinctively reached for the dagger she kept under her pillow and clutched it close to her side. "This isn't one of those houses; now get out!"

He kept walking toward her, covering the short space between himself and where she stood by the bed. Claire glanced toward the door, wishing she could get to it or that Maggie would come in.

Backing up slowly, Claire felt the window at her back. Panic suddenly rose in her; there was nowhere else to go. She could feel her knuckles turning white as she clutched the weapon in her hand, resolved she would use it if he got any closer.

Unaware of what she was holding, Frederick Harris lunged toward her, only to be met with a sharp object piercing the space between his shoulder and heart. Stunned, he stumbled backward, pulling out the dagger just before tripping over a chair and crashing to the floor. His head met with the corner of the vanity on the way down, causing him to land with even more of a loud thud.

Feeling out of breath and shaken up, Claire just stared at his body for several seconds. A small pool of blood gathered near his shoulder on the floor. Suddenly, the door opened, and Claire's eyes met Maggie's.

"What in the world?" Maggie looked from the body on the floor to Claire.

"I didn't know what else to do!" Claire said, still trembling from her place by the window.

"Is he dead?" Maggie was afraid to ask as she went to stand over the body. She saw Claire's dagger on the ground beside him, still covered in his blood.

Claire moved slowly toward him and then knelt to feel his pulse. "He's still alive."

"Should we send for a doctor?"

Claire nodded, her eyes still on the man who lay motionless on the floor. Maggie left the room and returned a moment later with two men who worked at the saloon. Claire briefly explained what happened as they picked up each end of him and carried him out of their room. Claire cleaned off the dagger once they'd left and threw a towel over the blood on the floor. That's when she noticed a set of keys lying near the vanity. Picking them up, Claire realized they must have fallen out of Frederick Harris' pocket.

A Debt to Pay

An idea suddenly sprang to her mind and seemed to overshadow every fiber of her being. "Maggie, these are Frederick Harris' keys."

Maggie looked at them. "So?"

"One of these is probably a key to his shop."

"So, what?"

"Don't you see…I could finally get out of here, out of this city!"

"Claire, what on earth are you talking about?"

"I could take just enough jewelry as I need. There's plenty of pawn shops in this city. I could trade the jewelry in for cash and then get on a train, putting a hundred miles between me and Chicago."

"Are you crazy?" Maggie's hands came to her hips as she shook her head incredulously.

"I will be if I stay in this place another day!"

Claire suddenly went to the window, pushing the threadbare curtains to the side.

"What are you doing?" Maggie asked.

"I'm getting out of here, Maggie." At those words, Claire pushed the window open and stuck her head outside. "It's not going to be a hard climb down."

Maggie reached out and took her friend by the arms. "You can't just leave."

"And why not?" Claire looked back at her, her deep brown eyes daring her to come up with even one good reason.

"Because you have nowhere to go."

"I told you. I'll take a train west and find a town to start over in."

"You can't be serious," Maggie said as she watched Claire move quickly about the room, gathering her meager belongings.

"Please don't go!" Maggie suddenly panicked. She nervously played with the long auburn braid that hung over her shoulder. "What will I do in this place without you?" She looked pleadingly at Claire. While Claire had only been working in the saloon for a year, she had been the closest thing to a sister and friend Maggie had known.

Claire reached out her hand on Maggie's thin shoulder, her expression one of pleading. "Come with me, Maggie. I know you've worked in worse places than this saloon, but you have to want out of here as badly as I do."

Maggie was holding her breath, her green eyes wide as saucers as she seemed to be considering it. She instinctively glanced at the door as if fearing someone would come in to stop them. But the door didn't open, and Claire was pleading with her again. "Grab what you have and let's go! The jewels will give us more than enough to start a new life."

"But what if we get caught?"

"I'm not even going to think like that, Maggie. We've got to go, and we've got to go now. Once we get where we're going, we can pay back what we take," she tried to convince her.

Maggie suddenly found herself nodding and, within thirty seconds, had shoved a few items into a pillowcase, lastly reaching for a small hand purse that lay hidden under her mattress. Claire was already halfway out the window when Maggie returned to it.

"We could just sneak out the door," Maggie suggested when she saw how high they were from the ground.

"We can't chance being seen with these keys," Claire told her as she swung her other leg over the windowsill and reached out her hand to help Maggie.

Maggie apprehensively climbed over the windowsill and then gave a little gasp as a gust of wind surprised her.

A Debt to Pay

"Hold on to the wall like this," Claire told her. "And don't look down. Just follow me. There's a spot at the back where the ledge is just a few feet above a shed. We'll lower down onto it, and it will be easy from there."

Maggie nodded nervously, not at all persuaded this was a good idea. The only thing she knew was that she was as desperate for a new life as Claire was. "I can't believe I let you talk me into this," Maggie said with a whimper as the roof narrowed, forcing them closer to the edge.

"You'll be thanking me when we're on the train."

"If we don't die first."

"Shh!"

It wasn't long before they reached the back of the saloon, and just as she had said, the roof hung just a few feet above a shed. Before Maggie could say a word against it, Claire squatted down to scoot to the edge and made a quick jump onto the roof.

"I can't do that!" Maggie whispered frantically.

"Yes, you can!" Claire encouraged her. "C'mon, Maggie!"

With a little cry, Maggie followed Claire's example and soon jumped onto the shed as well. A few minutes later, both girls were landing on the ground and scurrying down the street.

"Everything's going to be fine," Claire reassured her as they moved quickly from the saloon, their footsteps seeming to echo in the night.

Claire hoped her words sounded more convincing than she felt. Her heart was pounding, and she forced herself not to think of what she would face if they were caught. Beneath the light of the streetlamps, Claire's eyes skimmed the row of houses and shops along the empty street. She had seen his shop before and knew it was close.

"It's that one right there," Claire whispered a few minutes later, pointing to the corner of the street where a large jewelry shop with glass windows and a newly painted sign seemed to call to her. Fumbling with the keys in her pocket, Claire pulled them out and headed to the front door. Glancing over her shoulder, she nervously tried the first key and then two more.

"This is crazy!" Maggie whimpered.

Ignoring her, Claire tried the last one and felt relief mixed with fear when the doorknob turned and the door opened. Closing the door behind them, Claire felt her way around the darkness, with Maggie close behind. The cash register caught her eye, so she moved toward the counter and slipped behind it. The smallest of the keys unlocked the drawer, and Claire could feel wads of cash inside. "We won't even need to pawn the jewelry," Claire whispered to Maggie, who had wandered a few feet away and was reaching inside one of the expansive jewelry cases. "There's plenty of cash in here!"

At those words, Claire grabbed two handfuls of the bills and shoved them into her pocket. Closing the drawer, she dropped the keys onto the counter. "Let's get out of here!" she said to Maggie.

They left the jewelry shop and headed toward the train station and, within a few hours, had put Chicago miles behind them.

Chapter Two

The town of Millcreek was situated like a T-shaped island amid a sea of tallgrass prairies. It was home to an assortment of shops and homes, a post office, livery, mill, and saloon, which was solicitously placed at the edge of town. Recently reconstructed buildings, rebuilt after a fire, lined a portion of the main street, which was no longer muddy from spring rain.

Lyddie Hall stopped sweeping her front porch for just a moment to admire the pink dogwood tree that was in full bloom at the corner of her boardinghouse. She loved this time of year, even though the season was a sad reminder of her late husband. Twenty years seemed like an eternity ago, and yet sometimes it felt like only yesterday that her husband had passed.

"Morning, Mrs. Lyddie."

Brushing away a loose brown curl that had escaped her chignon, Lyddie waved at the general store owner as he tipped his hat from across the street and called out a greeting.

"Good morning to you, too, Tom," she called back. "How's your wife's leg?"

"Doc says she'll be laid up a spell, but she's trying to keep in good spirits."

"I'll bring some apple pie her way to help with that."

"She'd appreciate that," he said with a kind smile before heading inside his store.

Lyddie glanced down at her watch pendant and finished sweeping with more haste. The stagecoach would be arriving soon, and she hadn't yet finished preparing her two spare rooms for prospective guests.

"Stop squirming," Claire whispered to Maggie.

"I'm sorry. This coach has about done me in. I don't know if my back can take another mile."

Claire's gaze rested on the older woman seated across from them in the stagecoach. She had been sleeping since they boarded the coach a few hours ago, and she still appeared to be. "Let's stay a night in the next town, and if we like it, maybe we'll stay longer."

Maggie perked up at this. "Really?"

"We could see what sort of place it is and if there are any job opportunities."

Maggie let out a sigh as she turned her head toward the window. The scenery was shaking up and down as the coach seemed to hit every pothole on the road. "Not sure what *opportunities* we can find."

Claire swallowed down her own uncertainty and tried to be optimistic. "Starting a new life isn't going to be easy, but something will turn up."

"Unless what we did brings a curse on us," Maggie whispered, a worried expression on her face. "If there's one thing my ma taught me, it's that thieves go straight to…"

"Shhh," Claire shushed her with a nervous glance at the woman across from them. Her head had dropped further

A Debt to Pay

forward, and she looked as if she was starting to wake up. A moment later, she shifted her bulky frame in the seat and reached for her spectacles that had fallen onto her lap as she slept. She put them on and, for the first time, noticed the two young women sitting across from her.

"Oh my! I must have been sleeping for some time." She glanced out the window. "And there still seems to be a longer leg in the journey." She sighed with irritation, removing her spectacles to dust them off. "I think there's more dust in this carriage than outside!"

"Where are you headed?" Claire asked kindly.

"A town called Millcreek. Have you heard of it?"

"No, ma'am."

"Well, we should be coming up on it soon."

"You have family there?" Maggie asked.

"No. There's a minister there who needs a nanny for his two children," she told them. "I'm too old to be traveling further west, but I'm doing it as sort of a favor for a relative of mine who knew the minister's wife, God rest her soul."

The woman continued to chatter about this and that, but Claire's thoughts were on the town the woman had mentioned. She was hoping it was the sort of place she had hoped to find, and with almost a month of travel, it could be they had put enough distance between themselves and their old life.

Jacob Myles reached around his daughter to smooth down his three-year-old son's disheveled blonde hair. The little boy was standing close to his sister, holding her hand with one hand and a small toy train with the other. Jacob Myles then glanced at his pocket watch.

"Just a few more minutes and the stage should be here," he said.

"I don't know why we even need a nanny," his seven-year-old daughter, Lilly, said. "I can take care of Lucas just fine when you're not home."

Jacob smiled affectionately at his daughter, thinking, as he often did, how much she reminded him of his late wife. "And you've been doing an excellent job at it, but there are times when you need someone to look after you, too."

Lilly obviously didn't agree, as she let out a sigh and looked away from her father. "I'll be eight in a few months. I suppose she can stay until then."

Jacob hid an amused smile. "I wish you wouldn't grow up so fast," he said as he playfully tugged one of her long, blonde braids.

"Heuh it comes!" Lucas' little voice said as he pointed to a stagecoach in the distance, dust swirling around its wheels.

"Be polite" were Jacob's last words to his daughter on the subject as the stage eventually pulled up near the platform where they stood waiting. As the driver climbed down, Jacob moved toward the door to be of assistance.

The carriage door swung open, and a woman, clearly not of the description of the nanny he was expecting, began to climb down. Thoughtfully, Jacob reached up to take her hand.

"Thank you," she said quietly as her feet landed on the ground.

Maggie followed Claire but was taken off guard by an attractive pair of brown eyes that met hers. The man extended his hand to take hers, but when Maggie reached for it, she somehow managed to miss the step below the carriage door. Her dress was tangled under her foot as well, and before she knew what was happening, she found herself falling out of the door and into the unsuspecting man's arms.

"Are you alright?" he asked thoughtfully, helping her find her balance.

Embarrassed, Maggie let go of his arms as soon as she could right herself. She could feel a warm blush creeping into her cheeks and quickly averted her gaze from the handsome stranger. "Yes, thank you." She cleared her throat as she shook out her dress and lifted the hem to keep from tripping on it again. The dresses she had worn in the saloon had never been this long and hazardous!

"And you must be Mrs. Newberry," Maggie heard the man say as the older woman they had been traveling with emerged from inside the carriage. Maggie moved to stand beside Claire as they waited for the driver to unload the luggage.

Jacob Myles smiled at the older woman, who was trying to smooth back unruly wisps of gray hair.

"Are you Jacob Myles?" she asked, her brow furrowed.

"Yes, ma'am."

"I couldn't tell since you're not wearing a white collar. You don't look like a minister at all," she told him bluntly.

Jacob grinned. "I'm afraid I'm not as conventional as some."

"What now?" Maggie whispered from her place beside Claire. As if on cue, Claire spotted an inviting establishment just across the street. A large white sign neatly hand-painted with black letters read *Lyddie's Room & Board*.

"Let's see if there are any rooms available," Claire said as she glanced about, liking what she saw. Men, women, and children were milling about the streets in a shuffle of morning activity, going in and out of the shops and houses that seemed well-kept.

Carrying a suitcase in each hand, Maggie and Claire

moved away from the stagecoach and toward the boardinghouse. They knocked and waited. A woman in her sixties appeared at the door with graying brown hair, bright blue eyes, and a friendly smile that dimpled her cheeks.

"Afternoon, ladies. Can I help you?"

"Yes. My sister and I are just arrived, and we were wondering if you had a room we could rent for a night or two."

"I certainly do. You can bring yourselves and all that dust you've collected right in."

Claire thought the parlor looked picturesque with its wing-back cushion chairs and elegant mahogany furniture. An ornate gold mirror hanging on the wall made the room feel even more spacious. The room smelled as pleasant as a florist's, causing Claire to notice vases of fresh flowers in several places.

"If you'll follow me up the stairs, I can let you take your pick from two rooms I have vacant."

"We're not picky," Claire said. "Either will be fine."

"Well, I'll pick for you then. The one with the single large bed is quieter since the others are above the kitchen. If you don't mind sharing."

"That will be fine," Claire said. She thought about all the noise of the saloon hall. A quiet room wasn't something she'd had the luxury of for a long time.

"I serve breakfast and dinner for an extra twenty-five cents. The room is fifty cents per night."

"Thank you. We'll take the room and the extra cost for meals."

"Very good." The woman clasped her hands together in front of her apron. "Most folks call me Mrs. Lyddie, but Lyddie is fine as well. If you need anything, I'm usually in the kitchen. I'll leave you to settle. Dinner is at six."

A Debt to Pay

"This is like a doll's house," Maggie exclaimed once the door was closed and they were alone in the room. "Just look at the flower-printed quilt on the bed and those lace curtains!"

"It is rather beautiful, isn't it?"

"OK, Claire, I'm going to say it."

"Say what?" Claire asked as she plopped her suitcase on the large bed.

"You were right! I've never felt so free in my whole life! Just think…back in Chicago, we would have been gearing up for another loud night."

Claire sighed as she went to the window and gingerly moved the lace curtains to one side. "It's a fine town from what I've seen so far. And if folks are anything like Mrs. Lyddie, then we've come to the right place."

Chapter Three

Claire ran her finger across the delicate plate in front of her. The hand-painted flowers on the edges made her not want to soil it with food. She looked across the table at Maggie, who also seemed to be taking in all the fine things of Mrs. Lyddie's dining room. At the table also sat an older gentleman and his wife.

"I hope you all like roast lamb and potatoes," said Lyddie as she entered the room carrying a silver platter.

"We journeyed straight through lunch," Maggie said, "so that sounds wonderful."

"Mr. Hobbs, will you say the blessing?" Mrs. Lyddie asked the older gentleman.

Claire and Maggie bowed their heads with the rest and closed their eyes. A few minutes later, Lyddie looked up from her plate. "Where are you two ladies from? If you don't mind me asking."

Claire could feel Maggie's eyes on her. But they had already discussed what their story would be. "My sister and I are from Springfield. We lost our parents a year or so ago, and we just needed a new town and a fresh start."

"Oh, I'm so sorry to hear that."

A Debt to Pay

"We aren't sure where we're going to settle yet," Claire told her.

"Well, I certainly hope you give our town a fair chance. It's been around for decades, but a fire a few years back led to rebuilding several of the shops on this side of the street. Gives it a nice fresh look, I think."

"What caused the fire?" Maggie asked with curiosity.

"As I recall it, there was a holdup at the bank, and the robbery led to a shootout. In the ruckus, a fire got started and took out near five buildings 'for we got it put out." Lyddie noticed Maggie glancing at her sister and rushed in to reassure them. "Not to worry. Sheriff Dunley does a fine job keeping things orderly, and we've had no trouble since then."

"I think we'll stay for a few days at least," Claire told her.

"Glad to hear it, hunnie. Now," she gestured toward the platter of potatoes. "Please, help yourselves to more. We got slathers of them."

The next morning, Claire woke up and thought she'd slept deep enough to make up for the last few weeks of travel. She and Maggie could almost feel the quietness of the house, a very welcome change from their boisterous life in the saloon. Before going to bed, they had each taken a turn in Lyddie's washroom, where a warm bath had removed the dirt and sweat from their long carriage ride.

"After breakfast, let's take a turn about the town," Claire said.

Maggie readily agreed. "I think we may have missed breakfast," she said around a yawn.

Claire looked toward the clock on the wall and gasped. "Ten-thirty!"

"I think I could keep sleeping," Maggie said as she laid back against the feather-filled pillows.

Claire slid out of the bed and went to open the window, as the room was getting a bit warm. She donned a light blue skirt and white blouse before moving toward a chair to lace up her boots. After leaving Chicago with nearly a hundred dollars, Claire and Maggie visited a dress shop where they each bought a modest but sufficient wardrobe for themselves, complete with new undergarments, stockings, and shoes. It pricked both their consciences, but as Claire kept reassuring Maggie, they would pay it back to Frederick Harris when they were settled. It was her plan to work, save, and one day mail him back the money they had taken. Even though deep down she felt he deserved what they took, she didn't like the idea of owing that man a cent.

Once they were both dressed, they headed downstairs, took muffins Mrs. Lyddie offered them, and then headed out into the warm June morning. A few wagons and people on horseback moved down the street.

"Mrs. Lyddie's is one of the last buildings on this end. Let's head down the other direction," Claire suggested.

They passed a tailor shop and a bank before their walk took them past a sheriff's office, post office, and several other establishments. There was a two-story hotel up ahead, and farther in the distance, it looked like there was a livery and mill down the road. Eventually, their walk took them across the street and back down in the direction they had come.

After passing other shops, including a bakery and a dress shop, the false front of the general store came into view. It was white with the porch rails and General Store sign painted dark green. It was large and inviting, but what grabbed Claire's attention was a sign in the window that said, *Help Wanted*. The girls were soon stepping up to the platform to go inside. A bell chimed as they opened the door.

A Debt to Pay

"Look at all their yard goods," Maggie exclaimed, and she headed in that direction. Claire moved around the store for a few minutes, taking in the floor-to-ceiling shelves that lined the walls on both sides. They were teeming with items, from shoes and overalls to things like lanterns, nails, and ropes. Harnesses and horse bits were located toward the back of the store, and she eventually ended up in an aisle of home goods near the front counter.

Not seeing anyone, she glanced around and noticed what appeared to be a storage room off to the right side. She could hear movement from inside and slowly made her way over. She noticed a middle-aged man at the far end lifting a flour sack onto the shelf. There were several piled at his feet, and after he had lifted a second one, Claire quietly cleared her throat to get his attention.

He turned around with a polite smile. "I'm sorry. Can I help you with something?" He wiped his hands on the apron hanging over his trousers and took a few steps toward her. Claire thought he seemed a friendly sort, and he looked clean-cut with his neatly trimmed mustache, combed hair, and tan striped Ballard shirt.

"I wanted to ask about the Help Wanted sign in your window."

"You're an unfamiliar face."

"My sister and I may be moving here. I was trying to see if there were any job opportunities before we make a decision."

"I see. Well, I'm afraid this position may only be temporary. My wife took a fall a few weeks ago, and the doc says she'll be laid up a month or so."

Claire liked the idea of giving the town a month's trial period. "I would be willing to work for that duration."

He looked at her uncertainly. "Have you experience?"

Claire opened her mouth to reply but hesitated. She doubted it would suffice but decided to offer it anyway. "When I was younger, I helped my uncle in his tack shop." It wasn't much, but it was true. "I've worked odd jobs all my life," she told him. "I'm a fast learner and strong enough to help with stocking shelves and such."

She was willing and eager enough, he thought. He sighed, and his expression showed he was obviously contemplating it. "How are you at figurin'?"

Memories of counting money as men paid for drinks flashed across her mind. "I'm fast," she answered.

"Hmm, OK, I'll give you a try."

A smile lit Claire's face. "Oh, thank you, Mr..." She let the sentence hang as she realized she did not know his name.

"Tom Maison. And what's yours?"

"It's Claire Wallace, and thank you, Mr. Maison! When should I start?"

"Well, we're closed on Sundays, so how does Monday sound?"

"That's perfect."

"Eight o'clock?"

"Yes, sir, I'll be here." Claire turned to find Maggie, nearly exploding with excitement to tell her the good news.

"Does that mean we're going to stay?" Maggie asked as they left the store and continued down the street.

As she said the words, Claire looked across the street and saw the town sheriff for the first time. With his thumbs resting on his holster, he seemed to saunter with deliberate steps as if making sure no one missed the gold star on his leather vest.

"For now," Claire said, and Maggie followed her gaze.

"Oh no, Claire, he's coming this way," Maggie said a moment later.

A Debt to Pay

"Relax, Maggie, you're making me nervous."

"Afternoon, ladies," he greeted with just a brief nod of his hat.

"Afternoon, sheriff," Claire said, managing something akin to a smile. While he was tall and robust, there was nothing in his features that suggested he was handsome and nothing in his manner that suggested he was friendly.

Claire heard Maggie breathe a sigh of relief when he continued walking past them. "We're nowhere near Chicago," Claire reminded her quietly.

Maggie glanced over her shoulder, still a little nervous. "My head knows that's true, but my heart just about thundered out of my chest."

"You can't get all jumpy every time you see the sheriff," Claire told her, unwilling to admit that she herself had felt anxious when seeing the lawman approach them.

"What do you think of our town so far?" Lyddie asked Claire and Maggie that evening at dinner. The other couple had left, so it was only the three of them at the table.

"So far, so good," Maggie replied. "Claire even found a job."

"Really?"

"Yes, at the General Store," Claire said. "It's only temporary."

"So, I take it that means you two will be extending your stay."

Claire nodded. "For now. Do you know of any houses for rent in town or nearby?"

Lyddie lowered her glass, and a thoughtful expression crossed her face. "Nothing in town that I know of. But you might want to check with Will Carter. He owns a ranch about a mile from town. He owns a lot of land, and at one time, there was a small cabin he rented out."

"Alright, thank you," Claire replied.

"I can give you a ride out to his place tomorrow if you like. Unless he's at church, in which case you could speak to him then."

Claire felt Maggie's gaze on her, and she knew just what she was thinking. The idea of stepping foot in church was nerve-wracking, to say the least.

"It's not as if the minister will know our past by looking at us," Claire tried to reason with Maggie later that evening when they were alone in their room.

"He might," Maggie replied, a look of anxiety in her eyes as she brushed through her auburn hair and then twisted it into a long braid.

"Nobody knows anything about us, Maggie. And we're trying to make a fresh start, remember? Maybe it will even help somehow."

"I doubt religion can erase our past, Claire, but I guess it couldn't hurt."

"At the least, it will save us from questions from Lyddie about why we wouldn't go."

Maggie nodded in agreement and then sighed, remembering the only minister she had ever known. "I can see it now. A gray-haired, white-collared, angry man thundering from his pulpit about the fires of hell."

But the next morning, as Maggie and Claire sat in a long wooden pew beside Mrs. Lyddie, Maggie was shocked to see quite the opposite. "It's that man from the stagecoach," Maggie whispered to Claire, her eyes not moving from his face.

"You mean the one that saved you from falling on your face?" Claire whispered back with a grin.

"He's too young and handsome to be a minister," Maggie replied under her breath.

"Good morning," Jacob Myles said, a kind smile on his sun-tanned face. "Will you all turn with me to Psalm nineteen? I wanted to read the chapter before Peggy leads us in a few hymns."

"You can share my Bible," Lyddie said as she extended a large, leatherbound book over to Claire and Maggie.

Nervously, Claire flipped through the pages. She didn't have any idea where the Book of Psalms was. She was surprised when Maggie reached over and turned a large portion of the pages at once. She found the exact chapter without any problem. "My ma used to make me read the Bible every Sunday," she whispered to Claire. Her words made Claire realize she knew very little of Maggie's past before her days working at the saloon.

Maggie noticed that in the pew right in front of her sat the two children she'd seen at the stagecoach two days earlier. She also saw Mrs. Newberry sitting beside them. It was so unfortunate, Maggie thought, that the children had lost their mother. The little boy's head didn't even reach the top of the pew when he sat back, and his sister's expression was very serious as she kept her face toward her father. Maggie suddenly heard a little thump and realized the boy's toy train had rolled under the pew just by her feet. Noticing he was anxiously trying to scurry off his seat to get it, she bent down, picked it up, and then reached over the pew to hand it to him.

She earned a smile from him but noticed he earned a scowl from Mrs. Newberry. "Sit still!" Maggie heard her whispered command.

Maggie returned her attention to the minister, who was still reading from the chapter he had referred to. He was quite a different picture than the minister she remembered from her childhood, and his voice was soothing somehow. Maggie then noticed that the little boy in front of her kept trying to turn around and look at her. She smiled sweetly at him and hoped he wouldn't get another scolding.

"I didn't see Mr. Carter," Lyddie said as they left the church an hour later. "I'll have to give you a ride out to his place."

Claire thanked her, her thoughts still on Reverend Myles's sermon. The way he talked about God wasn't what she had expected at all. A few children suddenly scurried past her, laughing and playing. She smiled to herself, wondering how different her life would have been growing up in a place like this. The overcrowded streets of Chicago were a sharp contrast to the wide-open spaces these children had to enjoy.

"That's Mr. Keets, the banker, and his daughter Amy."

Claire realized Lyddie was pointing out various people as they left the church. Mr. Keets was well dressed and clean cut, and his daughter, who seemed to be around the age of nineteen or twenty, was also fashionably dressed, bustle and all.

"You'll get to know them all in time," she said. "Some you will want to know better than others," she added with a wink. "My goodness, this sun is hot," Lyddie exclaimed as she removed her shawl and draped it over her arm. "I'm not sure what sort of summer temperatures you are used to, but our Missouri summers could boil a puddle!"

As promised, a few hours later, Lyddie was driving Maggie and Claire out to Will Carter's ranch. Claire enjoyed listening to Mrs. Lyddie's pleasant chatter and managed to answer any questions in a way that didn't divulge too much about their past.

"You girls are mighty brave traveling west alone like you did," she was saying. "Of course, I can understand the longing for a new start. My husband and I traveled west some forty years ago with the same itch."

"How did he die?" Maggie asked quietly.

"Bad streak of smallpox. Lots of folks died that year." She grew quiet for a moment and then asked them how they lost their parents.

"It was cholera," Claire told her. That was the truth in regard to her parents. She knew Maggie had barely known her father and that her mother had died giving birth to a child who also did not survive.

"So, you know what it's like to lose someone you love." Lyddie took a deep breath, shaking her head. "God's world is going to be a sight better than this one, that's for sure and certain."

"God's world?" Claire heard herself asking.

"The life after this one," Lyddie explained. "No pain, no death, no tears, streets of gold…It's gonna be worth the wait, I can tell you that."

Claire tried to imagine a place like that. How could a person even guarantee they could go to a place like that? She knew it wasn't likely she would qualify.

"Look how many horses and cattle!"

Claire's reverie was broken by the sound of Maggie's excited voice. She followed her gaze to the wide fields, where dozens of horses grazed, and just beyond the horses appeared to be just as many cattle. A large two-story house was off to the left, surrounded by several trees and a white picket fence. An immense red barn loomed just ahead, as well as several smaller buildings and a large corral. They passed under a large archway sign that read *Millcreek Ranch*.

Lyddie stopped the wagon near the corral, where several men were working. It looked to Claire like they were repairing the fence.

"Good afternoon, gentleman," Lyddie greeted. "Can you tell me where Will is?"

"Ain't here," one of them replied. He looked curiously at Maggie and Claire.

"Do you know when he'll be back?" Lyddie asked.

"Nope. The new colt got out, and he went to bring 'im back."

"I see. Well, thank you. Good day." Lyddie repositioned her bonnet on her head from where it hung down her back before turning the wagon around.

"Sorry, girls," she said as they headed back to town.

"I'm just sorry we wasted your time," Claire told her, glancing over her shoulder to get one last look at the breathtaking property.

"No time wasted," Lyddie replied. "It's been time well spent getting to know you two ladies."

Claire was touched by the woman's kind words even though her conscience stung under the realization that Lyddie didn't know them at all.

Chapter Four

"Good morning, Miss Wallace."

Claire closed the door behind her and moved toward the front counter of the general store, where Tom Maison was rearranging some items in the display cabinet.

"Good morning, sir."

"I thought we would start with getting you acquainted with where everything is stocked."

Claire nodded, eager to learn. She followed him to the storage room, and he showed her where and how everything was to be organized. When customers arrived and made purchases, she paid close attention as he showed her how to use the cash register. At noon, Mr. Maison gave her a lunch break. When she came back from Lyddie's, he asked her to help him load up an order he would be delivering later that day.

"Here is a list of things you can gather from the store," he told her as he handed her a piece of paper. "Put all the items in that crate at the counter, and then I'll help you carry them out to the wagon."

Claire took the list and finished the task in short order. Once the crate was loaded with sacks of flour, sugar, salt, baking soda, and other such items, Claire carried it outside and to the wagon where Mr. Maison was loading heavier items. He checked his pocket watch and frowned. "A friend of mine was supposed to have been here by now to drive this out to Millcreek Ranch."

"You mean Mr. Carter's ranch?" Claire asked as she set the crate in the back of the wagon.

Tom Maison latched the back of the wagon. "Yep."

"I could drive it out there, sir," Claire offered.

"Can you handle a team?"

"Yes, sir," Claire replied, hoping she could remember. She had driven her uncle's wagon several times, but that had been years ago.

Tom glanced at the full wagon of supplies and then back at Claire. Something about her made him feel as if he could trust her, and it would be a big help so he could stay back and manage the store. "Alright, young lady. If you think you can handle it."

Claire nodded. "I'll be careful, sir." She was hoping this would give her an opportunity to speak with Mr. Carter about his possible rental property without inconveniencing Lyddie again.

Lifting her skirt, Claire stepped up by the wheel and climbed onto the seat. Swallowing a sudden lump in her throat and ignoring her pounding heart, she took the reins in her hands and shifted the break.

"They're a good team," Tom told her, "A little slow but steady."

That's perfect, Claire thought. The slower, the better.

―――――

The route to the Carter Ranch was an easy one, nearly a

straight path from the town. Claire relaxed after a few minutes, feeling the rhythmic clip-clop of the horses and rumble of the wagon beneath her. She glanced back more than once to make sure the supplies were still in order. The June sun overhead was blazing hot, and she could feel the sweat dripping down her face. Shifting the reins to one hand for the moment, she unbuttoned the top buttons of her blouse so it loosened around her neck, then leaning forward, she pulled her skirt up to her knees and sat on the excess. It helped a little, but by the time she arrived at the ranch, she was longing for a cold drink and some shade.

Following the same path Lyddie had taken, Claire drove the wagon to the corral. She didn't see anyone right away but heard voices coming from the side of the barn. She climbed down from the wagon and secured the reins to a nearby hitching post. Then, glancing about and still not seeing anyone, she headed in the direction of the voices.

A small crowd of cowboys were gathered watching something, their backs to her as she approached. "Excuse me?" she said, but no one could hear her over the commotion that seemed to be going on in front of them.

"Where is it?" she heard a man ask, the tension thick in his tone.

"I don't know what you're talking about!" retorted another angry voice.

Claire moved closer, peering around the men. She saw a taller, muscular man with his hands grasping the collar of a thinner man. She gasped slightly when she saw him push him up against the barn wall. "Where is it?" he asked again, giving the man's back another thrust into the wall.

"Git your hands off me!" the smaller man yelled as he took a swing at the man who had him pinned against the wall.

"Only when you stop lying and tell me where it is!"

"I didn't take your darn watch!" the man said. His words earned him a punch in the gut.

"I know you took it! This is your last chance, Grady; now tell me where it is!"

Grady Higgs saw the fist about to encounter his face and gave in. "I don't have it anymore!"

Claire saw the taller man's jaw muscles jump as he pulled the man closer and gripped his shirt tighter. "So, where is it now?"

"I lost it in a card game."

"Who'd you lose it to?"

"Tim Merch! He has it!"

Claire watched as the bigger man pulled Grady away from the wall and gave him a shove before letting him go. "Pack your things and be off this property by the time I get back!"

The men in the crowd parted as the man who had won the fight came walking through. Claire took a step backward to get out of the way. She was a little uneasy when the tall cowboy stopped and looked at her, his eyes still brimming with anger. "Who are you?" he asked suddenly.

Claire felt all the men's eyes now resting on her, and she cleared her throat nervously. "My name's Claire Wallace. I have a delivery from Mr. Maison." She glanced back at the wagon several yards away. "And I was looking for Will Carter. I wanted to speak with him about—"

"One of the men will unload the wagon," he interrupted and continued to walk past her with fast strides. Claire watched as he strode toward a horse that was already saddled near the corral. In one swift movement, he mounted the animal and sped away.

Claire turned her attention back to the men who had

started to disperse. The man she'd heard addressed as Grady, who had seemed to be the center of the action, had moved in an opposite direction as the rest.

"What do you need help with, ma'am?" a man who looked to be in his thirties asked her, his high-crowned cowboy hat shadowing his face.

"I have Mr. Carter's order from the general store," she explained again as she led him toward the wagon. "Is Mr. Carter here?" she asked a moment later.

"You just saw him," the man replied.

"Oh." She hadn't realized that was the man she was looking for. His violent and rude behavior made her want to change her mind about even consulting him about a house for rent.

"If you'll drive the wagon over to them barn doors, Miss, I'll unload the wagon."

Claire climbed back up on the wagon and directed the horses toward where he gestured. She couldn't help but notice several of the men she had seen before were starting to mill around her wagon.

"You're a new face," the youngest of the men said, a smile crossing his sun-tanned face as he leaned against the wagon.

"You ain't married, is ya?" another of them asked.

"Either help me unload this wagon or git outta here," the man who had first spoken to Claire told them. The two fellows who had been gawking at her reluctantly moved to help him unload.

"Should I take the home good items over to the house?" Claire asked thoughtfully, glancing over her shoulder into the wagon bed and seeing only the crate was left.

"That's alright, ma'am. I'll see to it." After he had set the crate on the ground, the man came around to her side of the wagon. "Don't mind them," he said, nudging his head toward the two men who had talked to her. "They're harmless but ain't got no manners." He extended his hand. "My name's Jared Cooper, Miss. Nice to make your acquaintance."

Claire smiled politely as she shook his hand briefly. "I'm Claire."

He smiled, and Claire thought his face rather attractive. He was rough around the edges, but there was a certain charm to his features, and his eyes were kind. She thanked him for his help and managed to turn the team around without making a spectacle of herself. She could feel several pairs of eyes watching her, and she ordered herself to stay in control of the horses and not run the wagon into the side of the barn.

The sun was still warm but was starting to slope lower in the sky, and a breeze was moving across the prairie. Glancing around the open fields dotted with trees and brush, she felt a feeling of hope she had never had before. As unsuccessful as her trip to the ranch had been, she had much to be thankful for. She was far away from the busy city of Chicago, far away from the saloon and its torrent of untrustworthy men, and far away from a past she hoped to forget. Claire breathed in the clean air and knew things were about to change for the better.

Chapter Five

"You've had a job for a whole week, Claire. And look at me! I'm doing nothing."

"Something will turn up," Claire encouraged Maggie. It was Sunday morning, and they were getting dressed for church.

"I'm not lucky like you," Maggie said. "Remember back in the saloon? Your tips were always better than mine."

"That's ridiculous," Claire said. "There's no such thing as luck."

"When we got off the stagecoach, who tripped and nearly fell on her face?"

"That wasn't bad luck," Claire laughed. "You're just clumsy."

Maggie rolled her eyes, half smiling, and plopped on the bed. "I just don't want you to have to take care of us. I want to do my part, too."

"You will, Maggie. Just give it some time. Besides, you're not just doing nothing. I've seen the way you help Lyddie."

Maggie shrugged. "That's true. She did say she appreciated the help with the laundry."

Lyddie was waiting for them outside on the front porch and chattered pleasantly as they walked together to church.

"How long has Reverend Myles been your minister?" Maggie asked Lyddie as the conversation steered in that direction.

"He and his wife came here about five years ago. It was a sorrowful day when she passed. Weren't a dry eye at that funeral."

"That's so sad, especially for her children," Maggie said, the memory of her own mother's death still fresh in her mind.

Lyddie nodded. "Yes, indeed. Rose was a delightful woman. A wonderful mother, too. Breaks my heart to know her children will grow up without her."

As they neared the churchyard, Claire smiled a greeting at Tom Maison and exchanged greetings with several others she had met that week while working at the store. Claire and Maggie followed Lyddie to the seat they had occupied the previous week. As they sat down, Claire noticed a tall, familiar figure out of the corner of her eye. He removed his hat and ran a hand through his wavy, dark blonde hair.

"That's Will Carter," Lyddie leaned over and whispered to Claire. "We could speak with him after the service."

The memory of the man's temper flashed into Claire's mind, and she spent the duration of the service wondering if she should ask him about the house or just wait for something else to turn up.

"He doesn't ever stick around long, so we better catch him now," Lyddie said as soon as Reverend Myles had concluded his sermon. Maggie and Claire followed, and by the time they had reached him, he was outside, nearly about to mount his horse.

"Excuse me, Mr. Carter?"

Will Carter turned around and tipped his hat at Lyddie. "Howdy, Mrs. Lyddie. How are you this morning?"

A Debt to Pay

"Just fine, thank you, Will. I wanted to introduce you to two new friends of mine, Claire and Maggie Wallace." She smiled as she looked toward Claire and Maggie. "They've recently arrived and are considering settling here in Millcreek."

Will nodded in their direction, and then his eyes lingered on Claire. "I think I've seen you before."

"I work at the General Store and delivered an order at your ranch earlier this week."

A look of understanding crossed his eyes. "Oh yes. I do apologize for that day. I was preoccupied and don't think I made a proper introduction."

"I figured you were distracted by the situation at hand," Claire replied, her eyes holding his. He was all manners at the present, but she knew from experience how quickly a man's temper could change him for the worse. Her uncle had raised her and had had enough spells of rage to make her untrusting of any man.

"Was there something you were going to ask me that day?" Will asked, a little taken aback by how attractive she was. There was a solidity and tenderness to her features that made an impression on him.

"Yes. As Mrs. Lyddie was saying, my sister and I have recently moved here, and we are looking for a house to rent for at least a month. Lyddie mentioned that you may have something like that." Her nicely arched brows lifted questioningly as she waited for his response.

A woman Lyddie knew suddenly joined them and consequently pulled Lyddie and Maggie into a separate conversation.

"Yes. The man who was staying in it for a few months is no longer living there. It might need some repairs, but I can let you look at it and see what you think."

"We would appreciate it. Is it far from—"

"I can't believe it."

"What?" Claire realized Will Carter's gaze had shifted from her to someone behind her. Without another word, he suddenly mounted his horse and rode in that direction.

With her hands coming to her waist, Claire let out an irritated sigh. Will Carter was the rudest man she had ever met. Who just left in the middle of a conversation? She shook her head in vexation.

"What did he say?" Maggie asked a moment later.

"I don't know. He just…left." And then a sense of determination rose in her. "I'll meet you and Lyddie back at the house."

"Claire, where are you going?"

"To get us a place to stay," Claire called over her shoulder as she lifted her skirt and walked swiftly to where she saw Will Carter's horse down the street.

The town was in something of a T shape, with the road to the church branching off the main street to the left and the road to the livery branching off opposite it to the right. Soon, Claire was passing the livery and forge and crossing the street to where Will Carter's horse was standing. "Ugh, figures," she said aloud to herself when she realized his horse was outside the saloon. It was so far down the street and out of the way, it was the first time she had even noticed there was a saloon.

Nearing the double swinging doors, she could hear several voices from inside. Crossing her hands in front of her chest, she sat on a wooden stool on the porch area and decided she would wait for Will Carter to come out. After a few minutes, curiosity got the better of her, and she glanced through one of the two front windows. She could see Will Carter leaning over a table where a man sat, looking back at him calmly. Will Carter seemed less calm, and Claire saw him pound his fist on the tabletop before the other man set something on the table.

"Can I buy you a drink, Miss?"

Claire started at the voice, surprised to hear someone talking to her. A middle-aged man in a dark maroon suit and matching vest removed the cigar from his mouth. Something akin to a smile spread beneath his dark, horseshoe-shaped mustache. "Little early to start drinking," he said with a playful wink.

"Oh, I'm…I'm just waiting for someone."

The man's eyes didn't move from her face. "My name is Bruce Conway. I own the hotel…and the saloon," he added after a brief pause. "I don't think I've had the pleasure of meeting you, my dear."

Claire wasn't easily unnerved by men after spending so much time around them, but this man made her uncomfortable. "I'm Claire Wallace."

"Well, it certainly is a pleasure, Miss Wallace. Are you just visiting Millcreek, or are you here more permanently?"

"I'm not sure," she replied carefully.

He took a step closer. "Might I ask where you are staying presently?"

"I'm helping Miss Wallace with those arrangements."

Claire turned her head at the sound of Will Carter's voice. He had just stepped through the saloon doors.

"Good afternoon, Mr. Carter," Bruce Conway slightly tipped his derby hat, but Claire thought his expression and tone insincere.

"Conway," Will nodded his head slightly in acknowledgment but said nothing more. His gaze went to Claire. "I can walk you back so we can finish our conversation," he said.

Claire nodded, glad to escape Bruce Conway's rather overbearing presence.

"I wouldn't befriend that man if I were you," Will said a moment later as they walked down the street, his horse following behind them.

"I wasn't planning on it," she replied. "I was just waiting to speak to you."

"Yes, I'm sorry for running off like that."

"It's alright; I'm starting to get used to it," she said with just a brief smile.

He chuckled. "I'm not always this rude; it was just a matter of urgency."

"I understand, and I apologize for being a pest. We're just anxious to settle in."

"No, it's not a bother at all. I'd be happy to show you and your sister what I have. It's about a half mile from town."

"Thank you, Mr. Carter."

"Do you have plans this afternoon? I can take you and your sister now if you like."

"That would be wonderful." Claire glanced over her shoulder. "Does your horse always just follow you like that?" She'd never seen anything like it.

Will grinned. "Phoenix has always had a soft spot for me…and I trained him that way," he added.

Claire gently touched the horse's mane, admiring his tan, almost burnt orange coloring. "How did he get his name?"

"Shortly after he was born, we thought he wasn't going to make it. He surprised us all by making it through the night and becoming one of the strongest and fastest horses I've ever owned."

Claire ran her hand down his soft, velvet-like fur, thinking about the mythological bird the horse was named after. "The name suits him," she said.

A Debt to Pay

"I like to think everyone can be given a second chance," Will agreed.

Claire met his eyes and smiled slightly. "I like to think so, too."

———

The small house was more like a cabin, and even though primitive, it was quite charmingly situated in a grove of oak trees. There was a wooden swing hanging from one of the tree's branches and a well at the far side of the house.

"When Jacob Myles first moved to Millcreek, he and his wife lived here until they had built their own home," Will told them as he dismounted his horse and went to help the girls down from the wagon that they had borrowed from Lyddie.

"Before then, it belonged to my grandfather and then my father. Jacob made some repairs and updates with it, but you'll find it isn't fancy."

"We don't need much," Claire said, "And I like that we could walk to town if we need to."

"The swing is a nice touch," Maggie said, smiling as she sat on it.

"And the well," Claire mentioned. "Is there a spring nearby?"

"Just behind that tree line," Will replied, pointing. He led them through the front door.

Claire thought it was bigger inside than it looked. Despite its unkempt appearance, there was a sturdy-looking table with four chairs that sat adjacent to a fireplace, and to the left was a door that Claire assumed led to the bedroom. Will opened the door to let them look inside, and as Claire took a step toward the room, her foot met with an empty bottle.

Will leaned over to pick it up, an apologetic expression on his face. "I haven't been out here in some time. Unfortunately, the last person who stayed here didn't take care of the place." He glanced around, noting some dirty pots and pans still in the sink and more empty whiskey bottles lying about.

Claire looked at Maggie, who, reading Claire's mind, nodded her head in approval.

"We'll take it, Mr. Carter, dirty dishes and all," Claire told him.

"Are you sure?"

"Yes, sir. We're glad to have it. What would be the monthly rent?"

Will hesitated, not wanting to overcharge them when they seemed so desperate. "Is five dollars a month too much?"

Claire shook her head, an appreciative expression on her face. "No, Mr. Carter. Five dollars is very reasonable."

"Good. And you can call me Will." He was looking up to the roof, noting some vulnerable-looking areas. "I'll ask one of my ranch hands to patch the roof up there, and you should be able to move in by the middle of the week."

"That's perfect. Thank you," Claire said.

"So, where are you two from?" Will asked curiously as they made their way back to the wagon and Will's horse.

"Springfield," Maggie lied.

"So, this wide-open prairie must be pretty new to you then, huh?"

"It's quite a change for sure," Claire said.

"Travelling across the country is no easy feat. What made you want to leave the city?"

It had been easy to answer Lyddie's questions, but for some reason, Claire found herself struggling for the words. She was glad Maggie was managing the conversation. "We were heartbroken after our parents died a year ago and just needed a fresh start, you might say."

"I can understand that," Will replied, a distant look suddenly in his eyes. "Will you two be alright getting back? My ranch is the opposite direction of town."

"Of course," Claire finally found her voice. "Thank you for taking the time to show us the cabin. Just let us know when we can move in. We're staying at Lyddie's boardinghouse."

"Will do." He tipped his hat from astride his horse and made a clicking sound that started the horse forward.

"I think it's perfect!" Maggie exclaimed as they began their ride back to town.

"For now, walking will be fine, but eventually, we'll have to get a horse and wagon of some sort," Claire said.

"That Mr. Carter is quite an eye-catcher, wouldn't you say?"

"I don't know what I think of him," Claire admitted.

"Well, you have to agree he's handsome."

"I suppose," Claire said. "The only thing on my mind is paying off what money we took and making a life for myself that looks nothing like my past."

"Amen to that!" Maggie agreed, and then she gave a little groan. "Sometimes I'm afraid that preacher's gonna see right through me and call me out on all the wrong I've done."

"I don't think you need to worry about that," Claire assured her.

"My past is a darn sight more sinful than yours, Claire. You think working at that saloon was bad?" Maggie shook her head and gave a heavy sigh. "You weren't ever part of the world I was, and thankfully so."

"Well, it's behind us now," Claire reminded her.

"We're off to a good start," Maggie agreed. "Now, if I could only find myself a decent job!"

Chapter Six

"Would you mind the store while I help my wife with something?" Tom asked Claire one day that week. It was near noon, so he wanted to make sure Verra was able to get lunch.

"Of course, Mr. Maison," Claire replied. Once he'd gone, she turned around at the counter to finish arranging some new books that Mr. Maison had just got in. The shelf was a little high, so she pulled over a nearby stool and climbed up on it. As she stacked the books on the higher shelf, she noticed something sticking out on the shelf above it. Curious, she tried to get it, but it was just out of reach. Glancing down at the counter, she put one foot on it and boosted herself up while moving her other foot to a lower shelf. Balancing herself in a slightly straddled position, she was able to reach it.

A white, unsealed envelope. That's all it was, but there appeared to be something inside. Claire suddenly heard the jingle of the doorbell, announcing a customer. She knew she must look odd on top of the counter and quickly tried to get her feet back on the ground. She started to step down with the foot she had on the shelf, but it was more awkward getting down than it had been to get up.

"Do you need some help?" she heard a familiar voice ask.

A Debt to Pay

Glancing over her shoulder, Claire saw Will Carter making his way toward her.

"No, I'm fine," she told him as she found the stool with her right foot and slid her hands to the next shelf. But that shelf wasn't nailed into the wall like the rest, and it suddenly flipped forward, causing Claire to lose her balance and flail backward.

Will's hands were there to catch her and set her upright. There was a loud banging noise as the shelf and all the books that she had set on it fell to the ground, just missing her feet.

"Are you alright?" Will asked, helping her step to the side to avoid the shelf that had fallen.

She didn't even hear the question as her attention was on the mess she had made. "I've got to clean this up," she said, eagerly kneeling to gather the books.

"Here, let me."

Claire moved out of the way as he picked up the fallen board and set it back in its place. "I should secure this a little better," he said, giving it a little shake to test its security.

"It wouldn't have fallen if I hadn't put weight on it like that."

"What were you trying to do?" Will asked, unable to keep an amused tone from his voice. "You looked like some sort of acrobat up there."

Claire heard herself laugh outright. "I was trying to reach something," she tried to defend herself but couldn't keep the smile from her face.

"Next time, just use a ladder." He leaned over with her and helped her pick up the books.

"Thank you," she said, taking them from his hands and returning them carefully to the shelf.

"I can reorganize these later," she said. "Was there something I can help you with?"

"I wanted to speak with Tom. Is he here?"

"Just left a few minutes ago, but he should be back soon."

"Well, I was going to stop by Mrs. Lyddie's after I came here to tell you the house is ready."

"Really? That's wonderful!"

The sincere appreciation in her eyes made Will glad he was able to help her and her sister out. There was something about her that made him want to linger a little longer. "I did notice a few other things around the place that could use some repairs, so I'll send someone to get to it in the next week or so."

"Thank you, Mr. Carter. My sister and I will probably be over tomorrow when I'm through here."

"My ranch is only a mile west of the cabin, so if ever you two need anything, don't hesitate to come by."

"That's kind, thank you," she smiled, looking into his warm, hazel eyes and wondering how this could be the same man she had witnessed at the upper hand of a fight the other day.

The doorbell chimed as someone came inside the store, reminding Will that he had other things he needed to do that day. "Good day, Miss Wallace."

"Claire," she corrected kindly before slipping behind the counter and beginning to reorganize the books, a task she wanted done before Tom Maison came back. She suddenly remembered the envelope that had grabbed her attention in the first place. She glanced around and realized she had dropped it on the floor, and some of its contents had spilled out. Adjusting her skirts, she squatted down to pick it up and realized it was money that had fallen out. Making sure she had collected all of it, she slid it back inside and closed the envelope. She knew she couldn't risk a climb back up the shelves to put it back, so she tucked it in her apron pocket to give to Mr. Maison when he returned.

A Debt to Pay

As she stood again, she noticed Will had not left the store but was standing near the door talking with the young woman Mrs. Lyddie had pointed out to her at church as Amy Keets.

"Pa has been at me for weeks to have you over for supper again," she heard Amy saying with an enthusiastic voice. "Do you have free time this weekend? He just won't forgive me if I don't ask," she laughed softly as she flipped a ponytail of blonde curls behind her shoulder.

"Please tell your father I'm sorry. I'm just too busy right now. Maybe another time."

To Claire, it seemed he was trying to move past her and out the door, but she shifted slightly and appeared to wittingly block him. "My father also has been talking about taking a ride over to your ranch to see you about a new horse. Perhaps next weekend if you're not busy."

"That would probably work."

His voice sounded hesitant, Claire thought, and she had to smile to herself at the way the woman continued to hold him hostage with her conversation. Finally, she stepped away from the door, giving him a wave with her white-gloved hand. "See you next weekend, Will."

Amy Keets lingered at the yard goods before addressing Claire. "Excuse me, ma'am? I need some of this material cut, please."

Claire came over. "Certainly. How much would you like?"

"You're that new girl who came in on the stage a few weeks ago, aren't you?"

Claire met her blue eyes and nodded. "Yes. Was this the fabric you wanted?" she asked, gesturing to a bolt of light blue gingham the girl was holding in her hands.

"It is. I'll take a dress length's worth."

Claire tried to remember what Mr. Maison had told her about the fabric lengths. Having never made a dress herself, she really wasn't sure. She had mended her own clothing but never made one from scratch. Biting her thumbnail, Claire stared at the fabric she had carried to the counter. She glanced back at the young woman and saw her skirt was quite full and slightly bustled in the back.

"You don't know, do you?" Amy said in a voice that sounded both sweet and accusing at the same time.

Claire flipped over the bolt several times so the fabric could be laid out and cut. "About five yards?" she guessed, her voice feigning the confidence she didn't feel.

"That's right," the girl said smugly, leaning her elbow on the counter as she watched Claire. Amy Keets enjoyed the attention being pretty afforded her, and she did not like the fact that there was someone else in town to rival her. "The fabric will make quite a statement, don't you think?"

"It is very nice," Claire replied as she finished cutting it and gingerly folding it into a parcel.

"My name is Amy Keets. I didn't catch yours?"

"It's Claire Wallace." She smiled politely but got the feeling this woman didn't like her. "I've seen you in church but never got a chance to introduce myself."

"Yes, well, it's nice to make your acquaintance," Amy said as she took the parcel and turned to go.

"Excuse me," Claire said. "You forgot to pay."

Amy turned slowly and sighed with a condescending look in her eyes. "I didn't forget to pay, dear. My father has an account here."

Claire watched as she left the store and made a mental note to avoid Amy Keets whenever possible. Mr. Maison was coming into the store as Amy was going out.

A Debt to Pay

"How is your wife feeling?" Claire asked him as he joined her at the counter.

"Like a caged animal," he chuckled. "She's not one to stop and rest, so I'm afraid this issue with her leg has her out of sorts."

"Oh, Mr. Maison. Before I forget, I found this earlier."

Tom took the envelope that she reached toward him, and his mouth dropped open. "Where did you find this?"

"On the top shelf when I was organizing the books." She could tell by his expression that he was pleased.

"I spent weeks looking for this! Couldn't remember where I'd put it." He looked at her, sincerity in his light blue eyes. "Thank you for your honesty."

Claire hadn't considered any other option, but his words made her think of a not-so-honest thing she had done not very long ago. It bothered her until she remembered what sort of man Frederick Harris was. Eager to escape her course of thought, Claire went for the broom and headed outside to sweep the front steps.

"There's a pile of wood at the side of the house," Maggie told Claire the next day as they were settling into their new house.

"It wasn't there the last time," Claire replied. "Mr. Carter must have chopped some for us."

"Guess that's something we'll have to learn how to do," Maggie said, a look of concern in her eyes.

Claire began to unload the crate of food she had brought back from the store. Her wages from two weeks had enabled her to buy everything they needed, plus a few extras like cleaning supplies and pots and pans.

"I could tell Lyddie was sad to see us go," Maggie said as she unloaded the flour and sugar into a cabinet in the hutch.

"She was very kind to us," Claire added. "But the stage arrives tomorrow, and it's certain to bring her more boarders."

"There's the hotel at the other end of town, too," Maggie mentioned. "But I wouldn't want to stay there knowing the likes of Bruce Conway ran it."

"You met him too?" Claire asked.

"Mm-hm. I was out for a walk one day, and he walked past and introduced himself. Just made my skin crawl." She gave a little shudder.

"I know what you mean." Claire agreed. "We're done with that sort, Maggie."

Maggie nodded, and Claire thought her eyes looked like they were pooling with tears. "What is it?" Claire asked.

"Just that I'm so grateful to be here." She wiped her cheeks.

"Me too, Maggie, and I'm so glad you came with me. I'd feel lost without you."

"Really?" Maggie sniffed.

Claire hugged her. "Of course. You're the only sister I have, remember?"

Maggie laughed softly. "Well, I guess that's true."

The next day was Friday. After a good night's sleep, Claire and Maggie muddled to make hotcakes for breakfast, and then Claire started the half-mile walk into town. Maggie waved to her from the doorway and then turned back into the house to clean up the mess. She knew she'd have to get a bucket of water to wash the frying pan and dishes, so she headed outside toward the well. Soon, she had the breakfast mess cleaned and then decided she would sweep and mop the wide-planked wood floor of the cabin. Rolling up her sleeves and retying her apron a little snugger, Maggie set to work. She would get this place clean from top to bottom.

A Debt to Pay

An hour later, she was outside draping a rug over a tree branch and taking a rug beater to it. She coughed as clouds of dust surrounded her. A few minutes later, she walked around to the back of the house. There was a small plot for a garden on the one side. It was overgrown with weeds at the moment, but Maggie knew she could change that. A sudden memory of watching her mother in the garden came to her. Before moving to Chicago, they had lived in a rural town where Maggie had many fond memories. She had attended school and helped her mother around the house. She had only a few vague memories of her father being there, though.

She distinctly remembered the day her mother told her they were leaving to go live with her father in Chicago. She was around ten, and life after that had far less fond memories.

Kneeling down, Maggie pulled up a handful of grass and weeds and then another and another. Within half an hour, she had a decent pile and an aching back. Coming to her feet, she shook out her skirt, and that's when she heard a noise that sounded like a child crying. She tilted her head to listen, thinking she was imagining the sound. But then she heard it again, and this time it was louder.

Maggie moved to the yard's edge, where a forest area separated the yard from another open field. The sound of a creek got louder as Maggie moved through the woods and down a little ravine covered with brush. She suddenly noticed that there, by the creek, sitting on a fallen tree limb, was a little girl. Maggie thought the blonde braids down her back were familiar somehow. A branch under Maggie's next step snapped, causing the girl to turn abruptly. That's when Maggie recognized the girl as the one who had sat in front of her in church the last two weeks, the same little girl who had been present when she arrived on the stage.

"You're Reverend Myles' daughter, aren't you?" Maggie asked gently when she saw the girl stand up and prepare to bolt. "You don't have to rush off," Maggie added. "It's a rather nice spot to be alone."

Lilly Myles wiped at her tears, unknowingly transferring dirt from her hands to her cheeks. She heaved in a shaky breath and watched Maggie as she continued to move down the ravine toward her.

"Are you hurt?" Maggie asked with concern as she sidestepped a bulging tree root and moved in time to miss a briar bush.

"No," the girl finally spoke.

"Do you live around here?" Maggie asked, her eyes scanning the wooded area. Perhaps her house was on the other side of the field that lay behind them.

"Just over that field," Lilly confirmed her suspicion.

"You're out for a walk then?"

Lilly shook her head. "I'm running away."

Maggie's eyebrows hiked in surprise, and she quickly noted the girl hadn't brought any belongings with her. "Why would you do that?" Maggie asked gently.

"I'm running away until that mean old Mrs. Newberry leaves. I hate her!"

Maggie sat on the log that Lilly had been occupying. "She's that bad, huh?"

"The worst," Lilly replied as she sat next to Maggie. She sighed and crossed her arms in front of her chest. "It was better when she wasn't here."

"Have you talked to your Pa about it?"

"She's nice when he's around. He just says to give her a little more time."

"Maybe she'll improve."

A Debt to Pay

"No, she won't, and if she's not going to leave, then I will! Ma would hate her too…if…if she was still here. But if she was still here, then we wouldn't need Mrs. Newberry."

Her words brought on fresh tears and little sobs that moved Maggie to instinctively place her arm around her. It was heartbreaking to think of how much this girl was hurting from losing her mother at far too young an age. Maggie felt the stinging reminder of how she had felt losing her own mother when she was in her teens.

"There, there, sweetheart. It hurts now, but in time, you won't feel so sad." Maggie just sat there and let her cry for several more minutes, and then her sobs became sniffs, and eventually, she was breathing peacefully. That's when Maggie realized the poor girl had fallen asleep. She must have really needed it, and Maggie wouldn't wake her for anything, so she just sat there on the tree stump with the sound of the creek and the little girl's even breaths.

Birds whistled and chirped in the canopy of green leaves while the water made its own song over the rocks and the forest floor. It was so peaceful that Maggie could feel herself getting drowsy. She didn't know how long she sat there with the little girl's head in her lap. She gently pushed back strands of blonde hair that had fallen over the sleeping girl's face and just watched her sleep. The idea that anyone could be unkind to such an angel was frustrating. Maybe she ought to have a word with Mrs. Newberry.

Lilly began to stir and yawn softly; she sat up and looked at Maggie curiously until she remembered. "How long have I been sleeping?" she asked, her eyes darting around the forest as if she expected it to be night.

"I'm not sure. Maybe an hour."

"Oh. It felt like a long time."

"Maybe you needed it. Can I walk you home?"

The little girl shook her head. "My Pa will probably be home by now, so it's OK."

"Are you sure? I don't mind."

Lilly was already coming to her feet. "I'm sure." She paused, biting her lower lip as she seemed to be searching for words. "Thank you."

Maggie smiled warmly. "I'm Maggie. I live in that cabin just up aways." She pointed behind her.

"I'm Lilly."

"I've seen you in church, but it's nice to meet you again, Lilly."

The little girl offered a little smile before turning and walking away. Just as she reached the clearing, she turned and gave a little wave.

Maggie waved back, hoping the girl would find happier days.

Claire was almost home when she heard a wagon approaching behind her. She stepped to the side of the road to let it pass, but she heard a man's voice slowing his horses. "Can I give you a ride the rest of the way?"

Claire lifted her hand to shield her eyes from the sun as she looked up at who had spoken. She couldn't remember his name, but she knew it was the man who had unloaded her wagon at the ranch.

"Thank you, but I'm almost there."

"I'm headed there myself with orders to mend the fence."

Realizing it wouldn't be an inconvenience, Claire agreed. "In that case." She lifted her skirt slightly to climb up and took his offered hand.

Once she was seated beside him, he took the reins again and urged the horses forward.

"It's Claire, isn't it?"

"Yes, but I'm afraid I forgot your name."

"Jared."

"Thanks for stopping."

"Sure thing. It's hot 'nough to sunburn a horned toad. How are you settling in?"

"Just fine."

"I heard you were from a big city or something. You must feel like a fish out of water."

Claire smiled slightly, "More like a fish that's found water, I think. I prefer this to the city."

He grinned, glancing at her and then back to the road. "So do I."

"Have you lived here your whole life?" she asked.

"Missouri, yes, but Millcreek just the last five years or so. I was working a cattle drive for Will Carter, and I ended up staying on. He's a good man to work for."

"I don't know if that man he was fighting the other day would agree," Claire said aloud, though she had only meant to think it.

"Who, Grady? He had it coming to him for a while. If there's one thing Will Carter can't stand, it's a thief and a liar."

Claire shifted in her seat, a little uncomfortable with the direction of the conversation.

"He'd stolen his watch and then lost it gambling," Jared explained further. "But that was only one incident on top of others."

Understanding dawned on Claire. Even Will's visit to the saloon made sense now. He was in pursuit of getting his watch back.

The cabin came into view, and soon they were pulling up to the yard. Jared jumped down and made it around in time to help Claire finish climbing down.

"I'll be here for about an hour," he told her. "Let me know if you need anything done before I leave."

She thanked him and then went inside. It was obvious Maggie had made good use of the day, as the house smelled and looked clean and put together. There was also a delicious aroma coming from the oven.

"You've been busy!" Claire said with a smile at Maggie, who had stepped out of the bedroom, a rag in her hands. "I can't wait to eat whatever you have cooking."

"Don't say that until after you've tried it," Maggie warned.

Chapter Seven

Claire looked up from the catalog on the counter and smiled as Maggie entered the store the following day. "Can I help you with something?" she asked teasingly.

"I decided to take a walk and stop by with some lunch for you, since you forgot it."

"Aw, thanks, Maggie."

"Have you been busy today?"

"Not so much. Spent most the morning helping Mr. Maison unload an order he got in."

"Where is he now?" She glanced around the store.

"In the back room."

The front door opened again, and Mrs. Newberry entered with her two young charges in tow. Lilly's face lit up when she saw Maggie, and she gave her a little wave.

"Good morning, Mrs. Newberry," Claire said.

"Good morning, Miss Wallace. I'm here to get a few things for Reverend Myles."

"If you have a list, I'd be happy to get them for you," Claire said.

Mrs. Newberry handed her a piece of paper and turned sharply to Lucas. "Don't touch anything!"

The little boy put his hand down from where he had been touching a hat on the shelf. "I'll keep an eye on him," Lilly spoke up as she took her brother's hand and walked him to the other side of the store.

A few minutes later, there was the sound of a loud crash. Mrs. Newberry looked horrified as she stomped over to where the children were standing. "I said not to touch anything!" She promptly hit the boy's hand hard, and he immediately started to cry.

"He didn't knock it off the shelf; I did!" Lilly told her.

"You're a liar. I saw him touching it."

Lucas had been the one to knock it over, but Lilly was ready to take the blame if it meant her little brother was spared further punishment.

"Now, take your brother outside and wait for me there, and think about what it means to obey your elders. Go!" She gave Lilly a shove, and the little girl and her brother quickly scurried out of the store.

Maggie could feel her blood boiling watching the whole exchange. Then and there, she reasoned she was going to do something about it. Walking over to Mrs. Newberry, she waited until she had her attention.

"It would do you right to remember these children are still grieving the loss of their mother."

"Excuse me?" the older woman looked indignant, and her eyes narrowed.

"From watching your response just now, I wager this isn't the first time you've responded to them harshly."

"Children who misbehave need correction. But I really don't see how it is any business of yours." She turned and abruptly walked away, meeting Claire at the counter. "Is my order ready?" she huffed.

A Debt to Pay

"Yes, ma'am." Claire handed her a basket with her purchases in it as she glanced sideways at Maggie.

Mrs. Newberry slid some coins across the counter and left without another word.

"What was all that about?" Claire asked.

"I don't know what came over me, Claire. Maybe my mother was right about redheads having a quick temper! I wanted to switch that woman after she slapped little Lucas. If today was any indication, I know why Lilly was so upset the other day."

Maggie had told Claire about her happening upon the little girl. "Maybe Reverend Myles needs to know the nanny he hired isn't what he thinks she is," Claire said as she carried the broom and dustpan over to the shattered jar that lay in the middle of an aisle.

"What if he knows and he's in favor of her treatment?" Maggie said with concern, hoping she was wrong.

"I doubt that. Just by listening to his sermons, he sounds like a kind and reasonable man."

Maggie nodded in agreement. "If the opportunity presents itself, Claire, I just might say something."

Maggie stayed in town and visited with Lyddie until Claire finished work, and then the two girls walked home together.

"There's that Mr. Cooper again," Maggie pointed out as they neared the cabin and saw him on his knees beside a fence post. He stood and smiled by way of a greeting to them as they neared.

"Good afternoon, Mr. Cooper," Maggie said.

"Please, call me Jared," he replied. "I'm just about through here, and I'll be out of your way."

"Oh, you're not in our way," Maggie reassured him.

"Is there anything you need done before I leave?" he asked, looking from Maggie to Claire.

"I don't believe so," Claire replied. "But if you wouldn't mind giving something to Mr. Carter, I would appreciate it."

"Absolutely."

"I'll be right back." Claire returned with a sealed envelope addressed to Will Carter. "It's our first month's rent." She figured if Mr. Carter trusted Jared to do work for him, she could trust him to deliver the money.

"I'll make sure that he gets it," Jared told her as he put it in his trouser pocket and then tipped his wide-brimmed hat. "Good day, ladies."

"He's not bad looking either," Maggie remarked after he had gone.

Claire rolled her eyes.

"Well, not as striking as Mr. Carter, but…" Maggie let her sentence hang as she noticed a man on horseback coming across the field toward them. As he neared, they saw that it was Reverend Myles.

"Woah," he said to his horse as he pulled on the reins to slow her.

"I'm sorry to bother you. I'm afraid I'm looking for my daughter, Lilly. Have either of you seen her around?"

They shook their heads, and Maggie stepped forward slightly. "Has she run away?"

He looked surprised that she would ask that question but nodded just the same. "She left a note." He took off his hat and ran a distracted hand through his brown hair, his worried eyes searching the surroundings. "I don't know why she would do this."

"I think I do. And I think I might know where to find her."

Jacob looked at Maggie with both astonishment and hope. "Please, I could use your help."

"Follow me."

A Debt to Pay

Jacob dismounted quickly, and Claire offered to take the reins. She led his horse over to a hitching post and watched Jacob and Maggie disappear behind the house.

"It was a few days ago that I was out here and heard a child crying," Maggie began to explain. "When I followed the sound, I found her sitting by the creek, just through those trees." She pointed in front of them.

"You said you knew why she ran away?"

"It's that woman you hired, Mrs. Newberry."

She heard him let out a frustrated breath of air. "I knew I should have sent her packing. I just thought maybe she would improve with time, and the children so desperately need a woman's gentle hand."

"I know you mean well, Reverend Myles, but I don't think Mrs. Newberry has a gentle hand."

"What do you mean?" He watched her closely, hanging on her words.

"I've seen her be hard on them, and today, she slapped your son rather hard for accidentally dropping something."

"Ugh, this is all my fault." He slapped his hat against his leg.

"You couldn't have known."

"But Lilly tried to tell me."

She could hear the remorse in his voice and wished she had something to say to encourage him. They reached the tree line and, glancing down the ravine, saw Lilly sitting on the same log as the last time Maggie had found her. Maggie watched as Reverend Myles moved past her and descended the ravine effortlessly.

"Sweetheart, I was worried about you," he said as he immediately scooped her up into his arms. "Please don't ever run away like that again." He gently wiped the tear drops off her face. "Did you leave because of Mrs. Newberry?"

The little girl nodded and then buried her face in his shoulder. Turning around, Jacob carefully climbed up the slope until he was standing by Maggie. "Thank you so much for your help."

"I'm just glad she was here."

"I'm in your debt." Jacob's gratitude was so sincere that Maggie had to glance away from the warmth in his kind eyes. She wasn't used to someone looking at her like that.

"Are you going to make her leave?" Lilly suddenly asked, and they both knew who she was talking about.

"Yes, sweetheart. I'll talk to her as soon as we get back."

Lilly hugged him tight and then slid down to walk beside him the rest of the way. Once back at the cabin, Reverend Myles helped his daughter up on the saddle and then mounted up behind her.

"Thank you again, Miss Wallace."

"It's Maggie," she said, sending a reassuring smile in Lilly's direction. She watched as they rode away, wondering why her heart felt so pleased helping a little girl she barely knew.

―――

*T*hat Saturday, as the girls were in the yard hanging wet laundry, Claire looked up and saw Will Carter coming down the road in a wagon, leading a cow behind him. Wiping her wet hands on her apron, she walked over to greet him.

"Howdy." He tipped his hat with a friendly smile and hopped off the wagon seat.

"Good afternoon. Can we help you with something?" Claire asked.

"I'm hoping I can help you." He walked behind the wagon, untied the cow, and led it back to where Claire, and now, Maggie, were standing.

"Thought you could use this jersey cow for milk."

Claire glanced at Maggie and back to Will Carter. "How much is she?"

"She's a gift," he replied.

"We wouldn't know the first thing about milking her," Maggie spoke up, biting her lower lip uncertainly as she looked at the brown and white cow.

"I can show you how," Will said. "It's not hard once you get used to it."

"Fresh milk would be nice," Claire thought out loud. "But I want to pay you for her."

Will tried to argue with her but saw he wasn't getting anywhere. He named a price he thought was more generous than fair and hoped she'd go for it. "I'd like to throw in a few chickens, too," he said, tilting his head toward the back of the wagon. He went to the wagon and came back holding a cage with three brown hens. "But I won't let you pay me for these because you'd be doing me a favor taking them off my hands. We have too many at the ranch as it is."

"I don't know what to say," Claire told him. "That's so kind of you."

He shrugged. "Everyone needs a little help when they're startin' out somewhere new, and like I said, I'm glad to get rid of a few."

Claire gave him an appreciative smile. "I'll be right back." She ran into the house and returned with money to give him for the cow.

Will thanked her as he put it in his pocket and then said, "I wanted to check out the stable and make sure it doesn't need anything before we put her in there."

He lifted a straw bale from the wagon before leading the way to the small barn, standing just at the end of the backyard bordering a fair-sized pasture. After a few minutes, Will used a pitchfork to spread out the straw in one of the stalls and then led the cow inside. "This should work for now," he said.

"What about the chickens?" Maggie asked. "Will they know what to do by themselves?"

"Yup," Will replied. "But I'll work on building you a proper coop. For now, they can just use the barn. You'll have to just make sure the door is closed at night after they go in so the foxes and coyotes don't get 'em."

"Thank you so much," Claire said, and then remembering, said, "Oh, did Mr. Cooper give you an envelope from me?"

"He did, thanks," Will said. "Anything you ladies need help with before I go?"

"I think we're alright for now," Claire replied.

"Alright. I'll see you in church, then; good day."

Once he was out of earshot, Claire turned to Maggie. "Speaking of church, now that we're not staying with Mrs. Lyddie in town, it doesn't feel like we have to go."

"That's true, but I guess I don't really mind it," Maggie said.

"I guess I don't either," Claire agreed with a shrug.

That Sunday, as they came into the churchyard, Claire spotted some familiar faces, although there were still plenty of people she hadn't met yet. Mr. Carter was one of the familiar ones. He arrived just behind them and walked up the stairs with them.

"Good morning, Maggie, Claire."

"Good morning," Claire replied as she tucked a loose strand of nutmeg hair behind her ear.

"How's the milking coming?"

"Oh, it's coming," she smiled with a small laugh. "More on the ground than in the bucket, but we'll get the hang of it."

A Debt to Pay

They were inside the church at that point, and Will moved off to the right to his usual spot. To his surprise, he spotted Jared Cooper sitting in one of the pews. "It's nice to see you in church this morning," he said as he removed his hat and took the seat near him.

Jared shrugged. "Just thought it might be a good idea to start coming."

Will followed the man's gaze to where it rested on Claire Wallace and put two and two together. The man was clearly not there for the sermon, or at least that wasn't his entire reason for coming.

The congregation was led in several hymns, and then Reverend Myles came forward and preached from the book of First John. Will was like a sponge as he listened. It was only two years since he had given his life to the Lord, but he was eager to make up for lost time. He found himself glancing over at the Wallace sisters a few times. They seemed to be listening intently as well.

After the service, Claire was approached by Silvia Wendel, who she learned was the schoolteacher during the school season. She seemed a kind young woman, in her twenties, and from what Claire found out from their conversation, she had lived in Millcreek her whole life. As she talked with her, Claire noticed Amy Keets and her father lingering around Will Carter. She also noticed Jared Cooper for the first time that morning and politely met his smile with her own before turning to find Maggie. She saw the Reverend's children were talking to her and that there seemed to be no trace of Mrs. Newberry.

Maggie enjoyed Lilly and her brother's chatter, whose little words were so jumbled she could barely understand what he said. They were telling her about a cat near their house that had just had kittens when Jacob Myles walked up beside them.

"May I speak to you about something before you leave?" he asked her.

Maggie was surprised that he was addressing her but found herself nodding.

He looked down at Lilly and asked if she would take her brother outside to play. She did as he said, a little smile touching her lips, almost as if she knew what her father wanted to talk to Maggie about.

"I wanted to thank you again for helping me with Lilly a few days ago."

"Oh, it was my pleasure. She's a very sweet girl."

"I was hoping you thought so because…"

Maggie saw what seemed like uncertainty in his expression and wondered what he was going to say.

"Well, my daughter is very taken with you, and as you know, my wife passed away not too long ago, which makes it difficult for me to make house calls or find time to study with having the children all the time. I also work at the mill a few days a week and have had to leave Lilly in charge of Lucas on several occasions, which I don't feel comfortable with yet."

He cleared his throat nervously. "I hope it doesn't sound too presumptuous to ask you if you might consider…if you might consider replacing Mrs. Newberry?"

Maggie was so shocked and honored by his question that she just stared at him for a full five seconds.

"I would pay you, of course," he quickly added. "And if I'm out of line for even asking, if that's not the sort of the thing you would like to do, then it's completely…"

"I would love to, Reverend Myles."

"Really?" he sighed with relief, and a smile tugged at the corner of his mouth.

"Really. I'm honored that you would ask me to look after your children."

"We can give it a two-week trial, and if it's too much, then I completely understand."

Maggie nodded her agreement, thrilled to tell Claire she had a job and one she was excited about, to boot.

"When are you available?" he asked.

"I'm pretty free all the time, so whenever you need me to watch them, I can be there."

"What if I come by tomorrow morning and pick you up? And then I can show you the house, and you can get better acquainted with Lucas and Lilly."

"Tomorrow morning works just fine. Thank you."

Jacob smiled. "My daughter is going to be thrilled. Thank you. Until tomorrow, then."

Maggie nodded, a smile still on her face when she met Claire at the back of the church.

"You're grinning ear to ear," Claire laughed softly. "What are you so happy about?"

"I'll tell you on the way home," Maggie replied.

As they left the church, Claire noticed a few people still milling about, Jared Cooper being one of them. He approached them as they walked. "Can I give you ladies a ride home?"

They agreed, and he waited as they climbed into the wagon. It was a pleasant ride home, with him talking most of the way, but Claire couldn't wait to get back and hear what Maggie had to tell her.

"I think he's sweet on you," Maggie said once he had gone and they were heading into the house.

"Horse feathers, Maggie. Now tell me your news!"

"Reverend Myles asked me to care for his children! And he'll pay me to do it."

"That's wonderful! I told you something would turn up."

"You were right. I just can't believe he would ask me."

"I can. You're great with kids."

"What if he expects me to cook?" A look of horror came over her face.

Claire laughed. "You'll be fine, Maggie."

Maggie wasn't so sure, but nothing could dampen her spirits. She was excited to spend time with those sweet children and put an end to the lonely days she had been spending in the cabin.

Maggie was ready bright and early and couldn't keep herself from going to the window half a dozen times to see if Reverend Myles had arrived. She must have glanced into her handheld mirror just as repeatedly, wishing she had Claire's complexion rather than the freckles that dotted her nose and cheeks. She had heard more times than not that she was pretty, but for the life of her, she couldn't see it.

The sound of a wagon suddenly caught her attention, and she hurried to the door, grabbing her bonnet just before going out. The children were in the back of the wagon. Jacob Myles had climbed down and was waiting to help her up.

"We only live about a mile east of here," he told her as he helped her into the wagon.

"Hello, Miss Wallace," Lilly said, coming to stand behind the seat.

"Hewoah, Miss Wayis," Lucas echoed.

"Lilly, sit down with your brother," Jacob told her gently.

A Debt to Pay

Once she had sat back down, he flapped the reins and began the ride to his house.

"I hope I didn't come too early," Jacob said apologetically, trying to ignore memories of him and his wife living in that same cabin.

"Not at all," Maggie assured him. She took in the fields of tall grass on either side of the dirt road. Trees speckled the grassy scene, their leaves rustling in the morning breeze. Maggie wasn't sure what to say, so she was glad the ride there was a mix of comfortable silence and small talk.

It wasn't long before they pulled up into a beautiful yard with young trees on either side of a small but clean-looking, rectangular-shaped home. The house was white, and the window trim was painted a dark green to match the front door. Just to the side of the house was a small garden enclosed by a two-foot wooden fence. Maggie saw another enclosed area behind the house with a cow and several chickens. She couldn't miss the fragrant and vibrant red rose bushes along the front of the house.

"This is just beautiful," she said. "I love all the roses!"

"Ma and Pa planted them," Lilly told her proudly, and Maggie suddenly remembered Lilly's mother's name.

"That's very fitting," Maggie said softly, not missing the smile Lilly gave her.

"Me and Lucas share a room," Lilly told her as they walked toward the house.

"You'll have to show me," Maggie said in a tone that made Lilly feel she was genuinely interested.

"Would Monday, Wednesday, and Friday work for you to be here?" Jacob asked a few minutes later as they moved from a tour of the house to the backyard.

"Yes, that would be fine."

"I'll work at the mill two of the days and save all my house calls and other duties at the church for the other. The children can always go with me if I get called out on a day you're not here. I'll be home before dinner, so you won't ever have to stay late. The children would just need lunch, but I can make sure they eat breakfast before you come."

"That's no problem," Maggie said.

"And would two dollars a week suffice?"

"Thank you, Reverend Myles; that would be just fine."

"You can call me Jacob," he surprised her by saying. "Reverend sounds so formal."

"I must say, you're nothing like the minister I grew up with."

"And what was he like?" Jacob asked curiously.

"Everything you aren't: loud, stern, and very unattractive."

He laughed softly, and she suddenly hoped she hadn't made him uncomfortable. She was glad when Lilly ran over to her and changed the course of the conversation.

"Do you want to see our cat?"

Maggie was grateful for the diversion and followed the girl to the small barn. Lilly was enthusiastic as she introduced her to the large tabby cat and her five kittens.

"Mrs. Newberry wanted to take the kittens and drop them off in the woods," Lilly said in a tone of disbelief. "How could anyone think of such a thing!"

"I don't know," Maggie said as she petted a gray one that Lilly had put in her lap. "They are just adorable."

"I knew you would like cats," Lilly told her as she snuggled two kittens at the same time.

"How did you know that?"

"Because you're pretty, and you smile a lot."

Maggie laughed at her unexpected answer. They were off

A Debt to Pay

to a good start, and if the light in her eyes was any indication, Lilly thought so, too.

Chapter Eight

Claire finished washing the front windows and took the bucket of dirty water to the side of the general store, where she dumped it into a patch of grass. As she came back to the front of the store, she saw Bruce Conway crossing the street.

"Good afternoon, Miss Wallace!" He called before Claire could slip back into the store.

"Good afternoon, Mr. Conway."

"How are you and your sister settling into Millcreek?" he asked, admiring the way she had her dark hair pinned up with tresses cascading down her back.

"Just fine, thank you."

"I can see you're busy," he said, glancing at the bucket in her hands, "so I won't keep you long. I just wanted to make you an offer."

"Oh?"

"When Mrs. Maison is on her feet again, and you find yourself out of work, I'd like to offer you a job at the hotel." He lit a cigar as he waited for her response.

"What sort of job?"

"Oh, this and that…all *respectable*," he added with a wink.

"I'll keep that in mind," she told him in a tone that said just the opposite.

A Debt to Pay

"Please do," he replied as she turned and went into the store.

Claire didn't know exactly what it was about him that didn't settle well, but she hoped she never had to work for that man.

"Can you help me hang this banner?" Mr. Maison asked her as she came back into the store. He was holding a thick string with a dozen triangle-shaped American flags hanging from it. "Every year, we decorate for the annual Independence Day Picnic," he explained.

"The fourth of July is next Saturday, isn't it?" she asked, realizing she'd lost track of time.

"Sure is, and that's when we have the all-day picnic as well."

"Sounds like fun," she said as she returned outside to help him nail the banner from one end of the front porch to the other. "Should I bring something?"

"Oh, everyone brings something or other: a pie, a cake, whatever you like!"

"There's games for the kids…and adults." He grinned as he recounted to her how he had been on the winning team of the tug-o-war contest the previous year.

"Mr. Carter gives one of his young horses to the winner of the horse race, and Mr. Keets awards five dollars to the man who wins the log chopping contest."

"Any contests for women?" Claire asked with a smile, although she had no intention of entering.

"Oh, sure! There's a pie baking contest and a basket raffle to raise money for the town."

"I know I wouldn't win any contest having to do with baking a pie," Claire admitted, "but maybe I'll see what kind of basket I can put together."

Later that day, as Claire told Maggie about the picnic, she was thrilled to hear how good her third day of working for Reverend Myles had been. It seemed that they both had settled into a nice routine, and their first month in Millcreek had turned out to be a promising one.

"I've kept a careful record of how much money we used on the trip, our new clothes, and our first days here," Claire told her as they worked in the garden together. She pushed a wheelbarrow full of weeds over to the other end of the yard. "Shouldn't be too long before we can pay it all back."

Maggie looked concerned. "Will mailing it give away where we are?"

"Of course not. We won't put our return address on the letter."

Maggie nodded. "It will be nice to have that off our conscience."

"That's what I was thinking, too," Claire replied as she brought the wheelbarrow back. "I didn't think it would prick my conscience to steal from a man like him, but I can't seem to stop thinking about it."

"What was that?" Maggie asked.

Claire had also heard a horse whinny and joined Maggie's gaze toward the side of the house where it had come from. "It's probably Jared," Maggie grinned. "He seems to keep finding things to repair around here, but it's pretty obvious he just wants to see you."

Claire shushed her in case it was him, but a moment later, they saw a man who wasn't Jared ride into view. "Howdy, ladies." The man tipped his hat. "Didn't mean to startle you."

It took Claire a moment to place where she'd seen him, and then she realized it was the man who had been in the fight with Will Carter.

A Debt to Pay

"I'm Grady Higgs. I was, ugh, just passing by and was curious who was living here now."

"I'm Claire, and this is Maggie."

"Sorry if I left the place a bit run down," he said. "I wasn't given fair warning that I'd have to leave."

Claire looked at him curiously. "You mean you used to live here?"

"For a little while." He turned his head to one side and spat out a wad of tobacco.

Claire realized he must be the man Will Carter had referred to as occupying the cabin for a few months.

"I'll be on my way, ladies." He tipped his hat with an inkling of a smile and, with a click of his tongue, turned his horse around.

"That was strange," Maggie said as she watched him ride off.

"From what I understand, I think he got the boot from Carter's ranch and this homestead."

"Why would he care who's living here?"

Claire shrugged her shoulders. "Beats me." Her gaze rested on his distant figure, wondering what it was about his visit that made her uneasy.

"I feel like this lunch might be lacking something," Claire said as she looked inside the basket she had prepared for the basket raffle. She had followed Lyddie's recipe, but she still wasn't certain.

"Fried chicken and potato salad? I think any man would be happy to eat that," Maggie replied.

"I put a few oatmeal cookies in there, too," Claire said. "But I'm not sure they taste very good."

The two girls walked the half mile to town, immediately spotting a large crowd of people, wagons, and buggies. Everyone was making their way to the churchyard where the food and main celebration would take place. Claire liked how all the businesses and homes in the town had American flags or banners hanging from their porches and doorways.

Once they had arrived, Lyddie found them right away.

"Oh! I'm tickled pink you brought baskets for the raffle! Come with me, and I'll show you where to put them," she said, leading the way across the yard.

"Hi, Maggie!" Maggie turned at the voice and spotted Lilly and her brother waving enthusiastically from a group of children not far away. It looked like they were lining up for a potato sack race.

"Just set your baskets here on this table," Lyddie told them. Her curly brown hair was pinned up, but several loose curls bounced around her heart-shaped face.

"You look beautiful, Mrs. Lyddie," Claire complimented her. "I just love that red dress you're wearing, and it's very festive for the occasion."

Lyddie smoothed out the lace ruffle on the end of her sleeve. "Thank you, dear; I always did like this one. Speaking of beautiful … you two look simply angelic. There's sure to be quite a bit of money raised on your two baskets alone."

Claire and Maggie looked at her questioningly, not sure what she meant. They didn't get time to ask because someone was announcing that the pie contest was about to begin, and Lyddie excused herself and hurried off.

"Hello, ladies."

Claire turned around and smiled at Will Carter as he tipped his hat. "How are things at the cabin?"

"Just fine," Maggie replied.

A Debt to Pay

"I heard you're working for Jacob," he said to Maggie.

She nodded. "His children don't make it feel like work," she replied, glancing through the crowd as she wondered where they had gotten to.

"And how are things at the store?" he asked Claire. She lifted her dark brown eyes that seemed the identical color of her hair, which he noted hung in waves around her shoulders with the sides pinned back. She was rather striking in a royal blue dress that flattered her trim figure, and he found himself absently wondering where Jared Cooper was.

"Good. I think I finally have the hang of it."

"Mr. Maison said you're the best help he's ever had, aside from his wife, of course," he smiled. Claire wondered why this well-built, handsome man wasn't married yet. There had to be more than one woman in this town who would give an immediate yes to his proposal, especially Amy Keets. More than a few times, she had overheard chatter in the general store about how eligible a bachelor Mr. Carter was.

"Looks like the contests are starting," Will said.

"Will you be entering any today?" Claire asked Will.

He chuckled and reached over and rubbed his right arm. "Afraid I injured my arm the other day trying to break in an ornery bronc, so that disqualifies me from log cutting or horse racing. But I'm glad to be a spectator."

"Miss Maggie! You just gotta come see!" Their eyes went to Lilly as she caught up to them and grabbed Maggie's hand. Maggie let the girl lead her away, calling over her shoulder, "I'll catch up with you later, Claire!"

"Looks like your sister is a welcome replacement for that Mrs. Newberry woman."

Claire laughed softly. "We met her briefly on the stage. I could have told you in a minute she wasn't a good fit for children."

"Are you pretty good at sizing people up then?" Will asked her.

"Life's taught me a thing or two," she replied, a little smile tugging on her lips. "Sometimes, I get it wrong, though," she added, thinking back to her first impression of him.

"I'm a pretty good guess of character myself," he told her.

"Good afternoon, Claire. Good afternoon, Will." Sylvia Wendel had been passing by and stopped to greet them. "Fine day for the picnic, isn't it?" she smiled, only making her blue eyes brighter.

"Yes, it is," Will replied.

"Is Jared here?" Sylvia asked Will as she glanced past him to the crowd.

"I believe he's coming," Will replied.

As if on cue, they heard a cheerful "Howdy" as Jared joined them, a fresh smile on his sun-tanned face.

"Looks like the fun's already started." Jared gestured toward a nearby crowd cheering enthusiastically over a tug-o-war competition.

"You should be over there, shouldn't you?" Will said. "You helped win it last year."

Jared grinned. "I'll catch the next one. Guess your bout with that new bronc will take you out of those matches today."

"Afraid so," Will replied.

"Good," Jared chuckled. "I'll have a better chance of winning then."

Claire listened to their jovial banter and could tell they had a good relationship.

"Are you entering anything?" Sylvia asked Claire.

"Just my basket," Claire replied with a shrug.

"I aim to be the highest bidder," Jared said, and Claire noticed Sylvia's expression fall a bit.

A Debt to Pay

"I'm entering my basket too," she said quietly, her gaze bouncing over to Jared several times.

"Glad to hear it," he said. "They'll be many eager takers, I'm sure." He tipped his hat, "Well, I'll catch you folks later."

Sylvia also drifted off a moment later, leaving Will and Claire alone.

"I think she may be sweet on him," Claire said as she watched her weave through the crowd just a short distance behind him.

"I think so, too. It's too bad he's got his eye on someone else."

"That is too bad," she agreed, oblivious to the fact that he was referring to her. "She seems like such a sweet girl."

"Sylvia and Jared have known each other most their lives, so I don't think he sees her as more than a friend."

"Well," Claire said, pushing back wisps of hair that the wind had blown in her face, "Maybe he'll have a change of heart."

"Will!" A tall, thin man wearing a brown vest and grey slouch hat walked up and clasped Will on the back. "I've been looking for you. The horse race is about to start."

"Claire, have you met Doc Fletcher? Doc, this is Claire Wallace."

Claire extended a hand and a friendly smile. "Nice to meet you, Doctor Fletcher."

"And nice to meet you," he shook her hand, a smile under his graying, handlebar mustache. "I've been away visiting my daughter for a few weeks," he told her as he removed his spectacles and wiped dust off the lenses.

"Glad you're back, Doc. Folks will rest a bit easier, I think," Will told him.

He chuckled. "Yes, I'm glad there was no need for me

during my absence." Remembering his reason for coming over, he said, "They're waiting for you at the start line."

"Coming to watch?" the doctor asked Claire as they started to leave.

"Sure," Claire replied, lifting her skirt a bit to walk quickly and catch up with them. She glanced around the crowd for Maggie and ended up finding her at the race's starting line, which was drawn out across a dirt path. Claire stepped up beside her, noting that Lilly, Lucas, and Reverend Myles were standing near her other side.

"Isn't this exciting?" Maggie asked when she saw Claire.

Claire noted the row of cowboys, including Jared and a few of the other ranch hands she remembered from the Carter ranch, lining up, their horses nickering and snorting as they waited for the go-ahead. Claire's gaze then went to a small platform across the path where the doctor and Will Carter stood.

"Alright, boys! We're about to start!" Everyone's eyes were on the Doc as he made the announcement. "Winner of this six-mile race will win one of Will's prize mares!"

There was a round of loud cheering and excited applause. "Stay within the markers," the doctor continued when the noise had died down. "There are men stationed along the course to make sure there is no cheatin'! I'm looking at you, Henry!"

There was an eruption of laughter as everyone's attention went to one of the men lined up for the race. Claire assumed he had tried a shortcut in a previous race.

"Get on with it, Doc!" the man singled out hollered back.

"Alright, men! Get on your mark! Ready, set…"

There was a loud gunshot fired in the air, and a cloud of dust flew up as the riders took off. People in the crowd cheered until the men were out of earshot. Claire noticed the crowd simultaneously begin to move in another direction.

"Everyone's headed over to Pond Point," she heard Reverend Myles telling Maggie. "That's where the finish line is."

"How do you like our Independence Day celebration so far?" Lyddie asked, gently taking Claire's arm as she came to her side, walking with her.

"Did you win the pie contest?" Claire asked, hopefully.

"Nearly. Miss Jenny Tait took the ribbon this year. I do believe that sister of yours has found her niche," Lyddie added, nudging her head toward Maggie, who was holding Lucas and Lilly's hands.

"The Reverend's children have really taken a shine to her," Claire agreed.

"Maybe the Reverend will take a shine to her, too."

Claire didn't have time to reply because someone came over and began talking to Lyddie, but her words did make Claire wonder.

A few minutes later, after being jostled a bit by the crowd that was anticipating the riders coming around the bend toward the finish line, Claire found herself near Sylvia Wendel.

"I hope Jared wins," Sylvia said. "He's been talking of nothing else for weeks."

Claire could see by the anxious look in her eyes and the way she stood on tiptoe to see around the crowd that she wanted this win for him.

"Good afternoon, Miss Wallace. Enjoying the festivities?"

Claire turned to find Bruce Conway standing near her. She gave him a tight smile but said nothing. "You're looking even more beautiful than usual today," he complimented her.

Claire hated the feeling of his eyes perusing her and hated that his presence reminded her of her old life and the sort of people she knew in Chicago.

"Thank you, Mr. Conway," she replied emotionlessly, avoiding his eyes and pretending to be very interested in what was happening in the crowd.

She felt herself stiffen when he leaned closer. "Save me a dance," he whispered into her ear before moving away.

Claire released the breath she hadn't realized she'd been holding and told herself to head home once the dancing started. Sometime later, the crowd began to whoop and holler as the riders came into view. There were two riders in particular who were neck and neck. And then, as they neared the finish line, Jared's horse came through first. The entire crowd cheered and applauded as Will Carter led a black horse toward the finish line and handed Jared the reins.

Claire stood next to Maggie with the other women who had entered their baskets for the raffle. There were about ten of them lined up, holding their baskets. The first basket to be raffled off belonged to Jenny Tait, the young woman who had won the pie-baking contest.

"We'll start the bidding at ten cents," a woman was saying. "Do I have ten cents for Miss Jenny Tait's basket and company?"

While the woman's words were merely describing an innocent lunch, Claire felt a little panicked at the realization that she'd have to spend time with the man who would buy her basket. For a moment, her thoughts went to Frederick Harris and how he had paid her to sit with him at the table. He had offered to pay for more than that, causing her to feel sick just at the memory.

"You alright?" Maggie whispered when she noticed Claire's uneasy expression.

A Debt to Pay

"I didn't think the raffle would mean we had to spend time with whoever bought our basket," Claire replied.

"I didn't either," Maggie sighed, looking around. "But nothing we can do 'bout it now. 'Sides, shouldn't be more than half an hour for them to scarf down the food, and you probably don't have to actually sit with them if you don't want to."

Her words made Claire feel a little better. She noticed Jenny Tait was already stepping down from the platform, taking the hand of the young man who had outbid some others and won her basket. A woman Claire didn't recognize was the mock auctioneer. One by one, each girl and her basket were bid on. Claire looked behind her and saw Amy Keets and Sylvia were the last two after her and Maggie.

Nervously, she clutched her basket, wishing desperately to be anywhere but in that awkward position. And then she heard the woman calling her to step forward.

"OK, gentleman, we have the lovely Miss Claire Wallace. She and her sister are new to our town, so let's make them feel welcome. I'll start the bidding at…"

"Twenty cents!" Someone shouted from the crowd.

"Twenty-five!" came another man's voice. Claire thought he looked like one of the ranch hands who she'd seen when she'd made the delivery at Will Carter's ranch.

"Forty cents!" Jared Cooper called out.

"Forty-five cents!"

Claire felt like her cheeks were on fire as the bidding went higher and higher.

"One dollar," said a clear and even voice that Claire recognized as Bruce Conway.

"One and fifty!" Jared Cooper bid higher.

"My goodness!" the woman leading the bidding smiled, shaking her head in amazement as she looked at Claire.

"Four dollars," Bruce Conway called out, and the crowd went from rowdy to almost silent.

Claire saw him moving forward in the crowd toward the platform and suddenly felt lightheaded. Just as he came to collect his winnings, another voice from the crowd spoke up.

"Five dollars!"

Everyone turned to see who from the back of the crowd had made such a generous bid.

Claire felt her breath return to her when Will Carter weaved through the crowd and passed Bruce Conway. Pulling the cash out of his pocket, Will tossed it into the money box that sat on the front of the platform.

"Five dollars, Mr. Carter?" Bruce Conway sneered at the man with a mocking grin. "And I thought you were a stingy man."

Ignoring him, Will reached up his hand to help Claire down the steps. He could tell she was a little shaken up just by the flushed look on her face and the way she leaned readily on his hand for support. She didn't say anything as he led her away from the crowd and to a large maple tree's shade. There was a wooden bench that he led her to, and she very gratefully sat on it. She remained silent for a moment and then, seeming to gather her words, lifted her chin a fraction and looked at him.

"It's just fried chicken and potato salad. I can't promise it'll be worth anything near five dollars."

Will heard the slight tremor in her voice and saw a flicker of vulnerability in her eyes as she extended the basket toward him.

"I didn't pay five dollars for the basket of food," he told her gently. "I saw how determined Conway was and just wanted to spare you his company."

A Debt to Pay

Claire's expression was a mixture of relief and gratitude. She took in a steadying breath and thanked him. "I didn't know the raffle would be like that. I thought it was just about the baskets."

"They don't have basket raffles in the city?" he asked with a grin.

Claire laughed softly, "I'm afraid not." And then her eyes looked concerned as she glanced past Will toward where the basket raffle had been. "I wonder who bought Maggie's basket."

Will turned around and spotted her not far off. "Looks like Frank's with her." He pointed toward where they sat on a grassy knoll. "He's a friend of mine and works on the ranch." Turning back to face Claire, he noticed she relaxed visibly. He moved toward the bench and sat on the ground, wrapping his arms around his knees.

"Alright," he said, reaching for the basket. "Let's give this a try."

"The oatmeal cookie should be decent if nothing else is."

"What are you talking about?" Will asked her a minute later after his first bite of the fried chicken. "This is better than my cook, Hannah, makes it."

"I'm sure it isn't," she told him with a slight laugh, "But it's nice of you to say so."

Will hadn't been exaggerating at all. He ate two more pieces and then started on the potato salad. "Not sure I'll have room for the cookie."

"Aren't you going to eat anything?" he asked.

"I'll eat later. I think my stomach is still unsettled at the prospect of being alone with Mr. Conway."

"As it should be," Will said. "The man owns the hotel and saloon and would own the whole town if he could. He's not an honest sort, I'll just say that."

"Have you lived in Millcreek your whole life?" Claire asked him curiously.

"About twenty years of it. When I was ten, my parents and I moved here. We lived in that cabin you're in now while my pa made repairs on the house that's on the ranch. He'd been to the mines in California and struck some gold back in '49. When we came to Missouri, he used that gold to buy the ranch from an old farmer."

"Are your parents still in the area?"

"My ma died of the fever when I was around thirteen, and a few years later, my pa remarried a woman who had a son around my age. My pa died when I was around eighteen, so I just picked up where he left off with the ranch." Will suddenly gave a self-conscious grin. "I guess you didn't ask for my whole life story."

Claire smiled, glad to listen. His voice was soothing somehow. "I don't mind. So, your half-brother helps run the ranch with you, then?"

"Not exactly."

Claire heard something in his tone that told her there was more to the story.

"I'm not too sure where he is right now, to tell you the truth."

There was a distant look in his hazel eyes that made her curious. "What of your stepmother?"

"After my pa died, she went back east, along with my stepbrother."

He watched as she absently picked at the oatmeal cookie in her hand as he talked, putting small bits of it in her mouth. She still looked a little flushed. "Are you thirsty?" he suddenly asked, rising to his feet and dusting off his trousers.

"I am, and I'm sure you are too after the lunch."

A Debt to Pay

"Follow me," he told her with an inviting smile. "Let's get something to drink."

As the hot sun gave way to a cooler evening, a full moon and quickly appearing stars began to spangle the sky. The festivities continued, lanterns marking out the yard, which was made complete with a ragamuffin band of harmonica, guitar, fiddle, and banjo players. Claire had been having such a good time since Will rescued her from sharing a lunch with Bruce Conway that she completely forgot her resolve to leave once the dancing started.

She found herself laughing and enjoying the simple and fun dance steps that Lyddie told her they called the Western polka. She alternated linking elbows with everyone she passed in the large circle that had gathered to dance. She saw Maggie enjoying herself also as they attempted to follow in the steps everyone else was doing.

After almost an hour, there was a lull in the music, and it changed to something much slower, the fiddle taking the lead. Maggie and Claire found each other at the refreshment table, where several people were waiting in line to ladle water from the bucket into their cups.

"I've always liked to dance," Maggie said, her green eyes bright and her cheeks rosy from the excitement. "But this is a lot more fun than I ever had!"

Claire agreed, lifting her cup to her lips and relishing the cold water that rushed down her throat.

"Excuse me, Miss Wallace. Can I have this dance?"

Claire turned at the sound of Jared's voice and, having no reason not to dance with him, smiled kindly and accepted.

"Congratulations on winning the race."

"Thanks. It was a close one, to be sure."

Claire thought he looked like he was going to say something else and then changed his mind. "How'd you like our Independence Day celebration?"

"It's wonderful," she told him and then apologized for stepping on his foot. "I'm afraid I'm not the best at waltzing."

"Nah, you're great. It's me who has two left feet. I'm surprised I ain't tripped you yet," he chuckled. Claire listened as he chatted about this and that, her gaze meeting Will's for just a second as she noticed him dancing with Amy Keets a few feet away.

"If you need anything else done 'round the property, just let me know," Jared was telling her. "Come winter, I'd be gratified to keep your wood pile high." A moment later, he felt a tap on his shoulder.

"Care if I cut in?" someone asked.

Jared didn't even have time to reply as Bruce Conway practically brushed him aside to step into his place.

"I would have outbid Will Carter," he told Claire as he placed one hand on her waist and took her hand with the other. "But he seemed pretty determined."

Claire wasn't sure what to say as they settled into the waltz-like dance with the others. There was a minute of silence between them, and then Bruce Conway said, "You don't have to be afraid of me, Claire Wallace."

Her eyes flashed toward his. "I'm not afraid of you."

"Your eyes say otherwise."

"I don't know what you mean."

"You know, I think there's a fair bit of tenacity beneath your composure. Just like there's more to me than meets the eye."

She looked at him really for the first time; his eyes were a shade of gray that reminded her of a wolf. "I know just what sort of man you are, Mr. Conway."

"Do you, now?" He looked amused, and she could feel his hand on her back, gradually pulling her closer. "Tell me, Miss Wallace, is your discernment from first-hand experience?"

He was now much closer than she felt comfortable with, and she found herself wishing Jared would come back.

"I've been wondering," he went on, "what brought you and your sister to our fine town. Springfield isn't exactly a stone's throw."

"Our parents passed away, and we packed up and headed west. There's not much more to it than that. We were planning to stay a few nights in this town, but here we are."

"Well, I'm glad our town was able to persuade you to stay."

She could smell the whiskey on his breath as he leaned in to say the words.

"You look uneasy," he said as he watched her adverting his gaze.

"I'm getting tired. I think I'm done dancing," she told him, trying to loosen her hand from his. He made no effort to release her hand but squeezed it a little tighter.

"Mr. Conway, I'm not feeling well," Claire tried to sound believable. "Would you…"

"Mind if I cut in?"

Bruce Conway slowed their dancing and turned with an irritated expression. "Will Carter…again," he said, drawing out his voice. He stepped away with feigned politeness and tipped his hat by way of goodbye toward Claire. "Remember, my offer still stands."

Claire felt relief washing through her when Will Carter took her from Bruce Conway's arms.

"I feel like I can breathe again," she told him.

"I'm sorry I couldn't get to you sooner," he said.

"Well, it's not your job to rescue me from every awkward situation," she laughed softly, thinking back to her fall off the counter in the general store as well as the basket bidding.

"It is when that situation includes the likes of Bruce Conway."

"He is rather dislikable."

"Jared's dancing with Sylvia," Will told her, nudging his head in their direction.

A pleased smile touched Claire's lips as she glanced over and saw them. "I'm sure she's delighted."

"He might need a smack over the head," Will shook his head with a grin. "I don't think he sees her interest."

They waltzed for the remainder of the song, and Claire felt strangely at home in his arms. She liked the way some of his dark blonde hair tried to escape his wide-brimmed hat, falling just slightly over his forehead. As she looked up into his eyes and felt her hand resting on his broad, solid shoulder, she realized she'd never known anyone like him. They could converse and laugh easily, and she didn't feel any uneasiness about his intentions.

"How are you and Maggie planning to get home?"

"I hadn't thought about it, actually."

"Well, I can give you a lift when you're ready to go home."

"Thanks. I don't know that I could make that walk after such a long day."

"That brings me to something I wanted to talk to you about."

"And what's that?"

"I have an old buckboard you're welcome to have," he said.

"I just mentioned to Maggie the other day that we would need a method of transportation soon. How much would that be, and is purchasing a horse expensive?"

A Debt to Pay

"Well, I'd give you the buckboard, and as for the horse, you could have one on loan for now."

"That's kind, but I would want to pay for it."

"Just you and your sister living in the cabin and keeping it up is payment enough."

Claire was used to men offering things when they wanted something in return, so it made her a little unsure. Just from the short time she knew Will Carter, she knew he was unlike the other men she had known, but she still didn't want to feel obligated to him.

"You can pay for them if you want," Will said as he saw the uncertainty in her eyes. He knew he wouldn't charge her what they were actually worth anyway.

"You've been so kind. Thank you for all you've done to help Maggie and I."

"You're welcome," he said and, as he looked at her, felt something stirring in his heart that he hadn't felt for a very long time.

Chapter Nine

It was after nine o'clock when Will dropped Maggie and Claire home. When they woke up the next morning and were getting ready for church, Claire suddenly stopped by the table and glanced over the room.

"Something looks different," she said. "I didn't notice it when we came in last night because it was dark, but something is definitely different."

Maggie lowered her cup of coffee and looked at Claire curiously. "What do you mean?"

"I'm not sure, but something seems…" She nibbled her thumbnail as she thought. "Look at the rug," Claire said as she walked over to it and then glanced toward the table. "This rug is usually lying over there. And look!"

Maggie watched as Claire walked over to the window that was opposite the table. It was slightly ajar, just an inch or so. "There's mud under this window," Claire said. "And I didn't open it before we left. Did you?"

Maggie shook her head slowly. "What are you saying?"

"I'm saying someone was in this house while we were at the picnic yesterday."

She turned back toward the window. "I locked the door, so whoever it was came through the window."

A Debt to Pay

Maggie came to her feet and crossed her arms in front of her chest. "But who would break in? And for what reason?"

Claire was already moving into their bedroom. She reached under the mattress and pulled out the small, brown hand purse where she kept the money they had stolen separate from where she kept her earnings from the store. She had made a point not to use any more of the stolen money than they needed. Pulling out the money to make sure it was there, she sighed with relief. But then she noticed something else.

"Maggie?"

Maggie was already standing in the doorway.

"Maggie, what is this?" Claire turned around, a diamond necklace hanging from her fingers.

"Oh. I, um, I grabbed it out of the case that night. I had it hidden somewhere else and a few days ago put it in with where you kept the money."

"Maggie, why didn't you say anything?"

She shrugged apologetically. "I thought it would be good to have a little extra, just in case."

"This is too much, Maggie! You probably took the most expensive piece of jewelry in the store!"

"It was dark, Claire! I just grabbed a piece of jewelry."

Claire let out a heavy sigh as she put it back in the handbag and slid it back under the mattress.

"You don't think someone broke in to find it, do you?" Maggie asked nervously.

"No. No one around here knows we have it. Whoever broke in had other reasons, but it makes me realize we have to do a better job hiding this."

"I'm sorry, Claire. I didn't realize it was such an expensive necklace until after we'd left Chicago."

"Well, we'll just have to return it when we send the money," Claire said, tucking the blankets back where they'd been. "Until then, I'm gonna find somewhere better to hide this purse."

"It makes me nervous to think there's someone snooping 'round the property." Maggie brought up the subject again as they walked to church. "Are you sure those things you noticed weren't just coincidence? Either one of us could have tracked mud in, and maybe I did open a window and then didn't shut it fully."

Her doubts did make Claire question herself. "There's no explaining away the mud tracked in under the window." She sighed. "Let's give it a little time. The last thing I want to do is go to the sheriff and draw attention to ourselves. I'd rather him not even notice us."

Maggie agreed with that and with the idea of letting their suspicions go for the time being.

After the girls returned from church, it wasn't long before there was a knock on the door. Claire opened it and smiled a greeting at Jared, who stood on the other side. He took his hat off and held it in his hands. "If you ain't busy, I wanted to show you something. Just out 'ere in the yard," he added.

"Of course," Claire replied. Maggie joined as well, and they went outside and followed Jared to the backyard and toward the small barn.

"I took the liberty of getting her settled," Jared said over his shoulder as he replaced his hat and walked with quick strides to the barn.

Claire could hear the excitement in his voice and glanced back to Maggie, who shared her questioning look. They stopped at the barn's door, and then Jared opened it and led out the black mare he had won the day before.

"She's yours," Jared said to Claire, handing her the reins.

"What?" She gently laid her hand on the horse's back.

"I won her for you," he said with a surge of pride in his voice.

Claire met his eyes. "Jared, she's beautiful, and that's so kind, but I can't accept a gift like this."

His expression didn't fall in the slightest. "Of course, you can."

Claire shook her head and handed him back the reins. "You won her. She's yours. I…I don't know the first thing about keeping a horse."

"That's the easy part. 'Sides, I can teach you everything you need to know."

Claire opened her mouth to argue when they heard another rider approaching. They looked over to see Will riding into the yard. He was coming by with the materials to start the chicken coop he'd promised them. He climbed down and wasn't surprised to see Jared there. He noticed his ranch hand kept finding reasons to be at the cabin. A few days ago, Will had to ask him why it was taking so many trips to mend a fence that should have only taken a few hours.

"He's given Claire his prize mare," Maggie told Will.

Will's gaze switched from Jared to Claire. He could see the uncertainty on her face.

"It's too fine a gift," Claire tried to refuse again.

"If I know Jared, he won't take no for an answer," Will said. "Best just accept it."

"He's right," Jared said, still beaming from ear to ear.

Claire sighed, not seeing any way around it. Jared had been kind to them. Perhaps it was a gift with no strings attached.

"I brung some hay and chaff, too," Jared told her.

The horse suddenly pulled his head back and stomped around a bit. Claire stepped back nervously, avoiding his hooves.

"Don't be scared of 'er," Jared said. "She's just a little nervous being in a new place. Here…" He reached over and took Claire's hand and placed it on the horse's back, then he directed her to put her other hand firmly on the bridle near her jaw. "She just needs to get used to you. Just pat her gentle."

Claire did as he showed her, running her right hand softly along the mare's back while holding her by the bridle with her other hand. She smiled faintly, feeling the horse calming under her touch.

"There, she's already warming to you," Jared said reassuringly.

Will walked closer to them. "Guess you'll be in fine shape for that buckboard now," he said to Claire.

She nodded in his direction, still in shock that this large animal beside her was hers.

"Here, follow me," Jared said, walking with Claire and showing her how to lead the horse behind her.

"I can't believe he gave her a horse!" Maggie said to Will as they stood by the barn watching Jared help Claire get familiar with the horse.

"I can," Will replied quietly. Any suspicion he had before about his ranch hand's interest in Claire Wallace was now a certitude.

"I'll have to mend that pasture fence on the south end for her to graze," Will said as Jared and Claire rejoined them.

"I can do it," Jared offered.

"You'll have to write me a list of when to feed her and

A Debt to Pay

what she needs," Claire said to Jared, slowly becoming OK with the idea. "I would feel horrible if I didn't take care of her right."

"Oh, sure, it'll come naturally to you after a few days," Jared replied as he gave the horse's rump a sound pat. "Don't forget to give her a name."

Claire looked at the horse, still a little torn. She glanced over at Will and saw that he was watching her. He smiled reassuringly. "You'll do fine, Claire," was all he said, but the encouragement in his tone was what she needed.

A few days later, Claire saw that Jared was right. Tending to the horse was becoming second nature. She and Maggie shared the responsibility of mucking out the stable, feeding, watering, and leading the horse to the small pasture that Will and Jared had secured by replacing old or missing fence rails and posts.

Maggie and Claire agreed on the name Willow for the horse. "I'd like to learn how to ride," Claire said to Maggie one day as she climbed up on the middle fence rail and leaned against the fence to watch Willow roaming about the pasture.

"I think I'd be too scared I'd fall off," Maggie replied.

Claire smiled. "Can't be that hard." And then, once the idea had surfaced, she couldn't ignore it.

"What are you doing?" Maggie asked curiously when she saw Claire grab the reins dangling over the fence before she climbed the remaining way over it. She watched her pull up her skirt as she waded through the tall grass toward Willow.

Claire attached the reins to Willow's bridle and led the young mare back to where Maggie stood. "Jared mentioned that she was already broke, so it shouldn't be hard to sit on her back."

"Claire, are you crazy? You don't know anything about mounting a horse!"

"Here, hold these," Claire said as she handed the reins across the fence to Maggie. Then, climbing up to the top wooden rail, Claire balanced herself and instructed Maggie to pull Willow parallel to the fence.

"I think you need a saddle, Claire."

"Indians ride bareback."

"Yeah, but last time I checked, you weren't an Indian."

Claire laughed. "You're making me lose my balance."

"If you get hurt, I'm not taking care of you," Maggie threatened.

"Willow's such a gentle horse. She's not going to throw me off."

"I'm more worried about you falling off in general."

"Just hold her as still as you can while I climb over." Claire waited until Willow had taken a few steps closer to the fence before lifting her right leg and pushing off with her left in one smooth motion to sit on the horse.

She landed a bit harder on the horse's back than she had anticipated and immediately scrambled to grab the horse's bridle to keep from sliding off.

"Just pass me the reins," Claire told Maggie, who leaned forward and got them into Claire's hands. Sitting up a bit, Claire attempted to balance herself by using her legs to press on the horse's sides. With a smile of pride, she glanced over to Maggie. "See. I knew I could do it."

As she said the words, the horse took a few unexpected steps, and although slight, Claire nearly lost her balance.

"Woah, girl," she spoke to the horse. "Easy, now…I don't know what I'm doing."

Maggie watched, half amused, half apprehensive, as Claire struggled to remain seated on the horse.

A Debt to Pay

"Don't they always press their heels into the horse to get them to go?" Claire asked.

"I think so, but I think you're better just sitting still."

Claire gently hit her heels into Willow's sides anyway and then gave a little cry of surprise when the horse galloped forward. Clutching the reins so hard her knuckles were turning white, Claire tried what she'd seen riders do to make the horse stop. She gently pulled back on the reins. "Whoa, girl…Willow, woah!"

"Maybe you need to pull a little harder!" Maggie called out as Claire was halfway across the field and the horse didn't seem like she was going to stop.

Feeling a little panicked as she bounced around on the horse's bony back, Claire gave the reins a stronger pull, sighing with relief when she trotted to a halt. She looked over her shoulder and flashed Maggie a smile. Then, carefully, she pulled the reins to the right and nudged her heels in again. Like clockwork, Willow started walking again.

"I might be a cowgirl yet!" she said, laughing as the horse trotted closer to Maggie. Claire took her for another turn around the pasture, pulling back gently on the reins whenever the horse seemed to be going too fast. She wanted to get her close to the fence so she could climb off the same way she'd gotten on, but Willow didn't seem to understand.

"I guess I'll have to just dismount from here," Claire said, looking down. It seemed a bit high, but how hard could it be?

As she attempted to lift her right leg, the horse started moving, so she quickly leaned forward and remained on her back. She tried a few more things, but she couldn't keep the horse still.

"Need some help?"

Claire nearly fell off the horse when she turned her head abruptly at the sound of Will's voice calling to her. She hadn't seen him ride up to where Maggie was. He effortlessly swung over the fence and headed across the pasture toward her.

Willow recognized him right away and began to canter toward him. Will took the horse by the bridle and gently stroked her forehead as he looked up at Claire. "Are you stuck up there?" he asked, a teasing expression on his face.

"I hate to admit it, but getting down is harder than I thought."

"I'm impressed that you managed to get up. Especially with no saddle. Lift your right leg off, and I'll help you slide down."

Claire did as he said and could feel his hands behind her on her waist, helping her find her footing. As she turned around to face him, she used the back of her hand to wipe at the beads of sweat mixed with windblown hair from her face. "Thanks," she smiled, a slight blush creeping into her cheeks. "I guess it's a little humiliating to think I needed help to get off a horse."

"Not at all," he assured her as they walked back to where Maggie was waiting. "Riding takes time. How'd you get up anyway?" he grinned.

"Climbed up on the fence and sort of jumped off."

He laughed a little, imagining the scene. "I guess Maggie was your accomplice. Or were you just an innocent bystander?" he asked Maggie as they neared. He saw Claire didn't need any help to get over the fence, so he climbed up and sat on the top rail.

"She's usually the one with the crazy ideas," Maggie told him, rolling her eyes, but Will knew she wasn't mad. "I did help hold the horse still."

A Debt to Pay

"Well, we should see about getting you a saddle. That will make mounting a lot easier."

"And dismounting, I hope," Claire laughed softly at herself. "Do you want something to drink?" she suddenly thought to ask Will. "It feels like a hundred degrees out here."

"Nah, thank you. I was on my way into town and thought I'd stop by and see how things were going with Willow."

They walked beside him toward the front of the house as he led Phoenix behind him. He mounted in one smooth movement. "Do you ladies need anything before I go?"

"I think we're alright," Claire replied as she lifted her hand to shield her eyes from the overhead sun.

"Have a good rest of your Saturday." He flicked the excess part of the reins in his left hand, and the horse immediately spun around and started to trot away. "And maybe wait for that saddle before you try riding again," he called over his shoulder.

Claire smiled to herself as she turned to head back into the house and caught the look Maggie was giving her.

"What?" Claire asked her.

"You like him, don't you?"

"Will Carter? Of course not."

"You say his name as if it's out of the realm of possibility," Maggie laughed.

"It is out of the realm of possibility, and it's not like that between us. He's a friend, someone who treats me like I'm just a person."

"You are just a person," Maggie teased.

"You know what I mean, Maggie. You know how it was with men before. Will doesn't make me feel uneasy."

"I know what you mean," Maggie said, thinking about Jacob Myles. While she only saw him briefly before he left or when he returned, she was starting to enjoy his company probably more than she should.

"As Jesus was speaking, the teachers of religious law and the Pharisees brought a woman who had been caught in the act of adultery. They put her in front of the crowd. 'Teacher,' they said to Jesus. 'This woman was caught in the act of adultery. The law of Moses says to stone her. What do you say?'"

Maggie felt like she was holding her breath as she listened to Reverend Myles reading from the Bible the next morning at church. She had never heard anything like it; she didn't know stories like this were in the Bible. She waited for him to go on, to see what Jesus would do.

"As we read on, we see what Jesus' response was to these religious leaders of the day. 'Alright,' Jesus told them, 'But let the one who has never sinned throw the first stone!' When the accusers heard this, they slipped away one by one, beginning with the oldest, until Jesus was left in the middle of the crowd with the woman.

"Then Jesus stood up again and said to the woman, 'Where are your accusers? Didn't even one of them condemn you?' 'No, Lord,' she said. And Jesus said, 'Neither do I. Go and sin no more.'"

Maggie couldn't remember the last time she had been moved to tears, but in that moment, she could feel tears stinging the back of her eyes. She hadn't expected Jesus to say that. She knew bits and pieces about God, but she had never heard that He was like this.

With her own past, it was easy for Maggie to imagine the shame and humiliation the woman must have felt standing in the crowd of men accusing and ridiculing her. Then, to

A Debt to Pay

have Jesus put them in their place and save her from being stoned to death? It made her want to hear more about Him.

It was all she could think about the whole way home. Claire was unusually quiet, and Maggie thought maybe she was taking in the story as well. She wanted to talk about it with Claire but couldn't seem to move it from her heart to her lips.

"I really like Reverend Myles' sermons," Claire suddenly said as they were just about home.

"I was thinking along those same lines," Maggie replied quietly.

It was all they said about it, but it was enough knowing they both felt the weight such a story meant for each of them.

Chapter Ten

"Did you hear that?" Claire sat up in bed late that night and gently shook Maggie. "Maggie, did you hear that?"

"Hear what?" Maggie replied, still half asleep. "It's the middle of the night."

"It sounded like a horse."

"We have a horse, Claire."

"No, I mean walking near the house. Do you think Willow got loose somehow?"

Maggie yawned as she sat up in bed. "Can't we just look for her in the morning if she did?"

"No, what if she wanders really far?" Claire was already out of bed and lighting the lamp on the bedside table.

"You're not going out there, are you?"

Claire was pulling on her shoes. "We have to. What if you just stand in the doorway, and I'll go out to the yard," Claire suggested.

"Or I can just stay in bed."

When Claire went into the other room to get a lantern, Maggie forced herself to follow. She did as Claire suggested, standing in the doorway and looking out at the warm summer night lit by a bright, full moon.

A Debt to Pay

"I might not even need this lantern," Claire said once she'd stepped outside. She was thankful for the moon's light as she moved about the yard. "Willow! Willow!" She stopped and listened, lifting her lantern. She didn't hear anything. "I'll go check in the barn," she told Maggie before heading along the side of the house to the backyard. If Willow was there, then she knew it was just her imagination.

As she got close to the barn, she stopped dead in her tracks when she saw a light coming from inside it. There were no windows in the front of the structure, so she moved to the side where there was a window. Clearly, there was a lamp lit inside. But who had lit one, and who was in there?

She could feel her heart beating loudly in her chest as she went closer to the window to look. It was hard to see from that angle, but she could hear movement. She almost jumped out of her skin when she heard the sudden snort of a horse. It was then she realized there was an unfamiliar horse tied to a nearby tree.

Claire crept quietly back to the front of the barn, intending to make a sprint back to the house, but the barn door suddenly opened, and a man stood in the doorway.

"Who's there?" he whispered roughly. "Who's there?" In the moonlight, he caught sight of a woman standing just a few feet away. She turned and bolted toward the house, but he caught up to her in just a few fast strides, grabbed her by the arms, and yanked her into the barn.

"You can't tell no one that I'm here!" he growled at her.

Claire could smell the alcohol on his breath as she struggled to break free of his grasp. "Let go of me!" she cried.

Claire suddenly felt him loosen his hold and shove her toward the other end of the barn as he closed the door.

"I ain't gonna hurt you if you keep your mouth shut! Don't tell no one I was here!"

Even in the dim light, Claire recognized Grady Higgs. "What are you doing here?" she asked.

"I'm looking for something I forgot."

"You broke into the house the other day, too, didn't you?"

He didn't respond. "Soon as I know you ain't gonna open your mouth, I'll let you go back to the house," he told her.

Claire felt fear rising in her as he edged closer, covering the short distance to where she stood. Claire glanced around for the pitchfork or some other source of a weapon, but there was nothing within reach.

"I ain't one to hurt a lady," he said in a raspy voice.

Claire wanted to scream for Maggie but didn't want to put her in danger. She had no idea what this man was capable of.

"But if you tell anyone I was here…" he reached out in a quick motion and grabbed both of her arms firmly in his hands, "I'll make sure you regret it."

Even in the dim lighting, Claire could see the look of anger in his eyes suddenly turn into one of interest. He slowly brushed away hair that had fallen in front of her face, running a finger down her cheek.

Seizing the moment when he only had her with one hand, Claire pushed past him with all of her strength, and the unexpected motion caused him to stumble backward. His hand didn't let go of her arm, though, and she felt herself pulled backward as well. She lost her footing and gasped as her forehead collided with the corner of one of the wooden beams of a stall just before she landed on her hands and knees.

"Let her go!"

Claire heard Maggie's voice as she pushed open the barn door and stepped inside with a long rifle aimed in her hands.

"Get out of here!" Maggie ordered in a more authoritative voice than Claire had ever heard.

A Debt to Pay

The man chuckled as he lifted his hands in mock surrender. "I don't think you know how to use that rifle, hunnie."

"You're welcome to find out!" Maggie returned. She waited for Claire, who was scrambling to get beside her, and then they backed up together until they were outside the door. "Get off this property!" she told him.

Cursing under his breath, the man moved out the door and toward his horse. "You jest remember what I said!" he yelled back to Claire before he mounted his horse and rode off into the night.

"Maggie!" Claire finally exclaimed, throwing her arms around her friend as she gratefully lowered the heavy rifle in her hand. "Where did you find that?"

"I searched the house for some kind of weapon to use and found it up in the loft." She sighed with relief. "He was right, though; I have no clue how to fire this thing or if it's even loaded."

"Well, you scared him away."

The two girls moved quickly back into the house, bolting the front door and rechecking the back door and the windows to ensure they were locked as well.

"I should have gone out there with you right away!" Maggie began to cry. "I'm so sorry! Are you hurt?"

"I don't think so," Claire replied, but then she lifted her hand to her pounding forehead and felt something wet.

"Oh, Claire! You're bleeding!" Maddie exclaimed as she brought the lamp closer to Claire's face.

"It's not too bad," Claire assured her.

Maggie scampered about the room and returned with a bowl of water and a clean rag. "Looks like you might have some bad bruising," Maggie told her as she gently pressed the rag to the injured area.

"What was he doing out there?" Maggie asked.

"Looking for something," Claire replied.

"It's so strange. If he had left something behind from when he lived here, he could have easily just asked to get it."

"It's obviously something he doesn't want anyone to know about," Claire reasoned. She sighed, feeling the pounding in her head. "Let's just go to bed for now."

"Do you think he'll come back?" Maggie asked nervously.

"The doors and windows are locked, and besides, you scared him off with that gun you couldn't shoot."

Maggie laughed, "I don't know what I was thinking."

"I've never seen you so brave," Claire told her. "Thank you for coming when you did, Maggie. I hate to think what might have happened."

Her words sent a shiver down Maggie's back, and she knew they had to tell someone about this man.

"Does that look any better?" Claire asked Maggie the next morning. Trying to hide the large bruise and cut on her forehead, she had done her hair in a different style. She parted it off to the side and then draped her hair across her forehead, finishing it in a loose braid over her shoulder.

"Well..." Maggie hesitated. "Not really, Claire. It's still pretty obvious."

Claire sighed. "Well, if anyone asks, I'll just tell them I tripped and hit my head in the barn. It's the truth."

"Half the truth," Maggie reminded. They heard a wagon, and Maggie reached for her bonnet. "That's Reverend Myles." She paused at the door. "Will you be OK to walk to the store?"

"Of course," Claire replied. "It doesn't even hurt anymore."

A Debt to Pay

"Not just that, Claire. I know it must have shaken you up to … to be manhandled like that."

"I think we've both endured worse things than that," Claire replied, not admitting to Maggie that it had indeed shaken her up.

She walked to the general store and was grateful there were few customers that day. Mr. Maison did ask her about the injury to her head, and she gave him her rehearsed answer. He seemed satisfied and told her not to work too hard. Claire tried to ignore the throbbing pain near her temple, which didn't seem to let up all day. He told her he had to run an errand but then returned with Doc Fletcher.

"I thought you might object if I told you I was going to fetch him," Tom Maison said with an apologetic smile. "I just thought he should take a look before you leave." Tom had noticed all day that she seemed a little off, moving much slower than usual and having difficulty adding simple figures that she usually breezed through.

"That was thoughtful, Mr. Maison, but I'm totally fine."

"Why don't you let me decide that?" Doc Fletcher said. "Can we use the back room?" he asked Tom, who nodded and stepped out of the way.

Claire sighed as she followed the doc and then sat on a stool. "I really don't think it's anything to fuss over." She winced a bit when he touched near the swollen area.

"Must have been quite a collision," he said as he reached into his bag and pulled out a bottle of antiseptic and a clean cloth. "Might sting just a second," he warned as he gently pressed it on the cut. "It's a tricky spot for a bandage," he told her. "I think it's OK to leave it uncovered, but I want you to keep it clean with this." He handed her a small bottle.

Claire nodded and thanked him as she took it.

"Do you have a headache or feel dizzy at all?" He looked into her eyes using a small instrument. "Any vomiting or blurry vision?"

"My head does hurt, and the numbers I was adding were blurry," Claire admitted hesitantly.

"I think you have a slight concussion, young lady. Nothing a little rest can't cure, though."

Claire stood to her feet when the examination was over and followed the doctor back into the main room. "I want you to come see me if your symptoms worsen or if that headache doesn't lessen by tomorrow, alright?"

Claire nodded. "I will, and thank you, Doctor."

He gave what Claire would describe as a grandfatherly smile and gently patted her shoulder. "Take care of yourself, young lady."

"I think you've done enough for today," Tom Maison said once the doctor had gone. "What if you let me give you a ride home?"

"It's not a far walk at all, but thank you, Mr. Maison."

"I think I would feel better knowing you made it back," he told her.

"But what about the store?"

"I'll close for a few minutes." He was already heading out the door, and Claire realized she had no other option but to follow.

"This is really too much fussing over me," she told him.

He told her he was going to hitch up his horse when Will Carter pulled up in front of the store.

"Looks like I made it," he said from the buckboard seat. "I was trying to get here before you left," he said, looking at Claire. "I wanted to give you a ride home in your new buckboard."

A Debt to Pay

"Well! If that isn't perfect timing," Tom Maison exclaimed. "I was just about to give her a lift myself."

Claire moved down the steps of the General Store platform and toward the buckboard. Will had described it as an old buckboard, but she thought it looked next to new.

Tom Maison followed to help her up to the wagon. "Mr. Maison," Claire laughed softly. "I promise I'm fine."

Will didn't understand her words until she sat next to him, and he saw the swollen lump on her forehead with a rather deep cut down the center of it. "What happened?" he asked with concern.

"Took a nasty fall," Mr. Maison filled him in. "Doc thinks it's just a slight concussion, though."

"I'm fine," Claire said, feeling like it was all she had been saying for the last several minutes.

Will flipped the reins, and the horse walked forward, pulling the buckboard.

"Thank you for loaning us this nice buckboard," Claire said, setting her hands in her lap and leaning back against the seat.

"No problem. I'll show you how to hitch Willow to it when I unhitch Phoenix." He glanced at her. "Did you just fall in the store?"

"No. Last night, I tripped in the barn and hit it on one of the stall rails," she answered carefully.

"Looks like it must have hurt. Willow wasn't giving you any trouble, was she?"

"Oh no," Claire assured him. "Nothing like that." Something inside her told her just to tell him the truth about what had happened. "Can I ask you a question?"

Will nodded, "Of course."

"That man you were fighting with the day I came to the ranch, who was he?"

"Grady Higgs? What made you think of him?"

"Well, he came by a week or so ago. He said he wanted to see who was living in the house."

"That's odd. I thought he had left town. Should have known better," Will added quietly, and Claire could hear the tension in his tone. "You said that was just over a week ago?"

Claire nodded, wondering how much she should share. She didn't have proof he had come into the house that day they had been at the picnic, but everything pointed to him being there, namely his being there the night before.

"With any luck, he's headed back east by now."

"I don't think so…" Claire replied quietly. They had just pulled into the yard. Maggie came out the door and moved toward the wagon. Her worried expression prompted Claire to immediately reassure her. "He just gave me a ride home to bring us this buckboard."

Will returned to their conversation as he climbed down from the wagon and moved to the other side to help Claire down. "What did you mean when you said you don't think so?"

"We probably should have said something earlier, but we weren't positive someone had been in the house."

"I'm so glad you're telling him," Maggie said as she came closer and overheard.

Will looked confused. "Wait, what are you saying?"

"The day of the picnic, it looked like someone had been in the house. Things were moved around a bit, and there were signs of someone coming through the window."

"We dismissed the idea until last night," Maggie chimed in.

"Why? What happened last night?"

"You didn't tell him that part?" Maggie asked.

A Debt to Pay

"I was getting there," Claire said. She could feel Will's eyes on her. "Last night, that man, Grady Higgs, was in the barn. I heard a horse and thought maybe Willow had somehow gotten loose, so I went outside to make sure she was still in her stall. When I got close, I saw a light coming from the barn..."

"That was just before that horrible man grabbed and threatened her," Maggie interjected.

Will's eyes flew to the wound on Claire's forehead. "Did he do that to you?" he asked, and Claire could see the muscles in his jaw jumping.

"Not entirely; I did trip and bang it into the stall when I was trying to get free."

Will was shaking his head, anger in his eyes. "You mean he wouldn't let you go?"

Claire's silence and faint shake of her head was all the answer he needed. It infuriated him that Grady would put his hands on her. *What was he doing there in the first place?*

"He seemed like he was looking for something," Claire answered his thoughts.

"He has no reason to be here and certainly no reason to cause harm to either of you."

Claire lifted her hand self-consciously to her face when she felt his eyes on her forehead again.

"How did the night end?" Will was almost afraid to ask.

"Maggie came out with a rifle she found in the cabin loft and scared him away," Claire said.

"That's my father's old gun. I need to load it for you."

"Do you think he'll come back?" Maggie asked nervously.

"If you don't mind, I'd like to spend the night in the barn just in case he does."

The girls didn't object and were honestly grateful for his

presence when nightfall arrived. The night came and went without incident, and in the morning, Claire went out to see if Will wanted to join them for breakfast. The barn door creaked only slightly on its hinges, and she found him just coming to his feet, arching his back in a stretch.

"Good morning," he said with a half yawn, running his hand through his disheveled hair. He leaned over and picked up his hat, dusting the hay from it.

"Good morning," she replied with a smile. "Was it terribly uncomfortable?"

"Yeah," he laughed slightly.

"I'm sorry you had to do that. Do you want to join us for breakfast?"

"Depends on what you're making," he teased.

"Bacon and eggs and coffee?"

"In that case, I'll be right in," he winked at her, rubbing the small of his back as he followed her out of the barn.

Jacob Myles always felt a sting of pain when he came to the cabin. He and his wife had lived there for a year while they built a home for themselves. Memories of her with their young children were never far off, even after almost two years. Now, as he waited outside for Maggie, he averted his gaze from the house, hoping to direct his thoughts to something less disheartening. A moment later, Maggie's cheerful voice greeted him, and she climbed up to sit beside him.

"Good morning, everyone." She turned around and smiled at Lilly and Lucas.

"Good morning, Maggie." Jacob smiled warmly, flicking the reins. "How are you today?"

It had been a week since their ordeal with Grady Higgs,

A Debt to Pay

so that wasn't as heavily on her mind. "I think I've mastered milking the cow," she laughed softly.

"Well, that's something, especially for a city girl like yourself."

"It sure is. You should have seen me the first time I tried. More milk on me than in the bucket, I think."

"You mean, you didn't know how to milk a cow?" Lilly asked with surprise, coming to stand behind them, holding onto the back of the seat as she often did.

"Nope," Maggie replied with a smile at the girl.

"It's not something you're born knowing how to do," Jacob told his daughter, tugging playfully at one of her braids.

"It is if you grow up in Missouri," she replied, which caused both Jacob and Maggie to smile.

"I have to make a delivery today, so I may be a little bit later than usual," Jacob told them a few minutes later when they reached his home.

"That's fine," Maggie climbed down from the wagon and joined Lucas and Lilly, who were already on the ground. "Take all the time you need."

He waved as he turned the horses down the road, thankful his children had someone taking good care of them.

"Bye, Pa!" Lilly called out, her voice echoed by Lucas.

"Well, what should we do today?" Maggie scooped Lucas up in her arms and planted a little kiss on his chubby, rosy cheek.

"Could we make another fort like we did last week?" Lilly asked, a smile in her big, brown eyes.

"I want to play hide-n-go-sweek," Lucas told her. He put each of his little hands on her cheeks to get her full attention and make sure she was looking at him.

"Alright," Maggie smiled. "We'll do both of those things."

"When will Pa be back?" Lilly asked, standing at the window with the curtains pulled to one side. "He said a little late, but it's almost eight o'clock. He's never been that late before."

"I'm sure he's fine, Lilly. Remember, he had to make a delivery. Maybe it just took him longer to get there and back than he thought."

Lilly sighed as she turned from the window and went over to the rocking chair where Lucas had fallen asleep on Maggie's lap.

"I'm going to lay him in bed; why don't you go get your nightgown on."

Maggie carried the sleeping toddler to a small bed in the room he shared with his sister. Lilly quietly took her nightgown from where it hung on a hook in the room and slipped out of her dress. After tucking the boy soundly in his bed, Maggie went to Lilly and helped her button the back of her night dress.

"Are you sleepy yet?" she asked the girl.

"I want to wait until Pa gets home."

"Alright. Let's go wait for him. I could read to you if you like."

Lilly nodded and quickly retrieved a book from a small table in the room. Once in the living room, she sat on a cushioned chair near the rocker and handed Maggie a Bible storybook.

Maggie opened it. "Have you heard this one?" she asked, pointing to a picture of a woman holding a bundle of wheat.

"Yeah, that one is about Ruth, but I like it."

Maggie had only gotten through the first page when she

noticed Lilly was starting to fall asleep. "You want to sit on my lap?" she asked, afraid the girl might fall off the chair if she continued to sit there.

Lilly nodded and climbed up, laying her head back against Maggie's shoulder as she read to her. Maggie heard a little yawn, and within minutes, Lilly was sleeping soundly. It was only a few more minutes before Maggie heard a wagon pulling up to the house. Momentarily, Jacob came through the door, an apologetic expression on his face as he took off his hat and hung it on a hook behind the door.

"I am so sorry," he said quietly. "I got lost a few times, and that delivery ended up taking me three extra hours!"

Maggie gave him an understanding smile. "It was no problem," she said as he came close.

Jacob walked toward them, trying to ignore an unexpected feeling in his heart seeing Maggie holding his daughter so tenderly. It reminded him of how Rose used to be with her.

"Here, let me take her," he said quietly as he leaned down and scooped her up in his arms. He carried her to her room and then returned, feeling uncertain of what to do. He needed to take Maggie home but didn't want to leave the kids alone, even though it was only a fifteen-minute horse ride there and back.

"I tried to keep supper warm for you," Maggie said as she went to the black iron stove where a pot of stew sat. "You must be starved."

Jacob's stomach growled as if on cue. "Thank you for makin' supper."

"Of course," she replied, turning towards him with a bowl she'd scooped potato stew into.

Jacob couldn't remember the last time he'd been served dinner, except when Mrs. Newberry was there, and her food was hardly edible.

He thanked her quietly, appreciative of her thoughtfulness. "I'll eat this quick and then run you home before it gets too late."

"Oh." Maggie bit her lower lip uncertainly. "That means the children will be left alone."

"Can't really see any way around it. I'll leave a note for Lilly in case she wakes up, and if Lucas wakes up, he'll just crawl in bed with her."

There was suddenly a knock on the door, and they simultaneously turned their heads toward it. Maggie was closest, so she opened it, smiling when she saw Claire on the other side. Maggie could see their buckboard just a few feet away.

"I got a little worried about you," Claire said as Maggie opened the door wider and gestured for her to come in.

"Perfect timing, Claire," Maggie said as she explained their predicament.

"I'm sorry for keeping your sister so long," Jacob apologized from the table. "I just got back a few minutes ago."

"Oh, I don't mind," Claire said easily, "I just started to get worried when Maggie hadn't gotten back yet."

"I'll see you Friday," Maggie said as she grabbed her bonnet from a chair.

"Alright, thank you. Goodbye, ladies," he replied.

"I really didn't want him to have to leave the children alone just to drive me back, so I'm so glad you came when you did," Maggie told her when they were outside.

"You're usually home before five, so when it hit eight, I started to get worried."

"Afraid I'd walked home and ran into a pack of coyotes, were you?"

"Not quite," Claire laughed softly. "Just with that Grady fellow somewhere about, I don't rest too easy."

A Debt to Pay

"I wonder who Will's going to have sleeping in the barn tonight," Maggie thought aloud. For the last week, he'd had one of his ranch hands take turns staying the night in the barn.

As they pulled into the yard, Jared was also arriving. He dismounted his horse and waved to them. "Evenin', ladies," he greeted with a cheerful smile. "Looks like I'm up for the night watch duty."

Claire smiled apologetically. "Hopefully, this is the last night. I hate puttin' you boys out like this."

"Oh, we don't mind," he said as he met them at the wagon and lifted his hand to take hers and help her down.

"You may think otherwise when you wake up with a sore back," Claire warned him.

He chuckled. "Just so long as you ladies are safe. Grady Higgs ain't biddable, and when Will cleaned his plow, he left the ranch madder than a hornet."

"Cleaned his plow?" Maggie asked with confusion.

"Licked him in a fight," Jared explained with a chuckle.

Claire knew he was referring to the fight she'd happened upon.

"He's got a nasty temper," Jared said. "Hard to believe him and Will is brothers."

"Brothers?" Claire looked at him with astonishment.

"Well, not by blood," Jared said. "Grady's Ma married Will's Pa when Will was a boy. Here, I'll unhitch Willow," Jared offered, taking the reins from Claire.

"Have they always been at odds?" Maggie asked, also surprised that the man who would cause Claire harm was any relation to Will Carter.

"He moved east with his ma after John Carter died, and he'd just come back this spring. Will let him live in this here cabin and offered him a job at the ranch. Didn't take long to see Grady was still a no-account thief and troublemaker, though. That's why Will sent him packin'."

"Will mentioned he had a stepbrother," Claire said quietly, thinking about their conversation at the Independence Day picnic. "But I didn't realize it was Grady."

"I don't think he's too keen on folks knowin' Grady's any relation, even if it ain't by blood."

Jared headed off to the barn, and the two girls went inside the house. Claire and Maggie were grateful for the protection of having a man sleep in the barn, but Claire also knew she didn't want to keep inconveniencing Will's ranch hands. She decided she would talk to him about it tomorrow. After all, if Grady was going to come back, he surely would have by now.

Chapter Eleven

The next day, Claire was surprised to find Verra Maison in the storeroom when she arrived. Claire had met her a few times before and thought her just as amiable and obliging as her husband. She was a petite woman with auburn hair graying at the temples and just a few noticeable wrinkles around her blue eyes. She greeted Claire warmly when she walked in.

"Glad to see you're up and about," Claire told her.

She leaned against the counter, a cane in her hand. "Not quite there yet, but at least I can limp now. My husband tells me what a blessing you've been."

Claire shrugged. "It worked out well for me, too." She didn't want to think about what she would do for a job once Mrs. Maison was up to working in the store again.

It was a slow day at the store, so Mr. Maison let her go early. Instead of heading home, Claire headed toward the Carter Ranch. A few people tipped their hats or waved greetings as she passed down the street on her buckboard. She hadn't attempted to ride Willow again but was hoping to purchase a saddle eventually, after she paid back Frederick Harris.

As Will's ranch came into view, she was once again in awe of the number of horses and cattle on either side of the property. The fencing that contained them looked like it went on for miles, and even beyond the fence, there were cattle roaming on the open range. In the center of it all, a two-story brick house with a double front porch stood perfectly situated between several towering oak trees.

There seemed to be a lot of activity, just as there had been the last time she was there, with half a dozen men working in various parts of the ranch. Claire caught sight of Will near the corral, his worn, leather cowboy hat giving him away. Hearing the approaching wagon, Will turned and waved.

Claire pulled up and hopped down from the seat. "Good afternoon," she greeted as she smoothed back some hair that had come loose during the ride.

"Howdy, Claire. What brings you out here?"

"Well, when you have a minute, if you're not busy, I just wanted to speak with you about something." Claire felt a little foolish all of a sudden for driving out there. "I won't take much of your time," she promised.

"I've got some time," he assured her. He turned back to a young man who had been standing near him. "Cody, why don't you finish up with Barnum and then start with Apollo."

Claire watched as the man nodded and then slipped into the corral where a large black horse was waiting.

"What is it you wanted to talk to me about?"

"It's about the men you have staying at the barn each night. I think…"

"Has anyone bothered you?" he interrupted, an alarmed look flashing across his suntanned face.

"No, no," Claire quickly clarified. "I only meant I feel terrible for the inconvenience, and Maggie and I both feel like if Grady was going to come back, he would have done so already."

"You don't know him like I do," Will replied.

"Yes, Jared explained to us the connection."

"I should have never given him another chance," Will said, more to himself than to her, Claire thought. "Before he left to go back east with his Ma, he caused a lot of trouble in town and around the ranch. Most folks think he may have even been the one who robbed the bank. Weren't enough proof to convict him, though. When he came back a few months ago saying he had changed and wanted to prove it and find his place at the ranch, I wanted to believe him."

"I thought you were a bully when I saw you tearing into him that day."

Will looked surprised, and Claire could feel her cheeks redden. She hadn't meant to say that aloud. "I realized soon after that I'd made a mistake, though."

He chuckled. "First impressions aren't always the best to go by. I think I was pretty rude that day and rushed off, as I recall."

"You were just preoccupied."

"To get back to what you were saying, I can't in good conscience leave you two alone at night knowing he's lurking around."

"We'll keep the doors locked, and now he knows we have the rifle. We're not as helpless as you might think. Maggie and I have…" Claire caught herself from finishing her sentence. Years of experience with rough and drunken men was definitely not something she wanted to divulge. Instead, she replaced it with, "…no problem taking care of ourselves."

He sighed thoughtfully, crossing his arms over his chest. The rifle had scared Grady off once before. He also reasoned that the men at the ranch were about to start rounding up the cattle that open ranged on his property, a task which was time-consuming, sometimes taking weeks. "I'll let up on the night watch under one condition."

Claire's brows rose a fraction as she waited to hear it.

"You let me know if there is even the slightest possibility you have seen or heard him on the property."

Claire nodded in agreement and promised she would.

"Now, while you're here, can I show you something?"

Claire was surprised at the question but readily said yes, curious as to what it was.

"I know you aren't one to accept a gift, but I hope you'll hear me out on this one."

Claire followed him around the corral and past a massive white silo toward the immense red barn. The smell of clean hay and horses greeted her once inside, and she spotted a man mucking out a stable at the far end. She continued to follow Will until they ended up in a tack room off to the side.

"This saddle is an older one that gets little to no use. If you would take it, it would be doing me a favor because it's just taking up space."

Claire looked at him incredulously, and he laughed, saying, "I know you don't believe me, but it's true."

"I think you're just trying to be generous without me knowing it," Claire told him pointedly, lifting one hand to her waist.

"Maybe, or maybe it really is just taking up space." He shrugged sheepishly, and Claire thought he looked rather boyish at that moment.

She sighed through a smile, shaking her head slightly. "If I took it, I could start learning to ride Willow, and if I paid you for it, I could also start learning to ride Willow."

"But if you paid me for it, I would be insulted."

A Debt to Pay

"Well, I wouldn't want you to feel insulted," she said with mock sympathy.

"Then you'll take it?"

"I guess I have to."

"Good!" He lifted it right away from the rail it hung over. "I'll put it in the buckboard now."

As he said the words, a loud crack of thunder caused even the bravest of horses in the barn to whinny. When they reached the barn door, a threatening cover of gray clouds was looming overhead.

"That rolled in a lot faster than I thought it would," Will said. "I think I'll wait to put this saddle out there. You don't mind waiting out the storm here, do you?"

Claire was about to object and tell him she didn't mind a little rain, but as she opened her mouth, another round of thunder rumbled, followed by a bolt of lightning that lit the darkening sky.

"I'll take that as a no," Will said as he set the saddle down on a nearby stool. "I'll get Willow to shelter, and why don't you head for the house?"

Large raindrops were already starting to fall as Claire moved across the yard. A forceful wind grabbed at her skirt and threatened to yank all her hairpins out. Claire moved a little faster when the rain began to fall harder and soon found herself on the front porch. She watched as men scurried to the barn and, a few minutes later, saw Will running toward the house, his hand on his hat as the wind almost took it.

As a loud bang of thunder seemed to shake the ground, a torrent of rain poured from the sky. Even on the porch, Claire could feel the pellets of water blowing toward her.

"Come on!" Will said as he took her gently by the arm and led her through the front door. He shook out his shirt sleeves a bit and hung his drenched hat over a hook near the door.

Claire was struck by the fine furnishings in the entryway and adjoining rooms on either side, tastefully situated in a manner that felt warm and inviting. It was spacious and cozy all at once.

"Do you think it's a tornado?"

The question came from Hannah Reed, a woman whose plain but young-looking face hardly looked to be her age of sixty-seven. Her blonde to gray hair was parted in the middle and formed a single, long braid—the same style it had been in since she was old enough to braid it herself. She had just come out of a room at the end of the hall, opposite the front door, when she heard Will come in.

"Hannah, this is Claire Wallace. Claire, this is Hannah. She takes care of the house and cooks and pretty much tells us all what to do," he added with a wink in Claire's direction.

"I don't know about the last part," Hannah said with a raised eyebrow in Will's direction, "but it's nice to meet you, dear. Got caught in the storm, did you?"

Claire nodded. "I'm afraid so."

"To answer your question, Hannah, I'm not sure," Will said as he glanced toward the window. Rain was hitting hard, soon turning to the sound of small hail.

"Hail's not a good sign," Hannah said as she wiped her hands on her apron. "I was in the middle of baking a pie, but maybe I should be heading to the cellar."

"A little early for that, but I'll keep an eye on it," Will assured the woman who had been more like an aunt to him than a housekeeper and cook.

"Why don't you two follow me into the kitchen, and I'll get you something to snack on. Besides that, we can get to the cellar from the kitchen," Hannah said to Claire.

Claire tried not to show her concern, but all their talk

about a tornado made her nervous. And that sound of ice hitting the roof and windows wasn't making her any less worried as she followed Will into the kitchen and sat across from him at a large rectangular-shaped oak table.

A loud crack of thunder caused Claire to jump a little, and she nearly spilled the glass of lemonade Hannah had put in front of her. Will stood from the table and went to the window. The rush of rain against it made it difficult to see, but then he noticed how large the hail had become.

"I think it might be a good idea to head to the cellar," he said in a tone that was so calm that Claire thought he might be joking. But then she saw Hannah hastily grab a lantern from a nearby shelf.

"You're serious," Claire said, her eyes growing bigger.

"Afraid so," Will told her.

Suddenly, there was the sound of a loud shatter as a large tree branch came hurling through the window where Will stood.

Hannah let out a little scream at the sound and ran to Will as he bent over, falling to his knees. Claire jumped up as well, in shock that there was a fairly large branch on the kitchen floor amidst shattered glass. Wind and rain rushed through the window, and there was an eerie howling sound outside that was getting louder.

"I'm alright," she heard Will say as he straightened up. The next thing Claire heard was a loud gasp from Hannah, and then the woman began to back up and turn white as a ghost.

Claire frantically grabbed a dishcloth that was on the table and rushed to Will, where she reached up and pressed it to his bleeding forehead. Blood was gushing down his face, and he was trying to wipe it from his eyes.

"Hannah, are you alright?" Claire all but shouted over the

roar of the wind. The woman was holding on to the table and looked like she might pass out.

"She can't handle the sight of blood," Will grunted, turning back to the window and making an effort to close the shutters. "Get to the cellar!" he yelled to Hannah and Claire.

"I'll do it!" Claire said, stepping in front of him and taking over. She slammed them closed over the open window and latched them together. She could tell Will was a little dazed as he looked around for something more to stop the bleeding.

Claire saw the dishcloth she'd given him was already soaked with blood.

"In there!" Hannah said, pointing to a hutch on the far wall, and Claire ran to it quickly. Opening drawers and cabinets, she found a basket with various wrappings and what appeared to be medicine bottles and grabbed it.

"C'mon!" She heard Will's voice as he lifted the lantern off the table and opened the cellar door. The three of them made their way downstairs and into a cold basement lined with shelves of canned goods and crates of food.

Hannah had found a stool to sit on, and Claire asked again if she was alright.

"I'm sorry, dear. I'm no help at all at the sight of blood. I'm afraid I get terribly lightheaded."

"That's alright," Claire said sympathetically. "Can you hold the lamp light close and just look the other way?"

Hannah saw that Claire meant to bandage Will's wound and immediately stood to comply. "I certainly can, dear."

Will was still standing, the rag pressed to his wounded head. Claire surveyed the dim room and saw the only stool was the one Hannah had been sitting on, so she retrieved it and brought it to where Will was standing. "Sit here," she ordered softly.

A Debt to Pay

As he sat down, she went through the basket and found scissors, bandages, and some antiseptic. Her recent visit from the doctor helped her know what to do. Once Hannah was near with the light, Claire gently put her hand where he was holding the rag.

"It's just a scratch," he said, lifting his hand so she could see.

"It's a bit more than a scratch," Claire replied, feeling a little horrified at the sight of a sharp piece of glass wedged in his forehead. It was only about an inch in diameter, but she didn't want to say how bad it looked out loud in case Hannah became queasy again.

"Just hold still if you can," Claire said to Will. She heard him wince as she pulled the glass piece out. She tried to do it quickly, but she knew it was still painful. She poured some antiseptic on a cloth and gently wiped it before putting another clean bandage over it. In the lamplight, she could still see there was blood coming from somewhere other than the gash from the glass.

"Can I see that?" she asked Hannah, who handed her the lamp. With the lamp poised just above his head, Claire was able to find the source of the bleeding. Handing it back to Hannah, she grabbed another bandage and applied light pressure to a wound just above his temple. It seemed rather deep, and she wondered if there was glass in that as well.

"You'd best see a doctor, then," Claire told him as she finished tying the bandage securely around his head. She then took a clean rag from the basket and gently wiped the blood off his forehead and cheek.

"Thank goodness you have a stronger backbone than I do," Hannah said as Claire stepped back.

"Amen to that," Will said. "Hannah would have let me bleed to death on that kitchen floor."

"It's not a time to be joking," Hannah scolded Will.

"I wasn't," Will replied with a slight smile. "Thank you, Claire." He gently touched her arm for a moment as she was still standing close to him.

"Of course," she replied, not thinking much of it. She suddenly had a distant memory of wrapping a head wound her uncle had acquired while collapsing during a drinking binge. It had happened more than once, as she recalled.

Even in the cellar, they could hear the roaring sound of wind outside. Now that Claire wasn't concentrating on doctoring Will's wound, her thoughts raced to the tornado outside.

"What will the others do?" Claire asked with concern, thinking of the men who worked at the ranch.

"There's another cellar by the barn. They'll take shelter in there."

"I hope Maggie's alright," Claire voiced her thoughts aloud.

"Is she at the cabin?" Will asked.

"At Reverend Myles."

"He's east of here, so with the way the wind was coming, I'd say she'd be fine. The storm may have missed his house completely. Don't worry," he tried to reassure her, "This will be over soon."

"This is something we never had to worry about in Chi… Springfield," Claire quickly corrected, wrapping her arms around herself against a sudden chill. There was another loud crack of thunder, and the sound of rainfall seemed to increase for several minutes.

"I've survived at least half a dozen tornadoes in my lifetime," Hannah tried to be reassuring. "We'll be fine."

About twenty minutes later, Will went up to the kitchen

and then called them up when he saw the storm had passed. He immediately picked up the four-foot branch that had flown through the window and carried it outside. The sky was still a little gray with some leftover drizzle falling from it, but just behind the clouds, a clear blue sky was beginning to take over.

Claire noticed some drops of blood that had fallen onto the floor when Will had first been hit, so she quickly wiped them up before Hannah could notice them. "Just some water, mud, and glass," Hannah remarked of the mess in the kitchen. "Could have been a lot worse."

"I'm going to go see if there was any damage done to the barn," Will said from the door.

"Go on then," Hannah said, "Claire and I will clean up this mess."

Claire smiled in agreement, glad to be of help. When Will returned a few minutes later, she was relieved to hear his good news.

"The barn looks virtually untouched. Just some damage to the fence and some debris in the yard."

"What about the stock?" Hannah asked.

"All fine and accounted for," he replied with a relieved sigh. "I'd like to follow you home to check if there was any damage to the cabin," Will said to Claire.

Claire nodded as she laid the broom against the wall. The mess was almost cleaned up. "It was nice meeting you, Hannah," she told the older woman sincerely.

"And nice meeting you, although the circumstances weren't ideal," she smiled. "Glad to know you're a good one to have around in the event of needing some doctorin'."

Claire gave her a quick hug goodbye, feeling like the last hour and a half had been much longer.

Later that night, Hannah was finally getting back to her baking when Will returned from following Claire home. He was thankful to find that besides a few trees down, there wasn't any damage done to the cabin. Coming into the house through the kitchen, Will took off his muddy boots and set them by the door.

"Now, if she isn't just the sweetest thing," Hannah said to Will.

"Who, Claire?"

"No, the jersey cow," Hannah retorted with a chuckle. "Of course, Claire. I've seen her in church but never talked to her until now. She's quite a delightful thing, and she's ain't squeamish or afraid to get her hands dirty."

"Or bloody," Will winked at her as he went to the sink to get himself some water.

"That too," Hannah added with a shake of her head. "Something I can't say for myself. What's her story?"

"I don't know too much about her, except that she and her sister headed west after their parents died, and they ended up here."

"Hmm."

"I know what you're thinking," Will said as he took off his hat and carefully adjusted the bandage near his eye.

"And what might that be?" she asked with a pointed look at him, her hands on her thick hips.

"Never mind," he replied.

"If you think that I'm thinking that you ought to start thinking 'bout a wife, then you're right."

"Too much thinking."

"Seriously, Will. Why not get to know her a little better?"

"We're just friends, Hannah, and I like it that way. Why complicate things?"

A Debt to Pay

"Because she's sweet and gorgeous, and there ain't a fellow in this town who can't see that. She won't be single for long. And if you don't make a move, you might miss your chance."

Will sighed. He knew Hannah was just looking out for him, but his experience with romantic relationships hadn't done him any favors. "We'll see," was all he said as he moved toward the doorway.

"I'm heading off to bed. I'll order a new window tomorrow," he told her.

"Stop by Doc Fletcher's while you're in town and have him look at you. Lord knows you'd be on your own if you needed me to change your bandages."

"Alright."

"Or you could always ask Claire to come by and…"

"Goodnight, Hannah."

Chapter Twelve

"Is anyone here?"

"I'll be with you in a minute," Claire called from the back room of the mercantile. She was trying to clean up a mess of sugar that had spilled when Mr. Maison accidentally caught the fifty-pound bag on a nail. He was making a delivery to the Feed and Seed, and she wanted to surprise him and have it cleaned up before he got back.

"I'm sorry for the wait. What can I help you with?" Claire asked as she came into the storeroom. Her smile fell when she saw Bruce Conway standing by the counter.

"Good morning, Miss Wallace," he smiled, tipping his derby hat slightly. His left hand was in the pocket of his silk Sutter vest, and he leaned on the counter with his other elbow.

"Good morning, Mr. Conway. Is there something I can help you with?"

"Just some tobacco, if you don't mind."

Claire moved to the back of the counter to a shelf with various tins containing tobacco. She set the three different brands they had on the counter.

"Which do you want?"

A Debt to Pay

"I saw Verra Maison in the wagon with her husband just a few minutes ago. Looks like she is on the mend."

"Yes," Claire tried to offer a polite smile. "She's starting to get around."

"I guess that means you'll be out of a job shortly."

"You must really be hard-pressed to find help in your hotel," Claire said. "You've mentioned this to me at least three times."

He chuckled. "I just want to make sure you don't forget."

"Mr. Conway, I do appreciate your offer, but I'm not interested in working at your hotel."

"You wouldn't even have to get your hands dirty. Merely greet guests with that pretty smile of yours and work at the desk."

"Thank you, but I'm just not interested. That will be twenty cents for the tobacco."

"Is there anything I could do to persuade you to have supper with me?" Bruce Conway's voice had softened to an almost tender tone, and for just a moment, Claire thought his expression looked sincere. His narrow eyes held hers a brief moment, and then the bell over the door chimed, and someone entered the store, causing Claire to look past him.

"You can think about it," he said as he dropped the necessary coins on the counter and took his tobacco. Turning around, he nodded politely toward Will. "Mr. Carter."

"Mr. Conway," Will returned the greeting with less than a smile. Will had reached the counter around the time Bruce Conway exited the store.

"How are you feeling?" Claire asked him, grateful for the breath of fresh air he brought in with him.

He touched the clean bandage the doctor had just put on. "Better. Just stopped by Doc Fletcher's. He said he may have to consider hiring you as a nurse."

"I'm sure," Claire laughed softly.

"Is Tom around?"

"He should be back in just a few minutes."

"Alright, I'll wait. Is there anything you could use help with while I'm here?"

"Actually…" Claire led him to the back room. "See that bag of sugar? It has a huge hole. We need to pour it into another sack or just set it in another sack."

"The second option sounds easiest. Where's the sack?"

Claire fetched it from a shelf. "I can hold it open if you can maneuver the other one inside. But…try to hold the hole together as you do."

As Will leaned over and picked up the fifty-pound bag, sugar began pouring out from the bottom. Claire reached over quickly and put her hand near his to try to plug the hole.

"There must be two holes!" Will said. "It's going everywhere."

"Here!" Claire opened the sack she was holding, but as Will tried to fit the leaking bag of sugar inside, it was too tight a squeeze.

"Grab a bigger sack!" he started to laugh.

"This one will work," she found herself laughing as sugar poured over their feet. They managed to finally get it in the new sack and then stepped back to look at the mess.

"It's definitely not a fifty-pound bag of sugar anymore," Claire said as she reached for the broom.

Will grinned. Out of nowhere, he heard himself say, "Would you want to come to the ranch for supper sometime?" He couldn't quite read her expression, but for a moment, he thought he saw something akin to disappointment, or was it reluctance?

"Hannah asked me to ask you...and Maggie, of course," he quickly added and saw relief fill her eyes.

She smiled and nodded. "I would love for Maggie to meet Hannah. She was so kind."

"Great. Why don't we plan for next Saturday?"

Claire nodded in agreement. "Oh, I think Mr. Maison is back," she said, looking around his shoulder into the storeroom. Will said goodbye and went to talk with Tom, leaving Claire alone with her thoughts. She had felt almost panicked when he first mentioned supper. Will had been the only man she'd ever known whom she considered a good friend. She certainly didn't want that to be ruined with him taking a further interest in her. She wasn't ready for that kind of relationship and, at this point, felt more than content with her independence.

Maggie wiped her flour-covered hands on her apron and smiled at Lilly, also covered in flour. She was wearing her mother's apron, and Maggie had bunched it up to size and wrapped the tie strings around her little waist several times to secure it. Lilly had been begging Maggie to make apple muffins, a task Maggie thought would be daunting until Lilly assured her that she would talk her through it. Maggie couldn't believe a seven, almost eight-year-old, as Lilly often reminded them, knew so much about cooking. Maggie thought it a good indication of her mother's influence.

"Next, we bake them for about twenty minutes, but Ma used to check before twenty minutes just in case."

"Alright," Maggie picked up the muffin pan and walked to the oven. She stepped back after she'd slid them onto the rack and closed the iron door. "I guess we could play hide and go seek with Lucas while we wait."

Lilly's eyes went to the table, and she looked back at Maggie uncertainly. "Shouldn't we clean this mess up first?"

Maggie laughed softly. "You're absolutely right!" She immediately went to the sink and used the water pump to fill the sink. "I'll wipe the table; what if you bring those bowls over to the sink for me to wash."

Lilly was already bringing the dirty utensils and bowls over before Maggie suggested it. She had watched her mother closely and spent nearly every waking moment with her for six years, so she knew the order of things.

"We still have ten minutes left," Maggie said after they had finished cleaning up. "Poor Lucas has been waiting. Why don't you take him and hide, and I'll come find you both?"

Lilly nodded with a smile and grabbed her brother's hand. Lucas was playing on the floor with a toy train he rarely parted from. "Let's hide," she whispered. He immediately jumped up and scampered across the room with his sister.

Maggie laughed to herself as she watched him, loving the way the curly blonde hair on his head bounced when he ran. She had yet to meet two children she liked more than Jacob Myles' children. After a minute or so of pretending to search for them, Maggie went into the bedroom and pounced on the bed, knowing they were hiding under the blankets.

"Found ya!" she said, tickling Lucas as he squirmed and giggled.

"The muffins!" Lilly jumped out of bed and ran to the kitchen.

"We should still have a few more minutes," Maggie said, coming up behind her. "But let's check." When they pulled out the muffins, Lilly squealed with glee. "They're perfect!" she exclaimed.

"They are perfect," Maggie agreed, more surprised than

she would admit to the little girl. "Thanks to your guidance, Lilly."

Lilly smiled proudly, and then her attention went to the door as it opened. "Pa! We made apple muffins just like Ma used to!"

Jacob Myles felt the arms of his little girl fly around him in a hug and then leaned over to scoop up Lucas, who had been close behind Lilly. "I was wondering what that wonderful aroma was," he said, looking past the kids to Maggie. Her presence there in the kitchen, mixed with the familiar smell of his wife's favorite muffins, caused an ache in his heart. He was thankful for Maggie and her help with the children, but he couldn't help but wish he'd come home to find Rose instead.

"Come try one, Pa." Lilly grabbed his hand and led him toward the table.

"They probably need time to cool," Maggie said as she used a fork to pop them out of the muffin pan and set them on a plate.

"How was your day?" Jacob asked Maggie thoughtfully.

"Great. Lilly is such a help."

Jacob smiled at his daughter, who reminded him so much of his wife in appearance and personality. "Yep, she's always been that way."

"How about yours?" Maggie returned the question.

"Well, after I left the mill around noon, I headed to the widow Parker's house. She's approaching eighty, and her niece has a hard time getting her anywhere, so I usually go by on Fridays to visit with her."

"That's kind. I'm sure she appreciates it since she can't make it to church."

"Come on, Lucas," Lilly said. "Let's go play outside."

"Stay in the yard," Jacob told them. "We're going to take Maggie home soon."

"Speaking of church," Maggie said a moment later as she started washing the muffin pan in the sink. "Are there any more stories like the one you told the other Sunday? About the woman who almost got stoned?"

Jacob swallowed the muffin bite he was chewing. "You mean the woman caught in adultery?"

"Yes, I didn't know there were stories like that in the Bible."

A faint smile tugged at Jacob's lips. "There are other stories like that. Here…look at this one," he said as he gestured for her to come over.

Maggie wiped her hands on a dish towel and joined him at the table as he opened his Bible and began to flip through it. "Have you read the whole thing?" she asked in awe of all the pages.

"Yeah, but it's not as hard as you might think." He opened to a book called Hosea. "In this book, God tells a man named Gomer to marry a prostitute to show us His own heart towards His people. While they have turned aside to other lovers and abandoned their faithfulness to Him, He is trying to draw them back like a husband would continue to love an unfaithful wife."

"That's beautiful," Maggie said quietly, amazed that God would do that.

"The story of the prodigal son is another one that shows God's heart. Have you ever heard that one?"

Maggie shook her head and watched as he flipped toward the back of the Bible, stopping at a book called Luke.

"'There was a man who had two sons'…"

Maggie listened intently as he read, completely expecting

the father to punish the son in the end. She felt like crying when the story's ending turned out much different.

"So, the father not only forgave the son for squandering his inheritance, but he had a celebration simply because his son had come home. That's how God feels when we come back to Him." Jacob saw something in her expression that made him ask her if she had ever had a relationship with the Lord.

"My ma used to make me read from the Bible when I was young, but once I was a teenager, things changed a lot, and I haven't read it since. I don't think I've ever had a relationship with the Lord," she admitted to him. "The only preacher I ever heard growing up made God sound so angry, I figured I'd just stay away from Him."

"Well, that preacher wasn't conveying the entirety of God to you. God does get angry, and He doesn't turn a blind eye to sin and evil, but His love for humanity far outweighs his anger. That's why he sent his son, Jesus, to take the punishment for sin, so we would all have a way to be with Him." Jacob paused, but seeing the hunger in her eyes, he found himself going on. "Adam and Eve's disobedience brought sin into the world and to every human, but the obedience of Jesus shedding his blood brings forgiveness for anyone who puts their faith in Him."

"It sounds too good to be true," Maggie said, hoping it wasn't.

"I know, but that's because God is so much better than we can imagine."

Maggie was left to ponder his words as Lilly and Lucas came running into the house. Jacob closed the Bible and stood from the table.

"I should be getting back," Maggie said, also standing.

"Do you have a Bible of your own, Maggie?" Jacob asked.

She shook her head and then watched as he went into his bedroom and came back with one. "Here, I have several extras." He placed it into her hands. "You may not understand everything you read right away, but keep at it. God will show you."

She looked down at the thick brown leather book in her hands, gently running her fingers over the leather. "I'll take good care of it, thank you."

His words to her that afternoon lingered in her mind even late into the night as she lay in bed, Claire sleeping soundly beside her. If God forgave the woman caught in adultery, if he forgave an unfaithful bride, and if he forgave a prodigal son, maybe her sins could be forgiven too.

Chapter Thirteen

"Where did you get that?" Claire asked Maggie a few days later as she saw her sitting at the kitchen table, bent over the Bible one morning after breakfast.

"Jacob gave it to me. Did you know that Jesus healed everyone who ever came to him? Blind people, cripples, mute…" Maggie flipped through the pages, looking for more examples.

"No, I didn't know that," Claire replied with a little laugh. "I can't say I know anything about that book. Oh, I forgot to tell you; we were invited to eat supper with Will and his housekeeper Saturday night."

"Alright," Maggie replied absently, not looking up from the page she was reading.

"We're close to halfway to paying back what we used to get here," Claire said as she knelt on the floor by the fireplace and used her fingers to pry up the corner of a loose floorboard. She had noticed it the other day when she was washing the floor by hand. When the corner of the board easily lifted, she noticed a nice space inside, which she thought was a better place to hide the money and necklace. Now, as she pulled out the bag, she took the dollar bills she had earned that week and stuffed them inside.

"I can't wait to send it back and be done with it," Maggie said.

"Hopefully, once Harris gets the money and necklace back, he'll be content enough to not set the law on us."

"Then we best send it back sooner than later."

"Another few weeks with both of us working, and we should be able to mail it all back to Chicago," Claire said with a sigh of relief. She glanced at the clock on the mantle and gasped. "I've gotta get going! I'll see you later, Maggie."

She quickly hitched the buckboard to Willow and headed toward town. After just a few minutes on the road, she saw a rider approaching on the other side. As he neared, she realized it was Sheriff Dunley. She'd seen him a handful of times in the streets and had done her best to stay off his radar.

"Good morning," he greeted, tipping his black slouch hat and giving her barely a glance.

"Good morning, Sheriff," Claire replied, glad when he rode by. His manner always seemed aloof, but it suited her just fine since she wanted to keep her distance. She knew the trouble she'd be in should he find out about their burglary.

Besides occasionally putting a drunken man in jail overnight for disrupting the peace, there hadn't been much cause for Jake Dunley to exercise his authority in the town of Millcreek. Of course, there was that bank robbery a few years back, but he'd managed to turn that around to benefit himself. He was pleased with how he kept order and pleased with the connections he'd made which helped him to do so.

That morning, he was heading out to meet Bruce Conway. The business owner had proven to be a sly opportunist who had brought quite a bit of monetary profit to him. Knowing

A Debt to Pay

the weight he carried as a sheriff also gave him plenty of leverage in their dealings.

Twenty minutes later, Sheriff Dunley dismounted, threw the remains of his cigarette on the ground, and made his way into a shack-like building. It was half-hidden beneath overgrown vines and shrubs, making it an ideal place to meet undetected.

"Mornin'," Sheriff Dunley said as he entered the abandoned house and saw Conway sitting at the table.

"Mornin', Sheriff. Pull up a chair." Bruce Conway lit his cigar and leaned his elbows on the table.

The chair scraped against the floor as Dunley slid it out and sat down opposite Bruce Conway. "So, what's on your mind?"

"Grady Higgs."

The sheriff's eyebrows furrowed together. "Last time I checked, he weren't in Millcreek."

"The fool came back."

"I know that, and I kept an eye on him like you said. But he's gone again. His brother ran him off, what I heard."

Bruce shook his head. "He's still here. I don't know why, but he's here. And if he talks..." he let his sentence hang and exhaled a thick cloud of smoke.

"He'd only implicate himself to bring up that bank robbery," Sheriff Dunley said. "He won't talk." Only the sheriff and Bruce knew it was Grady who had robbed the Millcreek Bank two years ago. When the sheriff had gone after him, there was some gunfire involved which injured Dunley but enabled him to get ahold of the stolen money. He told the townsfolk that the criminal had escaped, not disclosing that it was Grady nor that the money had been recovered. Sheriff Dunley kept all of it until Bruce called him out on it and ended up with half the take.

"You better make sure he don't talk. You should have killed him when you had the chance," Bruce said. "Although, I guess that bullet he sent through your arm made you look credible."

The sheriff grinned. "It did help quiet any suspicions about the money."

"I want to know why he's lingering 'round Millcreek."

"He's probably just barkin' at a knot, but I'll find him, and then I'll find out why."

"That's what I was hoping you would say."

Grady Higgs drained the rest of his whiskey and signaled for the bartender to get him another bottle. The Millcreek saloon was bustling that Saturday night, mostly regulars gambling, drinking, and having a good time.

"I thought you'd run away with your tail between your legs after your brother gave you a thrashin'."

Grady looked up as Sheriff Dunley took the stool beside his at the bar. "I'll leave when I'm good and ready."

"Some dispute about a stolen watch, was it?"

"Carter thinks he's a big gun, but he ain't gonna tell me what to do."

"So, you're planning to stick around then?"

"What's it to you?"

"Not much. Just like to know you ain't here to stir up any trouble like usual."

"What kind of trouble you worried about?" Grady asked, his eyes narrowing as he tried to read the sheriff's expression. As far as he knew, not even the sheriff knew it had been him behind the Millcreek Bank robbery. When the sheriff had caught up to him, and they'd fought and exchanged gunfire, Grady had managed to keep his mask intact.

A Debt to Pay

"I ain't a fool, Grady, and I know who that robber was who put a bullet through my arm."

"Then why haven't you arrested him yet?" Grady asked, his eyes taunting him.

"I don't have enough proof," the sheriff said, hoping that would suffice.

"I don't have any reason to believe that bank money didn't get returned to the good folks of this town, now do I?"

"No reason at all," the sheriff replied, holding his gaze.

"Humph." Grady reached for the bottle in front of him, not convinced at all that the sheriff was telling the truth.

"So, why did you come back to Millcreek? And don't give me any bosh about wanting to work at Carter's Ranch."

"I don't gotta tell you nothing."

"I could arrest you right now if I really wanted to, Higgs." Sheriff Dunley leaned forward and whispered, "Proof or no proof."

Grady sighed impatiently. "I'm looking for something. Soon as I find it, you won't see me again."

"I hope that's a promise," the sheriff said, moving away to join a poker game at a table across the room.

Grady dismounted, tied his horse to a tree about twenty yards from the cabin, and approached the rest of the way on foot. For the time he'd lived in the cabin, he'd searched countless times for the gold he'd recently learned was hidden there. His mother had overlooked a letter from Will's father, John Carter, addressed to Will, unintentionally stashed away in a box of his old belongings she had kept. It explained that Will's father had hidden some of the gold he'd found in California in the little cabin. "You know where I hid it," the letter had said to Will.

Grady had no idea what hiding spot the letter referred to. After Will had kicked him out, he'd been forced to creep around during the night, breaking in when no one was home to continue his search. Then, the other night, when he'd been caught in the barn, he'd had to stay away for a few weeks just to throw them off his trail. Now, he was starting to run out of money, and he wasn't about to head back east without the gold he'd come for.

Grady relaxed a little when he saw there were no lights on in the cabin. A glance in the barn told him their horse was gone, too. Confident that no one was home, he tried all the doors. Finding the windows locked as well, he pulled out his pistol, shot at the doorknob, and then kicked it open with his booted foot.

With his lantern poised in one hand and his pistol in the other, he entered the house and began what he hoped would be his last search. Not wanting to bother with pretenses or waste time, he knocked over whatever was in his way. Moving into the bedroom, he flipped the mattress and other furniture in the room. When he returned to the main room, his eyes shot around desperately, asking himself where he hadn't looked yet and what he might have missed.

He felt along the walls, searching inside and around the furniture. Sometime later, his gaze lowered to the floor, and that's when he noticed something a little strange with one of the floorboards. Dropping to his knees, he ran his hand along it until he came to the one protruding corner and, with a sharp motion, popped it up. Excitement building, he reached his hand inside and pulled out a small bag. He quickly emptied its contents into his hand, his eyes growing large at the sight of money and a diamond necklace shining under the lamplight. He shoved them into his pocket and then reached further into the hole. His next find was exactly what he'd been hoping for: a bag containing several gold nuggets inside.

For the next few minutes, Grady pried and kicked up the wood planks surrounding it to make sure he wasn't leaving anything behind. Finally satisfied that there was nothing more, he headed to the door. But as he stood under the door frame, he hesitated. Without a reproving thought, he walked back to the bedroom and tossed his lantern onto the mattress, watching as flames began to consume it. With a pleased smirk on his face, he left the cabin, everything he'd wanted and more tucked safely inside his pockets.

"Thank you again for supper," Maggie said to Hannah as she and Claire walked out to the front porch. It was after nine, and they had enjoyed every bite of her chicken dumplings and raspberry pie.

"You two are welcome anytime," Hannah said with a kind smile in her eyes.

"Will!"

Will was walking with Hannah, Claire, and Maggie on the front porch when they all heard Jared's voice shouting Will's name. He was moving fast on his horse towards them.

"Jared, what is it?" Will asked with alarm as Jared reined in his horse.

"I just came from the east field, and it looked like fire over by your cabin."

"What on earth?" Will jumped the steps leading away from the porch and climbed up into where Claire and Maggie's buckboard had been waiting. "Do you mind if I drive?"

he asked them, already reaching for Claire's hand as she moved quickly to climb up in the seat beside him. Maggie hastily climbed into the back seat.

"I'll follow you there," Jared said.

"And I'll tell the men to head over…with buckets!" Hannah said, already running towards the bunkhouse.

"Hold on!" Will told them as he flicked the reins and took the wagon on the fastest ride it had ever been on.

Claire and Maggie held tight to the side of their seats, feeling like they were holding their breath as they waited for the cabin to come into view. They could smell the smoke before they saw the flames. By the time they pulled into the yard, half of the house was ablaze, fire licking up the sides.

Claire jumped from the wagon before Will had even pulled it to a stop and ran full speed toward the house.

"Claire!" Maggie screamed, trying to scramble down from the wagon.

Claire could feel the heat from the fire before she reached the door, which was already wide open. She ran inside, lifting her arm instantly to shield her face from the heat of the flames just to the left of where she stood. Without even glancing toward the bedroom, she knew it was lost, but the hiding place, where the money and the diamond necklace were, was only feet away and not yet touched by fire. The roar of cracking flames was almost deafening and the light from the fire almost blinding.

"Claire!"

Claire ignored Will's voice as she tried to see through the smoke. She dropped onto her hands and knees and crawled as fast as she could toward it. She'd almost passed the table when she felt hands grab her by the waist and pull her backward.

A Debt to Pay

"No! I can still get it!"

"Claire! C'mon! The roof's about to go!"

Claire struggled against his hold on her, pushing the hands that went around her waist and practically dragged her out of the house. The warm summer air felt cold compared to what she had just been in.

"It's too late!" Will shouted over the blazing fire, now consuming the roof and back side of the house. They heard a loud crash, and through the open door, they could see a huge ceiling beam falling into the center of the house.

Will slowly released his hold when he felt Claire stop pushing away from him. He watched as she sank to the ground on her knees, coughing and crying with her head in her hands.

Jared came running from the side of the house, a bucket of water in his hands from the well. "It's too late," Will told him, staring in disbelief as his father's house burnt to the ground. "Let's just dig a ditch and pour water around the house to keep it from spreading!"

It was getting hotter as the fire took over every square inch. "Claire, we've got to move back." Will leaned down and reached for her arms. "Claire, come on." He pulled her up to her feet and led her away from the burning cabin.

The men from the ranch arrived and immediately began helping Jared, running to the well with the buckets and pouring water around the perimeter of the yard.

Jared had already run to the barn and let the animals out in case the fire spread.

Will ran to help the others, leaving Claire with Maggie.

"It's gone, Maggie! Everything. Everything's gone!" Claire's voice broke as she watched all they had worked for burn with everything else. Not just the money they'd saved but the money left over from the burglary and the diamond necklace. There was no way to replace that!

"Oh, Claire, what are we gonna do?" Maggie began to cry.

"Is everyone alright?" Maggie turned at the voice to see Reverend Myles dismounting his horse. He looked with concern from the cabin on fire to the two young women.

"The house was already half gone when we got here," Maggie explained with a trembling voice.

"Then no one was inside when it started? Thank God." He saw Will and other men pouring buckets of water around the property, the fire's bright flames illuminating them even in the dark. He joined them, asking Will if he knew how it started.

"It was too late when we got here," Will told him somberly. "We have no idea how it started." Even as he said the words, something in Will felt uneasy. He realized he did know; he just wasn't ready to admit to himself that even his stepbrother could do something so dastardly.

"I smelled the smoke from my place," Jacob told him. "I'm so sorry, Will." He knew there was nothing left they could do now but make sure it didn't spread.

"I'm just glad Maggie and Claire are alright," Will said, trying not to think of the sentimental value of his father's home, where he had spent several years of his childhood.

"Yes, but how distressing for them to lose all their things."

Will looked over his shoulder toward Claire and Maggie and saw they hadn't moved that whole time. He felt compassion seeing them stand there, watching the fire consume all their belongings and the cabin that had become their home, albeit for just a short time.

Will walked toward them. "I'll take you ladies back with me to the ranch for tonight. We can figure things out in the morning."

A Debt to Pay

Maggie nodded and thanked him, but he saw that Clare's gaze was yet to move away from the fire. She didn't say a word then or the whole way back to the ranch. Hannah greeted them in a wind of worry and empathy. She took Maggie and Claire each to a room and got them settled in.

Once alone in the bedroom, Claire lay on the bed and sobbed, feeling the overwhelming veracity of what that fire had taken from her and the ominous prospect of how hard it would be to get it back.

Chapter Fourteen

It was a light tapping on the door that awoke Claire the next morning. Her eyelids felt heavy when she tried to open them, and a headache was resting in her temples.

"Claire? Claire, are you awake yet?"

Claire sat up slowly at the sound of Maggie's voice. Blinking, she glanced around in a moment of confusion. The memory of the fire came rushing in, and she flopped back down on the bed. "I don't think I want to wake up, Maggie."

Maggie came in, closing the door behind her. She saw the bed covers hadn't even been turned down. "What are you always saying to me, Claire? Things will be OK; they'll work out somehow. We can't just give up."

"We should have never left Chicago," Claire said, sitting up again and pulling her knees into her chest. "This was all a mistake."

Maggie looked at her with a frown. "You can't really believe that, Claire."

"All that money is gone, Maggie."

"We can work hard and still pay it back. It just might take longer than we thought."

"It's not just the money, Maggie. What about the necklace? Sure, we can work and save and pay back the hundred dollars, but it would take us years to make enough to pay back the necklace."

Maggie slumped down on the bed with a heavy sigh, knowing she was right. "I'm sorry. The necklace is my fault."

Claire shook her head. "I'm not mad at you, Maggie. It was all my idea in the first place."

Maggie laid a comforting hand on Claire's knee. "We'll figure out something, Claire."

Claire nodded faintly, not feeling any confidence that they would.

"Thank you for breakfast," Maggie said to Hannah an hour later.

"A little closer to lunch," Hannah smiled. "But after last night, you needed a good rest. We all skipped church this morning." She collected their dishes from the table. "I'm so sorry about the fire, girls." And then having both of their attention, she added. "Will and I both agreed you can stay here at the ranch for as long as you need to."

"That's very kind," Claire thanked her.

"Will rode out to the cabin about an hour ago to see if there was anything to salvage."

Claire shot Maggie a glance. "We'd like to head over there as well," she said.

Hannah nodded, understanding in her eyes.

When they rode up to it about thirty minutes later, the sight of the smoking rubble brought a brand-new sense of loss.

Maggie's breath caught in her throat when she tried to speak. It really was a devastating sight. Will turned from the rubble and watched them walk into the area that used to be the house.

Claire's eyes went immediately to where she had hidden her handbag. The floorboards were burned up. There was nothing left but ashes, smoldering wood, and small bits of burned furniture.

"Look here," Will said, gesturing for them to follow him. He led them to where the bedroom used to be and pointed to the remains of a lantern on the ground in an ash heap. "That's where the bed used to be."

Claire bent down and looked closer. Shaking her head, she looked at Will. "We didn't have a lantern in the bedroom."

"I figured as much. Remember, the door was wide open when we got here, too. Someone started this fire deliberately."

"Would anyone have a reason to do that?" Claire asked with confusion.

"Grady would."

"But why?"

"To get back at me," Will answered. "My father was good to him, treated him like a son, but Grady was always vindictive. My father couldn't trust him with the ranch. Grady's never forgiven him or me for that." He looked at Claire, his heart in his eyes. "You and Maggie can stay at the ranch as long as you need to. I feel like I'm partly responsible for this. I should have found Grady and forced him to leave town before any of this happened."

"It's not your fault. You had no idea Grady would do this." Claire sighed, her eyes still searching through the blackened rubble as if her handbag full of money and the necklace would somehow materialize.

"He's lucky no one was home," Will said, and Claire could

hear the anger in his tone. "He could have seriously harmed someone with his foolishness. He'll pay for this."

Claire saw the determined resolve in his facial expression and thought she'd hate to be on the receiving end of his disapproval.

"I'll bring your livestock back to the ranch for now," Will told her before she and Maggie headed back.

Once at the ranch, Claire and Maggie drove their wagon to the barn, where Jared greeted them and told them he'd unhitch Willow and put her out to graze. Maggie and Claire began walking over to the house, but Claire turned when she heard Jared say her name.

"I'm really sorry about the fire," he said, his expression solemn. "Maybe we can make the most of it while you're here."

She looked at him, perplexed by his words.

"I mean, even though it ain't on good circumstances, you could learn how to ride horseback while you're here."

Claire nodded, a faint smile on her lips. It was the last thing on her mind, but she was touched by his kindness. "Thanks, Jared."

"I'd be obliged to show you," he added, running a hand down Willow's mane.

"Alright," Claire replied simply. "I don't know how long Maggie and I will be here, though. Just until we can make other arrangements."

"Then we better not waste time." He smiled. "What if I throw a saddle on her and meet you in the corral in a few minutes?"

Claire bit her thumbnail uncertainly. She didn't feel in any mood to socialize or learn a new skill.

"C'mon, it'll take your mind off of the fire," Jared coaxed, a hopeful glimmer in his light blue eyes.

Claire sighed and heard herself agreeing.

When Will rode into the yard, he spotted Claire astride Willow. Jared was leading the horse around the corral. After Will put the cow and chickens in the barn, he returned to the corral and leaned up on the fence next to Maggie.

"Jared's trying to take her mind off the fire, I think," Maggie said.

"Aren't you going to try it?" Will asked.

"I don't think I'm brave enough for that."

"Sure, you are. It's not as hard as you think." He paused a minute and then said, "What if I saddle up one of my calmest mares and help you at least to sit on her back?"

Maggie bit her lip nervously, watching as Claire made it look so easy. "I'll probably fall off and break my arm."

Will laughed softly. "I won't let you fall off. Just wait here."

A few minutes later, he returned with a bay horse walking beside him. He opened the gate to the corral, motioning for Maggie to follow him.

From her place across the way, Claire smiled as she watched Will attempting to help Maggie mount the horse. She heard Maggie give a little squeal when she landed on the horse's back.

"We can just stand right here until you get used to how sitting on her feels," Will told Maggie.

"Am I holding the reins right?" Maggie asked.

"Put your thumb on top like this," Will instructed her as he reached up and adjusted her hand position slightly. "Would you be OK if I walked her slowly?"

"I'm not sure," Maggie replied honestly.

Will grinned. "Just tell me to stop if you feel frightened at all." He took a few steps, leading the horse behind him. He glanced back to make sure Maggie was still OK and found her smiling. "Not so bad, right?"

"You can walk a little faster," she told him, feeling more confident.

"And you said you'd never be able to ride," Claire called to Maggie.

"Don't distract me," Maggie playfully scolded back. "It's taking all my concentration to stay on this animal."

Claire laughed under her breath. Thirty minutes later, as Jared helped her dismount, she gave him a grateful smile. "Thanks, Jared, this did help." She turned away and walked toward Maggie before she saw the look of satisfaction cross his eyes.

Maggie's dismount was a little more awkward, and she practically fell into Will's arms. He steadied her on her feet. "Not bad, Maggie. After a few more times, it'll be a breeze."

"I'll take your word for it," she said, smiling up at him in a way that made Claire feel just a little leery. She'd seen Maggie smile that way at men before, usually when she was trying to persuade them to buy a more expensive whiskey.

"That was fun!" Maggie said, looping her arm around Claire's as they walked toward the house. "Either I'm better than I thought, or Will's an excellent teacher." She glanced over her shoulder toward where he still stood in the corral. "It's going to be a lucky girl who ends up on his arm."

Claire let out a short breath. "Well, it sure won't be the likes of you or me, so I wouldn't waste my time if I were you."

Maggie stopped suddenly and dropped Claire's arm. "What on earth are you talking about?"

"Nothing, Maggie." Claire folded her arms across her chest and averted her gaze.

"It wasn't my idea for him to show me how to ride, if that's what this is about."

"I don't care about that. I just thought I saw a look on your face that…" Claire rolled her eyes and continued walking. "Ugh, never mind." She felt foolish for even bringing it up.

"What look?"

"You know what I mean, Maggie."

"No, I don't. I didn't have any look!"

"Alright, I'm sorry." Claire stopped walking and turned again to face her friend. "Sometimes, the past just…" Claire shook her head, and Maggie could see tears pooling in her eyes. "Sometimes, it all just catches up with me, and I wish my life would have been different."

Maggie reached up a tender hand to Claire's shoulder. "This fire just has you worked up. Things were getting better."

Claire nodded, but it didn't quite reach her eyes or her heart. Somehow, when that fire had destroyed all they had worked for the last few months, it also seemed to have burned up what hope for the future she had been holding on to.

―――

When Claire went to work the next day, Verra Maison greeted her with a hug. "I heard about the fire, dear. I'm so glad you're alright!"

Her genuine concern was touching, and Claire thanked her. Lately, Tom's wife had been spending a few hours here and there getting back into the swing of things at the general store. Claire enjoyed working with her, for she always seemed pleasant and patient. Claire also liked the way she was with customers and how generously she extended credit to those who needed it. Working with her, however, was a reminder that her temporary position was coming to an end.

A Debt to Pay

"I was so sorry to hear about the fire," Tom told Claire just before she finished for the day. Shaking his head, he sighed. "It's a darn shame."

Claire tried to smile optimistically. "Oh, we'll be alright. Just have to sort of start over, I guess." She noticed he looked a little uncomfortable as he rubbed the back of his neck.

"Mr. Maison, I knew this job was temporary when I took it." She saw her words brought a relieved look to his eyes.

"I just feel bad about the timing with the fire and all. I don't want you to be hard run."

"It's OK," Claire quickly assured him. She had never been one to accept a handout. "The time I've spent here has been so helpful, and I'm glad your wife is ready to take back her old job."

He smiled, appreciating her words. "I'll keep my ear open for any job openings in town, and you can stay on the rest of the week."

"Thank you, Mr. Maison."

The money that he would pay her for that week would feel like gold in her hands. She knew she would have to ration it carefully until she found another job. As she left the store, she was surprised to see Will waiting for her outside in his wagon.

"Thought you might need a ride back to the ranch," he said.

Jared had business in town that morning and had given her a ride since Maggie used the buckboard to get to Reverend Myles'. Claire hadn't even thought as far as a ride home.

"Thanks," she said, climbing up to the seat. "I hope you didn't make the trip just for me."

"Nah, I had to come into town anyway," he lied. He backed his wagon up and turned it around. A minute later, they were heading out of town and toward the ranch.

"I feel so bad about what happened," Will told her, shaking his head at the disappointment of the situation.

"It wasn't your fault," Claire assured him.

"I hate to think you and Maggie got in the middle of Grady's offense with me. I should have never given him a second chance when he came back here."

"Were you ever close?" Claire asked.

"Not really. Even as kids, it felt like he always had a reason to be angry with me. I know I have my faults, too, but I did make an honest go of being his brother."

"I know you said before that his Ma married your Pa. Did Grady's father die?"

"Yeah, after spending most of Grady's childhood in jail, his father went back to crime after he was released and ended up dead not long after."

"Well, if your father was anything like you, I'm sure Grady's mother was much happier in her second marriage."

"My father was a better man than me," Will replied, a surge of pride in his voice. "There isn't a day that goes by that I don't think about him."

"What was Grady's mother like?"

"Rebecca was kind and fair and did everything she could to make up for Grady's father."

"I guess sometimes even parents' best attempts don't always pan out."

Will glanced at her. "What about you? What were your parents like?"

Claire had a vivid memory of herself at eleven years old, waking up the morning after her parents had died of cholera. During the night, her father had gone first, followed shortly by her mother. It still brought a chill to her heart to think of it. An uncle she had only seen twice showed up at the funeral and was kind enough to take her in.

"Claire?"

Claire realized she hadn't answered his question. "They were good and loving," she finally replied.

Will sensed she was far away in her thoughts and wondered what memories his question had invoked.

"Their death must have been hard for you and Maggie, and it being so recent, I'm sure it's still hard."

Claire simply nodded, knowing she wasn't at liberty to share a past that contradicted their story. "You can't change the past, so might as well forget it and move on."

"Sometimes that's easier said than done," Will replied, thinking of situations in his own life.

"I'm surprised there's not a Mrs. Carter," Claire said teasingly, surprising Will with the change of topic.

He grinned, "The ranch keeps me too busy, I guess."

"Well, I'm sure Amy Keets is hoping you'll find some time."

Will gave an exaggerated sigh. "In that case, I may run a few extra cattle drives."

Claire laughed softly. "I'm sorry, but she's just so obvious I couldn't help myself."

"I think I've used up all my excuses for her invitations."

"I don't think she's deterred. She made a point to let me know you were off limits," Claire told him.

"Sees you as competition, does she?"

"I don't know why."

"I do."

Claire shrugged off his compliment. "Well, you did buy my raffle basket."

"And I danced with you," he reminded. "I'm sure she didn't like that."

Claire grinned, enjoying the banter. "Well, you're not the only cowboy in town."

"So, you're saying I have some competition, too?"

Claire laughed. "No, I'm saying if you're too busy for marriage, she might just have to look elsewhere."

"She's gonna have to look elsewhere whether I'm too busy or not."

"I'm glad to hear it because if she were the kind of girl you could be interested in, I don't know if we could be friends."

"Well, I'm glad our friendship is secured by our mutual dislike for Amy Keets."

Claire laughed, enjoying how easy it felt when she was with Will Carter. She felt almost disappointed when they reached the ranch and their conversation ended. He dropped her off by the house before taking the wagon to the barn. Claire walked through the house to the kitchen and found Hannah peeling potatoes.

"Need some help?" Claire asked.

Hannah looked up from the table. "Not really, but I'd love the company."

Claire smiled and went to the sink to wash her hands before joining her at the table. "I'll help you and keep you company," she said cheerfully as she reached over and picked up a potato and an extra knife.

It wasn't long before Will came through the back door in the kitchen. He tossed his hat onto a chair and went to the sink to wash his hands. "Putting her to work, are you Hannah?"

"She's putting herself to work, and I don't mind one bit," Hannah said with a smile in Claire's direction.

"These cookies look good," Will said as he dried his hands on a dish towel and glanced at a basket of freshly baked chocolate chip cookies. "Can I have one now, or are they for something special?"

A Debt to Pay

"They're for something special, alright," Hannah replied with a little smirk. "Amy Keets dropped them off for you while you were out."

Will exchanged an amused glance with Claire, giving her a wink. "They smell good enough to win my heart," he joked as he lifted one out of the basket and took a bite. He swallowed it rather painfully.

"But they taste bad enough to lose it?" Claire asked when she saw the expression on his face.

Will laughed. "Exactly."

"Well, maybe the boys will like 'em," Hannah said, not missing Claire and Will's friendly exchange.

"Or the chickens," Will said.

———

"Did I do that right?" Claire asked Will the next day as she stood in the corral with him and Willow. It was Wednesday morning, and since Will had lent Maggie a horse to hitch to the buckboard, Claire wanted to ride Willow to work. Will had helped her lift the saddle onto the horse and then talked her through securing it.

"Looks good!" He gave the horse a sound pat on the rump, smiling at Claire. "She's ready to go. Need help getting up?"

"Maybe, but let me try." Claire put her left foot in the stirrup and held the horn of the saddle as she hoisted herself up and swung her right leg over to the other side of the horse's body.

"Nothing much to it, is there?" he said, stepping back to look up at her. "All you need now is a cowboy hat, and you'll be one of us," he joked.

"I may just pick one up while I'm in town," she teased, gently nudging her heels into the horse's side and riding her out of the corral as Will opened the gate.

Once she entered town, Claire headed to the livery, where she handed Willow off to Eli Greene, the man who owned the livery. The walk to the General Store was only interrupted when she stopped to admire a dress in the window of Mrs. Murry's Dress Shop. The older woman saw her through the window and waved. Claire smiled and waved back before continuing down the street.

A dress like that wasn't in her reach for a very long time. Just the thought that today was her last day working at the General Store was discouraging enough. What was she going to do to make money? They didn't even have what they stole to lean on. They hadn't touched that money once Claire had started working for Mr. Maison, but it had been nice knowing it was there if they needed it.

Claire was surprised to find Maggie in the store when she got there, little Lucas and Lilly beside her. She was grateful they at least had the money that Maggie was making.

"We felt like a walk this morning, and Reverend Myles needed a few things," Maggie explained and then stepped back in time to catch a box of soaps that Lucas accidentally knocked off a shelf.

"Well, good morning," Tom Maison greeted Maggie and the children as he came out of the storage room. "I was hoping some children would stop by today," he said with a wink at Maggie before turning his attention to Lilly. "We've gotten in some new licorice sticks, and I wanted to make sure they were fit to sell. Would you and your brother mind trying one for me?"

Lilly glanced at Maggie for permission and received an agreeable nod before moving toward Mr. Maison, who was reaching inside a glass jar on the counter.

"What can I get for you?" Claire asked Maggie.

A Debt to Pay

"Just some coffee and sugar."

Claire went to fill her order, noticing Amy Keets entering the store a few minutes later. As Maggie left, Amy made her way to the counter to pay for her purchases.

"She's become quite the little mother," Amy remarked as she cast a glance at the children following Maggie out the door. "If I'm perfectly honest with you, some folks aren't so comfortable with the amount of time the Reverend's been spending with your sister."

"She's taking care of his children while he's at work," Claire replied evenly.

"Yes, but when he comes home, they would be alone together now, wouldn't they?"

"Not with the children there."

"Well, they are just children, after all. It wouldn't be difficult to…"

"That will be forty-five cents," Claire cut off her sentence, sliding her basket of purchases toward her.

"How are you enjoying life at the ranch?" Amy asked next, her lips in a sort of tight smile that matched the irritated look in her blue eyes. "Seems it would be a little tiresome being around so many cowboys at once. Watching you ride into town today…well, looks like you're turning into one yourself." She laughed softly. "And that was so sweet of Jared to give you that horse he won." Her white gloved hand came over her heart in feigned tenderness.

"My sister and I have only been there a few days because of the fire. As soon as we can, we'll find somewhere else to live." She wanted to tell her she had no interest in Jared or any other cowboy for that matter, but she didn't think she owed her an explanation.

"Well, you probably should, sooner rather than later. Not

quite proper, if you know what I mean, well, with Will and you and your sister in the same house. You know how folks talk. I wouldn't want anyone to get the wrong idea."

"How considerate of you."

"Just being a good neighbor," Amy said. She turned with a smug smile and left the store with her full satin skirt swishing behind her.

Amy Keets' visit did nothing to help Claire's mood and, in fact, only made her more discouraged about her situation. As she headed to the livery late that afternoon, her thoughts seemed to run wild. She was quite preoccupied with her musings and nearly collided with Bruce Conway as he stepped out of the barbershop. His dark hair was slicked and parted down the middle, and his mustache looked recently trimmed.

"Excuse me," he said, taking a polite step to the side.

"I'm sorry, I wasn't paying attention."

"No harm done. Glad to see you're unscathed and unsinged after that unfortunate fire."

"Thank you."

"Might I walk with you wherever you are going?"

"Just to the livery."

"Very well."

Claire reluctantly fell into step beside him, not seeing any way around it.

"So, you and your sister have been staying at the Carter Ranch?"

"For now," Claire answered carefully.

"I'm assuming you lost quite a bit in that fire."

Claire wasn't fooled by the concern in his voice. She knew this kind of man, and anything they said or did was to gain something for themselves.

"We did."

"It's such a shame. Do you know how the fire started?"

"We don't know for sure," Claire told him, not wanting to get into Will's business with Grady.

"I heard from one of Will's ranch hands that Will thinks his stepbrother did it."

"I really couldn't say," Claire replied. She saw that his hotel was just to their left across the street. Her eyes lingered on its tall false front, painted a bright yellow, and its eye-catching sign, reading *Millcreek Hotel*, painted in bright red. As much as she told herself not to ask, she suddenly heard herself say, "Mr. Conway, what sort of position were you offering in your hotel?"

He stopped abruptly and turned to her, his narrow, gray eyes registering surprise. "A desk clerk, to be blunt. I may have dressed up the position in previous conversations, but you'd be merely that."

Claire's gaze settled on the hotel again.

"Am I to believe you're reconsidering my offer?"

Something in his tone snapped her back to herself and made her remember why she didn't want to work there. "Not yet," she said, lifting her chin just a fraction and walking a little faster as the livery came into view.

Bruce Conway smiled to himself, not at all put-off. In his mind, her 'not yet' was as good as a future yes.

Chapter Fifteen

"Do you have a minute for a question?" Maggie asked Jacob after he'd gotten home that Friday.

He turned from where he'd just hung his hat, a smile on his face. "Of course."

Maggie went to the table where his Bible lay and flipped it open. "Are Matthew, Mark, Luke, and John pretty much the same book?"

"It's four different eyewitness accounts of the life of Jesus," Jacob explained. "So, they are all a little different but all true. Think of it like this: if we both went on a walk, you might later tell someone how beautiful the trees looked and how warm it was, while I may describe the blue sky and green grass. They're both true accounts of the same day and the same walk, but different things stood out to us."

"That makes a lot of sense."

"Luke was a physician, so if you notice, he gives more details about the miracles Jesus did, while Matthew was writing specifically to the Jews and spent a lot of time detailing the genealogy of Jesus so they would see his lineage, that Jesus is descendent from David."

"It makes it more complete to have four accounts rather than one," Maggie agreed.

A Debt to Pay

"I think God thought so, too," he said.

"Pa, can Maggie stay for dinner?" Lilly had just come through the door holding a handful of berries in her hands. "We could make a raspberry pie for dessert," she added, smiling at Maggie.

"I'm sure Maggie has things to do, sweetheart."

"Do you?" Lilly asked genuinely.

Maggie laughed softly. "Not really."

"So, can you stay for dinner?" she asked again.

Jacob gave her a warning glance. "Don't make her feel obligated," he told his daughter gently. Looking at Maggie, he said, "You can if you want, but they're fine either way. Lilly and Lucas love my son-of-a-gun stew."

"I've never heard of that," Maggie said curiously.

"Well," Jacob said, moving toward the stove. "Prepare to be amazed."

"Maggie must have decided to stay for supper at Reverend Myles'," Claire said as she helped Hannah set the table. "Don't you get tired of cooking for so many men?" She glanced at the nine plates she'd just set across the table.

"Most nights, they eat in their bunk kitchen and Rusty does the cooking, but on Fridays and Wednesdays, they get a little treat in my kitchen." Hannah winked at Claire.

"How long have you been here working at the ranch?" Claire asked.

"Since Will was young and his father started the ranch. John Carter hired me when his wife's health began to decline, and she couldn't do as much around the house. After she passed, John remarried, and he kept me on.

"After Will lost his father and his stepmother and stepbrother moved back east, Will asked me to stay."

Claire watched as Hannah moved about the kitchen, effortlessly whipping up deliciously smelling chili and cornbread.

"Now, you won't hurt my feelings if you decide you don't want to eat with the lot of ranch hands. They can be a little rowdy, but Will makes sure they mind their manners."

Claire smiled to herself, thinking if Hannah knew how used to rowdy men she was, she would have never made such a statement. Compared to the saloon in Chicago on a Friday night, seven men in Will's kitchen were nothing to be concerned about. Within a few minutes, they were making their way inside, greeting Hannah with familiar ease.

"Jeb, those boots better not be caked in mud like last time," Hannah warned when she saw him trail in. The nineteen-year-old grinned and proudly lifted his boot for her inspection.

"This smells amazing," Jared said, sitting across from Claire.

"You're a decent cook, Rusty, but no one cooks like Hannah." This remark had come from Cody Reese, who was in his late twenties and had been working at the ranch for close to four years. Claire noted that there were two others she had never seen before. Halfway through supper, she learned their names were Henry Hughs and Frank Travis.

Will blessed the food, and then everyone began to dig in, jovially laughing and joking. Sometime toward the end, the conversation turned more serious. "The boys and I've been talking, Will, and we decided one or two of us oughta go with you." Cody leaned back in his chair as he said the words, adding, "I'm up for it."

"Go where?" Hannah asked, looking from Cody to Will. When he didn't reply, Rusty filled her in. "Will's planning to go after Grady."

A Debt to Pay

"I appreciate the sentiment, boys, but I plan on doing this alone," Will told them.

"Not to disagree with you, Will, but having another man there might not be a bad idea," Rusty said, and Claire could see something in his eyes that reminded her almost of how a father would look at Will. Even though he worked for him, she knew Rusty was old enough to be Will's father.

"To put it bluntly," Jeb spoke up, "We don't want you going to jail for murder."

Some of the men chuckled, and Claire could tell he was joking in part but also concerned for Will's welfare.

"I see." Will leaned back in his chair. "You're not worried about me gettin' hurt; you're worried about Grady."

"We all saw you lick 'im more than once, so we know you can take care of yourself," Cody said.

Will stood from the table, his voice even but kind. "Don't worry, I won't lose my temper. I'll just bring him back for the sheriff to deal with."

"A lot of good that'll do," Frank Travis spoke up for the first time.

"What makes you say that?" Hannah asked.

"Sheriff Dunley's shady is all," replied Frank before he scooped another bite of chili into his mouth.

"But there ain't no proof," Rusty said, although he agreed with Frank's statement.

"Do you boys still think he had something to do with the bank holdup a few years back?" Hannah asked. She remembered the rumors surrounding the mysterious bank robber, but they had died down fairly quickly.

"A few years back, a masked man held up the bank and got away with hundreds of dollars," Rusty explained to Claire when he saw her questioning expression. "The robber also

Alexandra Miller

started a fire that spread and burned several stores and houses along the main strip."

"Sheriff Dunley went after the robber," Frank continued to explain. "But he came back with a gunshot wound and said the robber had gotten away with the money. He never tried to apprehend him again after that."

"In fact, he discouraged the posse who wanted to ride out after him," Will added, remembering he had been one of the men prepared to go. He carried his plate to the sink and thanked Hannah for the meal. "I'm gonna turn in early so I can leave first thing," he told them. "And don't worry," he added. "I won't shoot unless I have to."

Hannah looked worried as Will left the kitchen. "Maybe one of you should follow him," she said, looking at Rusty, who nodded reassuringly. Rusty had been working at the ranch longer than any of them and had been a close friend of John Carter. Before he died, Rusty had promised to look after his son. Even though Will had been a teen then, Rusty still keenly felt the responsibility to keep his promise.

"Need any help with them dishes?" Cody asked as he started collecting them from the table.

"Since when do you offer to wash dishes?" Hannah asked, looking at him suspiciously.

"Since the prettiest girls in town started livin' ere," Jeb said, laughing even as Cody elbowed him.

Several others joined in the laughter, causing Hannah to send them a scolding glance. "Get on outta here, all of ya."

Claire pretended like she didn't notice their glances or comments as she quietly helped Hannah clear the table. She knew their raillery was lighthearted and innocent enough and much more tolerable than what she had become used to.

Rusty lingered, and Claire saw him and Hannah talking

quietly by the door. She assumed it was about Will going after Grady.

"Is he going with Will?" Claire asked Hannah once Rusty had left.

"Yes, whether Will wants him to or not."

———

When Monday came around, Claire found herself feeling useless and discouraged. Working at the store had given her a purpose and a hope that they would soon be able to pay back the money they stole. Now, without any work, she felt she was wasting every hour that seemed to crawl by. All week long, she helped Hannah in the garden and in the house, even learning some cooking tips, but that feeling of complacency continued to gnaw at her.

"Did you never marry, Hannah?" Claire asked her one afternoon as she helped her clean up the lunch dishes. With Rusty away with Will, Hannah had taken on the responsibility of feeding the ranch hands almost every meal.

"I almost did," she said, drying the plates as Claire washed them. "It weren't meant to be, though. He wanted me to move east, and I just knew I'd never feel at home anywhere but Missouri."

"I guess if you didn't love him enough to leave, then you didn't love him enough to spend your life with him," Claire reasoned aloud, knowing Hannah wouldn't mind her frankness.

"Exactly what I realized, too." Hannah sighed. "Sometimes I regret it, but most days I don't." She smiled at Claire and shrugged her shoulders. "The good Lord has me here, and I reckon I'm content to stay. I'll probably never marry at this rate."

"Rusty isn't married either," Claire remarked casually, but Hannah picked up on the suggestion in her tone.

"Rusty's a good friend, but I think we're both too set in our ways to be more than that."

"I don't know, Hannah. I could see it."

Hannah shook her head, but Claire didn't miss the smile that lingered in her eyes.

"What about Will?" Claire asked a few minutes later. "I'm surprised he isn't married by now."

"There's plenty of women in this town who've been draggin' their rope where he's concerned," Hannah said. "But after Olivia Kendle, he hasn't shown interest in anyone."

"Who's Olivia Kendle?" Claire asked curiously. She'd never met anyone in the town by that name.

"Oh, she and Will grew up together. They fancied themselves in love and talked about getting married once they were of age, but then Will's father got sick, and Will spent the better part of a year taking care of him." Hannah dried the last dish and set it in the cabinet. "I guess Olivia felt neglected during that year, and after the funeral, when Will was able to focus on wedding plans again, it was too late."

"What do you mean?"

"She had engaged herself to another feller and told Will they were heading east after the wedding."

Claire watched as Hannah shook her head disapprovingly, a sad look in her eyes at the memory. "I think it 'bout broke his heart, well that on top of losing his father."

"How horrible," Claire agreed, imagining the pain he must have felt.

"Still, her loss is going to be another woman's treasure," Hannah said with a smile and a wink. "Took him some years to get over, but I think he's mended."

"So, you think he'll marry eventually?"

"Land sakes, I hope so!" Hannah said, bringing her hands to her hips. "I'm hoping for at least one baby in this house."

Hannah gestured for Claire to follow her out to the front porch. "Fhew, it's hotter out here than I thought," she said, fanning herself with her hand. They ended up on the wide chair swing on the porch, the chains that secured it to the porch roof creaking rhythmically as they swung.

"What about you, Claire Wallace? I know you haven't been here long, but do you have your eye on anyone in particular?"

Claire shook her head. "I don't think I've ever had my eye on anyone."

"Well, good things come to those who wait, or so I've been told," Hannah said with a little sigh. "I'm sure there's plenty of fellers who'd be honored to settle down with you."

"I don't know, Hannah. It's hard to imagine myself married. Men can be so…"

She paused, not really sure what she was going to say. "I don't know. I just can't see it."

"Well, once you meet the right one, I'm sure you'll feel differently."

Claire could feel the turmoil that lived in her heart starting to rise. Most days, she could stuff it back down, keep busy, and ignore it, but sitting there with Hannah made her want to suddenly talk to someone about her past. "Hannah, if I were to confide something in you, would it be a sin to ask you to keep it a secret?"

"My dear, keeping secrets is one of my specialties." She smiled, but upon seeing the somberness in Claire's expression, Hannah became more serious. "What is it, hunnie?"

"Well, maybe I can't see myself married because the only men I've ever really known in my life have been the sordid kind. I wasn't raised in a beautiful place like this. You see..." Claire paused, biting her thumbnail nervously as she tried to find the words. "My life up to this point isn't something I'm proud of. I hated the city and only moved there because..."

"Evenin'!"

At the sound of Jared's greeting, both Claire and Hannah looked simultaneously to their left. He had come around the corner on his horse, bringing the gelding to a stop in front of the porch.

"I was just about to take a ride out to the west pasture. Wanted to see if you wanted to join me, Claire?" His expression was hopeful as he waited for her response.

Claire exchanged a glance with Hannah and thought maybe the diversion was for the better. She suddenly realized how close she had come to sharing too much information with Hannah. Why, what on earth had gotten into her?

"I'd love to," Claire heard herself say, coming to her feet. She gave Hannah a kind smile before heading down the porch steps and following Jared to the barn.

Watching them move away, Hannah shook her head in vexation. "Ugh! Will Carter, you better open your eyes before it's too late." She glanced heavenward and sighed. "Lord, please don't let this one get away!"

The next evening, after supper, Claire slipped away to a large willow tree she had been admiring since coming to the ranch. Stepping behind its long, drooping branches, she felt almost hidden. Sitting against the trunk, she pulled her knees into her chest and, not for the first time, looked in awe at her picturesque surroundings. She tried to imagine what it would be like as a child growing up on a farm like this.

A Debt to Pay

Her conversation with Hannah the previous day still lingered in her mind. She had been eleven when the death of her parents forced her to live with her uncle. He had tried to raise her the best he could, but that wasn't saying much. Claire recalled him being drunk as often as he was sober, and she'd been practically on her own. One thing she could thank him for was letting her attend the local school, at least until she was fifteen. By then, she was helping him so much in his tack shop she barely had time for book learning. It was the people he kept company with that were her greatest trouble. She shuddered even now, thinking about the men she had to elude as a teenager.

And then, when she turned seventeen, she'd had enough of her uncle's drunkenness and his friends' indecency, so she moved to Chicago with a friend who promised her they would get rich being waitresses at a new restaurant her aunt also worked at. That restaurant turned out to be a saloon that made Claire anything but rich.

"Penny for your thoughts."

Claire jumped a little at the voice, relaxing when she saw it was Jared.

"Sorry, I didn't mean to startle you."

"It's alright." She readjusted her skirt around herself as he sat down near her.

"I was hoping to catch you alone, so when I saw you heading for this tree, I thought it might be a good time."

"Is everything alright? Is Will back?"

Jared shook his head. "Not yet, and nothing's wrong; I just wanted to talk to you."

Claire wasn't sure why his tone and manner suddenly made her feel nervous. She looked back at him, waiting for him to go on.

"I know the fire must have set you and your sister back quite a bit, and you may be uncertain what to do next." He cleared his throat and took off his hat, turning it in his hands as he went on. "I'm not real good with words, so I'm just gonna come out with it. I've only known you for two months, but since I met ya, I haven't been able to stop thinkin' about you."

"Jared…"

"Just hear me out," He let out a short sigh. "I've never felt this way about anyone before, and if you'd be willin', I'd like to court you proper like."

Claire looked at the hopefulness in his eyes and felt terrible at the thought of hurting him. He had been nothing but a kind friend to her and Maggie, and Claire wished desperately it hadn't come to this. She chided herself for accepting the horse he gave her. She should have stuck with what her experience taught her, that gifts always had strings attached.

"Jared, you don't even know me. You…"

"Well, that's what I want…to know you better."

He looked so vulnerable and genuine sitting there, his heart in his eyes. "I'm not the girl for you," Claire told him as kindly as she could. "I'm flattered that you would ask, but…" She shook her head apologetically. "I can't."

"Are you saying you can't ever, or just right now? I know the fire was a blow and…"

"Ever." She saw the hurt flash across his eyes. "I much rather keep on being friends and leave it at that." She offered a faint smile.

"Is there someone else, then?"

Claire's eyebrows rose in surprise. "No. There's no one else." Even as she said the words, Will's face flashed in her mind, and she dismissed it. "I don't think I'll ever marry."

A cynical smile touched the corner of his lips. "I highly doubt that." He came to his feet and put his hat back on.

A Debt to Pay

Claire also stood, not knowing what to say but wanting somehow to smooth it over. He just looked at her, his eyes begging her to reconsider. And then he turned and walked away. Claire watched him go, releasing a shaky sigh and feeling just horrible. Had she done something to imply she cared for him in that way? She thought back and couldn't recall a particular instance, but maybe she had unintentionally.

Frustrated with herself and the entirety of the situation, Claire walked swiftly to the house. She flung open the back door and went inside the kitchen.

"Why Claire, what's wrong?"

Claire looked at Hannah with surprise, not expecting to see anyone.

"You look like you're about to burst into tears."

Her words were Claire's undoing, and she did as Hannah predicted.

"Oh, my dear," Hannah said as she went to her and hugged her. "Whatever is the matter?"

"Everything," Claire whispered as she cried into the woman's shoulder.

Hannah let her cry for a moment and then lovingly walked her to the bench by the table.

"I'm sorry," Claire sniffed, wiping her tear-filled cheeks. "All at once, everything just seems…so impossible."

"That fire was devastating; it's no wonder you're feeling this way."

"It's not just the fire," Claire said, taking the handkerchief Hannah offered her. "Somehow, I gave Jared the wrong impression, and then I had to disappoint him when he asked to…to court me."

"I see." Hannah sighed, her arm still around Claire. "You may not have given him the wrong impression, dear; it may have just been inevitable."

"He looked so hurt." Claire blew her nose and then sighed with frustration. "I should have never taken that horse! I should have known he was looking for something out of it."

"I don't think he was trying to manipulate your feelings by giving you the horse, dear. I think it was a kind gesture because he cared about you."

"Men don't make kind gestures unless they want something out of it," Claire replied bitterly.

"Not all men, dear," Hannah gently squeezed her hand. "Don't lose heart."

"I need to leave here. Maggie and I should find somewhere else to stay."

"Now, don't let Jared run you off. You and Maggie are welcome to stay as long as you need to."

"You've been so kind, Hannah, you and Will, but it would be a mistake to stay here and make things harder on Jared."

"Where will you go?" Hannah asked with concern, thinking she wanted to give Jared Cooper a what for.

"I'll talk to Mrs. Lyddie tomorrow," Claire said, wiping her nose and feeling a new sense of resolve. "Maybe she'll have a room Maggie and I can rent again."

Hannah nodded, reluctant to see her and her sister go. Having the women's company around the house had been a breath of fresh air.

"Thank you, Hannah," Claire said with a weak smile. She stood and hugged the woman one more time before heading out of the kitchen. In the doorway, she turned, a grateful look in her eyes. "I won't ever forget your generosity."

Hannah smiled tenderly, touched by her words. There was something so vulnerable about her, something so loveable. She seemed lost and hurting, and Hannah wished there was some way she could help her.

Chapter Sixteen

"I was so upset to hear of your misfortunate fire, but I'm tickled pink to have you girls back at the boarding house."

Claire and Maggie smiled at Mrs. Lyddie, grateful she had a room to spare. It was the following day. After Claire told Maggie about her conversation with Jared, Maggie understood her wanting to find somewhere else to stay.

"We'd be willing to help with the cooking or cleaning to offset some of the rent," Claire said carefully, hoping Lyddie would agree.

"Yes, I'm sure we can work something out that will benefit both of us. Now, why don't you two take the room you had before."

"You can take the buckboard to Reverend Myles' on days you work," Claire said to Maggie once they were in the room.

"Do you think we can afford to keep her at the livery?" Maggie asked uncertainly.

"I plan on getting a job this week," Claire told her confidently. "But it will be in town, so I won't need Willow like you will."

Maggie looked at her curiously. "You sound like you already have something in mind."

Claire didn't reply but quickly changed the subject. They had nothing to unpack, save a few clothing items Hannah had generously lent them.

"I'm going to see if Mrs. Lyddie needs any help for dinner," Maggie said as they headed downstairs.

"I'm just going to take a quick walk, and then I'll be back to help as well," Claire told her.

The late afternoon sun was sweltering and made the already muggy and dusty air even more unbearable. Claire tried to keep in the shade as she moved down the street, walking quickly before she changed her mind.

Minutes later, swallowing down her pride and better judgment, Claire marched inside the hotel. It was decorated with more taste and style than she had expected. There was a dark green oriental carpet in the center of the lobby and plush velvet cushioned seating along the walls. A crystal chandelier dangled from the ceiling and added to the elegant ambiance of the room.

"Excuse me?" Claire called out, glancing toward the hallway that led away from the lobby. She then noticed a little bell on the counter and hesitantly touched it. The noise seemed to echo through the large room, followed by the sound of a nearby door opening.

"Good afternoon, Miss Wallace," Bruce Conway greeted politely, coming out of a nearby room and closing the door behind him. He stepped across the lobby toward the desk where she stood.

"Are you here for a room or for a job?" he asked.

"The latter, if it's still available."

"It is. When can you start?"

"I'm staying at the boardinghouse again, so I can start whenever."

A Debt to Pay

"Monday? At nine?"

Claire nodded. "I'll be here."

"Good. I'll give you a tour of the place then. You can meet the other staff on Monday as well."

Claire nodded, thinking his manner oddly void of its usual conceit. She preferred this side of him to what was his norm. "Thank you, Mr. Conway."

He nodded and went back into his office. Claire left, half relieved she had gone through with it and half regretting it already. She was glad to know there were other staff in the hotel so she would not be alone all day with Conway. Maybe he wasn't as conniving and corrupt as she had thought. At any rate, she'd be making money again. Right now, that necessity was all that mattered to her.

―――――

"Will! You're back!" Hannah rushed down the hallway from the kitchen to meet him at the door. "I was starting to get worried!"

"Rusty and I followed his trail for days and thought we were close, but..." he let the sentence hang and let out a heavy sigh.

"So, you didn't find him, I take it?"

Will shook his head, hanging his hat on the nearby hook.

"You must be starving," Hannah said. "Follow me into the kitchen, and I'll make you something."

"Are Claire and Maggie asleep?" he asked. He knew it was close to ten o'clock that Tuesday evening.

"They're not here anymore," Hannah told him.

"What do you mean?"

"They thought it best to go and stay at Lyddie's. They left on Saturday."

Will was a little surprised at the sudden disappointment that he felt. He didn't realize until that moment that he had been looking forward to seeing Claire. "I guess that makes sense," he said as he sat at the end chair. "As long as they knew they were welcome to stay here."

"I think Claire felt it would be easier on Jared," Hannah said before explaining what had happened.

Understanding—and something else Hannah couldn't quite place—dawned on Will's face. "I should kick him in the pants for his lousy timing," Will said.

"I suppose seeing her here every day would work on any lonely man's heart," Hannah said as she placed a pot of beef stew on the stove to heat up. "I thought Maggie might be next with as many times as Frank found an excuse to talk to her."

Will shook his head. "I feel bad I wasn't here and worse that we didn't find Grady."

"You could always invite them back," Hannah suggested.

"You like the company, huh?" Will asked, already knowing the answer. He knew Hannah had taken a keen liking to the girls, especially Claire.

"I did," she answered simply.

"It's not likely they would," Will thought aloud.

He went to bed that night discouraged about not finding Grady and irritated that Jared would put Claire in a position to feel she had to leave the ranch. He knew she and her sister had lost everything, and he hated to think of them scraping to get by when there was ample room in his home for them to stay while they got back on their feet. He also felt responsible for putting the Wallace sisters in the middle of his fight with Grady. If he had it to do over, he would have spared them by not letting them stay at the cabin.

A Debt to Pay

Lacing his hands behind his head, Will lay on his bed, looking up at the ceiling. He was tired but found himself praying, a habit that had begun to form over the last two years. He'd spent most of his adult life thinking he could handle everything on his own, but after Jacob Myles had come to Millcreek and become his friend, he started realizing there was a peace and joy Jacob had that was nothing like he'd ever experienced.

It was around that time that Will realized he'd been holding on to the pain of losing his parents, more recently his father, and on top of that, the heartbreak of losing the woman he thought he'd marry. Hearing Jacob talk about his relationship with the Lord and seeing his example, Will eventually surrendered his own heart to the Lord. It proved to be the best decision of his life. Now, as he lay awake, Will found himself not only praying about the situation with Grady but also for wisdom about how to help Claire and Maggie.

"Before everyone leaves, I wanted to mention two needs in our congregation." Jacob Myles waited until he had everyone's attention before continuing. "A few weeks ago, a tornado came through our area, and while it left most buildings untouched, Uriah and Rebecca Swanson's barn was damaged severely to the point that they are going to have to rebuild. I'd like to bring forward the idea of all of us men working together next Saturday to help them rebuild. Many hands make light work," he added.

There were simultaneous nods and words of agreement.

"Wonderful, and now to the second thing I wanted to mention," Jacob glanced at Will briefly since both ideas had come from him. Will had approached him at the beginning of the service that Sunday to see what he thought.

"As you know, two of our newest neighbors experienced a horrible fire not long ago that took everything they owned." Jacob met Maggie's gaze for just a moment before continuing. "While I know they would be the last ones to ask for help, I'd like us to take up a collection for them. Even the smallest amount from each of us can add up to be a huge help to them as they get back on their feet."

Will watched Maggie's reaction to see if she appeared uncomfortable. He wondered why Claire wasn't with her but felt, for some reason, maybe it was best since he felt she would be more likely than Maggie to refuse the monetary gift. A basket was passed around, and Will smiled to himself as he watched people willingly drop money inside. He put in a generous sum himself, knowing the bulk of it would be anonymous and more likely received.

He'd been praying all week for a way to help Claire and Maggie, and that Sunday morning, when he woke, the idea of helping the Swansons and the Wallace sisters came to him in such a way that Claire and Maggie wouldn't feel singled out.

Maggie didn't know what to think or say. She'd never seen such kindness in all her life. She lingered at the end after everyone had left and shook her head in disbelief when Jacob walked over to her with a tin can full of the collected money.

"This is for you, Maggie."

"I feel like it's too much to accept," she said as he placed it in her hands.

"It's not too much," he assured her. "That's what a church family does. If someone's in need, we can all pull together and help each other."

Maggie had never experienced that in her own family, so the concept was completely unfamiliar. She ordered herself

A Debt to Pay

not to cry as she looked at Jacob and thanked him. "Wait until I show Claire," she said.

Jacob grabbed his Bible off the podium and then walked with her toward the door. "My kids want me to ask you if you'd stay for dinner again tomorrow," he said.

Maggie smiled. "Of course. I can even make it," she suggested.

"I guess I can't argue with that."

Will mounted his horse and rode away from the church and toward the main street in town. As he passed the livery, an idea came to him, and he went to speak with Eli. As he left the livery, Bruce Conway was exiting the saloon across the street. Seeing Will, Bruce made it a point to get his attention and fell into step beside him as he moved down the street.

"Afternoon, Will Carter," he greeted.

"Bruce," Will gave him a courteous nod and nothing more.

"Just come from church?" Bruce asked with a mocking grin. "I almost went to church myself this morning."

Will eyed him suspiciously. "And what would compel you to do that?"

"To thank the good Lord for my new employee," he replied, pulling a cigar out of his breast pocket. "Claire Wallace is going to be quite an improvement."

"What?"

"Oh, didn't you know? Miss Wallace is working for me now." He could tell by Will's expression that it was the first time he had heard of it. He felt quite a bit of satisfaction catching the other man off guard.

Bruce changed the subject. "Oh, I heard you were off looking for that ornery brother of yours? Any luck?"

"Nope," Will replied, his gaze resting on the hotel across the way.

Bruce followed his gaze, a cocky smile on his face. "Well, I'd love to stay here and chat, but I should be getting back," he said, tipping his hat. "It's Miss Wallace's first week, so she still needs my *close* guidance."

Will felt his blood boiling as he watched the arrogant man walk toward the hotel. Swinging up into his saddle, Will's mind raced. What was Claire thinking? Why would she lower herself to work for Bruce Conway? He realized she hadn't been in town long enough to know the extent of the man's seedy reputation, but still, just a few minutes in his presence should be enough to know he wasn't trustworthy.

He wanted to ride over to the hotel that instant and tell her what he thought but reasoned maybe it would be better to talk with her when Bruce Conway wasn't around. It took all the self-control he had to ride past the hotel without going inside to see her and force her to quit!

———

"How was church?" Claire asked when she came back to Lyddie's late that afternoon.

"Oh, Claire! I wish you could have been there."

"Well, Mr. Conway said he'd pay extra for me working on the weekends since it's busier."

"So, you'll be missing church every week?" Maggie sounded incredulous.

"I don't get paid to go to church, Maggie, so if I can make some extra money, it's worth it. Besides, it doesn't have to be like this forever, just until we catch up."

Maggie sighed disapprovingly. "I still don't like it that you're working for that man."

A Debt to Pay

"It hasn't been as bad as I thought," Claire told her.

"Well, to answer your question about church..." Maggie walked over to her and put the tin of money in her hands.

"What's this?"

"Open it."

Claire looked perplexed as she stared at the bills and coins. "I don't understand."

"The church took up a collection for us!"

Claire closed the lid and handed it back to Maggie. "We can't take this."

"I felt like that at first, too, but we weren't the only ones in need. The Swansons' barn fell in the tornado, and they're going to help them rebuild. It's just like family helping each other," Maggie tried to explain it like Jacob had.

"And what would that *family* do if they knew the truth about us?" Claire rolled her eyes and flopped down on the edge of their bed. "What would they do if they knew that money is just going to go towards paying a thieving debt?"

Claire's words definitely put a damper on things. "Well, we won't use the money toward that then. We'll use it for room and board and food and such."

"We do need some new clothes," Claire said as her finger met up with a hole in her skirt. "Ugh, I hate to think that all those fine dresses we bought in Chicago were burned in the fire!"

"I know." Maggie came and sat beside her. "And what we have on is all we have left, so new clothes are pretty essential right now."

Claire nodded in agreement. "Alright, Maggie. As much as I hate accepting charity, we'll keep the money and put it towards what we need to get by. Anything I make from the hotel, I'll put away to cover what we owe Harris."

"And we have my money from Reverend Myles, too."

Claire nodded. "First thing I need to do with this church money is pay Eli Greene for boarding Willow."

"I'll take it to him when I go to get her in the morning," Maggie said.

"I'll walk with you since the hotel is just across the street."

The next morning, the girls walked there after breakfast and found him mucking out a stable. "Good morning, Mr. Greene," Claire said.

He turned around and wiped the sweat from his forehead. "Morning. What can I help you with?" He leaned his pitchfork against the stable and took a few steps toward them.

"Maggie's here to collect Willow, and we wanted to pay you for a week's boarding." She handed him some bills.

He shook his head and wouldn't take the money. "It's all paid for, Miss Wallace. I'll get Willow for you." He moved toward her stable and began opening the gate.

Claire followed him, confused by his words. "I'm sorry, I don't understand."

"A fellow who wishes to remain anonymous paid for a months' worth of boarding, so you is all paid up, Miss Wallace."

Maggie looked at Claire and shrugged.

Claire didn't understand who would have paid for it. A loud raucous from the saloon broke her reverie and caused her gaze to flash toward the hotel. Maybe she did know. "I'll see you later, Maggie," she said suddenly as she strode quickly to the hotel.

Bruce Conway was at the front desk when she arrived.

"How dare you interfere in my business," Claire said, walking toward the desk. "I can handle my own bills."

Bruce looked at her with a puzzled expression. "I had a

late night last night and am still a bit hung over, my dear; would you mind talking a little slower? Whose business did I interfere with?"

Claire's hands came to her hips. "I'm talking about you paying my bill and then some at the livery!"

"I didn't, Miss Wallace."

"You didn't?" Claire dropped her gaze and bit her thumbnail by habit.

"Of course not. I would never do something so underhanded." He paused and then added, "But I think I know who did."

Claire's eyes looked up at him as he said, "Will Carter."

"Are you certain?"

"Saw him over there yesterday talking with Eli, so I assume it had to be him."

Claire didn't know Will had returned. She wondered how long he had been back and felt disappointment that he hadn't come to see her. She dismissed it quickly; she was probably the last thing on his mind. Claire slowly lowered her arms. "I'm sorry for the mix-up," she said quietly, feeling strange to be apologizing to him.

"Not at all," he said with a little wave of his hand. "I'll be in my office if you need me. Oh," he stopped and took out his pocket watch. "The stage should be here in about an hour, so things will get a little busier for you."

Claire was grateful for the distraction that the new crowd brought. Around noon, two gentlemen and two ladies arrived looking for rooms. She recorded their names on the ledger and gave them the keys to their rooms. The rest of the day continued as usual, but when five o'clock came and she was done for the day, Claire felt like a teapot needing to blow off steam. She walked quickly back to the boarding house, hoping to run into Maggie before she returned Willow to the livery. As she neared Lyddie's, however, she remembered Maggie had told her she was staying at the Reverend's for supper.

Stamping her foot slightly on the porch in irritation, Claire made a quick decision to walk to the ranch. She could get there in half an hour if she walked quickly. Just a few minutes into her walk out of town, she was rolling up her sleeves, desperately longing to feel a breeze of some sort on any part of her body. That first week of August was brutally hot, and to her sudden chagrin, she realized she didn't even have her bonnet.

Undeterred, she continued. Within fifteen minutes, she was near where the cabin used to be, so she decided to cut across the field just before it so she wouldn't have to be reminded of all she lost. The field proved rougher than she realized, the combination of overgrown foliage and dirt leaving their imprint on her clothing. Breathing heavily, Claire hiked her skirts up as high as she could and draped them over her arm and shoulder. She could feel the sweat rolling down her forehead and cheeks and rested a few minutes under the shade of a maple tree.

She walked the second mile and finally came upon the lane leading to the Carter Ranch. She was grateful not to see any of the ranch hands, particularly Jared. As she entered the yard, she paused, not sure if she should go to the house or the barn. That was when she saw Will coming out of the front door of the house. He stood on the porch for a moment and then must have seen her because he waved and moved across the yard toward her.

"Claire?" He took in her disheveled hair and flushed cheeks and was concerned something was amiss. Her clothes were also covered with briars and dirt.

A Debt to Pay

"I needed to talk to you," she said.

Will looked past her and saw no horse. "You came on foot?"

"Maggie has Willow, so I had no other option."

"You look tuckered, Claire. Why don't you come in the house and sit a spell?"

"I'm fine," she replied in a tone Will had never heard before. He watched as she reached into her skirt pocket and pulled out a handful of dollar bills. "Here," she said, putting them in his hand.

"What's this?" he asked, looking at her with confusion.

"This is what we owe you for what you paid Eli Greene at the livery."

Will sighed, and his hands slipped into his pockets, knowing it had to be what the church had collected. "I'm not taking that money, Claire."

"We don't need any more handouts," she told him, the look in her eyes daring him to disagree. "It's bad enough that the church took a collection for us."

"Why is it so hard for you to accept a gift?"

"I don't want to feel indebted to you or anyone! And you paid the entirely of a month's worth of boarding, which makes it an even larger debt."

"Claire, you're not indebted to me. If anything, I owe you and your sister. It was my stepbrother who set the fire!"

Claire shook her head. "That wasn't your fault. We can take care of ourselves." She extended the money again, her eyes begging him to take it.

Will wouldn't take his hands out of his pocket. "I'm not taking it, Claire."

Exasperated, Claire threw the money down by his boots, whirled around, and started to walk away. Will went after her. "Wait!" he said, taking her by the arm and turning her to face him. "Wait. If you didn't need anyone's handouts, why would you go and work for Bruce Conway?"

"Because it's a job that pays money."

"If anyone's giving you a handout, it's him. You know he only hired you because…because he likes the way you look."

Claire's jaw dropped a fraction, surprised he would be so blunt. "What! Are you saying his hiring me has nothing to do with my capability to do the job?"

Will exhaled a sharp breath. "I'm not saying you aren't capable, but that's certainly not the reason he hired you! I thought you had more sense than to work for a man like him! You have to know full well what he's after."

Claire looked up into his hazel eyes, feeling something in her heart between conviction and shame. She jerked her arm free from his hand. "He's been very professional, and as long as he is, I'll continue to work there."

"You haven't been in this town long enough to know what he's like. I have. He's dishonest and can't have any good intentions where you're concerned."

"I've dealt with his kind before."

"Oh, really?" He looked like he didn't believe her.

"Yes," she answered in an even tone. "You don't know anything about me, Will Carter. Trust me, I can take care of myself."

Will heard the confidence in her voice, but it didn't seem to match the look of weariness in her eyes. She started to walk away again, so he ran back to where she'd thrown the money and brought it back to her. "Take this, and I promise I'll go and speak with Eli tomorrow and ask him to give me back what I paid."

Claire felt him gently press the money into her hands.

A Debt to Pay

"Please let me at least give you a ride back into town."

It was on the tip of Claire's tongue to tell him she would be fine to walk back, but she suddenly realized how weak and overheated she felt. "Alright," she agreed quietly, wiping sweat from her forehead before it dripped down her face.

"I'll be just a minute," Will told her and then added, "You look ready to pass out, Claire. Why don't you get a drink from that bucket over there while I hitch up the buckboard?"

Claire knew he was right and walked with him toward the barn, readily drinking from the ladle lying in a bucket of cold, fresh water. She had been feeling lightheaded and knew it would be difficult to walk back in this heat. She also hadn't eaten since breakfast and could feel her energy waning.

Will resurfaced in a buckboard a few minutes later, and Claire climbed up beside him. "When did you get back?" Claire asked after a minute of uncomfortable silence.

"Saturday night."

"I take it you didn't find him."

"Afraid not. I wired his mother to let me know if he returns to Ohio."

"That's where they live?"

Will nodded. "Her family is from there, so when my father died, she moved back, and Grady went with her."

"I'm sorry he got away," Claire said quietly.

"Me too."

They were quiet for the rest of the ride until the town came into view. "I'm sorry if what I did seemed presumptuous," Will told her, and Claire could hear the sincerity in his voice.

She felt bad for being so angry with him. "It was a thoughtful gesture," she replied.

"Just an unwelcome one," he grinned slightly.

Claire let out a sigh. "I'm sorry for making a fuss; I just don't like feeling indebted to anyone."

"I don't know what sort of people you're used to, Claire, but I promise I don't have some hidden agenda."

Claire didn't know what to say, but she was grateful for his words. He had given her no reason to doubt his integrity, and she knew she was responding from past experiences. The debt she and Maggie owed Frederick Harris already loomed over her like a dark cloud, so any additional debt felt suffocating. The sort of men she had known also made it feel very hard to trust anyone. She wished she could explain that to him but knew it was out of the question.

"Thanks for the ride," she said minutes later, taking his offered hand and climbing down the side of the buckboard.

"No problem, Claire." He tipped his hat with a brief smile and then turned the horses around and headed back the way they had come.

The entire way back to the ranch, he couldn't stop thinking about her. There was a strong fight in her to be independent, which made him wonder if she was trying to prove her self-sufficiency to others or to herself.

Chapter Seventeen

Claire headed down the hotel steps with her arms full of sheets to be washed. She had just remade the beds with clean linens and now headed toward the washing room. Sarah Brooks, a middle-aged woman she had met earlier, was already up to her elbows in sudsy water.

"I'm sorry, Sarah," Claire apologized. "I have another load for you."

"Just set 'em there," she motioned with her head to a similar pile as she raked laundry up and down on the washboard.

"I'll come back and give you a hand after I'm done," Claire promised.

"No, you just stick to what you gotta do. No sense both of us falling behind," the woman said.

Claire ignored her and returned about twenty minutes later. "I'd just be standing behind a desk doing nothing," she told her as she lifted a basket of wet, clean clothes. "I'll start hanging these out to dry."

Sarah thanked her and continued with the wash.

There was a small, grassy backyard behind the hotel with a clothesline running its entire length. Putting a clothespin in her mouth and one in her hand, Claire tossed a sheet over the line and smoothed it out to dry before securing it to the line. Once she had finished with all the laundry, she returned the basket to Sarah and headed to the lobby to make sure no one was waiting on her.

Bruce Conway was just coming out of his office when she came into the lobby.

"Miss Wallace," he said, approaching her and handing her an envelope. "Here is your pay for the last two weeks."

Claire took the extended envelope and thanked him. When he returned to his office, she opened the envelope and counted the money. She gasped softly, not believing how much he'd given her. His office door was ajar when she walked over to talk to him.

"Mr. Conway, I think you overpaid me. This is far too much."

"Not how I see it. Besides that, you've worked almost two weeks without a day off, so take off tomorrow."

Claire was surprised by his generous demeanor, which, unfortunately, just made her suspicious.

"I'm the boss, so don't argue with me, Miss Wallace." He returned to the stack of papers on his desk by way of telling her the conversation was over.

Claire thanked him quietly and left. She had made twice as much as she would have working at the general store, but as she slid the money into her handbag and headed to the boarding house, something didn't feel right. She dismissed her unsettledness and resolved not to overthink every little thing Bruce Conway did or said.

When the stage arrived that Friday afternoon, it brought in a slew of customers to the hotel, as did a group of cowboys that rode into town around the same time. Claire had never seen the entire hotel full until that weekend. She had also

A Debt to Pay

never heard it so noisy. Just before she was about to leave for the evening, Bruce Conway approached her.

"Can I have a word with you before you go?"

"Certainly," Claire said as she tucked the ledger in its place on the shelf and turned to face him.

"Can you work evenings?"

Claire's reluctant expression caused him to go on. "Come in at three and stay until ten," he clarified.

"I'd prefer to work the earlier shift, sir."

"Yes, well, I'll pay extra. I have some business that will take me away from the hotel for the next few evenings and would appreciate your flexibility in the matter."

"Just for the next few evenings?" Claire asked cautiously.

"Yes, a week at the most."

Claire knew his 'business' more than likely would take place at the saloon. "I suppose I could for a few days."

"Good." His eyes drifted over her dress. "There is one more thing, Miss Wallace. Your attire."

"My attire?" Claire looked back at him incredulously.

"Yes, it's rather drab for my fine establishment. I'd like you to look a little more, shall we say, done up?"

"Done up? I'm not one of your saloon girls," Claire reminded him, a bit of fire in her eyes.

"Yes, what a shame," he replied with a jeering smirk, his eyes lingering on her a little longer than Claire felt comfortable with. He was suddenly the Bruce Conway she remembered.

"I just bought this dress, and I have no intention of changing my wardrobe to suit your taste."

Bruce sighed. "Very well. But I'm certainly paying you enough to buy something that's a little more…" He paused as if looking for the right word. "…flattering," he finished.

"I'll expect you at three tomorrow," he said before moving to his office.

Claire let out an agitated breath when he'd gone. Bruce Conway had been tolerable since she started working there and had even surprised her by being professional and keeping his distance. His behavior just now, however, was more like him and reminded her of why she didn't want the job in the first place. She hoped she hadn't made a mistake in agreeing to stay later into the night, but she reminded herself it was only for a few days and would mean extra money.

"And this way, we can give her some hair." Maggie smiled proudly at the little yarn doll she was helping Lilly to make. She finished tying yarn to the head and then explained they would use small buttons for eyes.

Lilly giggled as she watched the pile of yarn come together as a doll. "How did you learn how to do that?" Lilly asked.

"Oh, my mother taught me when I was around your age," Maggie told her.

"Was your mother nice like you?"

Maggie smiled. "Nicer."

"What about your Pa?"

"I didn't see him but a few times."

"In your whole life?" Lilly asked with astonishment. "I see my Pa every day!"

"And you're lucky you do," Maggie told her as she finished gluing the eyes and then handed Lilly the doll. "Why don't you set her somewhere safe to dry."

"I wish we could make my Pa something," Lilly said as she came back from laying the doll on her bed. "It's his birthday on Friday."

A Debt to Pay

"Is it? Hmm, we could make him a cake?"

Lilly jumped up and down. "Oh yes! Let's make him a chocolate cake!"

"Alright, I'll get everything we need, and then we can surprise him on Friday when he gets home."

"But don't tell Lucas!" Lilly warned, glancing to where her little brother was napping on his bed. "He can't keep a secret to save his life!"

"Alright," Maggie laughed softly. "It'll be our secret."

In the days between then and Friday, Maggie talked to Lyddie and got a recipe and the ingredients she would need to make a cake. She even stopped at the general store Friday morning and purchased a few candles, thinking how excited Lilly would be. And then another thought occurred to her. Lingering in the aisles, she glanced around for some sort of gift she could get for Lilly to give her father. She had no idea what he would like. She was having a hard time when suddenly she remembered hearing him tell Lilly a story about when he was a boy and used to play the harmonica. As the story had gone, he had ended up losing it and told her he cried like a baby for two weeks straight. It had made her giggle and feel better about the item she had just lost.

Excited, Maggie picked up a silver harmonica lying nicely in a little brown wooden box. She couldn't wait to show Lilly. After she paid for it, Maggie headed to the Myles' house, excited about the day ahead.

A few hours later, she and Lilly were combining ingredients, laughing and enjoying every moment. "I don't know, Lilly; this is my first attempt at a cake."

"I think it's going to taste great! The batter does," she said, taking a quick swipe with her finger against the inside of the bowl.

"Let's pour it on those pans you dusted with flour." Maggie waited with the bowl poised above them and then gently scraped the mixture into each. After she had put them in the oven, she turned to Lilly with a smile. "Why don't you get Lucas so you two can lick the bowl."

Lilly jumped up from the chair she'd been kneeling on and ran into their bedroom. She returned a moment later with a puzzled expression. "He's not in there."

"What?" Maggie turned from the sink, wiping her hands on her apron. "He has to be."

"I think he might have climbed out the window," Lilly said, looking back at the room.

Maggie was outside in a flash, calmly calling his name and then more frantically as a minute passed. Just as she was about to feel really alarmed, she spotted him through some bushes that grew on the bank along the creek. "Lucas!" she called again, moving swiftly toward him. His little blonde head turned to face her, and he had a huge smile on his face.

Maggie noticed he had taken off his socks and shoes and was dangling his feet in the water. The creek had a deeper section just a few feet away, and her mind raced with the *what-ifs* had she not found him any sooner.

"You can't come down here alone," she scolded him gently. "That water is too deep right there." She pointed, but he didn't seem to understand.

"Lucas wants to swim," he told her.

She sat down next to him and put him in her lap. "Don't ever go outside by yourself; do you understand?"

His blonde curls bobbed up and down as he nodded. Maggie planted a quick kiss on his cheek and then stood, balancing him in her arms. The dirt under her feet suddenly gave in, and she realized she was on a slipperier spot than she had realized. She managed to get Lucas to his feet on the bank before she stumbled backward, falling on her backside into the water.

Lucas laughed as if it was the funniest thing he'd ever seen, but Maggie screamed as the cold water soaked her dress and shoes. Lilly had reached them by now and gasped. "Oh, no! Are you alright?"

"I'm fine," Maggie said, shaking her head and then laughing as well. "What a mess!"

She splashed her way out of the creek, feeling the mud mixed with water running down her legs. Once back at the house, she began to wring out her skirt. An entire bucket's worth of water was wrung out from the material, but she still felt drenched. Next, she removed her stockings and shoes. "What on earth am I going to do?" she wondered out loud.

"I know!" Lilly exclaimed. She disappeared into the house and soon reappeared with a light pink cotton dress. "You can wear this!"

"Was that your mother's?" Maggie asked gently.

"Yep. And she was the same size as you are. I know it will fit!"

Maggie held the dress she had pushed into her hands and looked at it hesitantly. "I don't know if your father would be alright with me wearing this."

"Oh, he won't mind. Better that than you getting the house all wet," she smiled.

She seemed so sure about it that Maggie agreed. She slipped into the house briefly to put it on and then took her wet dress and stockings and hung them on the line in the backyard.

"The cake!" Lilly shouted out the back door.

Maggie came running inside, grabbed a dishcloth, and

hastened to take the cake pans out of the oven. She sighed with relief. "They look perfect!"

"Can we put the icing on now?" Lilly asked.

"Let's let them cool first, and then we will. In the meantime, I have something to show you!" Maggie went over to her handbag and pulled out a little brown box. "I thought you might like to give this to your Pa."

Lilly gasped in awe when she saw it. "He's going to love this!" And then she threw her arms around Maggie's waist. "You smell like mama," she said.

Maggie's heart broke. "It's probably the dress."

Lilly nodded, and then the sad expression that had suddenly filled her eyes vanished when she looked again at the harmonica. "I'm gonna wrap it up in something. I just can't wait until Pa gets home!"

―――

Jacob unsaddled his horse and led him into the stable, making sure he had water before he headed to the house. It was a long day at the mill, and he felt especially tired that evening. It didn't help that his birthday was also his and his wife's wedding anniversary. He'd been missing her more than ever as memories of their life together seemed to flood him at every turn.

He walked into his house, and for a moment, he felt his heart slam against his chest. Standing by the stove, with her back toward him, it looked just like Rose as she had been so many times before when he'd come home. And then Maggie turned around, and Rose's death hit him fresh all over again.

"Happy Birthday, Pa!" Lilly jumped up and down. "We made you a cake!" she exclaimed.

"Where did you get that dress?"

A Debt to Pay

His tone was like nothing Maggie had ever heard before, and it cut through her like a knife. She could feel even Lilly and Lucas had frozen in place.

"Lilly said it would be alright, that is, I mean, I had nothing else to…"

"Change out of that dress," he interrupted her. "You had no business going through her things."

"I wasn't…I…" Maggie dropped her gaze, unable to look into his eyes for another second. Suddenly, no explanation seemed like it would suffice.

"I think you should leave," he said, and for a moment, the words seemed to echo through the room.

Maggie couldn't have been more stunned if he had shot an arrow in her heart. Methodically, she took a few steps forward and slid the tray in her hands onto the table. Then, without a word, she ran out the back door. She could feel hot tears streaming down her cheeks and could hardly catch her breath. She ran to the barn and hitched Willow to the buckboard as fast as she could. She felt so shaken up she couldn't even think straight enough to grab her dress off the clothesline. She climbed up to the seat and flicked the reins so hard Willow nearly took off in a full run. Maggie cried herself the whole way home, her heart breaking into a million pieces.

"Da! How could you!" Lilly's brown eyes had never flashed like fire before that moment. "She fell in the creek and got all wet! I gave her ma's dress!" Lilly was crying now, sobs shaking her little shoulders as she looked at the cake they had made him. "She was afraid you'd be mad, but I told her you wouldn't mind."

Jacob was in a daze as he watched Lilly cry, Lucas soon

joining in when he saw his sister's tears. Jacob realized he had barely moved from the doorway since walking in.

"We were gonna give you this! But I don't even wanna celebrate your birthday now!" Lilly threw the harmonica she'd wrapped down on the ground and ran out the door.

Slowly, Jacob moved to where Lucas stood crying and picked him up, giving him a comforting hug. Once the boy was consoled, Jacob set him down and picked up the gift Lilly had thrown to the floor. Feeling like he had handled the situation in the worst possible way, he slumped into a chair and just stared at the cake. He'd made a terrible mess of things, hurting Maggie and breaking his daughter's heart on top of it. He had never seen her so angry.

"Come on, Lucas," he said as he came to his feet a moment later and headed to the door. "Let's go find Lilly." He found her just by the creek, with her arms around her knees and her head down, crying. After apologizing and coaxing, he got her to come back into the house with him. He knew it wasn't the evening she had planned, and there was no way he could make it right.

"Let's just pretend like your birthday is another day," she ended up saying and went into her room with Lucas. The sound of the door closing and the silence that followed made Jacob feel the weight of his actions even more. He chided himself for reacting so emotionally, and sleep was hard to find that night. He was in and out, with dreams about his wife, Lilly, and Maggie. When morning finally came, he was at least grateful to be done wrestling with sleep. He slipped on his trousers and made coffee. As was his habit, he sat at the table with his Bible open, reading. His thoughts were distracted, though, and he couldn't read more than a sentence without losing interest. Thinking maybe some fresh air would help, he went to the front door and opened it.

A Debt to Pay

The cool, early morning breeze was refreshing, but he didn't even notice. All he saw was his wife's pink dress folded neatly and lying in a basket on the doorstep. He glanced around for Maggie but realized she must have dropped it off much earlier. Picking up the basket, he returned to the house and felt half sick with himself. From the beginning, it had probably been a mistake to ask Maggie to care for the children. They had formed such a close bond; it would feel terribly difficult to take her away from them.

Jacob couldn't ignore the fact that he had formed a bond with her, too, unintentionally, but it happened so easily. Was it Maggie, or was it just having a woman's gentleness in the house again that had brought happiness that they had been missing?

Jacob mentally shook his head, sighing as he paced the length of the house. He couldn't let them get any closer to her than they had already become. Someone as pretty and pleasant as Maggie was likely to get married eventually anyway, so her absence was inevitable. Jacob had seen Frank Travis talking to her on more than one occasion. The man could be courting her for all he knew. Jacob resolved that school would be starting in a few weeks anyway; that would take care of Lilly, and he could find someone in town to watch Lucas while he worked at the mill.

It was settled. He would apologize to Maggie but explain that he had thought things over and realized with school coming, she wouldn't need to care for the children. It seemed to make sense in his mind, but for some reason, it made his heart heavy to think of her not being there anymore.

Chapter Eighteen

The church service was shorter than usual that Sunday, and as Claire was leaving, Will approached her. He hadn't seen her since the day she'd walked to the ranch.

"Get all those briars out of your dress?" he joked.

Claire couldn't help but smile. "I'll not take that field ever again," she replied, grateful for the way he made light of the situation. She had half expected him to distance himself after getting a taste of her temper.

"Are you busy this afternoon?" he asked.

"No," she said, thinking of Maggie. She hadn't come to church that morning after what had happened on Friday at Reverend Myles'. She had explained it all to Claire, finishing by telling her she could never face Jacob again.

"Would you want to go for a ride?" Will asked.

"Sure," she replied, feeling he was offering her an olive branch. She had hoped her reaction to him paying her bill at the livery wouldn't alter their friendship.

"Great, what if you just ride out to the ranch when you're ready."

Claire checked on Maggie and then headed to the livery for Willow. Within an hour of talking to Will, she was at the

A Debt to Pay

ranch. She saw him already saddled up and ready to go when she got there. "I asked Hannah to pack a few sandwiches and things in case you didn't eat yet."

Claire appreciated his thoughtfulness and thanked him. They started off at an even pace, heading east of his house.

"Let's follow the creek," he suggested. It wound through one of the pastures on his property and down a slight ravine that led to another open field. "I doubt Willow has gotten much of a chance to run. Do you think you can handle a faster pace?"

"Absolutely," she said, already tapping her heels into her side and flicking the reins. The wind in her face, mixed with the steady jolting of the horse's motion, was invigorating. She could see Will beside her, trying to keep up at first and then passing her. Determined, she urged Willow to go faster until she was at least neck and neck with Will and his horse. As they reached a wooded area, they both pulled on the reins and slowed their animals, who were breathing heavily and in need of a drink.

Will and Claire dismounted. They led the horses to the nearby creek, letting their reins dangle to the ground while they drank and munched on the bank grass.

"There's a grassy spot over there," Will said as he lifted a leather satchel from his saddle bag.

Claire lifted her skirt slightly off the ground, stepping over branches and rocks to follow him. They settled on a shady spot, with the sun splashing between the awning made of leaves overhead. Will handed Claire a sandwich and then unwrapped one for himself.

"I'm sorry about Jared running you and Maggie off," Will suddenly said. "Hannah told me what happened."

Claire shrugged. "It was probably for the best anyway, with me working in town again."

"I still don't like the idea of you working for Conway."

"I don't really have another option at this point."

Will sighed, crossed his ankles, and leaned back on his hands. "Maybe something will come up that you've had experience in. Did you have any sort of job in Springfield?"

Claire swallowed a sudden lump in her throat. "In Springfield?" She didn't mean to echo his question but was struggling with a reply.

"Yeah. You never really told me what your life was like there."

"I've worked in a tack shop with my uncle," she heard herself blurt out. "When I was younger, but that's about all."

Will watched her fiddle with her sleeve and thought she seemed nervous. "You don't like to talk about your past, do you?"

She looked up at him and, holding his gaze, replied, "I haven't heard you share much about yours, either."

Will sighed, realizing she was right. "I was almost engaged once."

Claire didn't tell him Hannah had told her as much. "What happened?" she asked, curious to hear the story from him.

"We talked about getting married, but then my pa unexpectedly took sick, and it was all I could do to run the ranch and take care of him, so I unintentionally neglected our relationship. I thought she would understand and wait for things to settle down, but by the time they did, she was engaged to someone else."

Claire shook her head sympathetically. "I'm sorry."

"He was someone I didn't really know, but they ended up getting married and moving." He shrugged. The distant look in his eyes suddenly evaporated when he swung his gaze to hers. "As much as it killed me at the time, I guess it wasn't meant to be."

"So, you lost your father and the girl you loved at the same time?"

Will nodded. "They were dark days for me, but looking back now, I know the Lord used it to prepare my heart for Him."

Claire wondered at his words. "Do you think God does that? I mean, let us go through things that are hard to show us we need Him?" Claire was a little surprised she could verbalize what she was thinking.

Will nodded. "I do. Every person needs the Lord, but some of us don't reach out to Him unless we feel the sting of pain."

"But what if it's our choices that bring the pain, and God had nothing to do with it?"

Will smiled softly, liking the question. "When we turn to God, he redeems even our worst sins and choices."

Claire thought he sounded a lot like Reverend Myles, and it surprised her. "I thought only ministers talked like that."

Will laughed a little, a grin on his face. "Anybody can love God and know Him."

"Anybody?" she asked, looking off toward the creek water splashing over rocks in its path. "Don't you think some are born into situations that keep them from ever knowing God?"

"I think God is fair, and He gives everyone a chance in this life to know Him."

Claire sighed, biting her thumbnail for a moment. "So, you don't think some folks are just too far gone?" She felt like she was holding her breath, waiting for his answer.

"Jesus' sacrifice was enough for anyone to be forgiven."

Claire held his gaze for a moment, wanting to believe his words were true. She had been on a mission to make a new life for herself but hadn't really considered how much the past still lingered in her heart. It just seemed so unlikely that God would care what happened to her. After all, she was just one person on the earth.

Will could sense she was wrestling with his words. "There was a time not so long ago in my life when I thought I didn't need God. Turns out, he was the only thing I needed."

Claire thought it sounded very personal as if Will was talking about a close friend. Maybe that's what having a relationship with God was like.

"Knowing God isn't just attending church," he went on. "It's much deeper, like getting to know someone. You have to spend time with God like you would a friend."

His words practically echoed what she had been thinking. "I've never met anyone like you or Reverend Myles," she told him. "I guess I never gave God much thought before coming here."

"Well, maybe that's one of the reasons he led you to Millcreek."

Claire wondered if he was right. She and Maggie had come there to escape their life and find a new one, so maybe, ironically, this was part of God's plan if such a thing was indeed real.

Maggie blew her nose for what seemed the hundredth time and wiped again at the tears streaming down her cheeks. It had been two whole days since Friday, and she still couldn't seem to stop crying. She told Lyddie she wasn't feeling well and would just take to her room for the weekend. The kind woman left trays of food outside her door, but Maggie could barely eat. The look on Jacob's face when he saw her in his wife's dress still haunted her.

"How could I have been so stupid!" she spoke to the empty room, not for the first time. "What did I think? That I would just keep going on like that, playing house as if I were Lilly and Lucas' mother?" She laid back down on the bed and buried her face into the pillow as she cried. "I'll never be anyone's mother," she sobbed, feeling the heartache of years of loneliness and disappointment.

The bedroom door suddenly opened, and Claire came inside, shutting it quietly behind her. "Maggie? Are you still awake?" It was after ten o'clock that Sunday evening, and Claire was just returning from the hotel.

"How can I sleep knowing Jacob is angry with me?" She didn't lift her head from the pillow, so her words came out muffled, but Claire heard them. Going to the bed and sitting beside her, Claire smoothed her hair away from her tear-stained cheeks.

"Maggie, he was just surprised to see the dress on someone else, and it probably just brought back painful memories. He'll get over it, and so will you."

Maggie's sobs became sniffles as she sat up. "I don't think he'll have me back there anymore. Oh, Claire, I feel like my heart is breaking, and I don't even understand why."

She began to sob again, and Claire put her arm around her. "Because you came to love Lilly and Lucas and care about Reverend Myles, I think."

"I do like him better than any man I've ever met. I tried not to, but he's just so wonderful…and good-looking, too," she added before blowing her nose.

"What about that Frank Travis fellow? I wondered if you were starting to like him."

"Frank? Not in your life!" Maggie said, almost irritated that Claire would suggest it. "He's nice, but he's not anything compared to Jacob. Oh Claire, until this happened, I didn't realize it."

"Realize what?"

"That I'm in love with Jacob Myles! And I can't bear to think he's thinking ill of me."

Claire watched helplessly as she dissolved into a pile of tears again. She wouldn't dare mention how improbable it would be for the Reverend to marry her anyway, not with the past she had and with the kind of man he was.

Will Carter's face suddenly popped into her mind, and she mentally shook away the thought. It wasn't likely Will could love her like that, either, so she was glad she wasn't in love with him.

The following day, Claire convinced Maggie to eat something for breakfast and then persuaded her to take a walk with her. "We can just walk the road that leads away from town," she told her. "I know you'd rather not see anyone, so at least this way, you can get some fresh air."

Maggie reluctantly agreed but, once outside, was glad for the change of scenery. The warm breeze felt good as it passed them on the road. Claire tried to keep her mind on anything other than her situation, but it wasn't easy. About fifteen minutes into their walk, Claire felt Maggie's hand grip her arm.

"Oh, no! Claire, here comes his wagon!" Maggie had stopped dead in her tracks as she saw it drawing closer.

"Calm down, Maggie. He's just heading to town." As Reverend Myles came closer, Claire waved and smiled politely, noticing his children were in the back of the wagon.

"Good afternoon, ladies," he said, noticing Maggie wouldn't lift her eyes to look at him.

A Debt to Pay

"Good afternoon, Reverend. Hello Lilly. Hello Lucas," Claire returned. She watched as the Reverend's gaze continued to slide to Maggie.

"I was, ugh, just heading into town to get a few things and to, um…come talk to you, Maggie."

Maggie looked up at him for the first time.

"If you like, I could sit with the children if you two need a few minutes," Claire offered cheerily, acting as if their conversation was nothing more than a howdy do.

Jacob was already climbing down from the wagon. "Thanks, Claire."

As Claire went to talk with the kids, Jacob took her spot on the road. "What if we walk just a bit?" he asked quietly.

Maggie nodded, willing herself not to shed a single tear even though just seeing him and the kids provoked her emotions to come to the surface.

"I was out of line the other day," he said. "I realize now I spoiled a thoughtful celebration the kids wanted for me. I should have never reacted like that when I saw you…" he cleared his throat. "…in Rose's dress."

"Oh, I completely understand," Maggie heard herself say in a surprisingly even voice. "It was an unexpected reminder of the past, and please know I would never go through your wife's personal things."

"Of course, I realized that right away, and Lilly explained to me what had happened. Oh…" A small smile tilted the corner of his mouth. "…and thank you for the harmonica. It was very thoughtful. The kids have been making me play it almost every day."

Maggie smiled, "I'm glad you liked it."

He looked into her eyes, making him momentarily forget what he was going to say next. "Oh, one more thing, I'm going to be working a little less at the mill now, and with school starting in a few weeks…well…the kids won't need someone at the house as much."

Maggie couldn't find any words to reply, so she was glad when he went on.

"You've been such a blessing to the children, I want you to know I really have appreciated it."

"It's been a pleasure," Maggie managed, trying to keep her disappointment from showing on her face or in her voice. "Lyddie has been needing my help at the boardinghouse anyway lately, so it really works out rather well that you don't need someone to watch the children anymore."

"Oh good," Jacob replied, and Maggie thought he looked quite relieved. She suddenly wondered if maybe he had wanted to ask her to leave for some time and just had kept her on to be kind and charitable. He was a minister, after all.

"Well, I won't keep you any longer," she said, a forced smile on her face. Maggie waved to the children as Jacob climbed in the wagon and forced herself not to make too much eye contact with Lilly. The little girl suddenly jumped down and ran to Maggie, throwing her arms around her waist in a hug before returning to the wagon.

"How did it go?" Claire asked once the wagon was out of earshot.

"Exactly like I thought it would."

———

"I'll be with you in a minute," Claire said when she heard the hotel door open. She was hanging the keys on their proper hooks and didn't see who had come in. When she turned around, she was surprised to see Amy Keets.

"Good afternoon, Amy. Can I help you?"

A Debt to Pay

"My goodness, Claire. You're a jack of all trades, aren't you?" She smiled, but it didn't quite reach her eyes. "Where will you be working next?" she gave an amused laugh.

"Is there a reason you're here?" Claire couldn't keep the irritation from her tone.

"Of course, there is. I need two rooms for my father and myself. We are having our home remodeled, and the work will get done quicker if they don't have to work around us."

"I see." Claire glanced through the book, looking at what was available. The men who had been staying there since Friday were still in town, as were the two couples from the stagecoach. "There are a few vacant rooms on the first floor," she told her, reaching for the key. "It's just down the hall to the right. Room three and four."

Amy gingerly took the keys from her extended hand. "Everything is clean, right? I don't particularly like the idea of living in a room someone else has already occupied."

"Yes, everything should be to your liking," Claire said simply.

"Good. We'll be by later this evening with our things. Good day, Claire."

Claire was glad to see the back of her and released a sigh when she had gone. "That girl really gets under my skin," Claire mumbled under her breath. Just for good measure, she went to rooms three and four and double-checked that everything was clean and tidy.

Hours later, Claire found herself staring at the clock, just waiting for it to hit ten o'clock. She felt so tired, and the noise from the saloon across the street wasn't doing her headache any favors. She couldn't wait to get to the other end of town and fall asleep. She knew most of the guests had already turned in for the night, except the cowboys, who she assumed were part of the chaos at the saloon.

As she headed to the front door, it abruptly flew open, and Bruce Conway all but collapsed on the floor. At first, she just thought he was drunk, but then she caught sight of a bright red stain on his shirt.

"Mr. Conway! Are you alright?" She rushed toward him and helped him to his feet. "What on earth happened?"

Leaning on her for support and with his right hand tucked over his bleeding side, Bruce Conway tried to walk across the lobby.

"I don't think I can make it home like this," he said, and Claire thought his face looked white as a sheet. "Just help me get to a room."

Claire walked with him down the hallway and to the nearest room. Once inside, she lit a lamp as he found his way to the bed.

"I'll go for the doctor," she told him, already reaching for the doorknob.

"No!" His voice was so pleading that Claire turned back.

"Please, it's not that serious. I just need a bandage."

Claire brought the lamp closer and set it on the bedside table.

"Help me," he said, trying to get his jacket and vest off.

Claire helped him and then gasped when she saw the large gash on his side. It looked like a knife wound. "I should get the doctor, Mr. Conway."

"No!" He unbuttoned his shirt, shook out of it, and balled it up, pressing it firmly on his side. "Just help me stop the bleeding."

Claire suddenly remembered the bits of fabric in a basket

A Debt to Pay

in the washroom. "I'll be right back!" she told him, already heading out the door. She moved quickly down the hall and into the washroom. Just a minute or so later, she was back, the makeshift bandages in her hand.

"Can you sit up?" she asked, watching him wince in pain as he pulled himself to a more upright position on the bed. She spotted a silver alcohol flask tucked in his coat pocket and, grabbing it, untwisted the lid. "Move your hands for a minute," she told him, and then she poured the liquid on his bleeding wound.

He sucked in air and grimaced at the stinging sensation. Claire then packed a folded bandage over the wound and told him to hold it there while she wrapped another around his back. She went around twice until it seemed secure and tied it off at the end.

"I finally get you alone, and it has to be like this."

"Shhh. Save your strength," she returned in a tone that he wasn't about to argue with.

Stepping back, she repositioned the pillows. "Try to lay back as flat as you can."

She hesitated and then just asked, "Do you want me to pull off your boots?"

"I'd be much obliged."

Claire pulled them off and then gathered his bloody shirt, jacket, and vest. "I'll take these to the washroom," she told him.

"You're an angel," he said, his eyes following her out the door.

Claire closed the door behind her and headed back down the hall, unaware that after hearing the ruckus, Amy had poked her head outside her door. She watched Claire leave the room with something in her hands. It was too dark to see and most certainly left her curious as to what Claire was doing at nearly eleven at night going in and out of Room Two.

Chapter Nineteen

When she got to the hotel the following day, Claire tapped lightly on the door to the room she knew Conway was in. Not hearing anything, she opened the door a crack and saw Mr. Conway still lying on the bed. She slipped into the room and walked quietly toward the bed. She breathed a sigh of relief when she saw his chest rise and fall as he slept. While she didn't care for the man as a person, she wouldn't wish death on anyone.

Her gaze traveled to his bandage, and she saw there was some fresh blood that had come through. It wasn't an excessive amount, which was a good sign.

"Are you leaving?"

Claire turned around at the door at the sound of his voice.

"I thought you were still asleep." She watched him lift his head from the pillow to check his wound. "I think the bleeding is under control," she said. "I'll go and get your clothes and then help you change your dressing."

"Your concern is touching," Bruce Conway said, his tone slightly mocking.

"I wouldn't like to see a dog bleed to death either, Mr. Conway."

He chuckled slightly as he stood from the bed, his hand holding his side. "Thank you for bringing me back to the reality of your feelings, Miss Wallace."

Claire slipped out of the room and came back shortly, his clothes in her hands. "Sarah washed everything this morning, and it's mostly dry. I'm afraid the shirt is stained for good, though." She handed him the clean bandage wrap, and he fumbled with it a bit while trying to keep a section of it pressed on his wound.

"Here, let me."

He lifted his arms slightly while she wrapped it around his waist and tied it. Claire ignored the amused expression on his face and finished quickly. "Alright, you should be fine on your own now."

"Thank you," he said in a tone that was akin to genuine. "I'm sure you're wondering what this is all about."

"It's none of my business," Claire replied.

"One of the fellows that rode into town recently isn't too keen on the way I run my saloon. He looked a lot worse than I did."

"Like I said, it's none of my business." And with that, Claire left the room.

Once she'd gone, Bruce slipped on his boots, ignoring the pain it brought to his side. Then he reached for the shirt Claire had tossed on the bed and slowly pulled his arms through it. He donned his vest to hide the blood stain on his white shirt and hung his jacket over his arm. His house was a few blocks away, and once there, he planned to just rest the remainder of the day. As he stepped out into the hall, still buttoning his vest, his eyes met with Amy Keets. She was just heading to her room across the hall.

"Good afternoon, Miss Amy," he greeted her with a nod and a flicker of a smile.

A Debt to Pay

"Mr. Conway," Amy acknowledged him before moving into her room. Her hand went to her throat in astonishment as she put together what she had seen the night before. She had never liked Claire, but she had never thought the woman capable of something that scandalous. Amy conceded that she wouldn't say anything to anyone right away, but she would certainly hold on to her newfound knowledge about Claire Wallace.

Claire didn't see Bruce Conway at the hotel for the next two days, so she assumed he was taking that time to mend at home. On the day he did return, he approached the front desk as she was working and leaned against the counter.

"Thank you again for your help the other night."

Claire nodded. "Did you end up seeing the doctor?"

Bruce grimaced. "He and I aren't on the best of terms. And you were such a nice replacement."

The main door opened, and Sheriff Dunley walked in. He tipped his hat toward Claire, and then his attention went to Bruce. She watched as they moved into his office, and she could hear their muffled voices from behind the door that had been left slightly ajar.

For some reason, Claire found herself walking carefully toward it and then stopping outside of it to listen.

"Where's the body now?"

Claire held her breath as she waited to hear the sheriff's answer to Conway's question.

"A few miles outside of Jefferson. It'll look like he got himself robbed and shot out there." There was a pause, and then the sheriff said, "You weren't expecting that knife, were you?"

"Obviously not," Claire heard Conway reply in a tone she thought sounded irritated. "You said you wanted to talk to me about something else as well?"

"Other night, I heard one of the boys say before Grady left town this time, he was blubbering about some gold he was here to get," the sheriff said.

"Gold?" Bruce sounded perplexed.

"When I asked him what he was doing here, he said he was looking for something and would be gone as soon as he found it. Maybe that's what he was referring to."

"Interesting. He burned the bank after he got what he wanted, so maybe what he wanted was in that cabin, and then he set fire to that, too. I'd heard rumors it was deliberately started."

"Could be. John Carter used to live there, and he started his ranch with gold he struck in California during the rush."

"If Grady's out there with gold in his pocket, might be worth a try to track him down," Bruce said.

"I don't know if it's gold he came back to find, but I do know he suspects I kept the money."

"Like you said before, talking would only implicate himself."

"True, but he might just be coot enough to do it."

"Then, by all means, sheriff, let's find out where he is."

Claire heard a chair scraping the floor and knew the conversation was coming to an end. She turned quickly and dashed toward the front counter. She got behind it just as Sheriff Dunley was stepping out of Conway's office.

She felt anxious the rest of the day, wondering whose body they were talking about. From what she had overheard, the man who had stabbed Bruce Conway was lying dead in some ditch near the next town. Her thoughts lingered mostly on what they said about Grady Higgs. She wondered if Will knew anything about Grady being back in Millcreek to look for gold or if he knew he had been the one behind the bank robbery and fire several years ago.

Claire couldn't ignore the feeling that she needed to tell Will what she had overheard. The next morning, she walked to the livery and saddled Willow for a ride out to the ranch. As she rode into the yard, she spotted Jared by the corral. She rode up beside him, relieved that he at least waved.

"Mornin', Claire," he said, his voice emotionless.

"Mornin', Jared. I was looking for Will; is he around?"

"In the field behind the barn, last I saw."

"Thanks." She offered a brief smile before turning the reins to the right and directing her horse toward the barn. She wanted to tell Jared she was sorry but didn't want to bring the subject up again. A moment later, as she came around the corner of the massive barn, she noticed Will on horseback in the field.

"Howdy, Claire." He looked surprised that she was there. "Everything alright?"

"Everything's fine. I just…well, I don't know if it's important, but I overheard something last night I thought I should tell you."

"Go on," he said, giving her his full attention.

She recounted the conversation as accurately as she could and saw the play of emotions on his face as she spoke.

"I had wondered if Grady was the one behind that robbery."

Claire could hear the remorse in his voice.

"I wish there was proof that Sheriff Dunley and Conway kept that money."

"Maybe some will turn up," Claire offered with a little

shrug. "Did you know anything about the gold they were talking about?"

Will shook his head. "No, but it makes a lot of sense now why Grady came back and asked to stay in the cabin." He sighed, thinking of the man who had been nothing but trouble. And then his gaze and thoughts switched to Claire.

"I still think you need a hat," Will said suddenly, noticing her squinting against the sun. "Then you'd really look like you belong on that horse."

Claire smiled. "A hat, huh? Next thing I know, you'll be asking me to go on a cattle drive or something."

Will gave a little laugh and shrugged. "Who knows, you handle that horse pretty well; you just might be cut out to be a wrangler."

"Well, first, I'd have to see if I looked good in one of those wide-brimmed leather hats you boys all wear."

"Trust me, you'd look good."

Claire looked away, trying not to let him see she was flattered by his compliment.

"Thanks for telling me what you overheard. I'll see what else I can find out. Hopefully, I'll find Grady yet."

Claire nodded her reply. "Well, see you later, Will."

"Before you go, would you do me a favor?"

"Of course."

"Stop by the house and say hello to Hannah. She really misses you."

Claire smiled, glad to hear it. "I'd be happy to."

―――

"Want to take a little hike this afternoon and have a picnic?" Jacob asked Lilly during breakfast Tuesday morning.

She shrugged as she set her glass of milk down. "I guess."

"What about you, Lucas?"

"I yes," he tried to imitate his sister, misunderstanding the words.

"Great. We could see if there are any raspberries left on the way back."

"Ain't nobody 'ere to make a raspberry pie with 'em," Lilly reminded him.

"We can just eat them," Jacob said, knowing she was referring to a time a few weeks ago when Maggie had made a raspberry pie.

"I was talking to Miss Wendel yesterday about school, and she is really excited to have you starting this year," Jacob said. He saw that Lilly was still uninterested. She had been like this ever since that night of his birthday.

"Pa?"

Jacob looked at her, eager for her to finally say something. "Yeah?"

"Why can't Maggie come here anymore? It wasn't her fault about the dress."

"I know, hunnie. It's not because of the dress."

"Then what is it?"

"You're gonna be starting school."

"Not for another two weeks!"

"Well, it's because…" his sentence died off. He really couldn't explain it to her. "You just have to trust me, Lilly. It's for the best."

"Everything was better when she was here," Lilly mumbled as she raked her eggs with her fork.

"It was nice having her here for a while, but she couldn't stay here forever."

"She could if you married her."

Jacob blinked with surprise, staring back at his daughter's

serious expression. "Wouldn't you feel uncomfortable with me marrying someone other than your ma?"

"Ma's not here anymore, and having Maggie here was almost like her being here."

Jacob looked into Lilly's pleading eyes. She had been six when her mother died and had spent the last two years with a broken heart, missing her. Jacob let out a heavy sigh, feeling torn. "I could ask Maggie to come back until school starts," he said hesitantly. He resolved at least her departure wouldn't be on such sudden terms.

Lilly was out of her chair in an instant. "Oh, please, Pa. Can you?" She climbed up on his lap and hugged his neck. "Please ask her, Pa."

"Alright. I'll ask her."

Bruce Conway walked out of the Sheriff's office and moved down the street with a determined look in his eyes. He barely noticed the evening street traffic or those who passed him on the way. On that Tuesday evening, his mind was bent on one thing. He passed the bank and was soon walking into the hotel he'd taken over some ten years ago.

Claire glanced up from the desk when he walked in but dropped her gaze and continued with what she was doing.

"May I speak with you a moment?" he asked.

There seemed to be a hint of urgency in his voice, so Claire nodded.

"In my office," he added.

Claire had never been asked into his office and felt uneasy as she followed him. He waited until she was inside and then closed the door behind them.

"I was just talking with Sheriff Dunley." He sat at his desk and gestured for her to take the wing-backed chair that was on the other side of his desk. "He showed me something that I think you should see."

Claire looked at him curiously as he reached into the inside pocket of his coat and pulled out a folded piece of paper. He very slowly unfolded it, laid it on the desk, and then turned it so she could see it. Claire felt all the blood drain from her face as she looked at a reward poster with her and Maggie's sketched faces.

"Three-hundred-dollar reward," Bruce Conway read the poster in a drawn-out voice. "It says here, *Wanted for Robbery and Attempted Murder?*" He looked at Claire with wide, curious eyes, waiting for her to say something. "Also lists the names of Claire Wallace and Maggie Clemmins. That wouldn't be your *sister*, Maggie, would it?"

Claire hadn't sat down yet, but she suddenly felt too weak to stand. Reaching for the arms of the chairs, she sank into the seat. She released a shaky breath and closed her eyes for a moment to the room, which seemed to be spinning. She knew she shouldn't be surprised about the poster, especially the robbery part, but attempted murder? She almost felt like she would be sick.

"I must say, I'm more than a little surprised. Attempted murder?"

Claire shook her head, at least in that she could defend herself. "It was self-defense, nothing more." She swallowed the sudden lump in her throat. "Is the Sheriff planning to arrest us?" Claire whispered.

"Well, that depends."

Claire lifted her eyes to meet his, not liking at all what she saw there. "What do you mean?"

"Sheriff Dunley and I have what you might call an arrangement. I keep my mouth shut about his secrets, and he turns a blind eye to some of my less-than-honest business dealings. I have some considerable leverage where he is concerned."

"But he's the sheriff."

"He's human, Claire."

It was the first time he'd ever used her first name. It radiated a certain familiarity she didn't like.

"It says here to contact a man named Frederick Harris and that you and Maggie were both last seen working in a Chicago saloon?" He looked up from the poster, his eyebrows raised questioningly. "Now that is interesting."

Claire dropped her gaze, feeling like a thousand pounds had just been laid on her shoulders.

"I didn't realize you had experience working in a saloon or in breaking the law." He leaned forward, his elbows on the desk and his hands laced under his chin. "I always knew there was something about you I liked, and now I see we have more in common than I ever imagined."

Claire felt like she was holding her breath. "I'm planning to pay it back. All of it!"

"What did you steal? And how much did you steal?" he asked.

"It was a jewelry shop, and we took just enough money to get out of Chicago and travel west." She suddenly thought of the diamond necklace Maggie had kept.

"Do you have any of that money now?"

Claire sighed heavily. "We hadn't even used it all, but the fire…" she let the sentence hang.

"Ah, I see." He took a deep breath. He'd never seen her so vulnerable and couldn't help but seize this opportunity. "Tell me everything. Maybe I can help."

A Debt to Pay

Claire reluctantly told him the events of that night, ending with, "There was a diamond necklace we kept, but that was destroyed in the fire, too."

Bruce Conner leaned back in his chair, a pensive expression on his face.

"Maggie and I have been working and saving to pay it all back. We just need more time."

"And you think this Frederick Harris will just take the money you give him and let you off the hook?"

"I hadn't planned on getting caught. I thought we'd send the money back to him, and it would be enough for him to forget."

"A diamond necklace? I doubt your money could make him forget that."

"I know. It's a mess. I should probably turn myself in to Sheriff Dunley and be done with it."

"I don't think you want to do that, especially since Dunley won't press charges unless I tell him to."

Claire's eyes met his again. "Are you saying neither you nor he will say anything?"

"I'm saying he'll stay quiet as long as I tell him to stay quiet."

"But if those posters are out, anyone could come across it."

"True. But you have a better chance of living under the radar when I ask Sheriff Dunley to stay on your side and keep those posters from ending up in our town."

"Why would you do that for me and Maggie?" she asked cautiously.

"Because you and I are going to have a special arrangement."

Claire stood from the chair as if it were on fire. "I'd rather turn myself in now than be blackmailed by you."

"Go ahead. You say the word, and I'll hang up these posters all over town. There's plenty of folks who could use three hundred dollars."

Claire could feel her heart pounding in her chest, and her temples were suddenly throbbing. She slowly found herself sitting back down. "What would this special arrangement entail?"

"I'm not going to put any specifics on it just yet. Let's just take it day by day, shall we?"

"It would still just buy us time, though," she thought aloud.

"You could be right. It's up to you. If you want to go telling people the truth, then why not start with… I don't know, someone like Will Carter?"

Claire felt sick at the mere thought of telling him the truth about what she'd done. At least for now, she knew she wasn't ready to tell him.

Bruce Conway silently congratulated himself for that final touch. He knew the prospect of having to tell him would win her over to his plan. "What's your choice, Miss Wallace?"

Claire nodded slowly. "I'll do it. At least for now, but only under one condition. You leave Maggie out of this whole thing. It was my idea. She had nothing to do with it."

"Very well. I'll keep this strictly between you and me and Sheriff Dunley." He took the poster and ripped it up before her eyes. "Glad we could reach an agreement. You may go now."

Claire stood slowly, still feeling weak. She felt dazed and nauseous the rest of the evening and was glad when she could finally go back to the boarding house. She expected to find Maggie asleep, so she was surprised when a very bright-eyed and excited Maggie greeted her.

"Oh, Claire, I have the most wonderful news."

A Debt to Pay

"Reverend Myles hired you back?" Claire guessed with a voice that didn't sound at all excited. All she could think about was her horrible news.

"Something better than that."

Claire looked at her curiously, wondering what Maggie could consider better than working again for Jacob Myles.

"For the last week, I haven't been able to eat or sleep. I was so distressed about what happened but also just broken over my entire life!"

"Shhh," Claire whispered, worried she'd wake the whole boarding house.

"Sorry." Maggie smiled, biting her lower lip in an effort to quiet some of her excitement. "Well, tonight, a few hours ago, I decided I would give it a try. Everything Jacob has been saying for the last two months finally made sense!"

"Maggie, you're talking like a crazy person. Give what a try? What are you going on about?"

"I prayed, Claire. I got down on my knees, and I told God everything. I don't think I moved for over an hour. I just knelt by the bed, crying and confessing everything I've ever done and asking for forgiveness. And then when I had finished, and I stood up, it was like I was a new person!"

Claire just looked back at her, not knowing what to say.

"When we came here, we wanted to have a new life, but deep down, I felt the same old way I've always felt. But for the first time, Claire, I feel new! I feel peace and joy and freedom!"

Claire forced herself not to tell her she wouldn't feel freedom if she knew they could be arrested at any moment. She didn't know what to make of Maggie's apparent transformation. There was only one lamp lit in the room, but even in the dimness, Claire could see the glow radiating from Maggie's eyes.

Maggie suddenly reached out and took Claire's hands. "You could feel this way, too, Claire. It's for everyone. Now, I understand why Jesus didn't throw the stone at that woman."

Claire watched as tears slid down Maggie's cheeks. Claire didn't understand, and her own heart had never felt more dead. It would be cruel to rob Maggie of her newfound joy, though, even if it only proved to be temporary. "I'm happy for you, Maggie."

"God isn't at all like I thought he was. He's kind and forgiving and wants to rescue us from sin so we can be close to him!" Maggie saw she was losing Claire's attention, but in her heart, she wasn't deterred. "Just you wait, Claire. I just know in time, you'll understand what I mean."

Claire didn't share her confidence, but she didn't want to discourage her from it, either. She had debated telling Maggie about her conversation with Bruce Conway, but now she knew with certainty that she couldn't tell her. Why put this burden on her as well?

Claire lay in bed wide awake that night, but she felt so desperately tired. Finally, in the wee hours of the morning, she felt her racing mind drift into a state of much-needed sleep.

Chapter Twenty

Jacob was greeting people as they came into church, moving from conversation to conversation, when he spotted Maggie settling into a pew nearby, Claire and Lyddie beside her. He was glad to see her, especially since she'd not come to church since the night of his birthday, but he also felt a little anxious as to what her response would be when he spoke with her.

His message was on the shorter side, and after he concluded with prayer and a final hymn, Jacob made sure to catch her outside before she left. "Can I talk to you for a second?" he asked.

Maggie turned around, surprised that Jacob had sought her out. Claire and Lyddie moved on, leaving her in the churchyard with Reverend Myles.

Suddenly feeling nervous, Jacob cleared his throat. "How have you been?"

"Good," Maggie replied, a smile in her eyes as she felt near to bursting to tell him about her experience with God a few nights ago.

He saw by her expression that she meant it, and he relaxed a little. "I feel I was hasty in telling you we don't need your help anymore."

Maggie hadn't been expecting those words at all and wondered what he would say next.

"Fact is, we still have a few weeks until school starts, and well, Lilly and Lucas are feeling your absence pretty hard. I'm wondering if you might think about coming back, at least for the rest of the summer. I think it would be easier for them if your leaving wasn't so abrupt, which was my fault," he added with an apologetic look in his eyes.

"I don't have to think about it all," she replied easily. "Of course I will."

Jacob released a sigh, unaware he'd been holding his breath. "Thank you, Maggie. It means a lot to the kids…and me."

Maggie wanted to tell him about her encounter with the Lord but wasn't sure how to word it. She heard herself say, "Everything you've been preaching about…it all makes sense to me now."

"What do you mean?" he asked with interest.

"The other night, I prayed for the first time, and something happened in me that I can't even explain."

Jacob smiled gently; his heart warmed by her words. "I'm so glad to hear you say that, Maggie!"

"I just wanted to tell you," she said softly, "since you're the one who's largely responsible."

"Well, I'm glad the Lord used me to help draw you to Him."

"He really did, in more ways than you know." She knew he would have no idea how heartbroken she had been over what had happened on his birthday or how that broken heart had been the final blow that had caused her to want the Lord.

"Maggie, I am so sorry for how I spoke to you that day. It's been eating away at me ever since. You didn't deserve that."

"I understand, truly, and it's OK."

A Debt to Pay

Jacob felt something rising in his heart as he stood there looking into her sea-green eyes. The way her auburn hair framed and flattered her pretty face wasn't lost on him either. He was a little afraid to admit it to himself, but he was glad she was coming back.

Claire paced her small bedroom and then stood at the window that looked out to the town street. Maggie had left for Reverend Myles hours ago, leaving Claire alone with her thoughts. She had considered telling Maggie after church, but she was so excited about Reverend Myles asking her to come back that she didn't want to dampen her happiness.

Now, as she wrestled with the weight of it all, she started to feel like she couldn't breathe. She decided to leave a little early for work, hoping maybe a walk and some fresh air would help. It was still a little before three when she arrived at the hotel. There was a small, jewelry-sized box on the counter that grabbed her attention. She picked it up curiously, noticing her name was written on it.

Gingerly, she removed the red ribbon and lifted the lid, revealing a thin, gold chain bracelet with a dangling, gold-leaf charm.

"I thought it would be a nice touch."

Claire was startled at Bruce Conway's voice as he came out of his office. She hadn't realized he was in there. "What is this?" she asked.

"Just a small gift for you."

Claire set the box down. "Thank you, but I can't accept it."

Bruce crossed the lobby. "I'd like it if you did."

For a moment, Claire met his steady gaze and realized he was testing her. She slowly reopened the box and lifted the piece of jewelry out.

"Here, let me help you. The clasp might be difficult to manage."

Claire laid the chain across her wrist and let him hook it together.

"There, now that looks nice." He stepped back, a smile lifting the corners of his mustache. "I thought it would serve as a little reminder of our arrangement," he told her.

"How could I forget?" The disdain in her expression was more than evident, but Bruce Conway didn't mind. He always got what he wanted in the end.

The following week, before Claire was about to leave for work, a medium-sized box was dropped off at Lyddie's with Claire's name on it. When Claire saw the familiar red ribbon, she didn't even want to open it. Eventually, she took the lid off and forced herself to read the card that lay inside. After throwing it away, she pulled the dress out of the box.

"Where did you get that dress?" The question came from Maggie a few minutes later as she entered their room.

Claire turned around from the mirror, wearing the dress she had pulled from the box. It was made of burgundy chiffon and gathered at the waist with a slight bustle in the back.

"I mean, it's beautiful, but where did you get it?"

"It's just for work," Claire said. "Mr. Conway wants his hotel represented in a more fashionable manner." She didn't mention that Bruce Conway had bought the dress for her.

"Since when do you do what he tells you?" Maggie asked, sitting on the bed and looking at Claire with a questioning expression.

"Since he pays my salary," Claire returned a little sharper than she had intended. She swept past the bed, her rustling dress the last sound before she closed the door behind her.

A Debt to Pay

Maggie watched her go, feeling concerned by the sudden change she had noticed over the last week. Claire had seemed moody and preoccupied, not at all like herself.

When Claire arrived at the hotel, Bruce Conway was speaking with someone in the lobby. The man left shortly after, and Bruce came over and leaned on the counter. "Now that's more like it," he said, openly admiring her. "I'm so glad it fits."

Claire sighed with frustration, turning her back to him as she pretended to be busy with some books on the shelf. She didn't turn back around until she knew he had left. She knew she couldn't survive this for long, living under his scrutiny and manipulation. She started thinking maybe she and Maggie should catch the next stagecoach. Would he send the sheriff after them? Would he hang the wanted posters all over town if she left? Frustrated, she tried to distract herself by doing things around the hotel, but there was no escaping the torrent of fear and anxiety that now seemed to follow her everywhere.

A few hours later, as Claire was on her way back from dropping off a pile of bed sheets in the washroom, Bruce Conway burst through the lobby door. Upon seeing Claire, he exclaimed, "I need your help!"

She took in his distressed expression. "What is it?"

"Come with me!"

Claire shook her head. "Mr. Conway, I'm not going to…"

"Please, Claire, it's not for me. It's for a woman at the saloon."

Claire heard the desperation in his voice and, against her better judgment, followed him outside and across the street. The loud saloon music rising with the ruckus of men's laughter and voices was a familiar sound that made Claire freeze at the swinging doors. Bruce moved through them and urged her to follow him. She swallowed down the anxiety rising in her throat and forced herself to follow him inside. Bruce moved up a staircase to the left that led to a landing that overlooked the saloon room. Claire ignored a few suggestive calls from the men below and stayed focused on where Bruce was leading her.

He stopped at the third door on the left and turned toward Claire. "She's in there. They told me she fell down the stairs out back and is pretty bruised up."

"Why not get the doctor?" Claire asked.

"Please, Claire, just help her," he pleaded, opening the door.

Claire stepped in and heard Bruce shut the door behind her. There was a woman lying on her side on the bed, her back facing the door. Claire approached her slowly. "Hello? Can I help you?" she asked gently. There was a little movement, and then the woman pushed herself to a sitting position.

Claire gasped when she saw her bruised face. A trickle of blood streamed down from a cut on her forehead and mixed with dried blood on her cheek, which was swollen and severely bruised. She looked no older than nineteen, and Claire's heart broke at the familiarity of this scene.

"What happened?" she asked softly, going to get the basin of water and towel that sat on the dresser.

"I tripped down the stairs," she told Claire in almost a whisper.

Claire could tell she was in a lot of pain as she gently began to use the wet rag to blot the blood away from her eye and face. "Does anything else hurt?"

"My shoulder is sore, but I don't think anything's broken."

Claire could hear the girl wincing and groaning as she

tried to clean the blood. "I need to get you something cold to put on those bruises," Claire said. "Why don't you lie back and rest, and I'll see what I can find."

The girl nodded and scooted herself back on the bed.

"What's your name?" Claire asked.

"Vivian," she answered.

"I'm Claire," she smiled kindly and then, after a moment of hesitation, said, "What steps did you fall down?"

"There's a set in the back. I think my foot caught on something."

"Vivian, you didn't fall down the stairs, did you?"

The girl looked back at her. One eye was almost swollen shut, the other filled with tears. Claire knew the second she had looked at the young woman that her injuries hadn't come from falling down the stairs.

"Somebody did this to you; am I right?" Claire probed further.

The girl barely nodded, but Claire saw it. She released a shaky sigh, feeling anger mound up in her that someone would beat this poor girl so. Her heart went out to her, and for a moment, she could see herself behind the girl's frightened and defeated expression.

"I'm going to keep checking on you, Vivian, OK? I'll come back tomorrow and make sure you're alright."

The girl nodded again, trying not to cry. It was comforting just hearing the reassuring words.

"I'm going to get some ice or something for the swelling. I'll be back," she promised, laying a gentle hand on the girl's arm. She smoothed away some brown hair from the girl's face. "Just rest."

Claire moved to the door and out to the hallway. Contempt rose in her just at the sight of the men below gambling, drinking, shouting, and cursing. Lifting the hem of her skirt, Claire moved down the staircase.

"Hey, you!" A man shouted from a table near the stairs. He set his glass of whiskey down and came to his feet. "Is she gonna be OK?"

Claire walked to his table, her eyes cold. "You mean Vivian?"

"Yeah, she's my girl," he said, and though his voice sounded concerned, Claire could see darkness in his eyes. "Clumsy little thing, fell headlong down them stairs out back." He slumped back into his chair and reached for the glass. "I just wanna make sure she's OK."

Claire beat him to his glass, lifting it by the handle and promptly splashing its contents into his face. "We both know she didn't fall down the stairs!" She yelled at him, so angry she wished she would have hit him over the head with the glass instead.

The man gasped against the whiskey drenching his face and wiped it out of his eyes, cursing loudly.

"If you lay a hand on her again, I'll…" Claire's words were cut short when he jumped up and grabbed her angrily by the arms. "Who do you think you are?" he screamed in her face, shaking her.

Claire struggled under his hold, unaware of the attention they were drawing from others in the room. "Let go of me!" She ordered but felt his grasp only increase as he pulled her closer.

"Let her go!" The command came from Bruce Conway, who had come up on the scene as soon as he saw Claire in distress.

The man didn't release his hold on Claire but glared at Bruce. "Mind your own business, Conway!"

A Debt to Pay

The sudden sound of a pistol being cocked secured his attention. The man felt the end of Bruce's weapon pressed against his temple and slowly dropped his hands from Claire's arms.

Once released, Claire staggered backward toward the doors, weaving through tables, chairs, and men who had gone back to what they were doing. Claire could feel the power of Bruce's authority in the room, and she suddenly realized no one would bother her as long as he was there. She whirled around to run out the door and collided with someone.

She gasped. "Will!"

The look in his eyes made her want to crawl into a hole. "Claire?"

She didn't know he had walked in just in time to witness everything that had happened. He'd been on his way to her when Bruce Conway pulled out his pistol.

"What are you doing here?" His eyes searched hers for an answer, and then he took her by the elbow and quickly walked with her outside.

"I was helping someone," Claire explained. "A woman upstairs."

Will still looked confused. He noticed her dress, which he thought seemed tighter and more revealing than what she normally wore. He just couldn't wrap his mind around why she would even be out at this hour, let alone in the saloon of all places. He had been heading to the saloon in hopes that a conversation with Sheriff Dunley or another regular would lead to some information about Grady's whereabouts. He hadn't in his life expected to walk in and see Claire.

"Who was that man?" Will asked, glancing past her to the saloon.

"I don't even know," Claire told him. She wanted to explain but couldn't find the words.

"I'll take you home," Will told her, his voice determined.

"That won't be necessary, Mr. Carter."

Will and Claire simultaneously swung their attention to Bruce Conway as he stepped out of the saloon's swinging doors, tucking his pistol inside his coat pocket. "I'll escort Miss Wallace home," Bruce said matter-of-factly as he moved past them a few steps.

Will sent him an irritated glance and looked back at Claire. "C'mon," he said, starting to take her arm.

"Claire." Bruce had glanced back at her and was waiting, a pointed look in his eyes.

Claire froze, hearing the tone of Bruce Conway's voice. She looked up at Will apologetically. "It's OK, Will," she said softly, pulling her arm free from his hand and stepping away to join Bruce.

Will was shocked to see her willingly go to him and more shocked when she allowed him to take her arm. It was as if he had some sort of power over her. He watched as they walked away, feeling like he should follow them to make sure Claire arrived home safely. He waited until they were almost out of sight before reluctantly returning to the saloon. His reason for being there suddenly felt unimportant as his thoughts and heart lingered on Claire.

"Do you know how late it is?" Maggie whispered when Claire came into the room that night. "You've got to tell Mr. Conway you can't work this late anymore!"

Claire slipped out of her dress, leaving it in a pile on the floor. She donned her night dress and climbed into bed beside Maggie. "I know."

"Then talk to him," Maggie encouraged. "You said you

were only going to have to stay late for a few days. It's been much longer than that, Claire!"

"You're right," Claire said absently, still thinking of Vivian. "I'll talk to him tomorrow," she told her but knew there was little she could do.

The following afternoon, just after helping Lyddie in the kitchen with the dishes, Claire made her way to the Millcreek Saloon. Taking a steadying breath outside the doors, she went inside and slipped up the steps. There were only a few people inside, so she managed to get past without anyone taking much notice. She knocked lightly on Vivian's door and heard her voice answer from the other side. Entering the room, she saw the girl standing by the window.

"How are you feeling today?" Claire asked.

Vivian instinctively touched her forehead, lightly running her finger over the gash. "I'm feeling a little better," she said. "Thanks…for last night," she added, a brief smile touching her lips.

"How long have you worked here?"

"Just a few months. Mr. Conway lets me stay here for almost free since I'm working every day."

Claire sighed, a familiar band going around her heart. "Had that man hit you before?"

Vivian turned to face the window and slowly moved the curtains to one side. "Not like this."

"Vivian, if he did this to you, it's only a matter of time until he does it again."

"He drank too much, that's all."

Claire touched her on the arm, gently turning the girl to face her. "You don't really believe that, do you?"

Vivian's eyes filled with tears.

"Is there somewhere else you can go?" Claire asked.

"I came here with Trent. I don't know anyone else here."

"Where is your family?"

"Kansas City."

"Vivian, what if you went back? Surely, your family is better than this man."

"My parents told me not to leave with him; I can't go back and face them."

"They'll forgive you, Vivian. If they didn't want you to leave, then that shows they love you."

Vivian looked as if she was considering it and then sighed, shaking her head. "I couldn't let them see me like this."

"Then wait a week or two, but I think you should go back to your family."

For a moment, the girl said nothing, but then turned her eyes to Claire and thanked her. "Why are you helping me?"

"I know what this kind of life is like," Claire told her, "And it's not for you."

"I think you're right," she said quietly. "Trent isn't the man I thought he was."

Claire saw the disappointment in the girl's brown eyes and hugged her gently. "I'll help you get on the stage, and if that man tries to keep you here, I'll…"

Claire let the sentence hang because she wasn't sure what she would do.

"Trent's drunk most of the time. He probably won't even know I'm gone. In the beginning, I thought he loved me, but…" Vivian let the sentence hang, wishing desperately she could rewind her choices.

"You'll find someone else who does love you, Vivian. Someone who would never hurt you like this." Claire wasn't sure where the words were coming from or if Vivian would even believe them, but there was a longing to help this girl escape a similar lifestyle that she and Maggie had also known.

A Debt to Pay

A few minutes later, Claire left the saloon and headed to the hotel. When she entered, she saw Bruce Conway's office door open and knew he was inside. Approaching it nervously, she stopped in the doorway and waited until he looked at her from his desk.

"I'd like to ask you if I can go back to my original shift? I don't want to work evenings anymore."

He stared back at her and looked like he was considering it. He removed the cigar from his mouth. "OK," was all he said before turning his attention back to the papers on his desk.

Stunned it had been that easy, Claire went to the desk. That night would be the last one she would have to stay late. She already felt a little better and knew Maggie would, too.

Chapter Twenty-One

"Are you alright? You don't seem yourself the last two days."

Will looked up from behind a newspaper at Hannah and realized she'd finished washing the dishes and was staring at him, her hands on her hips as she posed the question. After supper, he'd remained at the table, his thoughts anywhere but on what he was reading. "Just wondering why a woman like Claire would give Bruce Conway the time of day. There was something about the way she acted toward him the other night that I can't seem to shake."

Hannah sighed thoughtfully as she took the chair at the end of the kitchen table. Will had told her about running into Claire at the saloon two nights ago, and she'd been just as confused as him about the situation. "She hasn't been here long. Maybe she just isn't aware of how cunning and divisive Conway is."

"It's bad enough to work for the man, but to jump at his beck and call?" Will shook his head and ran a distracted hand through his wavy dark blonde hair. "Just doesn't add up."

"Why don't you talk to her about it?" Hannah suggested.

"She wasn't too happy the last time I interfered," Will replied, thinking about the time he'd paid the livery for keeping Willow.

"Well, pray for an opportunity, and then, when the time's right, say something."

Will found the opportunity the following morning when he was in town leaving the post office. He glanced up from the letter he was about to open and caught sight of Claire heading toward the hotel. Sidestepping the wagons and other traffic in the street, he crossed over, calling her name as he neared.

Claire turned around, feeling nervous at the prospect of seeing Will after the other night.

"I wanted to catch you quick," he said, stuffing the envelope into his pocket for later. He hesitated a moment, deciding to start with something else he wanted to tell her. "This Saturday is Hannah's birthday. She doesn't like being made a fuss over, but I know if you and Maggie could come for supper, it would mean a lot."

Claire smiled softly. "Of course, we'll come."

"Good." He glanced toward the hotel and then back to her, unsure how to say what he wanted. He was relieved when Claire opened up the conversation.

"Will, about the other night…I want to try and explain. I was about to leave the hotel for home when Mr. Conway asked if I would help one of the girls who worked in the saloon."

"You shouldn't be working for him, Claire."

Claire felt conviction when she looked into his eyes. "I don't have a choice."

"Sure, you do. I can help you find another job. I should have said as much the moment I heard you were working at the hotel."

Claire sighed. "It's more complicated than that, Will."

"What do you mean?" He was surprised when Claire's eyes filled with tears, and she looked away. "What is it?" he asked, instinctively taking a step closer and touching her arm.

"It's nothing. I'll be fine," she said, wiping quickly at a tear that escaped.

"Claire, no amount of money is worth doing something you hate."

"Trust me, Will, I know that. It's the reason I left Chicago."

He looked back at her, knowing there was more behind her words than she was willing to share. He also took note of something else. "Chicago?"

Claire fiddled nervously with her purse. "I didn't mean Chicago; I meant Springfield."

"But you said Chicago." He looked at her curiously as if he knew she was keeping something from him.

"I just need a little more time," Claire said, managing a watery smile. "Please don't worry; I'll be fine."

"You keep saying that, but I'm not so sure you will be fine if you keep working for him."

Claire looked up at him, deeply appreciating the concern and kindness she could hear in his tone and see in his eyes. She found herself wanting desperately to tell him what was really going on. She felt tears starting to sting the back of her eyes again and knew she had to escape his presence. "I've got to get to work. Maggie and I will see you Saturday."

Will watched her go, wishing there was some way he could help her not have to work for Bruce Conway. She clearly was keeping him at arm's length, though. He thought he'd proven that she could trust him, but there was something going on that she wasn't telling him. He mentally chided himself

A Debt to Pay

for expecting her to confide in him and reminded himself that she didn't owe him an explanation.

He forgot about the letter in his pocket until he arrived home. It was a response to the letter he'd written Grady Higg's mother, asking her if she had any idea where he would be heading once he left Millcreek. He was completely surprised by what he read.

> *Will,*
>
> *I was distraught to get your letter and learn that Grady had once again brought shame and disappointment on your family. You were kind enough to give him a second chance, and I'm sorry he chose not to honor that. To answer your question, I don't know where he is, but I do need to share something with you that I just discovered. I found a letter from your father when I was going through Grady's things. It was addressed to you, but somehow Grady must have gotten it. I pray he took it after you had read it, but in case you didn't, I've enclosed it in this envelope. I'm sorry my son has been a thorn in your side, but I will always remain grateful for the time I was given with your father and you. Take Care, Rebecca.*

Will unfolded the other piece of paper she had included and hastily read the letter he had never seen before.

> *Dear Will,*
>
> *There isn't much I haven't told you son, but as I lay here not sure how much longer I have on this earth, I want to make sure I leave nothing unsaid. Decades ago, when I returned from California, there were a few nuggets of gold I hid in the cabin. I felt certain the ranch would grow and be successful, but as a backup I hid the gold. If there is ever a need you have, I trust you to use it as you see fit. In case*

this falls into the wrong hands, I won't divulge where I hid it, but you already know where I would hide it. I love you, Will and have always been proud that you're my son.

Will looked up slowly from the letter, the sight of his father's handwriting stirring fresh emotion in his heart. Even with the time that had passed since his death, Will found a reason to think about and miss his father almost every day. Will suddenly remembered what Claire had overheard Conway and the sheriff talking about. Everything made sense. He assumed that after robbing and setting fire to the bank, Grady had left Millcreek and then returned two years later after finding this letter. Will didn't know how he'd gotten his hands on the letter, but it was certainly what had caused him to return and ask Will to stay in the cabin. His visits back to the cabin while Maggie and Claire lived there made sense now, too.

During the two months, Will thought Grady was trying to redeem past actions and gain his trust in helping to run the ranch; Grady had actually just been using it as a cover while he searched for the gold. Will glanced back down at the letter. He did know where his father would have hidden the gold; he'd once shown him the spot, but never had he mentioned before this letter that gold was hidden there.

Will sighed as he walked across the front porch and sat on a stool. Grady had stolen from him on more than one occasion, and to think of him stealing from his father was infuriating. If Grady set the fire after getting what he wanted from the bank, then most likely, he had found the gold before setting the cabin on fire. Will knew he had to get it back.

A Debt to Pay

Will watched Claire from across the table. She and Maggie had joined him, Rusty, and Hannah for supper that Saturday, and now Hannah was bringing out a cake she had baked for the occasion. While Maggie seemed in high spirits, Claire seemed in stark contrast. She was polite and kind, but Will couldn't help but feel there was a heaviness in her.

"This is right sweet of you all to celebrate my birthday like this," Hannah said, leaning back in her chair and smiling at those around the table.

"I got you a little something," Maggie said as she set a small box on the table in front of Hannah.

Hannah shook her head disapprovingly, but there was a smile in her eyes. "Now, you didn't need to go and make a fuss!" As she said the words, she was already pulling the lid off.

"Well, that's right pretty," she said, looking at the cameo broach that lay inside. She gently took it out and held it to her chest. "Right pretty, I must say."

"I'm glad you like it," Maggie said, going to give her a little hug.

Claire had gone to retrieve the gift she had gotten Hannah and handed it to her. "You can open it later," Claire said, but Hannah was too curious. She pulled back the wrapping paper, and then her eyes went to Claire's and said more than words could have. The gift was clearly a reminder of their conversation about Hannah loving her home in Missouri too much to leave.

"It's just beautiful, Claire. Thank you."

Will leaned in from his chair, curious as to what it was. He saw in Hannah's hands a crochet picture that said, *There's No Place Like Home.* He saw the emotion in Hannah's eyes when she opened the gift and knew it must be something between her and Claire.

"I'm not good with a needle," Claire confessed. "So, when Will told me it was your birthday, I had to work fast. It's probably a little crooked."

"I think it's perfect. Thank you, ladies."

"Alright, Rusty," Will said with a grin in the older man's direction. "What did you bring, Hannah?"

The man scratched his overgrown gray beard. "Since you put me on the spot…"

Hannah gasped when he handed her a box wrapped in white ribbon and tied in a bow. "I didn't know you had it in you," she told him.

"Well, I think I'm getting sentimental in my old age," Rusty chuckled.

Claire watched their exchange and glanced at Maggie, knowing they both were wondering the same thing about Hannah and Rusty. When they lived at the ranch, they could tell she had a soft spot for him and learned they had been good friends for nearly two decades.

"Why, they're beautiful!" Hannah exclaimed as she pulled out two matching gold hair combs. "But where am I supposed to put these?"

"In your hair, of course!" Rusty laughed.

"Rusty, I've been wearing my hair in a single braid for longer than I can remember, and I'm too old to start trying something different."

"I think they'd look real pretty," Claire spoke up, sending Rusty a smile.

"There, you see," Rusty said with a wink in Claire's direction. "I've got one lady's approval."

"Mine, too," Maggie added. "I'll even show you how to put

them in," she offered Hannah, who was shaking her head and trying not to smile.

"Mine's not as thoughtful as all theirs," Will spoke up. "But Hannah, as soon as you want that new material for the curtains you've been talking about, just say the word."

"That sounds just fine; thank you, Will." She looked at each of them. "And thank you all for your gifts." She came to her feet, trying to swallow down the emotion she felt at being so loved. "Now, let's eat this cake!"

After they ate the cake, Rusty left, and Claire offered to help Hannah with the dishes.

"How are things working out at Jacob's?" Will asked Maggie as they found themselves alone.

"Good," she smiled. "I just love Lilly and Lucas."

"I know they're fond of you, too."

"Did you know the Reverend's wife?" Maggie asked.

"I did. She was pretty wonderful," he said. "It's been difficult watching Jacob go through his grief."

Maggie sighed. "I'm sure."

"I'm glad you've been able to help him out with the kids. I know he really appreciates it."

Maggie smiled thoughtfully. "It's been good for me, too."

"Can I ask you something? Is Claire alright? She doesn't seem herself lately."

"I thought the same thing, too," Maggie said. "I told her to go back to her normal shift of working in the day, and I think she did, so that might help."

"Why is she so stubborn about working at the hotel?"

Maggie hesitated before she answered. Ever since the night that she had given her life to the Lord, she had felt even more convicted about the money they took. She also felt compunction about not telling their friends the truth and for not turning themselves in. She prayed inwardly for a moment for the right answer and then heard herself say, "I think in time, you'll understand."

Will thought her words cryptic but could only hope she was right. "In the meantime," he said, "I ran into Mrs. Murry this week, and she mentioned that she was in need of some help at her dress shop." Will glanced past Maggie toward the hall to make sure Claire wasn't in earshot. "Claire wouldn't take kindly to me interfering, but could you say something to her about it?"

Maggie nodded, thinking Claire had found quite a friend in Will Carter. "I will, and I'll even make sure she looks into it."

Chapter Twenty-Two

"Claire, is that you?"

Claire closed the door behind her as she entered Lyddie's and moved down the hall toward the sound of Lyddie's voice coming from the dining room. It was the following day.

"It's me," Claire replied. "I was just out for a walk."

"There was a parcel dropped off for you. I saw it on the front porch when I came back from the general store. It's just on that table there."

Claire thanked her and moved toward the side table she had mentioned. The rather large box simply had her name on it, and Claire took it to her room, feeling apprehensive about its contents. She was growing wary of Bruce Conway's gifts. Sitting it on the bed, she sighed and slowly lifted the lid off.

A smile immediately parted her lips when she saw the brown, leather, wide-brimmed hat inside. Gently, she lifted it out of the box, remembering Will telling her more than once that she needed a hat. She moved to the vanity, placed the hat on her head, and looked back at her reflection. It fit perfectly. Will's face came to her mind, and she wondered if he had sent someone to drop it off or if he was still in town. Instinctively, she glanced out the window that overlooked the street, hoping to catch a glimpse of him.

The memory of his expression when he had seen her in the saloon still played over in her mind. For some reason, she hated the thought of disappointing him or meeting his disapproval. What would his reaction be if she told him that she had spent a year working in a saloon and then stabbed a man before burglarizing his jewelry shop?

Claire took off the hat and laid it carefully back in the box. Looking down at it, she felt a familiar sense of despondency. Things weren't turning out the way she had planned. It had been a foolish idea to steal from Frederick Harris. She knew that now and scolded herself for acting on an impulse and out of her own desperation of the moment. But there was no going back, and from her current vantage point, there didn't seem to be a clear path moving forward, either.

"I'd like you to join me for dinner tonight."

Claire froze at the hotel door, turning slowly to face Bruce Conway, who had just walked out of his office. It was the following day, at five o'clock, and she had just been about to leave.

"I have plans," she lied to him.

"I think not."

Claire felt indignation rising in her chest. "I don't like feeling like you own me."

"But as long as I keep your secret, I do, don't I?"

Claire felt hot tears welling in her eyes. The tone of his voice made her want to just turn herself in and be done with the secrets and blackmail.

Bruce walked across the lobby to where she stood and seemed to sense her thoughts as he said, "Don't get ahead of yourself, Claire."

A Debt to Pay

She hated hearing him say her name. She wanted to leave, but he took her arms and turned her completely to face him as one would do with a child. "I'm not going to hurt you," he said, but the hungry look in his eyes didn't match his words. "All I'm asking for is dinner."

Claire lowered her gaze and nodded slightly. She breathed a sigh of relief when he'd let go of her and moved away.

"I'll pick you up at seven," he called over his shoulder.

Claire fought tears the whole walk home, feeling she had left Chicago for freedom only to be enslaved all over again. There had to be another way. It was only a matter of time until that poster found its way into someone else's hands. As she walked past the jail, she actually considered just walking through the door and turning herself into the sheriff. She could take full responsibility for the burglary so Maggie wouldn't be implicated. Maggie had tried to talk her out of it, after all. The sudden idea of having to face Frederick Harris made her skin crawl. He would be anything but merciful.

She knew Bruce Conway wouldn't stop until he got what he wanted, and she only hoped she could find a way out before it came to that. A bracelet, a dress, dinner, these were things she could handle, but if he asked for more…

Claire reached Lyddie's and walked to the backyard, where she leaned up against the wall of the house and tried not to be sick. The very idea of being at Conway's beck and call made her feel physically ill. If only she hadn't involved Maggie, she could just pick up and ride out of here in the middle of the night. Now, if she left, all the blame would fall on Maggie once the secret was let out. Maybe she should tell Maggie they had been discovered and ask her to leave with her. Claire sighed, knowing Maggie's heart would break at the thought of leaving Lilly and Lucas and Jacob Myles.

Inhaling a shaky breath, Claire told herself she would figure something out. A few hours later, as she made her way outside to meet Bruce Conway, she was still talking herself out of a state of panic. She kept reminding herself it was just dinner.

―――

"Where's Claire?" Maggie asked Lyddie. She had spent dinner at Reverend Myles's house and, upon returning, had gone to her bedroom expecting to find Claire.

"She said she was going out to dinner with Bruce Conway." Lyddie shook her head with a frown and then shrugged. "I don't understand what a sweet girl like your sister would see in the likes of him."

Her words alarmed Maggie. "I don't understand, either," Maggie said, but she was determined to get to the bottom of it.

―――

"How is your steak?"

"Good."

"You've barely had more than a bite."

"I'm just not very hungry," Claire told him, adjusting the white napkin on her lap. The Millcreek Restaurant was at the edge of town and wasn't as busy as usual that Friday evening. Claire glanced around the medium-sized room with its round tables and higher-end table settings.

"You know, I've never been one to believe in fate, but I'm starting to." He drained the rest of his whiskey and called the waiter over for another.

"The reason I asked you to dinner tonight was because I wanted to talk to you about your future."

A Debt to Pay

Claire looked him evenly in the eyes. "My future?"

"Why, yes. You see, Claire, I don't just hold weight in this community, but I can be very persuasive. I've had to bend some rules, make some compromises to get where I am today. Let's just say I'm no stranger to dodging the law. Someone like me could be very useful to you. We probably have more in common than you realize."

"I'm not like you, Mr. Conway."

"Aren't you? You put on airs, but I don't think you're as innocent as you pretend to be."

Claire averted his gaze, feeling the meaning of his words. "I may have worked at a saloon, but if you think…"

"I'd like you to consider becoming my wife."

Claire's eyes shot up to his, completely taken back. "You can't be serious."

"Why not?" He leaned back in his chair. "Every man needs to settle down at some point. I think I could be quite content with you," he added, a smirk on his face.

Claire couldn't believe he was even suggesting such a ridiculous thing. She leaned slightly forward, glancing around the room quickly to make sure no one would hear her. "I've gone along with this because I don't know what else to do and I needed to buy more time. But I'll think of something, and when I do…"

"Claire, you only have two options. You keep running from the law, or you let me help you work around it." He saw the look on her face and smiled as tenderly as he could. "I'm not as ruthless as folks might think I am. In time, you may actually come to enjoy my company."

"I highly doubt that," Claire replied.

Bruce chuckled. "I'd like you to consider my offer, nonetheless. If you married me, I would do everything in my power to protect you."

Claire slid her hand out from beneath his as he laid it gently over hers. "It's getting late," she said quietly.

"Very well." He tossed a few bills on the table and pushed his chair back. Standing, he followed her to the door. As they stepped outside into the night, he came up alongside her and offered his arm.

Reluctantly, she took it and let him lead her to his buckboard. They sat in silence as he drove her back to the boarding house. Once there, he jumped down and came around to help her. With his hands still lingering on hers, he turned her to face him. "I've been patient with you, Claire, but I'm not a man to be trifled with." When she adverted his gaze, he took her chin between his thumb and finger and forced her to look at him. "Don't pretend like you're too good for me."

Claire squirmed uncomfortably and tried unsuccessfully to turn her head when she saw him leaning toward her. She could smell the alcohol on his breath as he pressed his lips to hers.

Pushing him away, she stumbled backward. "Don't ever do that again!" she warned before turning and running up the stairs to Lyddie's porch. Once inside, she quietly closed the door and released a shaky breath. She forced herself to regain composure before she saw Maggie.

"Claire!"

Claire almost jumped at Maggie's voice as Maggie stepped out into the hall from the front parlor.

"I didn't know you were down here," Claire said.

Maggie's hands came to her hips, and, for a moment, she looked like a mother about to scold her daughter for being out too late. "What on earth are you doing going out with that man?"

"It was just dinner," Claire replied as she headed for the stairs.

"What's going on, Claire?"

Maggie followed her, determined to get some sort of answer. Once in their room, she tried again. "Claire, I'm your friend, remember? Please tell me what's going on between you and Bruce Conway."

"Nothing!" Claire returned a little sharper than she had intended. She reached behind herself and unlaced the back of her dress.

"Then why are you spending time with him?"

"He just wanted to talk about…some things with his hotel business."

"I can tell when you're lying," Maggie said. She paused and then asked her if she knew who Mrs. Murry was.

Claire tossed her dress over a chair and slipped into her nightgown. "The dress shop owner?"

"Yes. I found out she's looking for someone to work in her shop. It could be an alternative to working at the hotel. You should look into it."

"I doubt she pays as much."

"But you wouldn't have to work with Bruce Conway. That's got to be worth a pay cut!"

Claire sighed as she sat at the vanity and took the pins out of her hair. "I have a job, Maggie."

Frustrated, Maggie went to stand behind her and looked at her in the mirror. "If I didn't know any better, I'd think you wanted to work there. I'm even tempted to think you're enjoying Bruce Conway's attention!"

Claire slammed the brush on the vanity. "Maybe I do! Is that what you want to hear?"

Maggie stepped back as Claire stood and moved to the bed. She was shocked by Claire's answer and told herself it couldn't be true. "Claire, there has to…"

"Leave me be, Maggie. I don't want to talk about it."

Maggie walked slowly to turn down the lamp and crawled into bed. She knew something wasn't right and found herself praying silently long before she finally fell asleep.

Chapter Twenty-Three

From inside the hotel, Claire heard the stage rumbling down the street the next afternoon and knew she had about an hour before it left again. She hadn't seen Bruce Conway all day and hoped he would continue to make himself scarce. Claire hoped that if there was anyone getting off the stage and checking into the hotel, they would do it soon. She was grateful when a couple soon walked in and asked for a room. She got them situated and then sought out Sarah, who she found hanging wet laundry in the backyard.

"Sarah, I have to step out for a few minutes. If someone wants to check in while I'm gone, can you tell them I'll be back shortly?"

Sarah nodded and told her she'd listen out for the desk bell.

Claire felt her heart starting to race as she crossed the street and headed to the spot where she and Vivian had planned to meet. She sighed with relief when she saw the girl already there, a small suitcase in her hand. The bonnet she had on helped to hide the bruise and swelling that still lingered on her cheek.

"I don't know about this," Vivian said once Claire was near. "If Trent sees me leaving, I'm afraid he'll thrash me."

"He's not going to stop you," Claire said, confidence rising in her. "I'll get you on that stage no matter what."

"What about Mr. Conway? I signed an agreement, Claire."

"You leave him to me," Claire assured her. "Now, take this."

Vivian looked down at the dollar bills Claire pressed into her hands. "I can't take your money."

"It's not much, but just in case you need it to get home."

Vivian's eyes filled with tears. "If they could, my parents would thank you."

"Let's get you to that stage." Claire led her behind the hotel and along a back street that wound past a few houses and shops. The last thing she wanted was for Trent to look out of the saloon or wherever he was and spot her.

The stage was parked at the side of the general store, which was across from Lyddie's, so Claire's plan was to wait with Vivian in Lyddie's backyard until the stage was ready to go. The driver of the coach watered his horses and was waiting for new passengers when Claire walked up with Vivian.

The man tossed Vivian's suitcase into the back hatch of the coach and opened the door for her to climb in. Once inside, Vivian leaned out the window. "Thank you so much, Claire."

"You take care of yourself, Vivian."

The girl nodded, her heart in her eyes. The driver waited a few more minutes and then, after glancing at his watch, climbed to his seat and grabbed the reins. Claire followed the coach as it headed down the street, feeling like she was holding her breath until she saw it turn right and pass the saloon, the mill, and then disappear behind the bend. Vivian was safe now.

She had almost reached the hotel when she saw Bruce Conway walking quickly toward her from the direction of

A Debt to Pay

the saloon. A wagon blocked his path for a moment, but they still reached the hotel at nearly the same moment.

"Have you seen Vivian?" he asked.

Claire could hear the anxiousness in his voice. She lifted her gaze and looked past him toward the road that led away from town. Bruce turned around, noting the dust that still lingered in the air from the stagecoach.

"Was she on the stage?"

"You can't find her?" Claire asked, but there was a glint of pleasure in her eyes that Bruce noticed right away. He reached out and grabbed her arm.

"You helped her, didn't you?"

"You asked me to, remember?" she replied with a feigned expression of confusion on her face. She tried to yank her arm free, but he wouldn't loosen his grasp. Looking at him angrily, she said, "You knew she hadn't fallen down the stairs that night!"

Claire was shocked when Bruce suddenly pulled her into the hotel with so much force that she nearly fell over. Once inside, he pulled her across the lobby and then pushed her against his office door.

"You had no right to interfere like that!"

Claire struggled to break free from his hold, frightened by the look of rage in his eyes. Until that moment, she had never been afraid of him. "Let go of me!"

"You think you can do whatever you want!" He nudged her a little harder against the wall. "I'm the boss! I'm the one in charge!"

"Mr. Conway," Claire's voice was pleading, desperate. "Bruce...please let go of me!"

"I've tried to be kind to you!" he said through clenched teeth, his face pressed close to hers. "How dare you go behind my back! Who do you think you are?"

Claire winced as he gripped each of her arms tighter in his hands and pushed her harder into the door. "From now on, you'll do what I say!"

The back of his hand came across her face so suddenly it knocked Claire to the ground. Bruce was taken off guard as well when someone suddenly grabbed his arm from behind and whirled him around just in time to see the fist coming toward his face.

Will would have planted another punch but was too concerned for Claire. He helped her to her feet and kept his arm around her as they walked to the door. Then, before he left, he covered the distance between himself and Bruce Conway, who was just getting to his feet. Grabbing him by the shirt, Will slammed him against the wall so hard Claire was surprised the door didn't break.

"You touch her again, and I'll beat you within an inch of your life!"

"You think you know her," Bruce mumbled, blood running out his nose and down his mouth. "She's not what you think!"

Will clenched his jaw and delivered a final punch to Bruce's gut before meeting Claire at the door and leading her outside. His horse was waiting nearby, and without a word to Claire, Will helped her mount and then climbed up behind her. "You're coming with me," he told her in no uncertain terms.

Claire felt too shaken up to argue and had no reason to, anyway. A few minutes later, she let her back rest against his chest, welcoming the strength of his arms around her. No words were spoken the entire ride, and once at the ranch, Will dismounted from behind her and then helped her down before gently taking her arm and leading her into the house.

"Hannah's not here right now," he spoke for the first time since they'd left the hotel. "I'll be right back; why don't you go sit in the front room," he said, already steering her toward the doorway.

Claire did just what he said, going to the sofa by the window. Will returned just a moment later, a cold, wet cloth in his hands. "Put this on your cheek to keep it from swelling."

Claire held it onto her face, wincing at the throbbing pain.

"Claire, what's going on? What makes him think he can do that to you?"

"It's complicated."

"I don't care. I want to know. Claire..." he waited until he had her gaze. "Please, tell me what's going on."

Claire opened her mouth to try to tell him, but something seemed to choke the words from her. She'd lose his respect and his friendship the moment he learned about her past and about all she had done. Jared's words from months ago echoed in her mind: *the thing Will Carter couldn't stand for was a liar and a thief.* And here she was, both of those things.

"I just can't, Will." Her voice broke.

"I thought we were friends, Claire." He shook his head, a look of confusion in his eyes. "Don't you know you can trust me?"

Claire released a shaky breath. How could she explain without explaining? "Conway knows something about Maggie that he's threatened to expose unless I do what he says." Claire felt sick inside the moment she said it, but it was the only way she could see to make him half understand.

A sense of understanding dawned on Will's face. "I understand your love for Maggie, but you can't live under this another day. I won't let you."

Claire shifted her gaze, feeling overwhelmed by what

seemed like love coming from his eyes. Did Will Carter love her? It seemed impossible she could have gained love from a man like him.

"His behavior is inexcusable, Claire. He's dangerous!"

"There was a young woman working at the saloon that I helped quit and get on the stage today. That's what he was upset about when you came into the hotel."

The fact that Claire would do something like that just made him admire her more. "She's the woman you were helping at the saloon that night?"

Claire nodded. "I'd never met her before the other night. The man she was with had beaten her, and Bruce asked me to patch her up. He wouldn't get the doctor, so I had to help her."

"He keeps his distance from the doc for a reason. Years ago, Conway nearly ruined Doc Fletcher's daughter. Thankfully, she escaped him and doesn't live around here anymore."

It all made sense now why Conway wouldn't let her go for the doctor on both occasions that he had needed him.

"I'm glad you helped her get away!" Will said, the muscles in his jaw jumping in vexation.

"Me, too."

Will felt his blood boil, thinking what might have happened today had he not come when he did. He had been at the livery when he caught sight of Bruce Conway roughly pulling Claire into the hotel.

"I'm going to talk to Conway, Claire. I'll work this out."

Claire felt unnerved at the thought. She reached out her hand on his. "Please, Will. Don't do that. It will only make things worse, trust me. I'll tell Maggie he knows, and we'll figure this out."

Will suddenly felt distracted by her nearness and the

warmth of her hand on his. The desire to protect her was almost overwhelming.

"You've been so kind, Will. I wish you knew how much I appreciate it." And then something very unexpected came over her, and before she knew what was happening, she leaned forward and gently placed a kiss on his lips. It wasn't longer than a second, but she felt her heart pounding all the same. She quickly pulled away and came to her feet. "I'm so sorry," she said, embarrassed.

Will was on his feet as well. "Please don't apologize," he said quietly, taking her hands. "I'm the one who should be apologizing."

Claire looked up at him, her eyes puzzled. "For what?"

"For not kissing you first."

Claire's eyes widened a bit and then closed when she felt his lips on hers. It was a good deal longer than her kiss, and when he lifted his head, she felt a warmth settling in her heart that she'd never experienced before.

"Claire, I think I'm in love with you."

He whispered the words, but they seemed to echo loudly. "I think I'm in love with you, too." When she said it, she meant it with every fiber of her being, but then the reality of how much she was hiding from him snapped her out of her dreamlike state. "I should go."

"Not yet. I don't want you anywhere near that man."

Claire looked down and realized his hands were still holding hers.

"You should rest a little longer and keep that cold compress on her cheek."

Claire nodded and sat back down, still a little taken back that Will had just kissed her and told her he loved her.

Will sat back down beside her. "Claire, promise me you'll

stay away from Bruce Conway." He saw a look on her face that made him worry.

"I can't promise anything until I know Maggie is safe."

"I don't want Maggie or you to be hurt, but someone's got to put an end to this, and I'm glad to be the one to do it. He can't keep blackmailing you."

Claire wasn't sure what would happen now, with Bruce furious with her. As far as she knew, he had already decided to let the sheriff arrest her. When she returned to town, she could be met with the prospect of a jail cell. She knew she had to tell Will the truth but try as she might, the words just wouldn't come. Claire could feel Will's warm gaze on her and met his eyes. "I just need a little time to talk to Maggie and sort this out."

He nodded. "Alright, as long as you sort it out as far from that hotel and that man as possible. If I knew we could trust Sheriff Dunley, I'd go to him right now and have Bruce locked up for assaulting you."

"No, we can't go to the sheriff," Claire said as she felt panic rising in her.

"Well, just let me help you in any way I can," Will offered, gently squeezing her hand.

Claire looked away, worried that her eyes would give away all the guilt she felt inside. "Thanks, Will," she replied, knowing there was actually nothing he could do to help.

Jacob finished washing the dishes and hung the dishcloth over the back of a chair. Lilly and Lucas were waiting for him in the front yard since he had told them he'd take them fishing after lunch that Saturday.

"Ready, Pa?" Lilly asked.

A Debt to Pay

"Just about." Jacob grabbed the fishing poles that were leaning against the house. "You got the bait?" Jacob asked Lucas, still holding a small pail full of worms Jacob had shown him an hour ago.

"Someone's coming," Lilly said, lifting her hand to her eyes against the bright sun.

Maggie prayed under her breath the entire way to Jacob Myles' house. She knew what she was about to do was the right thing, but it was also terrifying. Since coming to the Lord, her heart had become softer than she had ever thought possible. With that new capacity to forgive those who had hurt her in the past came a new sensitivity to right and wrong.

As she rode into the yard, she waved back at Lilly and Lucas. Jacob reached for Willow's bridle to steady her as Maggie dismounted. She immediately saw the fishing rods in his hands. "I'm sorry, you all are on your way out."

"That's OK. Is there something you needed?"

Maggie bit her lip, feeling a little embarrassed for just coming by. "I just wanted to talk to you about something," she said to Jacob. "I can come back."

"Nonsense, come with us," Jacob invited. "We can talk while they play."

"Alright."

Jacob led Willow to the pasture and then came back, and they all walked together to the pond. It wasn't a far walk, and soon Jacob was helping to bait the fishhooks. Maggie sat down on the grass and smiled as she watched the children waiting with excitement for a fish to bite their line. She glanced around at the open field dotted with trees and wildflowers. A late summer breeze rustled in the large oak tree just beside them, making a melodic sound in the leaves.

Jacob sat next to her, bending his knees and leaning back on his hands. "So, what's on your mind?"

"Well, it's something that might take me a while to explain," Maggie told him, suddenly feeling a wave of dread wash over her. "And it's something I can't let the children overhear."

Jacob nodded, taking in the seriousness of her expression. "Just go ahead and start, and if it takes a while, it's OK."

Maggie took a steady breath. "I've told Lilly good things I remember about my mother because there were some good things, but the truth is she drank all the time and pined for my father, who had left us when I was around three years old. When I was around ten, he wrote to us from Chicago, and we moved there to be with him." Maggie shook her head as if to expel the memory still fresh in her mind. "My mother was so happy to finally know where he was and that he seemed to want us again. She stopped drinking for a few months when they were back together, but then…" Maggie quickly went on, trying to finish before she cried. "She realized he wasn't at all the man she had been missing all those years. He was out late almost every night and had a lifestyle that involved relationships with many other women." She paused, hoping she hadn't shocked him too much. "It broke my mother, whose health was already failing. The doctor said she died of pneumonia, but I knew she really died of a broken heart."

"How old were you when she died?"

"Sixteen."

Jacob looked at her, puzzled. "You said you and Claire moved here shortly after your parents' death?"

Maggie turned her gaze to him, her eyes begging for

forgiveness. "That was a lie. We aren't even sisters. We just thought it would be easier to say that and to keep our story simple. You see, after I lost my mother, I was so lonely and confused and hurting that I…I let myself become involved with a man who, I realized too late, was just like my father. He promised he'd take care of me, and I thought he loved me, so I moved in with him. I realized too late that the house he owned wasn't a home at all. It wasn't long before I just became another one of the girls who worked there."

She lowered her head and felt tears drop out of her eyes and fall to the grass. "I'm so ashamed of my past, but hiding it feels like keeping it alive somehow. I kept praying and praying, and finally, I felt like I was supposed to tell someone. I thought maybe if I was honest, it wouldn't feel so…dark."

Jacob was quiet, so quiet Maggie started to think she had made a mistake in sharing all of that. But then she felt his hand gently touch her shoulder and compel her to look at him. "That's because the Lord has made you new, Maggie. Bringing your past to the light is being truthful, and remember Jesus said the truth would set you free."

Maggie wiped the tears from her cheeks and gave a watery smile. "That's what I want." Just seeing the kindness in his eyes brought overwhelming relief. She cleared her throat and gave a shaky sigh, knowing she had to finish before she talked herself out of it. "There is more."

"Pa! I think I caught one!" Lilly called from the bank of the pond.

"Don't go anywhere," Jacob told Maggie as he came to his feet. "I'll be right back."

Maggie watched as he helped Lilly and Lucas for a few minutes and tried to rehearse how she was going to tell him about the robbery. She silently thanked the Lord for helping Jacob not hate her so far and prayed he wouldn't reject her after he knew about the robbery.

"People think because I'm a minister, I have a clean track record."

Jacob had just rejoined her and surprised her with these words. "Before I met the Lord, my life was a series of broken relationships, sin, and self-hatred. The war didn't help either. It had already been going on for two years when I enlisted. After it was over, I spent years trying to numb the horrors that I saw and the mistakes that I made with alcohol and just about anything else I could find. Pain causes people to do things that lead to more pain, and the cycle just keeps repeating."

Maggie met his gaze and saw a vulnerability she'd never seen before. "You seem so far along in the Lord, it's hard to imagine."

"That's because when He forgives your sins and gives you a new start, the old really does pass away."

Maggie smiled softly. "I know what you mean, and I'm so grateful."

"You said there was more?" he asked quietly.

"Yes." Maggie sat up a little straighter. "Claire isn't my sister, but she is the best friend I've ever had. After a few years of working in that house, I knew I had to get away, so I found a job across town working in a saloon." She glanced up at Jacob. "I know it sounds ridiculous to think a saloon was any better, but it was. I only had to sell drinks there."

Jacob nodded, his expression one of understanding. He knew exactly what she was implying.

"That saloon was where I met Claire. She came a few years after I had been there, and one night, she told me she was running away and asked if I would come with her. She stole the keys from a man who owned a jewelry shop, and… well…we robbed the shop so we would have enough money to travel and start a new life."

Maggie held her breath, waiting for him to at least scold her or show some sort of disapproval.

"I'm so sorry."

She looked at him in astonishment. Why was he apologizing?

"I know that's not something you wanted to do, but you felt like there was no other way to escape your situation."

"It was still wrong," Maggie said, "And even though our intention was to pay it back, the jewelry was destroyed in the fire."

"Wow," he sighed. "I can't imagine how difficult it's been for you two."

Maggie was floored that he would be so sympathetic. "Thank you for being so kind about all this, Jacob."

"I don't have any right to throw a stone, Maggie."

His words reminded her of the service when he shared that story from the Bible. It had meant so much for her to hear that story, and it was the first time she considered the possibility of the Lord forgiving her, too.

"I wanted to tell you sooner, but I was afraid you wouldn't want me around Lilly and Lucas."

"Well, I appreciate you telling me now. And it doesn't change the way I feel about you." He meant in terms of their friendship, but as he said the words, something else dawned on him. He didn't want her to ever leave their family again. Perhaps he had felt that way all along and just never allowed himself to realize it. Maybe that was the real reason he had sent her away. He was afraid he was falling in love with her.

Looking at her now, he knew it was true. The thought of loving another woman after Rose felt unfaithful, even as ridiculous as that sounded. He felt the wrestling inside his own heart as he finally admitted to himself that he was falling in love with Maggie.

"I should help Lucas," Jacob said, suddenly coming to his feet. "Looks like his line is tangled."

Maggie nodded, unaware of the thoughts and feelings he was grappling with. "Looks like Lilly could use some help, too," she said. "I don't know the first thing about fishing, but I'll see if I can help."

"What happened to you?"

Bruce Conway looked at Sheriff Dunley as he took the seat opposite him at one of the tables in the saloon. "Will Carter's what happened," he replied, instinctively touching his swollen face. "About an hour ago."

Sheriff Dunley's eyes narrowed. "What sort of trouble you get in with him?"

Bruce lit the cigar he'd pulled out of his vest pocket. "He just stuck his nose in where it didn't belong." He sucked his cigar and exhaled as he leaned back in his chair. "I hate that man."

"I hate his brother, too," Sheriff Dunley said. He leaned forward. "Which is why I wanted to talk to you."

"Go on."

"I found out he's been seen 'round Jefferson City. I aim to head there first thing tomorrow."

"Good." Bruce drank the glass of whiskey the bartender had brought him and then leaned forward and looked pointedly at the sheriff. "If we're dealing with gold, I'd like to come with you."

A Debt to Pay

"You saying you don't trust me to make an equal split?"
"That's exactly what I'm saying."

Claire felt like she was holding her breath when Will drove her back into town near evening. She half expected the sheriff to be waiting for her when she got back to Lyddie's.

"A letter was dropped off for you," Lyddie called to Claire from down the hall when she saw her come into the house. "It's on the table by the door."

Claire grabbed it quickly and ran up to her room, hoping Lyddie wouldn't see the bruise on her face.

Once in her room, Claire curiously opened the envelope and removed the folded paper from inside. She glanced first to the bottom and saw Bruce Conway's name before reading it from the beginning.

Dear Claire,
I have to leave town for a few days. You have that long to decide if you will become my wife or choose the other prospect.

Bruce Conway.

"Ugh!" Claire ripped the letter up and threw it in the waste basket. "What a detestable man!" she said to her empty room. The door suddenly opened, and Claire turned around to see Maggie.

"Claire, your face! What happened?"
"I'm fine, Maggie. It's nothing."
"Nothing?" Maggie put her hands on her waist, a determined look on her face. "You're going to tell me right now what's going on, Claire. There's something you're keeping from me; I just know it!"

Claire sat slowly on the bed, nodding her head in agreement. "I was actually planning on telling you today."

"I knew there was something." Maggie pulled a wooden chair from a corner to the bed so she could sit and face Claire. "Alright, out with it."

"Bruce Conway found out about us. He showed me a wanted poster."

Maggie gasped. "Oh no, Claire."

"He promised to keep quiet about it and stay on our side if I went along with whatever he wanted."

Maggie's hand shot to her mouth. "You didn't."

"I did, but it didn't get as far as you're thinking. And he just left for a few days, so we have a little time to think." Claire sighed. "He said he'll keep our secret and do everything he can to keep us out of jail if I marry him."

"Well, we know that's out of the question!" Maggie had come to her feet and was pacing the floor. "Oh, Claire, I'm so sorry you were carrying this alone! Everything makes sense now, and I feel horrible. You should have told me!"

"It didn't make sense to upset you with it; besides, it was my idea to steal the jewelry in the first place."

"I'm the one who goofed and kept the necklace."

"There's more." Claire took a deep breath. "It's not just robbery we're wanted for; it's attempted murder."

Maggie's jaw dropped for a full five seconds. "No! How could he accuse us of that? It was obviously self-defense!"

"Maybe the men who carried his body to the doctors will speak in our defense. If I had wanted to murder him, I wouldn't have helped him to the doctor!"

"Exactly!" Maggie had come to her feet and was still pacing the length of the room.

"We've got to do something. I just don't know what."

A Debt to Pay

"I think we need to turn ourselves in," Maggie said. She had been feeling it for a while and was glad to finally speak it out.

"Before we have the money to pay it back? I feel like the charge would be lessened if we voluntarily pay back the money first."

Maggie nodded. "We can't do anything about the necklace, but we could give everything we have."

"I wanted to wait until we had the entire one hundred dollars, but I'll mail what we have tomorrow," Claire said decidedly, thinking that she'd have even less now with what money she had given Vivian.

"It may not help, but let's include an apology letter to Frederick Harris and tell him we'll keep paying until the necklace is paid off."

Claire gave her a doubtful expression. "It'll probably come to nothing, but I guess we can try."

The following day, Will looked for Claire at church but wasn't surprised not to see her after the ordeal she had had the day before. After the service, he and Hannah left in the buckboard and went to the boarding house to invite Claire to join them for lunch at the ranch.

"I'm going after Grady again," he told Claire on the way there. His recent visits to the saloon had given him the information he was looking for concerning Grady's whereabouts.

"I'm not sure how long it will take, so I wanted to spend some time with you before I go," he told her.

The way he looked at her made her heart feel so full and so scared all at once. She wanted more than anything to spend time with him, especially after what had transpired between them the previous day. At the same time, she felt the turmoil of not being able to be honest with him. She knew she couldn't go on like this and suddenly resolved that today, when they were together, she would tell him.

As they were about to enter the house, Hannah noticed an envelope wedged in the front door. "Not sure what this is," she said, handing it to him. "But your name is on it."

Once inside, Hannah headed to the kitchen while Will led Claire into the front room. He watched as she sat on the sofa and thought back to their kiss the previous day. Her gaze found his eyes, and she smiled, as if knowing what he was thinking about. Still looking at her, he absently opened the envelope and pulled out the contents.

He was still looking at Claire when he unfolded it, and then his eyes fell on the paper in his hands. His heart slammed against his chest, and for a full ten seconds, he just stared at it. Finally, he looked up to find Claire looking at him with a concerned expression.

"What is this?"

"What do you mean?" Claire asked as she stood up and took a few steps toward him.

"You and Maggie are wanted for robbery and attempted murder?" He turned the wanted poster around to face her.

Claire could hear the disbelief in his tone as much as she saw it in his eyes. She felt immediately lightheaded and like her heart was in her throat. "Will, I..." She couldn't even find the words.

"I thought you were being honest with me yesterday."

"I was, partly. I was afraid to tell you the truth. But I was working up the courage, and today I was..."

"And the kiss? Was that the part of you being honest or the part of you lying?"

A Debt to Pay

Claire thought she'd never seen anyone look so betrayed. "Of course, that was real."

"Now it makes even more sense why Conway had such power over you. It wasn't just Maggie you were protecting; it was yourself." He looked at the poster again, reading its entirety, and then looked up at her. "Says you were last seen working at a Chicago saloon?" He immediately recalled her slip-up that day he had talked with her in town.

Claire nodded reluctantly, hearing the disappointment in his tone. "I wasn't there very long," she said, although she knew it wouldn't help. "It's where I met Maggie."

"I guess that part about you being sisters was a lie, too."

"We just thought it would make things easier."

"I guess this is why you never want to talk about your past. Is anything you've told me true?"

"Will, I wanted so many times to tell you the truth."

"Then why didn't you?"

"Because I know what you think of thieves, and I didn't want you to think badly of me."

Will looked at the poster again, shaking his head in astonishment. "Attempted murder?" He looked over at her and exhaled a heavy breath as if it was too much.

"I didn't try to murder anyone, and that's the truth! It was self-defense. He came into my room and would have..." Claire sighed with frustration, wishing she could make him understand. "He came at me, and I stabbed him."

"It says here a reward of three hundred dollars? How much did you steal? I just can't believe you're capable of this." He shook his head in disbelief. "I really don't know you at all, do I?"

Claire took a step toward him, hoping desperately that he would understand. She gently reached up and touched his arm, her eyes finding his. "Will, from now on, I won't keep any more secrets."

"I'm sure you had to go to great lengths for Conway to keep your secrets."

Claire knew exactly what he was implying and felt her cheeks become red and hot. She pulled her hand away as if she'd been burned. "No. It never came to anything like that."

"Considering your past work experience, that's a little hard to believe."

Claire could hardly stand the weight of his disapproval. "I didn't want you to know about my past because I wanted to start over and be known for who I am, not who I was."

"Is there even a difference between the two?"

Claire wouldn't have felt more injured if he had physically hit her. She ran out of the room and out of the house. It suddenly dawned on her that she had no way back to town. That's when she spotted Jared. He was already astride his horse by the barn and rode over when he saw her running away from the house.

"You alright, Claire?" he asked, seeing that she was crying.

"I just need a ride back to town," she told him in between sobs.

He immediately extended his hand and helped hoist her up behind him in the saddle. "I'll get you back," he told her, wondering what had happened to make her so upset.

Hannah had been coming down the hall when she saw Claire run out the front door. She walked into the parlor, looking at Will for answers. "What on earth just happened?"

Will sighed as he handed her the poster. "The usual. I've just been played for a fool."

Hannah watched as he left the room and then looked at what he had handed her. Shaking her head in disbelief, she

A Debt to Pay

slumped into a chair. There had to be more to it than what the poster portrayed. She suddenly remembered her conversation with Claire on the front porch a few weeks ago. Maybe this is what she had been working up the nerve to tell her.

Once back at the boarding house, Claire packed her things as fast as she could. She wanted to be gone before Maggie got back. She wouldn't mail the money like they had talked about; rather, she would return to Chicago and give the money to him herself. Then, she would turn herself in as the only one who robbed the store. That would get Maggie off the hook, and Claire felt that, finally, both of them would be free of this lie.

Stopping at the dresser, Claire scribbled a quick note to Maggie and left it sitting upright so she would see it. She slipped downstairs unnoticed and out the door, where she moved as fast as she could toward the livery. She reasoned after she reached the next town, she could take Willow to the livery there, where she'd be safe until Jared or Will could go and pick her up. She explained as much to Eli Greene and asked him to make sure they went to get her within a few days.

Once she had Willow saddled, Claire shoved her things into the saddle bag and mounted her quickly. Then she rode as fast as she could out of Millcreek, not looking back toward the town that held all the people she loved.

Will wasn't sure where he was going; he just knew he needed to get out. His mind felt like it was racing as fast as his horse was, the ground being torn up underneath him.

He had felt so close to Claire, like he could trust her, like he could love her. When they'd kissed yesterday, any question of his feelings for her had been answered. It was extremely discouraging to realize that the kiss probably meant nothing to her, that it had most likely been an attempt to distract him from prying into her secret past. She had worked in a saloon, so of course, she had experience with flirting and enticing men. Bruce Conway's face popped into his mind and made him angrier. Claire had said their relationship never crossed a line, but with them working so close, how could he be sure?

After a few hours, Will circled around the east pasture and realized he was close to Jacob's house. Feeling he needed to talk to someone, Will rode toward his house, hoping something Jacob would say would help him get his emotions under control.

Will knocked on the door and then stepped back, waiting for Jacob to answer.

"Will," Jacob smiled when he answered the door. "What brings you here?"

"I need to talk to someone."

Jacob noticed the upset look in his eyes. "No problem. Give me one second." He turned around and told his kids to stay in the house. Then, stepping outside, he fell into step next to Will as they walked a short distance away from the house.

"What's wrong, Will?"

Will suddenly realized that what he was about to say would implicate Maggie as well. He knew Jacob thought highly of her and hated to be the one to break the news. "I found out something about Claire…and Maggie that completely took me by surprise. I trusted her, Jacob. I even thought I…" he took off his hat and hit it against his leg. "I was considering proposing to that girl, only to find out she's not at all what I thought."

"What did she tell you?" Jacob asked carefully.

"Brace yourself." Will released a heavy sigh. "She and Maggie are wanted for robbery and attempted murder. Someone delivered a wanted poster to me, and come to find out, they both were working at some saloon in Chicago at the time."

Will turned to face Jacob. "You don't seem surprised at all."

"Maggie already told me."

"What?"

"Just yesterday, but she was very honest and repentant about it. It would seem they were trying to pay back what they stole, but the money and jewelry they took was destroyed in the fire."

The memory of Claire charging into the fire-filled house came back to Will. No wonder she had been so desperate to get inside. And all those times, she refused to be indebted to anyone, never accepting charity or help. She never took a day off work—it all made sense. She was driven to pay back what she had stolen. He understood why owing one more person felt so hard for her.

"I don't know what Claire's backstory is, but I do know what Maggie's is, and there's more than meets the eye, Will."

"If she had only been honest with me from the start, I could have helped her."

"She's trying to make things right on her own and doesn't realize yet that she needs help."

His words hit Will's heart hard and echoed in his head for the next twenty minutes as he left Jacob's and headed to town. He needed to see Claire and talk to her again. Jacob was right; there had to be more to it. Maybe she would have told him if he hadn't flown off the handle.

As he approached town, Lyddie's came into view, and he wasted no time riding up and knocking on the door. Lyddie answered and told him she hadn't seen Claire all afternoon. She even checked her room and told Will she wasn't there.

Will headed to the hotel next. She had agreed not to work there anymore, but he couldn't be sure if she had kept her word. He didn't find her there, either, and ended up outside the hotel, scanning the street and trying to decide where to look next.

"Good afternoon, Will."

Will turned to the voice and saw Amy Keets strolling toward him. "Afternoon, Amy."

"What brings you to town?" she asked, glancing at the hotel.

"I'm looking for Claire; have you seen her?"

"You look rather distressed, Will. Is everything alright?"

"If you see her, just let her know I was looking for her, alright?"

"I'll do that." She paused, watching him starting to move to his horse, and then said, "Speaking of Claire, there is something I've been concerned about regarding her."

Will gave her his attention again. "What do you mean?"

"Well, I don't want to gossip, but it's her reputation I'm concerned for."

"Go on," Will said.

"A few weeks back, when my father and I had to stay at the hotel for a few nights, there was a particular night I heard quite a bit of noise. I peered out into the hall and saw Claire coming out of the same room Bruce Conway was staying in. It alarmed me since it was nearly eleven at night." She saw by the look in Will's eyes that she had hit a nerve and continued. "It's not my business what she was doing in there

A Debt to Pay

so late, and maybe it's completely innocent. But you can see how that looks, right?"

Will walked away without a word, mounted his horse, and headed back to the ranch. He had let himself harbor just a little bit of hope that things weren't as bad as they appeared, but after hearing that from Amy, he resolved to maintain his initial reaction. Claire was a liar and a thief, with a character that was far from the woman he thought he knew.

Chapter Twenty-Four

"When will you go?"

"First light tomorrow," Will answered Hannah's question. It was several hours later that day, and after supper, Will had told Hannah he was leaving to find Grady.

"Are you sure you shouldn't wait?" Hannah asked. "I mean, at least until you get a chance to clear things up with Claire."

"There's nothing to clear up, Hannah."

Hannah sighed. "I know it was wrong for her to do what she did and then lie about it, but that doesn't mean her friendship or feelings for you were a lie. With this coming to light, more than ever, she's going to need real friends right now."

"She's never wanted my help, so I don't see what I can do. She's always wanted to do things on her own, so I guess she'll find a way."

Hannah knew it was Will's pain talking, making her see even more how much he actually cared about her.

There was suddenly a loud series of knocks on the front door. "Who can that be at this hour?" Hannah said, moving out of the kitchen and down the hall.

"Maggie," she said with surprise when she opened the door.

A Debt to Pay

"I'm sorry to come by like this. I know it's getting late, but I need to talk to Will."

Hannah opened the door and welcomed her inside. Will had followed Hannah to the door and was standing behind her.

"It's Claire," Maggie told them. "She's gone."

Will took the letter she offered to him and read it quickly.

Maggie, I'm going back to Chicago to make things right and clear your name. Will knows everything, and it won't be long before the whole town knows, too. Thank you for being such a good friend to me. Claire.

"What do you think she means by 'make things right'?" Will asked.

"I think she's going to turn herself in and say I had nothing to do with it, which isn't true. It's really because of me that things got so much worse. Claire didn't want to keep any of the jewelry, but I secretly held onto a diamond necklace. That's what's taken so long to repay."

"Where's that necklace now?" Hannah asked.

"It got destroyed in the fire."

"Unless Grady found it first," Will said.

Maggie gasped. "Do you think he could of?"

"Where did you have it hidden?" Will asked, thinking that if Grady had torn up the house searching for the gold, he may have also stumbled onto it.

"Claire found a spot under a floorboard," Maggie told him.

"Then there's a real chance he has it," Will said, knowing that's where his father would have hidden the gold.

"If we could return the necklace, Frederick Harris might drop the charges," Maggie reasoned aloud.

"Then we've got to find Claire before she turns herself in without it," Hannah said, looking at Will.

He had already been thinking as much. "I'll find her," he told them.

———

Claire hunkered down in an abandoned shed she had come across just before nightfall. She knew if she stayed on this road, it would take her to the next town. From there, she could take the stagecoach to the train station. There was some dry hay in one of the corners of the shed, and she settled on it after removing Willow's saddle for the night.

An hour later, she was feeling the loneliness of the prairie, and the distant howl of a wolf made her appreciate the fact that she hadn't had to sleep outside. She tried to sleep, but her mind kept hearing Will's words and seeing his face. The memory of how he looked when he'd seen the poster made her want to cry. Claire pulled her knees tight to her chest and leaned her head back against the wall, and finally, after what seemed like hours, she fell asleep.

It didn't seem all that long before she felt a bright light flicker across her face. Slowly, she opened her eyes and realized sunlight was coming through the window. She couldn't believe it was morning already. Rubbing her aching neck, she came to her feet and went over to Willow, who was standing only a few feet away.

Claire gently ran her hand along her mane, talking softly to her before she saddled her and led her out of the shed. For the next few hours, Claire traveled down the road. Her eyelids felt heavy, and a few times, she had to catch herself from dozing off. It was at one of those moments when she felt herself falling asleep that Willow suddenly began to knicker and stomp the ground so abruptly Claire lost her balance. She gripped the reins just as the horse reared up on her hind

A Debt to Pay

legs, but the motion was so fast, Claire felt herself sliding backwards off the saddle and toward the ground.

"Willow!" she cried as the horse began to run down the road in the opposite direction as they had been traveling. Claire jumped to her feet and tried chasing down the horse. "Willow! Willow, stop!"

After a few minutes of running as fast as she could, Claire slowed down to catch her breath. Willow was almost out of sight at this point. "Now what!" Claire yelled. "Ugh!"

She turned around to look down the road, realizing she couldn't go on without the money in her saddlebag. She knew she would have to find Willow in order to get anywhere. Claire alternated between running and walking in the direction Willow had gone. She hadn't the slightest idea what had caused the horse to startle and bolt.

The sun was beating down on her, and with it not even noon yet, she could only imagine how much hotter it would be in just a few hours. After about twenty minutes, she noticed a fresh pile of mud just off the road with hoof marks going through it. Veering off the road, she followed them into a field. She thought she could hear a stream nearby and paused to listen. The horse would probably go looking for water. Claire followed the sound, hoping to find Willow wherever the stream was.

Will had been on the main road since before daylight. He was sure Claire would have taken it as well since it was the road the stage traveled. Just a few minutes ago, however, a horse off in the distance had caught his attention. He rode toward it and knew almost instantly it was Willow.

"Claire!" He called her name continually as he searched the surrounding area. As the minutes went by, he felt his concern rise. Had she been thrown? Was she lying somewhere hurt? He chided himself for his words to her the previous day, feeling like he was the one who had driven her to leave so suddenly. He began to pray, as he had been doing since learning Claire had left. From the moment he started after her, he had been asking the Lord to do something that would hinder her from getting too far before he could catch her.

He reached Willow and dismounted to secure her reins behind his saddle. With her following behind him, he continued calling out Claire's name and searching the field. Minutes later, he heard the faint sound of Claire's voice yelling Willow's name. Riding in that direction, he eventually caught sight of her in the distance. She was treading through the tall grass and noticed him at almost the same moment.

As soon as he was close enough, he dismounted. "Claire, are you alright?"

She wiped the sweat and hair from her face, amazed to see him. "What are you doing here?"

"I was looking for you."

Claire met his gaze for just a moment before looking past him. "You found Willow!" She sighed with relief just before going to her.

"Maggie said you were heading back to Chicago."

"I should have never left Chicago in the first place," Claire replied as she untethered Willow's reins and began to lead her toward the road.

"Claire, wait!"

"It's the right thing to do, and you're not going to talk me out of it."

Claire stopped walking when she felt his hand gently taking hold of her arm. "Maybe the charges would be dropped or lessened if you could return the necklace."

Claire shook her head. "It got destroyed in the fire."

"I think it's possible Grady found it before he started the fire."

His words made Claire feel a twinge of hope, but then she thought of Frederick Harris. "I don't think Frederick Harris will drop the charges."

"It's still worth a shot," Will told her. "You returning what you stole could sway the judge's decision or at least make your sentence lighter."

Claire looked to be considering the idea. "Do you think so?"

"Why don't you come back to Millcreek and wait there until I find Grady."

"But if something happens to you trying to find him, I'd feel like it was my fault."

"I'm going after him either way to get back the gold he stole."

Claire was relieved to hear he wasn't going just for her sake. "Alright, I'll go back," she said after a moment of deliberation.

"We have a few hours of daylight left," Will said as he mounted his horse and watched her follow suit. They turned their horses in the direction of Millcreek and started back on the main road.

"You got pretty far in one day," Will said a few minutes later.

"I got an early start this morning. I would have gotten further if Willow hadn't startled and thrown me."

"How long were you looking for her?"

"I don't know, but it seemed like a few hours."

"Just enough time for me to catch up to you."

Claire wasn't even sure why he had bothered to find her.

He had been hurt and angry the last time she saw him, and she doubted anything had changed. Their conversation was next to nothing as they traveled, but Claire found her eyes continually resting on him as he rode just a few feet ahead of her. She couldn't help but wonder what he was thinking.

When twilight came, Will told her they would have to find somewhere to sleep for the night. They had already passed the shed that she had stayed in the night before, so that wasn't an option. She followed as he led them to a grove of trees just off the road. He gathered some wood for a fire and then laid out a bedroll he'd brought. Claire did the same, being careful to lay hers on the opposite side of the fire from his. He handed her something to eat he'd brought from home.

Claire thanked him but wasn't hungry at all. She sat on her blanket and pulled her knees into her chest, staring at the red flames starting to consume the kindling. She glanced up, and her eyes locked with Will's from across the fire. Her heart broke when she thought of how close she had felt to him recently, only to now feel so far.

The questions in his heart weren't going away, but Will felt like he couldn't trust the answers Claire might give. It pained him to think she was so desperate to hide the truth that she would yield herself to a man like Bruce Conway. He was mad at himself for falling in love with her, knowing now he'd have to move on. He could never be with someone he couldn't trust or respect.

Claire sat silently with her thoughts as well, chancing a glance once in a while toward Will, only to find him looking intently at the fire.

"I am sorry I wasn't more honest with you," Claire said quietly. "You've been nothing but a friend to Maggie and me, and you didn't deserve to find out this way."

A Debt to Pay

"How long has Conway known?"

"He showed me the poster just a few days after I told you about the conversation I overheard. Sheriff Dunley knows about it, too."

Will shook his head knowingly. "Those two have been conniving together for too long."

"Yeah, I've seen their kind before," Claire said.

"I'm sure you have. With working at the saloon, you've probably run into all sorts of men."

Claire felt his words like a sting. "It's not like I wanted to work there."

"Then why did you?"

"Because it's all I could find."

"So that part about you and Maggie losing your parents was a lie too, wasn't it?"

"Not completely. Both of our parents did die, mine when I was eleven. I think Maggie was older when she lost hers." Claire suddenly decided she'd share more, hoping maybe he'd get a better understanding of her. "I lived with my uncle after they died, and he was decent when he was sober, but that was less than half the time. I could overlook his fits of rage because he never extended it toward me, but some of the men he associated with frightened me, especially as I got older. When a friend offered me a job in Chicago, I went with her, thinking it could make my life better." She sighed. "Obviously, it didn't."

Will felt a pull of sympathy on his heart, knowing her life must have been anything but easy. He hated to think of an eleven-year-old losing her parents and then living with an alcoholic. No wonder things had turned out this way for her.

"So, this man Harris…how did you get involved with him?"

"I only knew him from his visits to the saloon, but the night I left, he had followed me up to my room after work." Claire saw a confused look on Will's face and explained further. "Maggie and I rented a room at the saloon, and I thought she was coming up since her shift was nearly over, so I didn't lock the door. I've been sleeping with a knife under my pillow since I lived with my uncle, so by habit, it was there. When he came at me, I had already grabbed it."

Will heard the tremor in her voice as she spoke and felt infuriated at the thought of someone trying to take advantage of her.

"We asked two of the men who worked at the saloon to get him to the doctor. After they'd gone, I noticed his keys had fallen out of his pocket." Claire avoided his gaze, feeling the guilt of what she was telling him. "I knew he owned a jewelry shop and, at that moment, felt desperate. I convinced Maggie that we should rob his store and take what we could to travel west and start a new life."

The way she told it made it sound not so terribly wrong. He could even argue that Frederick Harris had it coming to him after assaulting her. Still, she broke the law, which no judge would ignore.

"In your situation, I might have done the same thing."

Claire was surprised to hear him say that and felt a speck of hope that maybe he wouldn't despise her. She longed for him to know she wasn't as indecent as he thought. "I know it may sound hard to believe, but my job in that saloon was only to sell drinks, and it's all I ever did." She held his gaze, hoping he would see the truth in her eyes.

At that moment, looking into her eyes, Will felt like he could believe her, but then, like a wave, Amy's words about seeing her leaving Conway's room refreshed his distrust. It made him doubt everything she was saying. It wasn't that her life before had soiled her beyond redemption or even his love; it was the fact that she had lied to him, especially about her relationship with Conway.

"It's alright, Claire," he said. "You don't owe me any explanations."

His sudden indifference was even worse than his disapproval. To Claire, it felt like his way of saying nothing she had just shared altered what he thought about her. At that moment, she realized she would never change his opinion of her. She would have to accept that his love and friendship were lost forever.

Wordlessly, Claire turned to her side and pulled the thin blanket she'd brought over her shoulders. The sound of crickets and the crackling fire filled the August night. An owl hooted from a nearby tree, and the wind resting in the surrounding pines was a soothing sound to her troubled heart. As she lifted her eyes to the vast night sky speckled with countless stars, she suddenly felt insignificant in the middle of that wide-open prairie.

Maggie had recently quoted a Bible verse to her about God being mindful of even the sparrow that fell. She couldn't imagine a God like that. Even if he did exist, she knew he wasn't mindful of her.

Chapter Twenty-Five

"Claire! You're back!" Maggie threw her arms around her friend, hugging her tight as she walked into Lyddie's boardinghouse the following afternoon. "I've been worried sick."

"Me too," Lyddie said from just behind Maggie. She had heard the front door open and had followed Maggie to it. Lyddie also embraced Claire. "Don't you worry, hunnie. Things are gonna work out."

Claire looked from her to Maggie. "She knows," Maggie told her. Maggie had told her everything the night Claire was gone. And knowing the girls like she did, Lyddie could sympathize with their plight.

"I'll draw up a bath for you," Lyddie told her, already moving in that direction.

"I feel like the prodigal son," Claire joked, remembering the story from one of Reverend Myles' sermons.

Maggie smiled, but there was concern in her eyes. "I'm so glad Will found you. I was going out of my mind thinking of you alone out there." She took Claire by the arms. "Don't you ever think of facing this alone again. We both had a part, and we'll carry it together."

Claire sighed, touched by her friend's words. "Thanks, Maggie. I just wish there was something more we could do."

A Debt to Pay

"Did Will leave to go after Grady?"

"Yes."

"Let's just hope and pray he finds him and that he has that necklace!"

Jefferson City was about a day's ride from Millcreek. Riding into the crowded town and passing all the busy shops on either side of the street made Will thankful for Millcreek's calmer atmosphere. As he neared the end of the street, he spotted the West End Saloon, a two-story brick building with a roofed porch enclosed by a white railing. Will secured his horse's reins to one of the hitching posts and moved past a few men lingering on the porch.

Once inside, he moved around the tables and to the bar. A tall man behind the counter with a dark mustache and slicked black hair asked him what he wanted to order.

"Have you seen a fellow by the name of Grady Higgs come through here recently?" Will got right to the point of his visit.

"That the same fellow you was in here a month ago askin' about?" The bartender replied, remembering Will from his last visit to Jefferson City.

"It is."

"Lots of folks pass through here, mister."

Will slid money across the counter.

"But I'll be sure to keep my ears open," the bartender said, glancing down at the money Will had just passed to him.

Will turned around, leaned against the bar, and surveyed the room. He noticed a man at a nearby table looking at him. "The name Grady rings a bell," the man said loud enough for Will to hear. Will headed toward him, taking the empty seat across from him at his table. "You know where he is?"

"Maybe."

"When's the last time you saw him?"

"Why don't you buy me a drink, and I'll tell you."

Will placed some coins on the table but covered them with his hand. "You can buy yourself a drink after you tell me what you know."

The man didn't need much persuading. "He was in here two nights ago."

"You know where's he staying?"

"I don't know if he's still there, but you might want to try the Blue Moon Hotel."

Will lifted his hand and stood from the table. "Thanks for your help."

"You ain't gonna shoot him or nothin', are ya?"

"What's it to you?"

"Nothing," the man grinned from beneath an overgrown beard and mustache. "He's bested me more times than I'd like to count at poker." The man spit a wad of tobacco onto the floor and continued, "For a fair price, I could help you look for him."

"Thanks for your time," Will said by way of declining his offer. He headed out and toward the Blue Moon Hotel, not sure if he could trust the man or not.

Will walked down the street and into the Blue Moon Hotel. He approached the man behind the front desk and asked if someone by the name of Grady Higgs was staying there.

"He was until yesterday morning," the clerk answered. "Sheriff came and arrested him. You'll probably find him in the jail a few blocks down."

"Was it a sheriff from Jefferson?"

"Nope. I didn't recognize him."

Will left the Blue Moon Hotel, wondering if it had been Sheriff Dunley. Will rode down to the jail.

A Debt to Pay

"Morning, Marshal," Will greeted him as he walked into the jailhouse. He immediately noted there was a man in the cell, but it wasn't Grady.

"What can I help you with?" Marshal Montgomery asked, leaning back in his desk chair and scratching his graying beard.

"I'm looking for someone by the name of Grady Higgs. I heard he was arrested yesterday morning."

The sheriff looked surprised. "Not that I know of."

Just then, a younger-looking deputy walked in from the street. "You arrest anyone by the name of Grady Higgs?" the Marshal asked him.

The young deputy looked from Will Carter back to Marshal Montgomery. "No, sir. But I did see that Sheriff from Millcreek riding out of town with someone yesterday morning," he replied.

Marshal Montgomery swung his attention back to Will. "There ya go, son."

"Did you see which way he was heading?" Will asked the deputy.

"Seemed like they were heading east."

Will thanked him and was soon riding that same road. He wondered if they were heading back to Millcreek, but he wanted to scout out the surrounding areas just in case. An hour or so outside Jefferson City, he came upon an abandoned-looking house. It was Grady's horse that Will recognized first, having been the one to give it to him years ago.

Quietly, Will dismounted and secured Phoenix's reins to a tree limb so he wouldn't follow and then moved carefully toward the house. He rested his hand on the gun in his holster, glancing about for a sign of Sheriff Dunley. It seemed quiet and deserted, but the horse nearby told him Grady was inside.

As Will got closer, he noticed the front door was already open, hanging crooked off one of its hinges. Approaching it cautiously, he stepped inside. His eyes perused the shadowy room and almost immediately spotted Grady lying motionless on the floor. In a moment, Will was kneeling beside him, checking his pulse, even though the gunshot wound to his heart left little room for hope. Sighing heavily, Will removed his hat and just stared down at the man whom he had tried to form a brotherly bond with. As much trouble as he had been, it grieved him to think of the man's life ending this way, and it grieved him to think of having to tell his mother.

After a few minutes, Will checked his pockets for the necklace or the gold, finding neither. He also searched the house and came up empty. He did find the butt of a cigar, though, a brand he recognized as the same Bruce Conway smoked. Will knew he would have to bring Grady's body back to Millcreek to be buried, but before he did, he needed to ride back to town and see the marshal.

"You're back," the marshal said as Will walked in an hour later.

"I'm going to need your help," Will told him. "My stepbrother's been murdered, and I know who did it."

"They really are the sweetest kids," Claire said to Maggie as they headed home from a day at Reverend Myles. Maggie had invited Claire with her since she had more time on her hands with no longer working at the hotel. Claire wasn't sure who Bruce had put in her stead, but she was determined to stay away from anything pertaining to him, the hotel included. It appeared he hadn't shown the poster to anyone save Will Carter, and Lyddie and Hannah wouldn't tell.

"I'm not sure they'll be able to do without you," Claire said, glancing over her shoulder at the Myles' house behind them.

Maggie sighed wistfully. "I hope not."

Claire laughed softly. "So, you're hoping Reverend Myles proposes to you? Did you ever imagine you'd be the wife of a minister?"

It was Maggie's turn to laugh. "That does sound crazy, doesn't it?" She shook her head as if coming to reality. "He would never ask me, but I find myself sometimes imagining what it would be like to have my own family."

"Maybe it's not a complete fantasy. I mean, you said he didn't even bat an eye when you told him everything. That's quite an opposite reaction as Will had."

Maggie glanced at her sympathetically. "It was probably the way he found out."

"And I can guess who sent him that poster," Claire said, her tone angry.

"He had to find out at some point, Claire."

"I guess I was just hoping to resolve it and put it in the past with everything else."

"It won't stay there."

Claire looked at her curiously. "What do you mean?"

"Claire, we came here to get a fresh start, but for me, my heart couldn't get new until I'd turned my past over to the Lord."

"You really have been spending a lot of time with Reverend Myles."

"It's not just that, Claire. There's a real change that happened in me that night I gave everything to the Lord and asked him to forgive me."

"But most of the stuff you did was because your circumstances forced you into it."

"Even if I would have had a perfect life and never stepped foot in one of those houses, my heart would still have had sin in it, Claire."

The faces of people who had hurt her throughout her life flashed across Claire's mind. She didn't want to think about it. She just wanted to move on and pretend her life up to this point had never happened.

"I know you want to just forget and move on," Maggie said as if reading her mind, "but God's the only one who can really give you a fresh start."

Claire didn't know what to say, so she just sat in silence the rest of the way back to Lyddie's. She knew Maggie was only trying to help, but right now, she didn't feel she was worth God's time or intervention.

Claire dropped Maggie off at Lyddie's and then continued to the livery. On her walk back, she spotted Bruce Conway walking down the street. It had been such a relief not to see him for a few days that just a glimpse of him made her want to hide. Unfortunately, he spotted her, too.

"It's been far too long," Bruce said as he met her on the street.

"Not long enough."

He removed the cigar from his mouth, a feigned expression of hurt on his face. "You aren't still mad at me, are you?"

Her eyes were indignant as she looked at him.

"Remember, it was you who went behind my back and helped one of my employees sneak off without so much as a goodbye."

"You knew she hadn't fallen down the stairs that night," Claire retorted. When he didn't answer, she shook her head in frustration. "All you care about is the money you would lose with her not being there."

A Debt to Pay

"Some new verve has gotten into you since I've been gone," he remarked, looking at her curiously. "In my absence, maybe you've forgotten our deal."

"I didn't forget, but apparently, you did."

"What do you mean?"

"It was you who sent that poster to Will Carter's house, wasn't it?"

"I just thought he needed a little touch of reality."

Claire walked faster, hoping he would leave her alone.

"I expect your answer by tomorrow evening."

Claire stopped, turning to look at him. She knew she had to be careful until Will got back. She didn't want anyone else to know about the robbery until Will had returned with the necklace, if indeed it could be recovered. "Why tomorrow evening?"

"You'll see." His smile was oozing with self-confidence, and as he walked away, Claire felt as if he knew something she didn't.

The following day, Claire offered to pick up an order for Lyddie at the general store. She paid Mr. Maison the money Lyddie had given her and then headed to the door holding a basket full of supplies. She had heard the rumbling of the stagecoach pulling up near the store, knowing Lyddie had already prepared her extra rooms for possible boarders. As she stepped down from the platform to the street, the carriage stopped, and a man stepped out of the coach. His eyes almost immediately locked with hers.

The unexpected sight of Frederick Harris caused Claire to drop the basket, sending its contents spilling over the ground. Mr. Maison had been following her to the stagecoach and immediately began helping her pick up the items.

"I'm so sorry," Claire apologized absently, dusting off the tin of crackers as she put it back in the basket. She handed the basket to Mr. Maison as he picked up the rest and mentally told herself not to bolt as Frederick Harris sauntered towards her.

"Hello, Claire."

His expression was direct as his eyes seemed to paralyze her to her spot.

"Mr. Harris," Claire practically choked on his name.

His left hand was holding a suitcase, but with his right, he reached out and took her by the arm. "Would you mind walking with me to the hotel?"

"Claire?" Mr. Maison looked curiously at the strange man and back to Claire. A protective instinct jumping to the surface.

"It's alright, Mr. Maison," Claire said quietly. "Can you see that Lyddie gets her things?"

Claire felt like her legs were led as she walked beside the man she had hoped to never see again. He eventually let go of her arm, but his nearness was almost suffocating.

"You won't believe me, but I intended to pay you back everything. I was going to send it earlier, but there was a fire and…"

"Save it." They were passing the jail when Frederick Harris nudged his head in that direction. "I wonder how comfy that cell is in there."

Claire could hear her heart pounding in her ears. "I'll give you all the money I have, I swear it."

"Thought you were pretty slick, didn't you?" He grabbed her arm tight and leaned closer. "I don't like being cheated!"

"Mr. Harris, please!" Claire begged him under her breath, not wanting to draw too much attention from others on the street. As they neared the hotel, Bruce Conway was making his way from the other end of the street.

"Stage was a little early," Bruce said. "I was just on my way to meet you."

Claire's mouth dropped, and her eyes grew round with astonishment. "You knew he was coming?"

"Of course. I invited him. Weeks ago."

"I don't understand," Claire said, looking from one man to the other as they continued toward the hotel. "Why would you come all this way? I could have just been arrested and sent to Chicago to stand trial."

They entered the hotel, and Claire found herself led into Conway's office. Frederick Harris finally let go of her arm, taking a seat across from Conway's desk.

"He came all this way, Claire, because I want you to know how serious my offer really is."

Claire glared at Bruce Conway. His words about getting her answer that night made sense.

"You can agree to marry me, and Mr. Harris leaves you alone forever, paid off and then some," Bruce added with a sneer in Harris' direction. "Or you reject my offer and get thrown into jail until a deputy can escort you back to Chicago."

As if on cue, there was a knock on the door, and Sheriff Dunley walked through the doorway. "Sorry I'm late," he said, glancing at Claire before shutting the door behind him and going to stand along the wall.

"You have this planned out just perfectly, don't you?" Claire said, shaking her head in disbelief. She turned her gaze to Frederick Harris, whose arrogant manner was just as she remembered. "I'm sorry for stealing from you, Mr. Harris; truly I am. I promise I will pay you back every cent!"

"That's not really how a crime works, though, is it?" He stood from his chair and walked towards her. "I do expect you to pay it back, but when you commit a crime, you must be punished. You tried to kill me so you could rob my shop. Any judge will see that." He had stepped closer to her as if hoping his nearness would further intimidate her.

"You know it was self-defense. You know it was!" Taking a deep breath, she looked Bruce Conway square in the eyes. "You want my answer?"

And then she turned to where the sheriff was standing. "Sheriff Dunley, I turn myself in. But it was me and me alone who robbed Frederick Harris' shop. Maggie is innocent."

A look of vexation crossed Bruce Conway's face and then settled into one of resolve. "Maybe a little time in a cell will change your mind." Then, looking at the sheriff, he said, "Lock her up and make a show of it while you do."

Sheriff Dunley immediately went to Claire and took her by the arm. "Let's go," he said, leading her out of the hotel and to the street.

Claire noticed he kept a firm hold on her arm and walked swiftly. "You know I won't run," she said with irritation, but he kept a hold on her all the same, pulling her roughly as if she was trying to resist him. Claire heard whispers and could feel eyes on her as they walked past people on the street.

Sheriff Dunley put Claire in one of the two cells and closed the barred door. The sound of the key in the lock almost made her jump. For a moment, she felt frozen in place, and then she slowly sat down on the slab of wood that ran along the back wall. With her head in her hands, she closed her eyes, feeling too hopeless to think or even cry.

Chapter Twenty-Six

"Claire!"

Claire looked up as Maggie and Lyddie came rushing through the door of the jailhouse and toward her cell. Claire stood and met them at the bars.

"We came as soon as we heard," Maggie was saying, tears in her eyes. "You shouldn't be in there alone!"

"Shhh," Claire glanced at the sheriff, who was sitting at his desk, a cigarette in his mouth. "It's as it should be, and don't go messing it up for yourself," she warned.

Maggie shook her head. "I hate that you're in there."

"Don't you worry, hunnie. We'll figure out something," Lyddie tried to be reassuring.

"I'm freer in here than being blackmailed by Bruce Conway," Claire said.

"Maybe Will'll be back soon and straighten out this whole mess."

"He might not be able to, Maggie. Even if he has the necklace when he gets back, I'll just have to pay the price. I broke the law, and this is only fair."

"But it doesn't seem fair at all," Maggie said, wiping at her tears. "I can't believe Frederick Harris is actually here in Millcreek," she whispered.

"I know," Claire said quietly. "I had hoped never to lay eyes on him again."

"That's long enough, ladies," Sheriff Dunley spoke up.

"I'll be back," Maggie promised, reaching through the bars to squeeze Claire's hand. As she and Lyddie left the jail, Tom Maison was just approaching.

"Is it really true?" he asked, his eyes looking past them toward the jail. "Claire's been arrested for robbery and attempted murder?" His tone radiated disbelief.

Maggie couldn't believe how fast word was spreading around the town. "It's true, but the circumstances are complicated."

"I didn't think she had a dishonest bone in her body," he said, remembering when she had found his misplaced money and returned it to him.

"There's more than meets the eye," Lyddie said. "Sometimes desperate situations can lead a person to do almost anything."

"I need to tell Jacob," Maggie said quietly. "I'll be back," she told Lyddie as she moved quickly toward the livery to get Willow.

The next morning, when Claire woke up, her aching back and neck told her it was all too true. She sat up, letting her eyes adjust to the little bit of sunlight poking through the shutters of the front windows of the jailhouse. The sheriff was still asleep on a cot and still snoring. As if sleeping on the hard, makeshift bed hadn't been bad enough, his loud snores had only made it worse.

Claire stood and stretched, taking a few steps around the pad. She wondered how long a sentence she would have to

A Debt to Pay

serve. One year? Two? Three? She shuddered to think of what it would mean to be behind bars for a long time. She paced the floor, telling herself not to think of it yet. Maybe Will would find Grady and recover the necklace. But would Frederick Harris drop the charges even if he was repaid? He may still want her arrested and tried by a judge.

"Oh, God, please get me out of this mess," Claire heard herself whisper out loud, but her words seemed to bounce off the cell walls and fall to the ground. God didn't listen to sinners; of that, she was sure. Why would he listen to the prayer of a thief? Claire sat back on the makeshift bed and pulled her knees into her chest, burying her head in them. "Please help me," she heard herself whispering again, even though she knew her chances were next to none.

A few hours later, Claire realized she had fallen asleep when she heard someone saying her name. She looked up, surprised to see Jared Cooper standing on the other side of the cell.

"Hi, Claire," he said, removing his hat and looking at her empathetically.

"Word's really getting around, isn't it?" Claire said as she came to her feet.

"I, um, just thought I should come see you. Hannah's on her way, too."

Claire sighed, wishing she didn't have to face everyone. "Thanks, Jared."

"Did you really do it?" he asked, and Claire thought he looked like he was holding his breath.

"Yes," was all she said.

"I don't believe it."

"Well, it's true. I robbed a jewelry store so I could have enough money to come west and start a new life."

"Weren't a bad motive."

Claire gave an airy laugh. "It was still wrong."

"I s'pose." He paused and then asked reluctantly, "And the murder part?"

"In that, I can defend myself. I never tried to kill anyone! I was just defending myself on that score."

He looked like he didn't know what to say, and then, "Is there anything I can do for you?"

Claire was touched by his kindness. "No, but thank you, Jared. You've been a good friend to me."

He sighed, putting his hat back on. "I did wanna tell you something." He was glad Sheriff Dunley had stepped outside. "I ain't mad at you no more."

Claire smiled softly. "I'm glad to hear it."

"I had hoped we'd be more than friends, but if it ain't in the cards, then I'll settle for just friends."

Claire couldn't believe he would say that even now that he knew her to be a thief. "That means a lot. Thank you."

He nodded. "I jest didn't want you to go away thinking I had any hard feelings toward you. Maybe eventually, I'll find someone else to settle down with."

"You may not have to look too far," Claire said. "Sylvia lives just up the road."

Jared chuckled at her words. "Nah, she's been my best friend forever. She doesn't got sheep's eyes for me."

"Are you sure about that?" Claire saw by his expression that she had gotten him thinking. "Just don't wait too long to find out," she added, hoping her words would nudge him in the right direction.

"I may just do that," he said, a grin tugging at his lips. He

A Debt to Pay

tipped his hat. "I'll be checking in with you later." He hesitated at the door, looking back at her before he left, wishing there was something he could do to help her.

Claire had just sat back down when, a few minutes later, Jacob walked into the jail. "I didn't realize how many friends I had," she joked, but Jacob could see the sadness in her eyes.

He talked with her for several minutes and then asked if he could pray for her. Claire agreed, noticing a moment of peace as he did. Then, before he left, he looked at her intently and said, "Claire, there's something I feel the Lord keeps impressing on me. You're to take my Bible and read Luke twenty-three."

Claire took the book as he reached it through the bars and thanked him, surprised at the specifics of his request. Before he left, he promised to come back and check in on her. Staring at the Bible he'd given her, Claire sat down and just held it in her lap. She wanted to open it but just couldn't bring herself to do it. It was almost as if she knew that opening the book would somehow force her to open her heart, and she wasn't sure if she was ready for all that would entail. She let her head rest against the stone wall, listening as the clock across the room ticked. The lonely sound seemed to echo through the jail cell.

At four o'clock, the door to the jailhouse opened, and this time Bruce Conway walked through it. He approached her cell and very slowly removed the cigar from his mouth. "You have enough time in there?" he asked.

"Mr. Conway, were it years in this cell, my answer would still be the same."

"And there's nothing I can do to change your mind?" he asked, his eyes narrowing as he studied her. "Nothing I can promise you? Because I could give you just about anything you wanted."

Claire lowered her eyes. "There's nothing you can give that I would want."

"Not even this?"

She looked up, gasping when she saw the diamond necklace in his hands. "Where did you get that?"

"I told you I would do everything in my power to help you." He slid it back into his pocket. "Say the word, and Frederick Harris goes away forever."

Claire took a few steps back and weakly sat on the bench. There was silence, and then she heard his footsteps as he left the jail, slamming the door behind him.

Minutes later, Frederick Harris walked in. "Why not accept his offer and be done with this?" he asked.

"Why are you trying to help him?" Claire asked.

"Because men like him, and men like me know how to benefit from each other's situations. You may fancy yourself a respectable lady starting a new life out here, but we both know what sort you are. Do you really think you can do better than him? Who would want you? A thief and a…"

"I'm not listening to this another minute. I'll just have to pay for my crime."

"Oh, no, you'll pay for more than that."

Claire heard something in his voice that made her look at him. Even in the dim cell, she could see a coldness in his eyes that scared her. "You made a fool of me, and that's not something I can forget. I'll be waiting for you when you get out of jail. Even if it's years, I'll wait. If you were to accept Conway's offer, however, you might find me to be more forgiving."

Claire released a shaky breath when he had gone. She realized she was clutching the Bible in her hands so hard that

A Debt to Pay

her knuckles were turning white. Slowly, she opened it and turned the pages until she found a page that was titled Luke. She flipped through the chapters until she saw the twenty-third chapter, and then she read. Every word seemed to jump out at her, and Claire felt her heart gripped by what she was reading. Jesus was innocent, yet they nailed him to the cross. When she got to the part where Jesus spoke to the thief on the cross, she had to wipe at her tears, trying to see past them to the words.

Just like that, Jesus forgave him, and just like that, Jesus forgave those who were killing him. She read on and, for the first time, realized his death on the cross was as much for her as it was for anyone. He paid her debt for sin so she could have eternity with God. He paid a debt He didn't owe because He knew He alone could pay it.

Claire cried into her lap, feeling the weight of the debt she owed, not just stealing the jewelry but her life of sin apart from God. She felt no condemnation, almost as if God understood why she had done the things she had, but she felt a conviction that almost physically made her heart hurt. She wanted to be free of guilt, shame, and loneliness. Claire found herself suddenly on her knees, clutching the Bible as she asked God for forgiveness.

Sometime later, as her tears stopped and she lifted her head, she felt almost as if a cool breeze had blown into the hot cell. She even glanced over her shoulder to see if Sheriff Dunley had left the door or a window open. But they were closed. Claire stood slowly from her knees, feeling oddly freer in that small cell than she had ever felt in her entire life.

Chapter Twenty-Seven

"Sheriff Dunley? Can you bring that bucket of water over here?" Claire waited a moment, thinking perhaps he didn't hear her. "Sheriff Dunley?"

"I have to go out for a little," he said, standing from his desk and heading out of the jailhouse.

Claire watched him go, and then her eyes fell onto the bucket of water just a few feet from the cell. She hadn't had anything to drink since she'd been put in the cell two nights ago. Lyddie had brought her a basket of food yesterday, but the sheriff had kept it on his desk. Claire didn't have an appetite anyway, but she was starting to feel dehydrated and in dire need of water.

The door opened sometime later, and she sighed with relief, thinking she could ask him again. Disappointment washed over her when Bruce Conway's frame filled the doorway. He walked over to her cell, and she backed up from the bars.

"Has your two nights in here changed your mind at all?"

"A hundred nights wouldn't change my mind."

"Why are you so stubborn?" he said between clenched teeth. "I offer you freedom!"

"I'm freer behind these bars than I'd ever be with you," Claire returned.

A Debt to Pay

"Is that what you think?" Angrily, he reached for a set of keys that hung on a nearby hook.

Claire stepped away as he unlocked the cell door and moved quickly toward her. She let out a little cry when he grabbed her arms roughly and shook her slightly. "If you won't marry me, I'll make sure no one else does either! I can do whatever I want with you, and not even the sheriff could stop me!"

"Let go of me," Claire begged in a hoarse whisper, feeling suddenly too weak to fight him.

"Maybe one more night without food and water will bring you to the realization that you need me." He pushed her back slightly, watching as she crumbled on the bed. He stepped toward her and took her chin in his fingers, forcing her to look at him. "You're a hard one to break, Claire, but I will break you."

When he had left, Claire felt the rest of her strength drain from her body. Her head was pounding, and all she could think about was how much she wanted water. Sheriff Dunley came in shortly after, and she begged him for water until he left again. She prayed Maggie or Lyddie or anyone would come to see her so she could ask them for a drink. But evening came without a visitor, and Claire felt herself sink into a state of near unconsciousness.

Maggie stamped her foot angrily as she stood outside the jailhouse. "And why not? You said to come back later, so I did. Why can't I see her?"

Sheriff Dunley rocked back on his heels, his hands on his holster. "Because I'm the sheriff, that's why not."

"I just want to visit with her for a few minutes!"

"I ain't allowing visitors, and that's final. She'll be fine. Now get on outta here."

Maggie released a frustrated breath, glancing back at Sheriff Dunley, who was still guarding the jailhouse door. It didn't make any sense why he wasn't allowing anyone in. "I'll be back," she told him, reluctantly leaving for the second time that day. Come morning, she was going to get Jacob and see if he had more sway with the sheriff.

The following afternoon, as Hannah was pinning up clean laundry on the clothesline, the sound of an approaching rider caught her attention.

"Will!" Hannah exclaimed, going to meet him in the yard. She immediately noticed the horse following behind him with a man's body lying on it.

"Oh, my Lord, is it Grady?"

Will dismounted and hugged Hannah as she came toward him. "I'm afraid so."

"I always prayed he would turn out different." She looked toward him and then turned away, overcome with emotion.

"I'm not going to bury him near my parents, but I thought it would help Rebecca to know he was at least buried on the property."

"Right you are," Hannah said, laying a hand on his arm.

"I'll be back in a bit. I'm going to get some of the boys to help."

"Will…Claire's been arrested. Conway had her thrown in jail."

Will closed his eyes as regret washed over him. "I took too long."

"You're here now, and you should go to her. The sheriff won't let anyone in, though, so be prepared."

A Debt to Pay

"What do you mean?"

"I tried to visit her today, and he won't let anyone in."

Will shook his head in confusion. "That doesn't seem right."

"I've never liked Sheriff Dunley, but he's more dogmatic than ever. Tom Maison's been concerned, too. He told me Conway's the only one he sees the sheriff letting in."

Will didn't need to hear anymore. He asked Rusty to oversee Grady's burial, and then he rode as fast as he could toward town. Minutes later, a cloud of dirt rose from under his horse's hooves as he came to a fast stop in front of the jailhouse. Dismounting, he strode up to the porch, where Dunley sat on a chair, his rifle lying across his lap.

"Afternoon, Carter," he said, not even looking up.

"I heard you arrested Claire. I'd like to see her."

"I'm afraid that's not possible right now." He slowly stood to his feet, bringing attention to the rifle in his hands. "This ain't any of your business, Will."

"I'm making it my business, and I'm going to ask you one more time to let me in that jail."

"You threatening me, Carter?"

"I don't want to make trouble, Sheriff. I just want to see Claire."

"Last time I checked, I was still the law 'round these parts. Now you get on your saddle and head back to…"

Will grabbed him so quickly that he didn't have time to lift his gun. Will grabbed that, too, just before he shoved him so hard he fell backward onto the street. Pushing the door open, Will stepped inside.

"Claire?" It was dim inside, but as he went to the cell, he saw Claire lying motionless on the bed. "Claire!"

Alarm pumped through his body when she didn't answer. He reached for the keys to the cell and had just inserted the key when Sheriff Dunley came up from behind. Will was expecting him and knocked him to the ground with a hard punch. Turning his attention back to the cell, Will unlocked the door and stepped inside.

"Claire!" He went to her and realized she was unconscious. Scooping her thin, frail body in his arms, he left the jail and headed toward Doc Fletcher's office. The doctor answered the door as Will continued to kick it with his boot.

"Bring her in here," the doctor sprang into action as soon as he saw Claire in Will's arms.

Will followed him and laid her on a cushioned table in the center of the room. He stepped back as the doctor checked her pulse.

"I think she's just severely dehydrated," Doc Fletcher said.

A few minutes later, Claire came to and drank the water he held to her lips. "Thank you," she said as she laid her head back down.

"What happened?" Will asked.

It was the first time Claire noticed he was in the room. "Will, you're back!" She sat up slowly, still feeling lightheaded and weak.

Will came closer and took her hand. She looked thinner and pale, her hair in disarray around her face. "I'm sorry I didn't get here sooner."

"I'm surprised Sheriff Dunley wouldn't have come to get me when he saw something wasn't right," Doc Fletcher said, his thick brows knotted together in a frown.

"He's too afraid of Mr. Conway," Claire told him.

The doctor looked confused, his gaze going to Will and back to Claire for answers.

"I think they thought if I were deprived of food and water, I'd come to a decision sooner."

"He wouldn't even give you water?" the doctor asked.

Claire shook her head.

"He's treated murderers better than that," the doctor said with frustration.

All three of them looked simultaneously to the doorway as Sheriff Dunley barged in.

"Is it true you wouldn't give this woman water?" Doc Fletcher asked, a scowl on his face. "She could have died if this had gone on another day!"

Sheriff Dunley walked toward them. "I've got to take her back now."

"No, you don't," the doc said, giving Will such relief that he could have hugged the older man. "She's not well, so she'll stay here the night. If she's OK by morning, I'll bring her over there myself."

Sheriff Dunley narrowed his eyes, glancing at Will and back to the doc. Reluctantly, he turned around. "I'll be back in the morning," he called over his shoulder. "And don't try anything, cuz I'll be patrolling this house all night."

"Thank you," Will said once he had gone. "I probably wouldn't have handled that so calmly."

The doctor was helping Claire to her feet. "I'll show you where you can sleep tonight."

Claire thanked him, grateful to be out of the cell and feeling a little more like herself. As the doctor led her from the room, she turned back toward Will.

"Frederick Harris is here," Claire told him quietly.

"In Millcreek?" Will asked with concern.

Claire nodded solemnly, and then she gasped softly upon remembering about the necklace.

"Conway has it! The necklace, he has it."

"You saw it?"

"Yes."

"I knew it," he said more to himself than to her. "Don't worry, I'll get it back," he told her, gently touching her arm.

Claire's eyes rested on the holster and guns on his waist. She'd never seen him wearing it before. "Please be careful, Will."

Will nodded and told her he would, before watching the doctor lead her away. He knew a lot had happened since that afternoon when he told her he loved her, but in his heart, those feelings hadn't changed.

Will went outside and headed toward the saloon, knowing he would most likely find the sheriff there. From the noise spilling out into the street, he knew it was busy before he even entered it. It looked like every table was occupied and the bar area full, too, but Will still found the sheriff easily enough. He was leaning against the bar, drinking and talking to Bruce Conway. There was another affluent-looking man sitting next to Conway that Will assumed was Frederick Harris.

Stopping in front of Conway and Dunley, Will waited until he had their attention and then said, "I'd like to know which one of you put a bullet through Grady."

Conway and the Sheriff exchanged glances before looking back at Will. "I don't know what you're talking about, Carter," Sheriff Dunley spoke first.

"Grady hasn't been in Millcreek for some time now," Conway said with a look of disinterest.

"He wasn't murdered in Millcreek, but you already know that."

"If anyone got tired of that fool and killed him, it was probably you," Sheriff Dunley smirked.

Will ignored the comment and kept his eyes glued to

A Debt to Pay

Conway. "Where's what you took from him? I know you were there, and I know you have it."

"We weren't on the same side during the war either, were we, Mr. Carter?"

Will glared back at him. "That's got nothing to do with this."

"Just trying to understand your vindictive behavior."

"One of you murdered him, and you better give back what you took."

"I don't know what you're blabbering about, but I can't help you," Conway said. "You know as well as anyone that Grady was a fool and a coward. So why don't you pour yourself a glass, and we can at least all drink to that."

Out of the corner of his eye, Will saw the sheriff reach for his holster. Will drew his pair of .45 Colt revolvers so fast no one saw it coming. Will noticed he'd also gotten the attention of the man sitting next to Conway. He squirmed uncomfortably as Will kept the gun in his left hand aimed at Conway and the one in his right at Dunley. "I'm not messing around. Give me what you took from Grady!"

"Don't be stupid, Will! After this little episode, I could lock you up," Sheriff Dunley told him.

"That's just what he wants," Conway said, thinking of Claire and looking Will square in the eyes. "I'm sorry to disappoint you, Carter, but I don't have anything that you could want. At least not yet anyway," he added, referring to Claire.

Will understood his meaning and wanted to wipe the smirk off his face but kept a level head and slowly lowered his guns. "Claire isn't a pawn in your game, Conway." Seeing that he wasn't getting anywhere, Will turned his attention to the man sitting beside Conway. "I'd be obliged to speak with you if you have a minute?"

Frederick Harris looked unsure as his gaze bounced from Will to Conway and then to the sheriff. Finally, he stood from his stool and followed Will to a recently vacated table in the corner.

"I'm assuming you're Frederick Harris," Will said as he took a seat.

"Your assumption is correct."

Will took in his greasy appearance and knew instantly he didn't like this man. The thought that he had tried to force himself on Claire only added fuel to the fire. "How's that stab wound healing up?"

Frederick Harris' thick eyebrows furrowed together in annoyance. "She left a nasty scar."

"You really think her intention was to murder you?"

"Of course. Claire knew I was a wealthy man, so she lured me up to her room, stabbed me, and proceeded to rob my shop. It's pretty obvious, don't you think?"

"I think she was shaken up after you came after her, and when she saw your shop keys on the floor, acted on an impulse, not only because you deserved it, but to get out of Chicago."

"That's an interesting way to look at it, but I don't think a judge would romanticize the situation like that."

"Besides the diamond necklace, how much money did they take from you?"

"Near one hundred dollars."

"So, if you get back everything that was stolen, would you drop the charges?"

"Someone has already tried to play that hand."

Will knew who that someone was. "I'm not trying to do anything underhanded, Harris. I'm just asking you to look at the situation for what it is and have a little mercy."

A Debt to Pay

"Mercy?" Harris laughed outright.

"Claire and Maggie had two men get you to the doctor after you were stabbed. They could have easily let you bleed to death."

"Then they stole from me."

"They know it was wrong; that's why they've been working and saving to pay you back."

"That's what they may have told you, but you can't trust women like them."

"They made a mistake, Harris. If you're recompensed, I don't see what benefit it is to you to have them stand trial and locked up."

Will watched as the man across from him appeared to be considering what he was asking, but his face was hard to read. After a moment, Will slid his chair back and stood up. "Think about it," was all he said before he left the saloon.

"What was that about?" Bruce Conway asked Frederick Harris as he came to take Will's seat once he had left the saloon.

"Do you really think your leverage with Claire will work? She's not appearing to budge."

Bruce Conway looked irritated by Harris' words. "It'll work if you stick with the plan. If she knows I'm the one who can get her out of this, she'll break."

"What if we amp up the pressure? Make her think things are getting worse."

"I like that idea. What do you have in mind?"

Will waited outside the saloon for Bruce Conway, hoping he'd make an appearance before too long. It was dark when he eventually stepped out of the saloon, and from a distance, Will followed him home.

A few minutes later, Bruce Conway stopped just outside his home and turned around. "I know you're there, Carter."

Will stepped out of the shadows. "Then you also know why I'm here."

"I already told you; I don't have what you want."

"You're not above the law, Conway. Sheriff Dunley might be pulled into your shady dealings, but he's not the only deputy around here." He took a few steps closer until he was standing near him. "One of you killed Grady, and one or both of you have the necklace and gold."

"Gold?" Bruce pretended to be surprised.

Will covered the space between them by grabbing Bruce by his coat collar.

"You know I can bust you up, Conway. Just give me what you took from Grady!"

"Let him be, Carter!"

At the sound of Sheriff Dunley's voice and a cocked gun, Will released his hold on Bruce Conway and stepped back. He was expecting the sheriff but not the other two men who came from behind and suddenly grabbed each of his arms. Will grunted as Sheriff Dunley came around in front of him and socked him in the stomach.

The sheriff delivered another hard punch to his face. "Hold him, boys!" he ordered as Will began to struggle. "Don't ever cock a gun in my face again!" he said as he clouted him in the jaw.

Bruce shook out his shirt collar and looked indignant as he stared down Will. "You touch me again, and you'll end up like your brother!" he threatened him through clenched teeth.

Will fell to his knees when the sheriff punched him again, and the two men restraining him released their hold. He

A Debt to Pay

could hear them moving away as he slowly stood to his feet. Conway was stepping into his home, and the sheriff returned to the jail. Will wiped the blood off his mouth and looked around the empty street. He could hear the distant commotion from the saloon, which got louder as he returned to get his horse. He had no other option but to head home and try again tomorrow.

Chapter Twenty-Eight

When Claire awoke the next morning, the sight of a cozy bedroom in contrast to the steel bars of the jail cell was confusing. She suddenly remembered everything that had happened and how she had ended up at Doc Fletcher's. Will's face came to her mind, and an ache to see him tugged on her heart.

There was a light knock on the bedroom door. Claire sat up and swung her legs off the bed. "Come in."

Doctor Fletcher smiled a kind greeting. "How are you feeling this morning?"

"Much better, thank you."

"I made some breakfast and wanted to make sure you ate something. I'm afraid that sheriff's itching to take you back."

Claire nodded. She accepted the fact that she had to go back. "I'll be right down," she told the doctor.

Doctor Fletcher had been right, and just as she finished her breakfast, Sheriff Dunley was knocking on the door to take her back to the jail.

―――

"Will." Claire stood and went to the bars when she

saw him enter the jailhouse an hour later. When he came closer, she gasped softly. "What happened to you?"

"It's nothing," he said, tilting his wide-brimmed hat forward to shadow a little more of his face.

Claire saw clearly that he had been in a fight. "I'm so sorry, Will."

"When did the sheriff bring you back?" he asked.

"Just an hour ago. I'm not sure where he got to," she said, glancing past him toward the desk and chair the sheriff usually occupied.

"Grady's dead."

"What?" She shook her head in disbelief, "But how?"

"Found him in an abandoned cabin a few miles outside Jefferson City. He'd been shot probably about a day before I got to him."

"Mr. Conway and the sheriff weren't in Millcreek around that time."

Will nodded. "I know one of them did it, and they were probably both there."

"That explains how Mr. Conway has the necklace," Claire mused.

"He won't have it for long," Will told her.

"How are you going to get it?"

"The Marshal from Jefferson is on his way here. I filed charges against Conway and Dunley, and he's coming to look into it. I'm hoping he can-"

"Visiting time's over," Sheriff Dunley said as he entered the jailhouse.

Will glanced over his shoulder at him before looking back at Claire. "I'll be back," he promised.

"What happened to you, Carter?" Sheriff Dunley asked as Will moved past him to the door. "Looks like you were in a fight or something."

Will ignored his taunting and kept walking until he was outside, hoping Marshal Montgomery would be there soon. Will hated to leave Claire alone in the jail but knew there wasn't anything he could do at this point. Before leaving town, he stopped at Lyddie's to talk to Maggie and make sure she was keeping an eye on Claire. He knew Doc Fletcher was planning to stop by as well, which made him feel better.

Claire looked curiously at Sheriff Dunley as he unlocked the cell and motioned for her to come out. "What are you doing?" she asked as he handcuffed her hands in front of her. It was later that day, and the sheriff had just come back after being gone for several hours. During his absence, Maggie had visited her, but she had just left.

"Looks like you're going back to Chicago to stand trial."

"What?" She felt panicked as he pulled her out of the jail. She squinted against the bright sunlight as they stepped outside. Almost immediately, she noticed Frederick Harris. He was leaning against the front porch post of the jailhouse, his arms crossed in front of his chest as he watched her.

"I'll see you back in Chicago," he said to Claire with a satisfied grin.

"Get in!" the Sheriff barked as he roughly pulled Claire away from the jail and shoved her into the barred carriage.

"Please! Sheriff Dunley! Please let me say goodbye first!" But the sheriff acted as if he didn't hear her as he walked around to the front of the carriage and climbed up to the driver's seat.

Claire felt her heart almost burst out of her chest when the carriage lurched forward, and the reality of what was

A Debt to Pay

happening washed over her. She clung to the barred window until they were out of town and then forced herself to sit back against the wall. The carriage was dark and stuffy, save the small amount of light and air coming through the barred window on the back door.

"Please, Lord, please help me," she heard herself whispering. "I know I was wrong to steal, but please rescue me from this mess!"

———

Will met Marshal Montgomery on the road when he saw him approaching the ranch. "Thank you for coming, Marshal."

Marshal Montgomery removed his hat and wiped the sweat from his brow before replacing it. "I started having suspicions about Dunley a few years ago. If everything you say checks out, it'll be my pleasure to put him away."

They rode side by side and had just about reached town when Tom Maison approached on horseback. He was moving fast, so Will immediately felt alarmed.

"What is it, Tom?"

"Sheriff Dunley left with Claire. Something didn't seem right."

The marshal looked at Will with a questioning expression. "I'll fill you in on the way to town," Will told him. "How long ago?" Will asked Tom.

"Just about a half hour ago."

By the time the three of them reached town, Will had explained the entire situation about Claire. Once in town, Will and the marshal kept riding through, taking the main road that Tom Maison said Sheriff Dunley had taken.

———

Claire tried to remember how many hours it was to the next town. She knew it was going to be a hot and uncomfortable ride, and the frequent potholes and rocks that met the carriage wheels kept her bouncing about. She felt that all she could do was pray, or else the gravity of the situation seemed to choke her.

Suddenly, the wagon slowed and came to a stop. Curiously, Claire went to the window and tried to peer out. She heard the horses' nicker and could hear footsteps coming around to the back of the carriage. She scooted back a little when she heard the door unlock. A fresh breeze washed over her when the door was opened, and it was all she could do not to bolt outside. The sheriff suddenly reached out and grabbed her upper arm. "Get out," he ordered.

Claire landed a little awkwardly and winced against the pain of the handcuffs against her skin. "Why did we stop?" she asked, glancing about.

The sound of an approaching horse grabbed her attention, and she suddenly spotted Bruce Conway riding up from where the front of the carriage faced. "Look at you," he said, shaking his head in apparent sympathy for her appearance. He dismounted and walked close to her.

Claire instinctively stepped back when he reached up to smooth away the sweaty hair that stuck to her temples. He looked at her empathetically, as if she were a lost child.

"I'm glad I caught up to you before you got too far."

Claire looked at him questioningly and was even more surprised when he ordered the sheriff to remove her handcuffs. Claire instantly rubbed her sore wrists. "I don't understand. Why did we stop?"

"I gave Harris the necklace and paid him enough to drop the charges and go away forever." He smiled almost tenderly.

"But how did you even come to have the necklace?" Claire asked suspiciously. Bruce Conway glanced toward the sheriff for a moment as if seeing if he was listening before he took Claire's hand and led her a short distance away from the carriage. "Sheriff Dunley murdered Grady Higgs," he whispered to her with another side glance in Dunley's direction. "He was bragging about what he took from Grady, and that's when I persuaded him to give me the necklace." He sighed, and his eyes looked at her pleadingly. "I've only ever wanted to help you, Claire. I'm sorry for trying to force you to feel something for me."

Claire wasn't sure what she thought about his sudden change in personality. His kindness made her feel more uneasy than his usual malice. She noticed he was still holding her hand and was attempting to take her other.

"Frederick Harris told me he would see me in Chicago. I don't think he's about to drop the charges."

"Trust me, Claire. I took care of it. Once I learned that Harris told the sheriff to send you back to Chicago, I went to speak with him."

"Mr. Conway, I don't want you to pay off my debt for me! I'd rather go serve my sentence than be blackmailed!"

"Do you understand what you're facing, Claire?" He took her arms in his hands and pressed his face closer to hers. "You'll go to trial, and you could be looking at a year or possibly several in jail! Harris will hire the best lawyer and see you do the maximum time. You'd rather that than let me help you? I can be different…I would be different if you would agree to be my wife."

Claire could see something akin to desperation in his eyes as he looked at her. "Mr. Conway, I can't ever give you what you want."

Bruce Conway paused a moment, his expression twisting into one of determination. "Then maybe I'll just have to take what you won't give."

Claire jerked her arms free. "Sheriff Dunley! I'm ready to go back in the carriage."

Sheriff Dunley looked to Bruce, waiting for his next order.

"She's coming with me," Conway said, grabbing Claire by the upper arm and attempting to lead her to his horse.

Will and the marshal caught up with them just as Conway was forcefully pulling Claire toward his horse. Sheriff Dunley noticed them first and called to Conway, who only slightly released his hold on Claire. She whirled around, grateful beyond words to see Will and the other sheriff.

"What's going on here?" the marshal asked Dunley.

"Just transporting this criminal to stand trial," Sheriff Dunley replied, sending a glance toward Claire.

"And what about you?" the marshal asked Conway. "What's your business here?"

Conway finally let go of Claire's arms and took a few steps toward the marshal. "I was just coming to say a proper goodbye," he told him, his gaze shifting to Will, knowing the man would understand what he was implying.

"I have reason to believe one or both of you is in possession of some stolen items which you lifted off of Grady Higgs after you killed him."

"I ain't killed nobody," Sheriff Dunley said, his hands resting on the guns in his holster. "But I can't say as much for Conway here."

Bruce Conway's eyes shot toward him. "You lying dog!" Then, looking at Montgomery, Bruce said, "He's dirty, Marshal. Go on and check his coat."

A Debt to Pay

"I ain't got nothing to hide," Sheriff Dunley said with confidence.

Marshal Montgomery dismounted, his .45-caliber poised in his hand as he walked toward Dunley. "Hand me your coat, Sheriff."

Dunley slid it off, a cocky smirk on his face, and tossed it to the marshal. A moment later, Montgomery pulled out the diamond necklace from one of the pockets.

"This the necklace you were telling me about?" Marshal Montgomery asked Will.

"What the devil?" Dunley stared at the necklace with surprise and then sent an accusing look to Bruce. "You put that in there!"

"And there's more..." the marshal said as he also held up a small leather pouch. He tossed it up to Will, who was still astride his horse. "This the gold that went missing?"

"Why, you double crossin' scoundrel!" the sheriff hollered at Bruce. "You planted all of that!" Looking at the marshal, Dunley tried to explain. "It was Conway who killed Grady and took the gold and necklace off his body!"

"The clerk at the Blue Moon Hotel says you arrested Grady, and my deputy says he saw you riding out of town with him the morning he was killed."

"I brought him to Conway, and he did the rest!" Dunley defended himself, his anger obviously mounting.

"I'm sure we'll get this all sorted out," the marshal said, his gun raised toward Dunley. "For now, you're both under arrest." He motioned for Dunley and Conway to get in the carriage.

"I ain't done nothing wrong, Marshal," Dunley held his ground. "It's Conway you want!"

Claire screamed when Sheriff Dunley suddenly drew his

pistol and fired toward Conway. Bruce saw it coming and promptly jumped behind the carriage, the bullet whizzing past Conway's horse and causing it to scare. Just a few feet away from the horse, Claire moved out of the animal's path but wasn't sure where to go as more gunfire pierced the air.

Will suddenly appeared, grabbing her and pulling her beside him. There weren't any trees or rocks nearby, just open road and the carriage, which Conway was firing from behind. Claire felt Will cover her as he pulled her with him behind Phoenix.

The shooting didn't last long, as the marshal quickly got the situation under control by taking out Dunley's weapon with a well-aimed shot that grazed the man's arm, making Conway stop shooting.

"He's in a rage!" Conway said to the marshal as he saw Dunley being moved into the carriage. "You can't put me in that carriage with him, or he'll kill me!"

"Fine. You can walk," the marshal said as he motioned for Will to put the handcuffs on Conway and then tethered him to the carriage.

Marshal Montgomery tied his horse and Conway's to the carriage as well and then climbed into the driver's seat. Will and Claire followed him back to town, where everyone on the street was curiously watching their return. Seeing Bruce Conway and especially Sheriff Dunley led at gunpoint into the jailhouse wasn't a sight the townsfolk would soon forget.

Frederick Harris was among the bystanders. Obviously, Conway's plan had blundered. He had been hoping Claire would reach such a state of panic at the reality of facing a trial that she would change her mind about his offer. Now, it looked like the only one facing trial was Conway and Sheriff Dunley.

A Debt to Pay

When the marshal stepped out of the jail, he approached Will. "This is the necklace that the young lady stole?" he asked him.

"Yes, sir," Will replied. "And it belongs to that man over there."

The marshal headed in Frederick Harris' direction and handed him the necklace.

With Conway and the sheriff now under arrest, Frederick Harris wanted to be rid of his ties with them as soon as possible. He took the necklace without a word and then waited until he could speak with Will and Claire alone.

"Since I got back the necklace, if the hundred dollars is returned to me, I've decided I'll drop the charges."

Claire looked at him, her eyes expressing her disbelief. She didn't even know what to say.

"If you'll just follow me to the bank," Will told him. "I'll get you your hundred dollars."

As they walked away, Claire felt almost weak at the realization that she was no longer facing criminal charges. She started walking toward Lyddie's when Maggie met her on the street.

"Claire!" Maggie burst and threw her arms around her. "I've never been so worried for you!" She stepped back and held her at arm's length. "My goodness, you're a sight, Claire. Let's get you into a warm bath and get some food in you!"

Claire let Maggie lead her, feeling exhausted and overwhelmed.

Chapter Twenty-Nine

"I can't believe it's really over," Claire said to Maggie the next morning as they woke up and dressed.

"I'm so glad it is! And what an outcome! Thank the Lord Will got the marshal involved."

Claire knew it was the Lord's intervention. The timing of the marshal looking into Grady's murder had benefited her more than she could have imagined. It had also persuaded Frederick Harris to move on.

"You seem so peaceful, Claire," Maggie said, smiling at her. "I know you must be so relieved."

"I am relieved beyond words. But it's not just that the prospect of jail isn't looming over my head. I found God in that cell, Maggie."

Maggie felt tears stinging the back of her eyes. "I think we all have our cells until God pulls us out from them, if we let him."

"I think you're right. I'm just so relieved he pulled me out of mine. Until recently, I didn't realize the debt I owed him, and as much as I could have tried on my own to pay it back, it would have never been enough."

"I'm glad you let him pay your debt, Claire."

A Debt to Pay

Claire met her smile, her own heart stirring as she remembered the love the Lord had shown her in that lonely cell. "Me too, Maggie."

"I'm so glad to be able to put all this past us," Hannah said that evening after supper. She finished drying the last dish and then sat at the table across from Will. "You must be relieved, to say the least!"

Will nodded, a brief smile touching his face before it fell. "I am glad things worked out as they did. The marshal was an answer to prayer for sure. I know he's planning to investigate as far back as their connection with the bank robbery a few years ago. Either way, they'll do some time for Grady's murder."

"I wonder how Claire must be feeling. She and Maggie are probably over the moon with relief."

"Gossip in town might give them a hard time for a bit, but folks will eventually move on, and hopefully, Claire and Maggie can settle into the new start that they wanted."

Hannah thought his eyes didn't match the optimism of his words. He seemed a little melancholy. Hannah didn't want to press him since she knew he had been through a lot the last week. His encounter with the sheriff and his ruffians still showed on his bruised face. By the middle of the week, however, when his mood hadn't changed, Hannah decided to probe him a bit.

"Have you been to see Claire since everything?" she asked him one morning at breakfast.

He shook his head just before bringing his coffee mug to his lips. "Not yet. I figured she might need some time after the whole ordeal."

"What she probably needs is to know her friends are still her friends," Hannah said. "I stopped by Lyddie's a few days ago, and she seemed in good spirits. She told me she gave her life to the Lord during those days in jail." Hannah smiled, thinking of their conversation. "There's definitely a new thing going on in her."

Will was glad to hear it, but even news as good as that didn't quite expel what he was feeling. He didn't even know how to explain it. Was it disappointment he felt, knowing that from here on out, she could only be a friend to him? He'd have to face reality when he saw her, so he'd as soon put it off. Maybe with time, they could just be friends, and he could forget about the feelings stirring in his heart for her.

He just couldn't share his life with someone he couldn't trust. She had lied to him not just from the start but also during their conversation after he had found her on the prairie. If Amy Keets hadn't told him what she had, he'd be more apt to open his heart to Claire again, but knowing himself like he did, he knew that was something he couldn't do.

Claire took a deep breath as she walked with Maggie and Lyddie past the folks in the churchyard. She could feel their glances and imagine their whispers. She told herself things would settle down soon and tried not to let it bother her. She was pleasantly surprised when Sylvia Wendel came up to her and hugged her. "I'm so glad you're alright, Claire. You must be so relieved all that is over."

Claire smiled at her, thankful for her kindness. "I am relieved and thankful. I got better than I deserved."

"The Lord gives us all better than we deserve," she replied. Her eyes then found Maggie. "I wanted to tell you that Lilly is constantly talking about you and drawing pictures for you at school. I wasn't sure if you were getting all of them."

Maggie smiled. "I have been getting them," she laughed softly. "I'm starting quite a collection." At those words, Maggie glanced around the church and spotted Lilly and Lucas. They were in the front row like usual but were sitting next to a young woman Maggie had never seen before. She turned around for a moment to talk to someone, and Maggie noticed she was rather beautiful. She also noticed the children seemed very comfortable with her. Lilly had her arm looped around her left arm, and Lucas was lying on the pew with his head resting in her lap. Maggie sat next to Claire, but even as Jacob started his sermon, her gaze kept wandering to the mysterious woman.

Claire followed Maggie's gaze and also wondered who the unfamiliar woman was. Her heart ached for Maggie a little, knowing she had fallen hard for Jacob Myles. Claire's thoughts soon found their way to Will, and discreetly, Claire glanced around the church. Unfortunately, her eyes met Amy Keets across the aisle. The girl smiled smugly, and Claire almost felt like she knew she had been looking for Will. Claire didn't see him sitting with Hannah or anywhere else. Maybe he had to miss church because he was behind with work. He had, after all, spent an ample amount of time helping her that week.

After the service, Claire tried her best to avoid Amy Keets, but the girl rather obviously cut her off at the door. "Oh, Claire, I'm so glad to see you're alright. You really had us worried for a while."

"Thank you, Amy."

"Tell me, did you really try to murder that man and then steal from him?"

Her expression was anticipating details. Claire mustered up her strength before answering. "I'd rather not talk about it now that it's over."

"Oh, of course not. It must be terribly humiliating. And I just can't believe the sheriff and Conway have been taken over to Jefferson City to stand trial for Grady's murder." She shook her head disapprovingly. "And to think you were working and spending so much time with that man. Folks are even saying they were involved with the money that was stolen from the bank a few years ago." She shook her head softly. "I must say, Claire, you two have a little more in common than I ever thought."

Claire couldn't verbalize a reply or defense, so she just moved around her and headed outside. Walking swiftly to avoid any further conversations, Claire headed back to Lyddie's. She knew she shouldn't pay Amy Keets any mind, but her words did sting. Knowing everyone must be thinking the worst about her was more than a little unsettling. Will seemed to be keeping his distance, too, and that was more disheartening than all the rest put together.

A moment later, Claire heard Maggie calling her name and telling her to wait up. "I saw Amy talking to you," Maggie said once she'd caught up. "I'm assuming something she said is the reason for you leaving so quick."

"It shouldn't bother me, but it does."

"Don't pay her no mind, Claire. She's just jealous that Will prefers your friendship to hers."

"Not anymore."

"You don't know that." She paused and then added, "Hannah came up to me and invited us for supper tonight. I hope it's alright that I told her we'd come."

Claire couldn't ignore the uncertainty she felt at the

A Debt to Pay

thought of seeing Will. The last thing she wanted was for him to feel obligated to be her friend now. "Of course, it's alright," Claire replied, hiding her reluctance.

But it was Maggie who became reluctant to go into the house a few hours later. She and Claire had just pulled up to the front of the house in their buckboard when Maggie saw the mysterious woman from church that morning swinging on the porch swing with Lilly. A quick glance in the yard caused her to spot Lucas on top of his father's shoulders as he stood by the corral with Will.

"I guess they were invited for supper, too," Maggie said.

Claire climbed down from the buckboard and wrapped the horse's reins around a post. By then, Will and Jacob were nearing. Claire found herself toward the back of the group next to Will as they went up the front porch steps.

"Nice hat," he said to her.

"A cowboy I know gave it to me," Claire replied as she adjusted the front with her thumb and index finger.

"That was thoughtful of him," Will replied.

"Yes, it was," Claire said, already feeling a wave of relief wash over her. Maybe their friendship wasn't completely ruined.

They reached the porch as Jacob was making introductions. "This is my sister, Alison. She's visiting for a few weeks. Alison, this is Maggie, Claire, and you already know Will."

Claire could almost feel Maggie's relief, knowing the beautiful stranger with Jacob was his sister. Claire thought she seemed very sweet. She now saw similarities in her and Jacob's appearance.

"It's nice to meet you all," Alison replied, her full lips forming a smile beneath her bluish-green eyes.

"Let's get inside," Hannah said, opening the door for them. "Supper's already on the table."

"Your ranch is as beautiful as ever," Alison said to Will after they had all settled around the table and said the blessing. "I know I was here last time I visited Millcreek, but I don't think I realized how vast it is, nor how many cattle you have."

"We've grown a bit since the last time you were here," Will agreed. "And we'll be bringing back a couple hundred more after the cattle drive."

"I hate to think of how lonely it'll be without you and most of the boys," Hannah dropped into the conversation from across the table.

"When do you leave?" Jacob asked as he helped Lilly cut up the steak on her plate.

"Middle of this week," Will replied, missing the look of surprise that crossed Claire's face.

"How long will you be gone?" Alison asked as she took the bowl of green beans being passed in her direction.

"Two or three months."

"It takes that long?" Maggie asked.

"Sometimes longer," Will replied. "Just depends on the weather and if we run into any trouble."

"Well, for what it's worth, I'll stop by and check on Hannah from time to time," Jacob said with a wink in her direction. "I wouldn't want those pumpkin pies she starts to make 'round this time of year go to waste."

"So, what brings you out here from Kansas City?" Will asked Alison a few minutes later. "Just visiting your brother, or do you have intentions of a more permanent stay?"

Alison smiled. "I know I mentioned possibly moving here the last time I visited, but this time, I really am considering it."

"Not sure Ma and Pa will take to that idea," Jacob warned her, "Although you have my vote."

She smiled thoughtfully, "They'll come around if it's meant to be."

"Well, for what it's worth, you have my vote, too," Will said kindly.

"Lilly and Lucas would sure like having their Aunt Ali around more," Jacob said with a glance in his daughter's direction.

"You both have recently come to Millcreek, isn't that right?" Alison asked, looking toward Maggie and Claire. "Would you say it's a good place to put down roots?"

"I think if I had a brother as kind as yours," Claire said, being careful to avoid an answer that was too personal. "I'd be quick to settle wherever he went."

"I'm glad we came," Maggie spoke up.

"Ali is a writer," Jacob told everyone. "So maybe if you do move here, Ali, you could get a job at Bell's Newspaper Press."

"Harold Bell could certainly use the help," Hannah added with a little roll of her eyes. "I think the man's half blind with as many errors as I find in that paper."

Claire listened to them continue to talk, not missing the easy way Alison and Will conversed. She kept telling herself to stop being ridiculous, but for some reason, she felt a strange feeling of jealousy rising in her heart. It wasn't so much that she thought Will liked Alison in that way, but it was the fact that he no longer cared for her in that way. She thought back to the kiss they had shared just a few weeks ago, yet it seemed like an eternity ago. Could she really live in Millcreek and be OK with him eventually marrying someone else?

Claire didn't say much during the meal and was still lost in her thoughts when she realized Maggie was saying her name.

"I'm sorry; what did you say, Maggie?"

"Just that we're heading outside for a walk. Did you want to come?"

Claire realized everyone was already getting to their feet and followed suit. Even Hannah left the dishes for a change and joined them. The warmth of the day had given away to a cooler September evening. Claire fell into step beside Hannah for a few minutes as they all walked to the west end of the yard, heading toward a pasture where Will said one of the mares was with her newborn foal.

"With my sister being here for a few weeks, you can get a break from the kids," Jacob said to Maggie as he came alongside her. Even with Lilly at school now, Maggie had continued to stay with Lucas during the days Jacob had work.

"Oh, I hadn't thought of that," Maggie replied, looking ahead as Lilly walked with Alison, her hand laced inside her aunt's. It suddenly occurred to her that if Alison moved to Millcreek, Jacob might not need her at all anymore.

"I hope she does move here," Jacob said. Maggie could tell just by the look on his face that he loved his sister very much.

"I'm sure it would be great for the kids, too," Maggie said, trying to sound optimistic.

"My parents are good folk, but they can also be a little controlling, so I think Alison is feeling that need to break free a bit."

Maggie felt his hand brush hers accidentally as they walked and forced herself not to think anything of it. Jacob Myles would never think of her as anything more than a friend and nanny for his children.

"I've been meaning to talk to you about something, but with everything that happened with Claire, I didn't get a chance."

A Debt to Pay

Maggie felt her heart drop. She knew he was going to ask her to leave again. At least this time, they could part on good terms.

"Would you have some time tomorrow? I thought Ali could stay with the kids while we have lunch. You know I'm not the best at cooking, but I could manage some sandwiches."

Maggie couldn't help but smile at his words. "As long as you don't bring any of those ginger cookies you tried to make the other day."

He chuckled. "I promise I won't bring any."

Claire watched as Maggie and Jacob talked, wondering what they were saying. He had seemed unable to take his eyes off her during dinner, but she didn't think Maggie even noticed.

"How are you feeling since everything?"

Claire glanced at Will, realizing he was beside her.

"So grateful it's over," she told him. "I finally feel like I can really start over."

"Hannah told me that you had an encounter with the Lord." He looked at her in a way that made Claire feel he truly understood. "That really does make all the difference," he said.

Claire smiled reflectively. "It really does and did. As horrible as it felt being in there, I'm grateful for it now, if that makes sense."

"It makes a lot of sense," Will said quietly, thinking of the trials in his own life that had brought him closer to the Lord. "I meant to come see how you were earlier this week, but I…" he let the sentence hang, not sure what reason to give.

"Oh, I understand," Claire reassured him. "I'm sure you had some catching up to do with as crazy as last week was. Especially with needing to prepare for the cattle drive."

Will nodded, glad he hadn't had to go into his real reason for staying away.

"I hope you weren't planning to leave without saying goodbye, though," Claire tried to say it almost jokingly so he wouldn't know how hurt she'd been if he did.

"Well, I'd planned to at church today, but…" he shrugged. "Just had a lot of catching up to do, like you said."

Claire nodded, not at all convinced. It was so odd that one moment she felt like they were close again, and the next, it was as if he was miles away. "Well, you certainly don't owe me a goodbye after all I put you through. And, even though you would never ask to be repaid, Maggie and I haven't forgotten about the money we owe you."

Will didn't care about being repaid, but he knew it was important to Claire. "I figured I would hire you both to help Hannah with all she does during this time of year. With me being away, it would make me feel a lot better knowing she had the company and help. That would more than pay me back."

Claire smiled softly, appreciating his thoughtfulness and generosity. "Will, I really am sorry for everything," she said.

"It's alright," he said. "We can just put it all behind us."

"Everything?" she asked quietly, her gaze on the ground as they walked. He had told her he loved her. She didn't want to put that behind them.

Will realized they had stopped walking and were facing each other. As he looked into her dark brown eyes, the desire to kiss her again was overwhelming. He was thankful there were so many others around to keep him from making an even bigger fool of himself. "I was hasty that day," he told her, realizing this was the closure he needed to move on. "I mean, I really haven't known you that long."

A Debt to Pay

It was the exact opposite of what she had hoped he would say, but it was also what she had been expecting. Looking into his hazel eyes as he said it just made it more painful to hear. "I understand," she replied, mustering up a weak smile. "And you're right. We better catch up with the others."

Will watched as she walked away, feeling worse than ever. Why was his heart on such a different track than his mind? He knew this was the right thing to do, so why was his heart screaming the exact opposite?

Chapter Thirty

"I want to talk to you, Maggie, and I want you to hear me out before you try to talk me out of it."

Maggie glanced over at Claire as they rode back to town. "I don't think I've ever succeeded in talking you out of anything," Maggie laughed softly.

"You've done well here, Maggie. You have a respectable job as a nanny, and no one can speak ill of you. You have Reverend Myles' respect, and that makes everyone else respect you as well."

"What are you getting at, Claire?"

"I honestly think I should move on."

"What!"

"Now, hear me out. With the past really behind me this time, I could settle someplace new and not have to deal with the rumors and the gossip."

"But rumors and gossip will fade away. Is there another reason you want to leave?"

"I just can't stay in Millcreek knowing Will Carter is only being my friend out of obligation. I can't stay here knowing he doesn't care like he once did."

Maggie heard Claire's voice catch and could tell she was

holding back tears. "I think he does still care, Claire. He just needs some time."

Claire shook her head. "No, I've ruined any chance I had of being with him. That's as plain as plain. He pretty much told me that tonight. I never told you, Maggie, but a few weeks ago, he told me he loved me, but tonight, he said those words were just spoken in haste. Every time I see him, it's like my heart breaks all over again."

Maggie sighed as she put a loving arm around her friend. "I don't think Will Carter is a fickle man. If he loved you a few weeks ago, I don't see how that could have changed. I think he just needs time to sort through what he's feeling."

"The way he looked tonight, I…I think I just need to go."

"Well, he's the one leaving, remember? He won't be home from that cattle drive until at least November, so don't go running off again, you hear? Promise me, Claire!"

"I promise, for now."

———

Maggie pulled the buckboard up to Reverend Myles' house the next day and hesitated for a moment before climbing down. For a moment, she just let her eyes sweep the quaint home with its flower beds and rose bushes. This place had been like a refuge the last few months, and it felt painful to think of not coming anymore. She thought it sweet of Jacob to go out of his way to plan a nice lunch while telling her. It was quite the contrast in the way he had asked her to leave before.

"Just stay there," she heard Jacob say to her as he came out the front door. He was holding a basket in his hands and closed the door behind him before meeting her. "If the kids see you, we'll never get away, so let's just go now while Ali has them occupied."

Maggie scooted over as he climbed up next to her in the buckboard and took the reins from her hands. He directed the horse down toward the creek and alongside it on a dirt path that Maggie knew led to an apple orchard.

"Claire doing alright after everything?" Jacob asked her.

"She is. Giving her life to the Lord has certainly changed a lot in her. I'm just so grateful for how merciful God was to work things out the way he did."

"Amen to that."

They talked for a few more minutes about all that had transpired and then about how Lilly was doing in school. Before long, Jacob was slowing the horses and parking them near a grassy area beneath a large magnolia tree.

"This look alright?" he asked, climbing down from the seat and going around to help her down. He took the basket as she handed it to him and then took her hand as she stepped down.

"It looks lovely," she said. She followed him and watched as he pulled a blue and white checkered blanket out of the basket and spread it over the grass. She thought he seemed especially cheerful and talkative as he set out the food and plates he'd packed.

"Don't worry. Ali made those cookies," he assured her.

Maggie smiled as she took the sandwich he offered her. They conversed easily while they ate, and Maggie found him making her laugh several times. She couldn't remember ever seeing him quite this happy.

"I'm glad Ali was able to stay with the kids. I feel like I can hardly get a word in with Lilly always trying to be in on the conversation."

Maggie laughed softly, knowing what he meant. "She's always listening, isn't she?"

"Quite the professional eavesdropper, for sure."

"It's nice your sister is so good with them."

"She and my wife were close before we moved here," he told Maggie. "Rose was actually her friend before she was mine."

Maggie had never heard him talk about his late wife and listened with interest. "Not sure we would have even met if it hadn't been for Ali."

Maggie watched as he took a deep breath and seemed to have a distant look in his eyes before they settled on her. "What I wanted to talk to you about has to do with the kids and I."

"I've really appreciated you letting me work for you all this time," Maggie told him, her sincerity in her eyes.

"Well, that's just it. I don't want you to work for me anymore. I want you to marry me."

"I knew it was only temporary, and I understand…" Maggie suddenly realized what he had said. "Wait, what?"

"Maggie, will you be my wife?"

He had shifted and was on both knees in front of her. Maggie couldn't believe he was taking her hands in his and looking at her with such affection. She couldn't believe the words that had just come out of his mouth.

"You mean, live with you and the kids?"

"Of course," Jacob laughed. "You look so surprised. What did you think I wanted to talk to you about?"

"I thought you were going to tell me you didn't need me to work for you anymore."

"Well, I guess I am saying that," he grinned.

"I'm just…I just can't believe this is really happening." She looked down at her hands in his. "I'd been dreaming of this and hoping for it, but…I didn't think you would be able to love me after what I told you."

"I don't care about your past, Maggie. God's used it to bring you to Him...and to me."

Maggie closed her eyes as tears escaped past her lashes. She told herself not to cry but just couldn't help it. She could feel Jacob pulling her to her feet and, a moment later, felt his arms pulling her into the sweetest and most endearing kiss she had ever known. Jacob Myles loved her. It was all she could do not to explode with joy.

A moment later, he took a step back and tucked a loose wisp of auburn hair behind her ear. "I can think of two little people who will be as happy as I am," he said with a tender smile.

Maggie smiled as well, thinking of Lilly and Lucas. "I can't wait to tell them."

"Me too."

"Jacob, I know I won't ever be able to replace their mother or your wife," Maggie said in a tone of resignation as she looked up into his eyes, wanting him to know she didn't expect him to love her as much as he loved his children's mother.

"I don't want you to replace her," Jacob said, feeling the love he had for her welling in his heart. "Rose was the best part of my past, but Maggie, you're the best part of my future."

"Oh, Jacob," Maggie said, loving the way he was pulling her close again. "I don't deserve you."

"Maggie..." he gently said her name contemplatively. "Is that short for Margaret?"

"No, for Magnolia."

"Magnolia?"

"Yes," she laughed softly at his surprised reaction. "Is it that unusual?"

A Debt to Pay

"I've never heard it before, but I like it." He glanced up. "Pretty fitting that we're standing under a magnolia tree right now."

"Is that what it looks like?" she said, excitement in her voice. "I've never even seen one."

"Come spring, I'll plant one in the yard," he promised her.

"I think that's just perfect," Maggie smiled before meeting his kiss again.

Chapter Thirty-One

"I heard that Conway was responsible for that other fellow who they found dead a few miles outside Jefferson City," Rusty remarked. It was the night before the cattle drive, and he and Will were in the barn loading up the chuck wagon and making final preparations. "I heard that there were eyewitnesses that saw that man murdered here in Millcreek. Someone must have thrown his body out that ways to throw the light off Conway."

Will suddenly remembered the conversation Claire had relayed to him that day she'd rode out to the ranch. "Claire overheard Dunley and Conway talking about a body they'd disposed of, so most likely, that's not just idle gossip you heard."

"Yep. Frank was at the saloon the night before that man went missing. Said he saw the man stab Conway after they got in some sort of argument. From what I heard, Conway left the saloon spittin' nails."

Will headed into the house a few minutes later, finding Hannah in the kitchen as she was finishing the dinner dishes. "You all set?" she asked.

"Yep."

"Then I guess you'll be off."

Will looked at her curiously, recognizing her tone as one he'd heard before when she was put off about something. "Got a bee in your bonnet, Hannah?"

The woman released a short, heavy breath and turned to face him. "Yes, I do! You're about to leave for months, and you're doing so without making things right with Claire first!"

Will was clearly surprised by her words. "Hannah, there's nothing to make right. In the midst of trying to hide her past and throw me off the trail, she pretended to be more interested than she was."

"She may have hidden what she did from you, but trust me, she wasn't pretending when it came to your relationship."

"How can you know that?"

"Because I have two eyes on my face, Will Carter!"

Will shook his head, knowing she wouldn't understand unless he explained further. "When I went to bring her back to Millcreek, she told me to my face that nothing had happened between her and Conway, that his blackmailing her had never crossed the line. She lied to me, Hannah. Amy Keets told me she saw Claire coming out of Conway's hotel room."

"And you're staking your future on Amy Keets' words?"

The question hit Will like a ton of bricks. Until that moment, he'd never stopped to consider the credibility of the source.

"I know we haven't known her long, but if Claire told you that, then I don't think she was lying."

"But that's the problem, Hannah. I can't be sure she's telling the truth, and you know how I feel about deception."

"I know how you feel about that girl, and if you go away

without telling her and hearing her side of Amy Keets' story, there's no guarantee she'll be here when you get back. Don't miss out on what God has for you because of your pride, Will."

Will looked at her wide-eyed and felt like he did when she had scolded him as a child. "It's almost nine o'clock," he said, taking off his hat. "She'd be asleep if I rode to town now."

"Then go tomorrow morning."

"We're leaving at first light, Hannah. This is just going to have to wait." He knew his words bothered her as she turned back to the sink. There were no dishes left, but she pretended to be busy with something so she wouldn't have to talk to him. Will went to bed then, but sleep was the furthest thing from his mind.

―――

Claire tiptoed about the room to avoid waking Maggie. It was just a little after six in the morning, and after a fitful night of sleep, she couldn't lay in bed another moment. After dressing and then grabbing her shoes, Claire quietly left the room. Stepping out onto the front porch, she sat on a chair and laced up her boots. There was a coolness to the late summer morning that hinted at a change of season about to come. The sun was just painting the sky as it rose, and Claire thought a ride would help clear her thoughts.

Twenty minutes later, she was astride Willow and riding her away from town. She passed the churchyard on her right before taking a back road toward the ranch. She knew Will was probably already gone, but she thought maybe she'd catch a glimpse of him before he left.

―――

A Debt to Pay

"You alright?" Rusty asked as he drove the chuck wagon.

Will looked over to Rusty from where he rode next to him. "Yeah, why'd you ask?"

"I don't know; you've looked back over your shoulder like three times in the last thirty minutes."

"I didn't even notice," Will replied. Again, his thoughts went back to what Hannah had said the previous night.

"A lot can happen in the space of two months," Rusty said, meeting Will's eyes when he looked at him. "The boys and I could keep going, and you could catch up by tonight if you're fast."

Will didn't have to think about it another second. Leaning his reins to the left, he turned his horse around and headed back to Millcreek.

"She's not here."

Will looked at Lyddie, disappointment written all over his face. "Do you know where she went?"

"She left before I saw her. You could check with Eli at the livery and see if she took a ride."

Will nodded, thanked her, and headed back to his horse.

"Thought you was on a cattle drive," Eli said when he saw him a few minutes later.

"Did Claire come by here?"

"Yep. 'Bout an hour ago. I think she headed out toward Pond Point."

"Thanks!" Will nudged his horse into a gallop and headed in that direction. He hoped he hadn't come back for nothing and prayed he'd be able to find her before too long.

About twenty minutes later, he thanked the Lord as he spotted her about a half mile away. As he neared, he realized she was walking, her hands holding Willow's reins.

"Will!" she said once he was near. "I thought you had left." She'd already been out to the ranch and knew he wasn't there.

"I did leave," he told her as he dismounted and walked to the front of his horse. "But I came back." He glanced down and saw she was holding something.

"She threw a shoe," she told him, looking at it in her hand. "I was heading back to the livery."

"Seems every time I have to chase you down, Willow helps me out."

"You came back to find me?" Claire asked curiously.

"Yes. Two months is too long not to know."

"Know what?"

"If you feel even half of what I feel for you."

Claire pushed back the hair that the wind had just blown in her face, wondering if maybe she had never woken up that morning and was dreaming. "But the other day, you said—"

"I know what I said, but it's not lining up with what I feel." He took a deep breath, not sure how to say what he wanted to. "I understand you having to keep the robbery a secret, but it was the fact that you lied to me about Conway that I can't seem to move past."

"Lied to you about Conway? Do you mean when I said he was blackmailing Maggie?"

"No. I mean, when we spent that night on the prairie, and you said the blackmail had never led to anything between you two."

"It didn't, Will. Once, when he took me home, he tried to kiss me, but I ran away."

"Then how can you explain Amy Keets seeing you coming out of his hotel room?"

"Amy Keets told you that?"

"Yes."

A Debt to Pay

Claire's hand came to her mouth, and she gasped softly. "I can see how that must have looked," she said quietly, then her eyes went to Will's. "That same night Amy was in the hotel, Bruce Conway was stabbed. I grabbed some clean towels and helped him bandage his wounds. It was late," Claire told him. "I remember because I was almost done my shift when he came into the hotel."

Will thought back to his conversation with Rusty the previous day. It all checked out. He knew then and there she was telling the truth.

"I promise you, Will. What Amy saw was me coming and going out of his room with bloody clothes and bandages."

Will nodded slightly. "I believe you, Claire."

Just hearing him say it made her sigh in relief. "You can't imagine how good it feels to hear you say that."

"I've been a fool," he told her, innately taking a step closer to her. "Please forgive me."

"Forgive you? Will, I'm the criminal, remember?"

"Were the criminal," he corrected, a slight grin pulling at the corner of his mouth. Suddenly, none of it seemed to matter. How could he care about the past when he loved her so much in the present? "The only thing you're guilty of now, Claire Wallace, is stealing my heart."

Claire was pleasantly surprised when he covered the space between them and kissed her with all the love and passion he felt. Then he wrapped his arms around her waist and hugged her, making Claire feel like she never wanted to leave his embrace.

"Do you really have to leave?" she asked, her arms going around him and settling around his leather belt.

"Don't remind me." He stepped back slightly, gently brushing back a wisp of hair in front of her face. "At least now, I'll be able to look forward to coming back."

Claire rose up slightly on her toes and placed a soft kiss on his lips. "You better drive those cattle faster than you ever have before."

Smiling, he reached behind her and pulled her hat back over her head. "Maybe I could sneak you along with all the other wranglers. You certainly look the part in this hat."

Claire smiled, "You have my permission to try," she said, loving the way he was looking at her.

"On second thought, I think you might be too much of a distraction."

"In that case, I guess I'll have to stay here and pine away for you."

"I hope you do," he said, kissing her again. Smiling, he took her hand and kissed the back of it. "I'll walk with you back to town."

"Alright, but let's walk slow," she said, feeling like she was in something of a dream while they talked and walked. They got back to the dirt road and, still holding hands, eventually arrived in town. Once at the livery, Claire handed Willow, as well as the thrown horseshoe, over to Eli.

Claire turned to Will, thinking it was goodbye.

"Not yet," Will said, "I want a few more minutes at least. I'll walk you back to Lyddie's."

Claire smiled warmly, taking his hand as he reached for hers.

"Don't look now," Will whispered a few minutes later, "But Amy's just outside the bank watching us."

Claire laughed softly. "Nothing she could do or say will ever bother me again."

"Good." Will quickly dropped a kiss on her lips as they walked, glad Amy was watching and would know her meddling had availed nothing.

A Debt to Pay

"Please be careful," Claire said minutes later as they embraced one last time before he left.

"I will," he replied, holding her close and kissing the top of her head.

"Just promise me one thing."

"Anything."

"Go by the ranch and let Hannah know we talked. I don't want her hating me for two months!"

Chapter Thirty-Two

Ten Weeks Later

"It's getting chilly out there," Maggie said as she came inside the kitchen and closed the door behind her. She put the basket of eggs she'd just collected from the chicken coop on Lyddie's table.

"Winter's definitely around the corner," Lyddie agreed. "It's only the beginning of November, and already it feels colder than usual." She had just finished peeling potatoes and was dropping them in a pot of boiling water on the stove when Claire came in from the other end of the house. She had just come home from Mrs. Murry's dress shop, where she'd been working almost daily for the last two months. Although she had been skeptical at first that she would get the hang of all the stitching and sewing it entailed, Mrs. Murry proved to be an excellent teacher, and Claire was now getting used to it.

"Maggie! Wait till you see the fabric Mrs. Murry just got in," Claire exclaimed as she met them in the kitchen. "If it's not made for a wedding dress, I don't know what is."

Maggie smiled just thinking about her wedding date in December. "I can't wait to see it!"

A Debt to Pay

"Mrs. Murry said to come in tomorrow if you can for a fitting. She wants to start on it right away." Claire glanced around at the dinner preparations that were being made. "Anything I can do?" she asked.

"Are Jacob's parents and sister coming for the wedding?" Lyddie asked.

"They're coming a few days before. I think they're planning to stay at Will's."

Just the mention of his name made Claire feel a little ache in her heart. She hadn't thought she could miss anyone as much as she missed him. It had been a little over two months, and she prayed each day that it would be the day he came home.

"Will you be seeing Hannah anytime soon?" Mr. Brewster, the postmaster, asked Claire just before she left the post office one Saturday afternoon. She had just stopped by to collect any mail for Lyddie.

"Because I've got a letter for her," he said, "and I know she doesn't come into town much."

"I'm due for a visit," Claire smiled. "What if I take it out to her now?"

Mr. Brewster handed her the letter, and Claire was glad for a reason to go by the ranch. She already had Willow out front and was soon astride her and heading out of town.

Claire pulled her coat a little tighter around her as a cold gust of wind swept past. She glanced up at the gray sky and wondered if snow was likely any time soon. She felt like Willow knew exactly where they were going once they started toward the ranch, so she relaxed her hold on the reins and let the horse practically lead the way.

As she often did, Claire smiled when the Carter ranch came into view. She couldn't believe she might live there someday soon. The contrast of her life in Chicago with this new life God had given her was almost too miraculous to be real. There were a few ranch hands who had stayed behind to care for the stock, but the ranch seemed so quiet and lifeless without Will and the rest of the boys.

Minutes later, Claire was at the house and knocking on the front door. Hannah answered with her usual friendly smile. "Just in time for lunch," she said, leading the way to the kitchen.

"You don't need to feed me," Claire smiled. "I was at the post office, and Mr. Brewster asked me to give this to you," she said as she handed her the letter.

Hannah looked down at it and seemed to recognize the handwriting immediately. "It's from my sister," she smiled, tucking it into her apron pocket. "I haven't hardly had to feed anyone for months, and I'm starting to forget the reason for my existence," Hannah teased. "So, you'd be doing me a favor by eating some chicken pot pie."

"I'd be glad to," Claire said, following her to the kitchen. They talked easily for the better part of an hour. Claire was just standing to go when Hannah stopped mid-sentence and said, "Do you hear that?"

Claire listened and could hear the faint sound of what sounded like multiple bellows and something akin to distant thunder.

"I think they're back," Hannah said, going to the kitchen door.

Claire was on her heels and standing outside with her in seconds. She beamed at the nearing sight of Will among the other cowboys amidst a hundred or more cattle thundering across the field. The cracks of their whips and shouts directed the cattle into the pasture behind the barn. They all headed in that direction except for Will. Upon seeing Claire and Hannah outside, he veered away from the rest and headed straight for the house.

It wasn't long before Claire felt his arms going around her in a hug that swept her feet off the ground. She returned his kiss with all the love she'd been saving up, so grateful his feelings for her hadn't changed.

"That was the longest two and a half months I've ever known," he said, stepping back slightly but not taking his eyes off her.

"It was a snail's pace for me, too," Claire told him, trying to blink away a sudden rush of tears. Deep down, she had thought his love was too good to be true and had been afraid the absence might make him question his feelings. She was so happy to be wrong.

―――――

"It's almost time, Maggie." Claire closed the door behind her and looked at her best friend in amazement. "You are the most beautiful bride I've ever seen!"

Maggie turned away from the vanity mirror and laughed softly with excitement. "I can't even believe this is happening to me!"

Claire walked to her and took both of her hands. "You deserve it, and you're going to be a wonderful wife and mother." Claire kissed her on the cheek and then picked up the veil that was lying on the bed. "I can help you get this on, and then we really should go."

A few minutes later, the two of them were leaving Lyddie's boardinghouse and meeting Tom Maison out front. He had offered to drive them to the church, where everyone else already there and waiting. Claire could feel Maggie's joy and excitement as they drove down the street and could tell it was mounting as they drew closer to the church.

As her maid of honor, Claire walked down the aisle, and behind her came Lilly, beaming from ear to ear as she tossed petals from her basket. Claire caught Will's eye as he stood beside Jacob, and she knew he was honored that Jacob had asked him to be his best man.

They had called in a Reverend from Jefferson City to do the wedding, and Claire stepped beside him on the other side of Jacob. Suddenly, all eyes in the room went to the back of the church. Maggie was standing there, looking radiant in her white gown of satin and lace, a delicate chiffon veil draped over her face.

Everyone in attendance stood as Maggie moved down the aisle and eventually stopped beside Jacob. Claire glanced around the room and didn't think there was space on the pews for one more person. Her eyes then rested on Jacob, whom she thought never looked happier. Just behind him stood Will, and her eyes locked with his. She knew what he was thinking and couldn't keep the smile from her face. In just a few months, they were going to have a wedding of their own.

Claire sighed wistfully, listening as Maggie and Jacob exchanged their vows. Even with the hope she had felt in her heart when they left Chicago, she could have never imagined their lives would have come to such a happy ending... or rather, such a happy beginning.

The End